Highest Pra. .... s Thrillers

THE COLDEST FEAR

"Everything you want in a thriller: strong characters, plenty of gory story, witty dialogue, and a narrative that demands you keep turning those pages."
—BookReporter.com

THE CRUELEST CUT

"Rick Reed, retired homicide detective and author of *Blood Trail*, the true-crime story of serial killer Joe Brown, brings his impressive writing skills to the world of fiction with *The Cruelest Cut*. This is as authentic and scary as crime thrillers get, written as only a cop can write who's lived this drama in real life. . . . A very good and fast read."
—Nelson DeMille

"Put this one on your must-read list. *The Cruelest Cut* is a can't-put-down adventure. All the components of a crackerjack thriller are here, and author Reed knows how to use them. Readers will definitely want to see more of Reed's character Jack Murphy."
—John Lutz

"A jaw-dropping thriller that dares you to turn the page."
—Gregg Olsen

"A tornado of drama—you won't stop spinning till you've been spit out the other end. Rick Reed knows the dark side as only a real-life cop can, and his writing crackles with authenticity."
—Shane Gericke

"A winner of a debut novel . . . Reed is a master of describing graphic violence. Some of the crime scenes here will chill you to the bone."
—BookReporter.com

Also by Rick Reed

The Deepest Wound

A Jack Murphy Thriller

RICK REED

KENSINGTON PUBLISHING CORP.
www.kensingtonbooks.com

LYRICAL UNDERGROUND BOOKS are published by

Kensington Publishing Corp.
119 West 40th Street
New York, NY 10018

First Lyrical Underground edition: April 2016

ISBN-13: 978-1-60183-638-0
ISBN-10: 1-60183-638-4

First trade paperback edition: April 2016

ISBN-13: 978-1-60183-639-7
ISBN-10: 1-60183-639-2

For my wife, Jennifer,
who has made so many things possible.

CHAPTER ONE

His hands stopped shaking, but every muscle in them ached as he knelt, clutching the toilet seat and tasting the bile that burned his throat. He looked at the body in the other room, sprawled on the floor, legs spread, arms bent, hands limp on either side of her head. Dark hair spilled across a face that five minutes ago was beautiful, now drawn into a rictus of death.

"Dear God!" He ground a knuckle into his mouth as his mind flashed back over horrible images—shoving her, her head hitting the brick fireplace, hands around her throat, thumbs driving deep into the flesh until something crunched. And the blood—he'd never seen so much blood.

He hadn't seen anyone outside when he came to her house—no lights on, no sound coming from any of the houses on the block—and in his panic he thought about fleeing the scene of the crime. But he knew that wasn't going to help him in the long run. He had undoubtedly left fingerprints, fibers—they could find all sorts of things these days. The most damaging evidence was the body itself.

Maybe he could dispose of the body. And there was that other problem he had to deal with.

Who am I kidding? I'm no killer. But that isn't true anymore. I am a killer. But she brought this on herself. I only wanted to talk to her, explain my side. All she had to do was keep her big mouth shut.

She had deceived him. Betrayed his trust. Women were like that. All nice when they wanted something, then baring their claws when they didn't get it the way they wanted. She had called him to come over, and it surprised him. It had been months. And just when he was feeling good about coming to see her, feeling good about himself, she dropped the bomb.

She told him she knew about the girl named Hope and that he'd gotten the girl pregnant. She wanted him to do the right thing. Let Hope have the child, and stop pushing her to abort it. She even went so far as to say he should pay Hope to raise the child. When he laughed at that ridiculous idea, she became angry and started with the threats of public exposure. The bitch had somehow found about the other affairs, and she threatened to go public, ruin his career. He couldn't allow that to happen.

That was when he lost it. Had gone into a homicidal rage. Any man would have. He could still feel his pulse pounding in his ears, and he felt the urge to retch again, but his stomach had nothing left. He wiped his mouth on the sleeve of his dress shirt, flushed the toilet, and buried his face in his hands.

I killed her. I'm a murderer!

And then he realized he knew someone he could call for help. Someone he trusted completely. They would know what to do. They knew people who could fix this.

He took his cell phone from his pocket and punched in a number.

CHAPTER TWO

Jack watched the festivities from Katie's kitchen window, thinking about how his life had changed over the last few years. He was still young, or youngish, but his solid six-foot-one build was getting a little soft, and this morning he'd spotted some gray hiding in his dark hair. This house was his childhood home. He and his wife, Katie, had lived here. But then came the divorce, and everything had gone to shit—his life, his marriage, his home, and his happiness.

Jack Murphy was a police detective, not a fortune-teller. He noticed if someone was right- or left-handed, calm or nervous, lying or telling the truth, going for a weapon or likely to run, but he'd never seen today coming. They didn't teach you in cop school how to react when your ex-wife got engaged to another man. If he were a fortune-teller, he wouldn't be here.

When he and Katie divorced, they had remained close because of the friends in common. She had dated and he had dated, but it was never serious for him until he met Susan Summers. He thought maybe she was the one. Three months ago, Susan accepted a position as chief parole officer for the state of Indiana, which necessitated moving to Indianapolis. It was only a three-hour drive, and they had promised to get together often, but neither of them kept that promise. The last time they spoke, Susan said she was dating someone, and he realized that he was happy for her. He also realized that when he was with Susan, he was thinking about Katie. Comparing Susan to Katie. Maybe Susan knew that. Maybe that was why she left.

Outside, Katie and her sister, Moira, were posing for photos. Katie was short like her mother, about five-foot-five, and she worried needlessly about her age because she possessed an ageless beauty, both inside and out. Moira was younger and taller, like their father. She was nearly Jack's height and he was over six feet tall. The one thing they shared, and their most striking feature, was their bright red hair—thick, wavy, and long.

Jack watched them standing together in the sunlight and thought about the telephone call he'd received from Katie two days ago.

KATIE: *Jack! I have some exciting news. Moira is coming home tonight and I thought we should have a celebration for her graduation from law school.*
JACK: *Wow! That's great, Katie. I'm proud of her.*
KATIE: *Trent Wethington has offered her a position as a deputy prosecutor. She starts next week.*
JACK: *She's living with you?*
KATIE: *She has some huge student loans.*
(Silence for a beat.)
KATIE: *Jack, will you come to the party? Noon-ish Sunday. Liddell and Marcie are coming.*

Of course he had said yes. Why wouldn't he? He and Katie were still friends. And he adored Moira, and she him. Plus, his partner and his wife had already committed to going. So he said yes. Then Katie dropped the bomb:

KATIE: *Jack. I'm getting married. I'm engaged to Eric Manson.*

She prattled on, but he didn't hear or remember any of the rest of the conversation, except her comment that her new fiancé had insisted on inviting Jack. Eric wanted them to be friends. Eric thought they should get to know each other. *Well, Eric can kiss my ass.*

Jack knew the real reason Eric wanted him to be there. Eric wanted to establish himself as the alpha male.

Jack had ended the conversation by congratulating her, promising to come to the party, keeping his tone light, going through the motions that he'd learned from a lifetime of giving and receiving bad news.

Since that call he had thought of at least twenty ways to kill Eric without getting caught. *Leave a trail of money leading into a wood chipper. Not allow Eric to talk about himself for a month. Keep him away from mirrors.*

Pulling himself back to the present, he thought about the look Katie's father had given him when the old man arrived. Her father thought that *anyone* was an improvement over Jack.

Maybe it was the Scotch, but Jack noticed several swarthy-looking characters out in the yard that he didn't recognize. Some of them looked like Eric's family, both from the resemblance and the holier-than-thou attitude. In fact, they resembled each other so startlingly, he wondered if incest . . . *Be nice, Jack,* he reminded himself.

Other people he didn't recognize. They were probably attorneys because they stood around with their hands in their pockets. Probably to keep the other attorneys' hands out of their pockets. They taught that in Attorney 101.

Everyone was having a good time. Liddell, Jack's partner, had of course taken over the barbecue grill, and his wife, Marcie, spread joy and smiles to whomever she touched. Some chatted, and some drank. Some played bocce ball while they drank. "At least I'm drinking," he said quietly, and lifted his glass of Glenmorangie single malt in a silent toast to Katie and Moira. "Here's to the Connelly girls. May the road always rise to meet you." Then he lifted his middle finger and said, "And here's to you, Eric."

He knew he should be sociable, but he couldn't make himself go out there and pretend he was happy about this. But, damn, if Moira and Katie weren't radiant! Not a care in the world. He hoped it could always be that way for them. Being a cop, he knew that life was something that happened *to* you, not *for* you.

Everyone was smiling like one big happy family. And he couldn't get his mind wrapped around it. *Katie's engaged to Eric Manson. What the hell was she thinking? She knows I hate lawyers.*

"Ready for another?" a man asked.

Jack turned and saw Eric Manson framed in the doorway, a full bottle of Chivas Regal in his hand.

Slightly taller than Jack, Eric was perpetually tanned, with a bright-white smile and what women thought was a ruggedly handsome face. The only physical defect was an ever-so-slight drooping of the left side of his mouth and eyelid. It made him look like a younger Sylvester Stallone.

Eric Manson was chief deputy prosecutor for Vanderburgh County, and Jack had worked with him many times. But even before his going after Katie, Jack didn't like him. Eric was a competent prosecutor, but he had a reputation for playing fast and loose with his female coworkers—married and unmarried alike.

Jack had three reasons to hate Eric. One: Eric was an attorney, no matter which side he pretended to be on. Two: he was offering Jack Chivas Regal, which was the same as offering a glass of lighter fluid to a man in hell. And the biggest reason: Eric was taking Katie out his life. Jack would be damned if he let her be hurt by anyone.

So you think you're good enough for Katie? "Brought my own," Jack said, and nodded at the half-empty bottle of Glenmorangie on the countertop.

Eric picked up the bottle and examined the gold and orange label. "I forgot you were a connoisseur."

"Every man has a hobby. What's *your* hobby, Eric?" *Besides chasing tail.*

Eric ignored his jibe and motioned toward Jack's empty glass. "It's a party. And yet here I am drinking Diet Pepsi." He made a show of looking at his watch and said, "But I guess it's five o'clock somewhere."

Jack resented the insinuation. "If you have something to say, counselor, spit it out."

"What do you think I'm saying, Jack?"

Jack's fists clenched, and Eric planted his feet.

"There you boys are," Moira said, walking into the kitchen.

The men stared at each other for a long moment before Eric said, "Tell my *fiancée* I'll be right there."

"But will you *always* be there, Eric?" Jack asked under his breath, his arms dropping to his sides.

"I didn't quite catch that, Jack," Eric said.

The accusation was on the tip of Jack's tongue when his cell phone rang.

"We've found an unusual item in a landfill. I'm afraid I need you to get over there pronto. It's a homicide."

CHAPTER THREE

A flock of white gulls circled in a cerulean sky, drawn by the rubbish in the Browning-Ferris landfill. On top of this no-man's-land, three massive yellow landfill compactors with enormous steel chopper wheels lumbered up and down the hills of newly collected trash.

Jack and Liddell stood ankle-deep in discarded waste outside the chain-link fence on Laubscher Road. The putrid smell was overwhelming. Twenty feet away, a half dozen crime scene and uniformed officers cordoned off a massive area with yellow and black tape.

"Another fifty yards and the Sheriff's Department would be working this," Sergeant Tony Walker said, pointing at where a line of trees began. Walker was fifty years old, but except for his salt-and-pepper hair, he could pass for twenty years younger. He didn't have an ounce of fat on his frame. He had been Jack's mentor and partner when he first made detective a decade ago, but then Walker was promoted to sergeant and transferred to Crime Scene.

Since Tony had taken over, the Crime Scene Unit ran much more smoothly. The brass was afraid to cross him, and the other detectives respected him. It was the best of both worlds, as far as Jack was concerned.

Liddell, like Jack, was still in the clothes they'd worn to the engagement party. He brushed some cake crumbs from his knit shirt and said, "My brother, Landry, and his family are visiting Friday, and I was planning a crawfish boil. Tony, do you think I'll get back home in, say, five or six hours to start making the roux?"

At six-foot-seven, weighing in at full-grown Yeti, Liddell was a big man by anyone's standards. Jack called him Bigfoot for obvious reasons, but everyone else called him Cajun because of his previous job with the Iberville Parish Sheriff's Water Patrol Unit in

Plaquemine, Louisiana. He and Jack had been partners since Liddell and Marcie had married and moved from Louisiana to Evansville, where she could be closer to her family and Liddell could do what he did best—work homicides.

Walker put his hands on his hips. "Friday? Friday is five days away. It takes you five days to make that stuff?"

"You've never tasted my roux. It's not 'stuff.' It takes time."

Walker looked accusingly at Jack. "We're standing outside a stinking trash dump, and he's talking about food. Don't you ever feed him?"

"Hey, he ate a whole cake today at Katie's. Besides, I don't even know what a roux is," Jack lied, knowing that it was the base of almost every Cajun dish. Liddell had missed his calling as a chef—he loved cooking and eating almost as much as he loved his wife.

Fifty yards away, at the main entrance to the landfill, a gaggle of reporters hovered. They jostled each other each time a car slowed to see what was going on. Cameramen and reporters would rush the passing car and, seeing it was no one of consequence, fight their way back to the entrance, anxious to get the gory details. Fear sold TV airtime and newspapers.

"Let's see the body." Jack noticed the other officers were wearing boots, and he glanced down at his deck shoes. He would have to throw them away after this.

Seeing his distress, Walker reached in the back of his SUV and came out with two pairs of yellow knee-high rubber boots. "Not a body," he informed them. "Body part. A head, to be exact."

Jack slid the boots on—they were large enough to swallow his shoes—and he and Liddell followed Walker down the shoulder of Laubscher Road. Walker pulled up where orange marker flags had been stuck in the ground inside a roped-off area of chain-link fence. Half of the flags were inside the fence, the other half outside.

It was over one hundred degrees, the sun was directly overhead, and the smell hit them first. Decaying human flesh has an unmistakable sickly sweet odor. Jack had smelled it as soon as they parked, but hadn't been able to pinpoint the source.

Walker pointed toward the edge of the fence where a head seemed to melt into the uneven vegetation and garbage. The skinless right side of the face, teeth, and jaw faced upward, and a piece of scalp with long dark hair flapped away from the top of the skull.

"How long?" Jack asked. The rate of decomposition suggested the head had been there for weeks, but he wasn't the expert here.

"There are five stages of decay," Walker said. "This is in the fourth or advanced stage." He pointed at the blackened vegetation around the skull, resembling an oil patch. "The body fluids purge and seep into the soil. The grass around the head looks like it's been cooked."

"Gee, thanks, Mr. Wizard," Liddell said. "But that doesn't tell us much."

"Sorry," Walker said, seeming to realize how technical he was sounding. "I just returned from a medicolegal death investigation school, and they brought in a forensic anthropologist who taught all this stuff. To determine the time of death, I have to factor in temperature, location, and any other preservation factors, plus age of the victim, manner of death—"

"In other words, Mr. Wizard, there are a plethora of factors to consider," Liddell interjected.

"Plethora? Did you really say that, Cajun?" Walker grinned. "Anyway, the short answer to your question is she's been down two days or less. The head was brought here in a plastic contractor's bag. We won't be able to tell until the autopsy if the head was stored somewhere else, maybe refrigerated or frozen, or if it was just done."

Jack looked closer and saw the black pieces of plastic that he had assumed were just more trash. The contractor's bag suggested the victim—a woman, judging by the length of the hair—had been killed somewhere else and dumped here.

"What lucky soul made this discovery?" Jack asked, but before Sergeant Walker could answer, a uniformed officer walked up holding a portable radio.

"Dispatch," the officer said, and handed the radio to Jack.

Jack punched the transmit button. "Two David five four," he said, giving his radio call sign.

"Two David five four. Call Captain at home," the police dispatcher said.

"Will do." Jack handed the WT back to the patrolman, who motioned over Jack's shoulder.

"Little Casket's here."

As Jack punched in the captain's cell phone number, he saw the coroner's familiar black Suburban arriving. It just missed striking a cameraman who had unwisely run into its path. The phone stopped ringing and the sound of someone cursing loudly in the background came through the line.

"Jack. Jack," Captain Franklin yelled over the noise.

"Captain, is everything okay?" Jack asked. Captain Franklin was in charge of the detective's office.

"That's Stinson raising hell," Franklin explained. "He's in the sand trap and about to break an iron over his caddy's head."

Jack had to grin at the mental picture of the former commander of the investigations unit swinging a golf club wildly and cursing.

"Look, Jack, I got the call from dispatch. What have you found out?"

"Walker said the murder is recent—one or two days at most. We've got a female head. Just a head and it's not a pretty sight. Looks like it was dumped here in a garbage bag and animals had a go at it, so it's going to be hard to say when she died. But Little Casket's here, and hopefully the autopsy will tell us more."

"Do you need more detectives or uniforms for the search?"

"Crime scene is setting up a search grid. I'll pass this on to Walker and see if he needs more people." Jack didn't have to tell the captain what the chances were of finding the rest of the body. It was a working landfill. That they had even found the head was pure luck.

"I called the chief. We'll both be at headquarters in an hour. Keep me posted." Franklin hung up.

There was a chain of command in police work, just like in the military. The brass was supposed to assist the investigator get the needed men or equipment, or to give the media a talking head—usually a lieutenant or above—to pass on information. This, in theory, allowed the detectives to work unobstructed.

In Jack's experience, though, the chain of command did just the opposite. Every time he followed SOP and called the brass, they felt compelled to come in, and would make him stop whatever he was doing and come to headquarters to have a meeting. They wanted to make their suggestions, worry about the media, and then sit around useless as a bra on a bull.

But Captain Franklin didn't interfere or try to direct the investigation from a telephone. He'd served in the field and knew what it was like. Plus, he would take the blame when Jack screwed the pooch, like a good leader. Of course, he got an extra twenty-four percent pay for his troubles.

Jack saw a familiar figure wearing hospital scrubs—complete with green medical cap, green paper booties, and a surgical mask—heading their way. Lilly Caskins, chief deputy coroner for Vanderburgh County, was a diminutive woman who had been dubbed "Little Casket" by local law enforcement officers because she was tiny and evil-looking and associated with death. Her large dark eyes stared out of thick lenses of horned-rimmed glasses that had gone out of style in the days of Al Capone.

Jack respected her work for the most part, but she had an annoying habit of being blunt at death scenes. He found it surprising that a woman could have no compassion for the dead, and no love for the living. She wasn't trying to protect herself. She just didn't like people.

"Who found her?" Lilly asked.

Liddell looked at the notes he'd been given by the first officer on scene. "A man and wife were dumping a mattress this morning. Apparently he stepped on it."

"They wouldn't have cut the fence," Lilly said, looking at the section of fencing that had been spread wide by the crime scene squad. She frowned at the busy crime techs. "Walker and his team are here, so there's nothing for me to do. I'll wait in the Suburban until they're done." Lilly turned and marched promptly back to her vehicle.

"Look at this, Jack," Walker said, motioning for a tech to bring the camera.

"Start taking pictures. I'm going to get a closer look."

On hands and knees, Walker crawled into the circle of flags toward the head, his arms buried up to his elbows in the stinking trash and uncut weeds. He stopped and tugged something, then lifted the object for the others to see.

"What the—!" Liddell's eyes widened.

Walker pulled an evidence bag from his belt.

"We need to back up, folks," he said. "The scene just got bigger."

CHAPTER FOUR

"Let's talk to the couple who found the victim's remains," Jack said, and they looked toward the St. Joseph Avenue entrance to the landfill, where a man and woman were sitting inside a yellow Chevy pickup.

A black Lexus sedan with dark-tinted windows approached the gate and was waved through by another uniformed officer.

"The eagle has landed," Liddell said under his breath.

"More like a vulture," Jack murmured.

The car rolled to a stop, and Captain Dewey Duncan—who was square-shaped and bald as a baby's ass with huge spaces between his peg teeth—literally leapt from the driver's side wearing his dress blue uniform, complete with a police-issue eight-point cap, and rushed to open the door for his boss, Deputy Chief Richard Dick. Duncan seemed to be attached to his boss by an invisible tether. Liddell once remarked that when Dick had his hemorrhoids removed, he promoted them to captain and taught them how to drive.

Duncan was called an administrative assistant, but in truth he was little more than an overpaid driver. Jack had really hoped Richard Dick—aka Double Dick—wouldn't show up at the scene, but the news media were involved, and the man was a media whore.

The deputy chief of police emerged from the back like a movie star—blond-haired, blue-eyed, tall and lean, every bit the Aryan poster child. He also wore formal dress blues, with a chest full of ribbons, spit-polished shoes, and, displayed on the shiny bill of his eight-point cap, the "scrambled eggs" that indicated the rank of a commanding officer.

Jack had given him the nickname Double Dick, not just because of his two first names, but because he was known to repeatedly "dick" those below him in rank. Dick nodded to Jack and Liddell, but the whole of his attention was on the news media in the distance. "Show me what we have," Dick commanded.

Liddell snapped to attention behind the deputy chief's back, giving an exaggerated salute. "She's over here, Deputy Chief, sir."

Sensing sarcasm, Dick started to turn in Liddell's direction, but Jack stepped between them. "You'll probably want to put some boots on. It's pretty messy." To which Dick made a dismissive gesture and nodded for Jack to lead on.

Dick followed Jack to the cordoned-off area. Jack stopped when they were almost on top of the decapitated head. Dick squinted in the bright sun, peering into the trash and weeds in the direction Jack was pointing. "What am I looking for?"

"The blackened area," Jack said. "A woman's head. Sergeant Walker found an arm next to the head."

Dick moved forward cautiously, peering down, then stopped and gasped. He turned and rushed back to his car, crushing several of the markers underfoot on his way past.

"My God," Dick said, leaning heavily against the car door.

Following behind, Jack felt no pity for the man. After all, he had insinuated himself into the crime scene. If he were anyone else, Jack would have told him to stay the hell out.

"We need someone to deal with the media," Jack suggested, and wasn't surprised when Dick quickly recovered his erect composure.

The deputy chief looked down at his dirty shoes, and Jack guessed he was weighing the impact they would make on the media. *Not afraid to get his shoes dirty.* Dick then snapped his fingers. "I'll need some details."

Liddell leaned down and, covering the side of his mouth, said, "We don't want to give details yet, chief. If we catch the monster that did this, we want *him* to tell *us* the details."

"Right. Good thinking." The deputy chief slid into the backseat and the Lexus made a U-turn toward the gate.

"Nice move," Liddell said as Double Dick approached the gathered media.

"Better him than us," Jack replied.

They turned back to the waiting witnesses, Larry and Donita Cannon. Yet the couple didn't have any new information that was helpful. They were mainly concerned that, because they hadn't reported it right away—because they were illegally dumping the mattress—they would be considered accessories after the fact. Jack assured them that the police only wanted their cooperation.

Twenty minutes and as many questions later, Jack watched the Chevy truck drive away, the Cannons' faith in police restored.

"They found the head about three o'clock this morning, and didn't call nine-one-one until noon," Jack said. "Nine hours. If Walker is right about the time of death, they just missed witnessing the killer in the act of dumping the body."

Liddell joked, "Can you imagine his surprise when he tripped over the head?"

When they made it back, Jack found Walker splashing water from a bottle onto his face. Several white-clad crime-scene techs were in a line, carrying more little flags—yellow this time—and walking off a search grid. They had started one hundred feet from where the cut was made in the fence, and the techs on each side of the line had stuck a flag in the ground to mark where they had already searched. They were about halfway finished.

Jack noticed Little Casket's Suburban was gone.

"In answer to your question, Lilly is taking the remains to the morgue," Walker said. "And she's calling Dr. John," Walker added, referring to the forensic pathologist, Dr. John Carmodi, who performed autopsies for Vanderburgh County.

"Find anything else?" Liddell asked.

Walker pointed to a white truck parked near the entrance. "That's the general foreman for the landfill," he said.

Jack and Liddell went to meet him.

"Sherman Price," the man said, pulling his bulk from the little truck and taking Jack's hand. He obviously didn't want to get any closer to where the remains were found. "I'm foreman here."

Sherman's name fit him well. About thirty years old, with a buzz cut, he was the size of a Sherman tank. Muscles strained the material of his T-shirt.

"When was the last time someone checked the fence?" Jack asked.

"We check about once a week. Do it myself," Price said. "It's fenced all the way around with solid fence or chain-link, and the only easy place to get inside is along St. Joseph Avenue. Someone coming in that way would have to walk past the scales and the office. But it's happened before. The fence doesn't keep them out if they've a mind to come in."

"Keep who out?" Jack asked.

"Thieves." Price spit on the ground, then looked at Jack. "Sorry. I shouldn't have spit down there, should I?"

"It's okay," Jack said, wishing shows like *NCIS* and *Cold Case* had never been aired. Everyone was a forensic specialist now.

"There's no reason to come in here," Price went on. "We put up lights and dummy cameras to keep people honest."

"Well, they came in this time," Jack said, "and they left what they considered garbage."

Price's eyes drifted to the blackened ground where the head had been found.

"I never seen nothing like this . . . this . . ." His words trailed off.

Jack understood. Most people never saw anything like this. He gave Sherman Price one of his business cards. "Pass word on to your crews that there may be more pieces out there."

Price didn't understand at first, but then the light went on in his eyes. "I'll sure tell them. We'll call right away if we come across something."

Jack turned to leave and then thought of another question. "Mr. Price. Those are dummy cameras near the recycle bins, but are there any security cameras that do work?"

Price scratched his head. "Nothing like this has ever happened around here."

Price agreed to get the work schedules and contact information for employees who would have been in the yard over the weekend, squeezed into his truck, and headed for the office.

CHAPTER FIVE

Dressed in the same dark slacks, deck shoes, and mauve polo shirt he had worn to his engagement party, Eric Manson sat in the chief of police's office. The impressive display of diplomas and awards on the walls all bore the name of Marlin H. Pope.

"I guess congratulations are in order, Eric," Pope said with a smile.

"Yes, I'm a lucky man."

"Katie will be good for you. Have you two set a date?"

Manson and Pope knew each other, having crossed paths at many political events and fund-raisers. Pope attended to protect budgetary concerns. Manson went because he was running for his boss's job—prosecutor of Vanderburgh County.

Eric had come to Evansville from Pennsylvania and started at the bottom, doing scut work, working weekends and long hours, while taking the cases no one else would touch. But in six short years he had moved up through the ranks, and was now the second in command of the most powerful office in the county. He'd survived a ball-busting divorce settlement eight years ago from his cold fish of a wife, and was now getting what he so richly deserved for his hard work and sacrifice. The only thing that had held him back from attaining the top spot was the scandal caused by his divorce.

Now, with a woman like Katie, things would be different. She possessed charm and poise, not to mention drop-dead gorgeous looks that turned many a head and loosened many a donor's grip on their wallets in his bid to replace the current prosecutor, Trent Wethington.

Trent was his mentor, his father figure, and a powerhouse himself. Trent, who was running for governor, had announced that he was stepping down at the end of this year, and had thrown his ample support behind Eric to replace him. Of course there were challengers, but none of them had Eric's qualifications, passion, or drive, and none had the one thing they would require to win—Trent's backing.

And that thought brought him back to the real reason he was paying a visit to the chief of police on a Sunday afternoon.

"Wedding date to be announced," Eric said. "But that's not why I'm here." His smile faded and he was all business. "I understand you're working a homicide."

Pope looked surprised. "I got a call from Captain Franklin just minutes before you called, Eric. Is the media calling you?"

Eric shook his head. "I need to know what you've got."

Pope still wasn't sure where this was going. "Well, we've found some body parts of a white female. A head and an arm," he said. "They're still looking for the rest of the body."

That confirmed Eric's fears. "Where?"

"BFI landfill."

"Identifiable?" Eric asked.

"Why are you so interested, Eric? If you don't mind me asking."

"I have a missing employee—and under suspicious circumstances."

"Just a minute." Pope picked up his desk phone and dialed a number.

Eric heard enough of the conversation to assume that Pope was talking to someone at the county morgue. When the police chief replaced the receiver, he had a bemused grin on his face.

"That was Lilly Caskins," Pope said. "I thought she might email us a photo of the head, but it seems we'll have to drive to the morgue if we want any information."

Eric was more than a little irritated by Lilly Caskins's rudeness, but he said nothing. She wielded a lot of political power, but even she had her limits. She'd do well to remember that. Political loyalties swing to whoever is in power.

"You don't have to go, Eric. I take it you want to verify the victim is or isn't your employee."

"I know it's unusual for the prosecutor's chief deputy to get involved this way," Eric replied, "but we may have a personal interest in the identity of the victim. I just pray it's not Nina."

"We?" Pope asked.

"I'm sorry, I thought I told you. I'm here at Trent's request."

"He sent you on his behalf? Why?"

"You know how the game is played, Marlin. Trent was worried his personal presence would imply something he didn't want to be implied. So I'm doing the legwork." He knew Pope would understand.

"By the way, Eric, how *did* you find out about this?"

"Trent was made aware that Nina Parsons, one of our deputy prosecutors, didn't show up this morning to do the weekend charging documents for tomorrow's court." Eric went on to explain. "As you know, when someone is arrested after regular court hours, a deputy prosecutor has to prepare affidavits and the 'charging information' for a judge to determine if the prisoner should be held over for court on Monday mornings."

"Who reported Nina missing?" Pope asked.

"Cindy McCoy," Eric said. "She was supposed to meet Nina at the office this morning. Nina was preparing Cindy to take over the weekend precharges. It had been Nina's job until recently. Anyway, when Nina didn't show up, Cindy called Nina's home and cell phone. When she couldn't reach Nina, she called Trent at home."

Pope raised an eyebrow, and Eric explained. "She tried to call me first, but when I didn't respond . . ."

"Because you were at your engagement party. That's understandable." Yet Pope surprised him by asking, "Aren't you jumping to conclusions that the body at the landfill is Nina?"

Eric leaned forward in his chair. "Trent called me at Katie's this afternoon to tell me Nina was missing from work. It was right after Jack left the party. I put two and two together, and . . . look, I may be wrong here, but I have another reason to believe it's Nina."

"I have the feeling you're going to tell me something I don't want to hear," Pope said.

Eric had finally worked around to the point he needed to make. "I may have screwed up, Marlin."

CHAPTER SIX

Somewhere on the East Coast a cell phone rang. "Yes," a woman's voice answered.

"It's done."

Under normal conditions she would have disconnected and destroyed the cell phone. The job was done. Payment would be made. But this time was different.

"Call back," she said, and hung up.

The next call would come from another public pay phone, and she would use another of her cell phone numbers. She pulled the battery from the back of the disposable phone, removed the SIM chip, and broke it in half. She would burn all of it later. Nothing would lead back to her.

Her job as a fixer required that she not leave anything to chance, and she was good at that. She had to be. A woman fixer was unheard of in the business a few years ago, but she had proven her worth to the organization. She did what needed to be done, no matter how undesirable.

Her crew had collected the body of the dead woman, and the same evening they killed the prostitute and her pimp. For her plan to work, the first body had to disappear entirely, and the other two bodies—or the heads, at least—would be left in a very public place.

The two contractors she had selected for this job were good. They did as they were told with no questions asked. In less than three hours, they had flown in to Louisville, rented a car, driven to the client's location, and sent him on his way before they cleansed the scene of evidence.

She wasn't happy that her crew had made personal contact with the client, but she needed someone to verify his condition, see if he could be trusted not to talk to anybody. Considering the tasks that were required of them, she'd had doubts they could pull it off.

Unfortunately, she was right. They'd been sloppy in the method of disposal of the first woman's body. They had deviated from her plan, and now she would have to make changes. Well, it couldn't be helped.

She sighed, picked up her glass of sparkling water, and added a twist of lime. When she reported the cock-up to her superiors, it would start a shit storm. They, too, were expecting a simple acknowledgment that the task was completed, and they were disturbed enough by the client's actions. Not to mention he had called *them* using his personal cell phone. If someone was tracing phone records, things could get messy.

She took a sip of the water and watched out the window the dark, streamlined forms of cormorants as they swooped down into the sea, then lifted back into the sky. Sometimes they would have a fish in their grasp, sometimes nothing. The symbolism wasn't lost on her. Life was like that. Sometimes you were the hunter, sometimes the prey. She'd been on both sides, and had fought for her position in the food chain. A mistake could cost her everything.

She began to run down a mental list of contractors who she trusted to take care of this botched job if it came to that.

CHAPTER SEVEN

Jack asked Detective Larry Jansen for the second time, "What are you doing here?"

Jack and Liddell had been waiting for Lilly to finish a phone call at the morgue when Jansen showed up in his scuffed lace-up shoes and permanently wrinkled trench coat.

Lilly had turned the air-conditioning down to subzero, and while Liddell and Jack were freezing their butts off, Jansen was sweating bullets. Jack, knowing Jansen had a heart attack not too long ago, asked him, "Are you okay?"

Jansen ran a hand through his greasy mop of hair. "I'm okay, Jack. Are *you* okay?" He looked offended. "I'm the missing persons detective, remember? I'm doing my job."

"So who's missing?" Liddell asked. "I mean besides missing a head and an arm."

Jack knew Jansen wasn't going to tell them anything. He was jealous of his cases to the point of leaving them unsolved rather than letting another detective get involved. He figured Jansen knew something they didn't and was waiting for that "aha!" moment to tell them. That's the way the man was wired.

Lilly came back in the room, poured her second cup of coffee, and added three heaping teaspoons of sugar. "That was your chief on the phone," she said to the three men. "Better put on your big-boy pants. He's on his way here."

"That was the chief?" Liddell asked.

She gave Liddell what passed for a smile, then blew across the top of the steaming mug and took a sip. "I told him this wasn't a pizza delivery joint. If he wants to view the remains, he has to come here, just like anyone else. Besides, I don't know where our digital camera is to take a picture. Maybe it's been sold to pay the electric bill."

Jack knew the coroner's office was struggling with the budget cuts, just like every other agency, but he also knew that it wasn't like Lilly to piss off the chief of police. She must be in a mood.

"Did you hear about the mayor signing a sweetheart deal with one of his buddies?" Liddell asked.

Jack had heard the scuttlebutt. The city was leasing two buildings from the mayor's brother at a cost of over one hundred fifty thousand a year, plus a hundred grand for the improvements needed to run computer and phone lines. The rumor was the mayor was taking the cost out of the police department's manpower and equipment budget.

"Things are tough all over, Bigfoot," Jack said. "Better drop it."

A buzzer sounded from the front door of the building.

"I'll have the receptionist get that," Lilly said, and then threw her hands in the air. "Oh, I forgot. We don't have a receptionist."

Jansen hurried toward the back door that led to the garage.

"Tell us how you really feel, Lilly," Liddell yelled as she left the room. He turned to Jack. "Where's Larry going?"

Jack said, "My guess is he doesn't want the chief to know he was trying to get paid for coming to work on a Sunday. He probably wasn't called in to help with this case, and Sundays are double overtime."

Chief Marlin Pope walked into the room, followed closely by Eric Manson.

"Jack. Liddell," Eric said to the detectives.

What the hell is Manson doing here? Jack thought.

"There's no need to use an autopsy table," Lilly said as she wheeled a steel gurney into the examination room. "We really should wait until the doc gets here. And I don't know when that'll be. We may have to sell the Suburban to pay for his gasoline."

"Have we identified her?" Pope asked, ignoring Lilly's remarks.

"No," Lilly said, scowling. "*We* haven't identified the head yet, but maybe if *we* weren't being interrupted by visiting dignitaries, *we* could get some work done. But don't mind me. I'm just a grouchy old bitch today."

"Not just today. Every day, Lilly," Pope said, and Lilly gave him an evil grin.

They all moved in closer to the gurney while Lilly folded back the heavy green evidence bag to reveal the decapitated head.

Twigs and viscid blood were matted into long dark hair, and a flap of uneven skin was peeled back along the exposed skull. The skin around the flap was ragged, as if it had been chewed. The sightless eyes were wide; the mouth a straight bloodless slash in what was once a pretty face.

Eric Manson gasped at the sight. He turned pale and his lips became tight, his eyes squinted into slits.

Probably the first time he's ever seen a dead body, Jack thought. If he didn't dislike Manson so much, he'd feel sorry for the man. *Or does he know her? Why is the chief deputy for the prosecutor's office at the morgue? Unless . . .*

"Well, Eric?" Pope asked.

Manson managed a strangled "It's Nina."

As Lilly rolled the gurney back to cold storage, the men went to the conference room to talk. That's when Jack found out Eric's link to the deceased.

"You did what?" Jack asked, and leaned across the conference table to glare at the chief deputy prosecutor.

"Look, Jack. I did what any good boss would do. I went to an employee's house to check on their welfare." The tone of his voice was challenging, not apologetic.

"You walked through a possible crime scene," Jack hissed through clenched teeth. He didn't add the word *moron* in deference to the chief of police, who was watching this exchange with interest.

"How was I to know Nina had been killed?" Eric asked. His eyes were still locked on Jack's.

"It's done, Jack," Pope said, with finality. "At least Eric told us about it, so let's work with what we've got."

Jack nearly muttered, *You mean I'll have to work with what he has done.*

"I'll need a taped statement from you, Eric," Jack said.

"Of course."

"And fingerprints," Jack added.

"DNA, too?" Eric asked sarcastically.

"Good idea."

Eric wasn't used to being treated like anything but a crown

prince. "I don't know what good it'll do, since I already told you I was inside the house, but I'll cooperate."

Damn right you will, Jack thought.

"Is this going to be a problem?" Pope asked.

They both knew exactly what he meant.

"No problem with me," Eric said.

"Or me," Jack added.

"Good. Do you need us here, Jack?" Chief Pope asked.

"No, Chief. Thanks for coming," Jack said. He turned to Eric and added a dose of harshness. "Just be sure you give those samples ASAP. I'll get back to you on the statement, but I expect you to be available."

"Sure thing, Detective Murphy." Eric glared at Jack and left in a huff.

After Pope and Manson were gone, Liddell put an arm across Jack's shoulders.

"Glad to see you've kissed and made up. I mean, you and Eric burying the hatchet and working together and all," he said with a grin.

"Shut up, Bigfoot," Jack said, thinking about burying the hatchet for real.

Lilly came into the room and stopped, staring at the men.

"What?" Jack asked.

"Unless one of you can do the autopsy, I'm getting back to work. Doc's in Illinois and won't be back for a couple of hours." She headed down the hallway toward her office.

"Call us when he gets here," Jack yelled at her retreating figure.

A short distance away, the outside door to the morgue's garage closed, and Detective Larry Jansen hurried along the street to his car. He hadn't been able to hear everything, but he'd heard enough.

So Eric knew the dead woman? She was a deputy prosecutor, no less. And, boy, did Jack get right in Eric's shit about going inside the victim's house!

This is great stuff. I can sell this.

CHAPTER EIGHT

It was one in the morning in downtown Harrisburg when the two men stuffed the two headless corpses in the trunk of a stolen Ford Taurus. The girl's body hadn't been a problem, but the guy was easily three hundred pounds and they were both out of breath by the time they finished wrestling the body into the trunk. They had driven seventy miles back to Evansville, where they dumped, and then gone back to the house. It was almost daylight before they finished cleaning up the client's mess. Book napped while Clint drove around on county back roads, crossed Interstate 64, and turned north onto Highway 41 toward Terre Haute.

He woke Book when they hit the outskirts of the city.

"Easy breezy," Book said, rubbing the sleep out of his eyes.

"Yeah. Easy," Clint said, checking the dashboard clock. He took the ramp down to Interstate 70. "I vote we go to Indianapolis. We can get something to eat and a few hours sleep before we get out of here."

"Where are we?" Book asked.

"Terre Haute. Two hours from the airport in Indy."

"Find a motel near the airport and we'll leave this evening," Book said.

They intended to leave the Taurus in the long-term airport parking and fly home. Clint knew distance was their friend—he'd learned that lesson in the military. Hit and run. No one would think to look for them, or the car, in Indianapolis. And by the time the Taurus was found, they'd be long gone.

As they approached Indianapolis, Clint noticed how much the city had grown. He'd last been here in 2006, just before enlisting in the Army. The Indianapolis Colts, with Peyton Manning at quarterback, were robbed of their bid for Super Bowl XLI by the Pittsburgh Steelers 21–18. The RCA Dome was gone now, torn down a few years after that amazing victory to make way for the expansion of the Convention Center. He had no interest in going to the new stadium, Lucas Oil. It had been built after he was already shipped to Iraq. No memories there.

"Find a phone," Book said.

Clint took the next exit and drove around a depressed area on the edge of town until they found a telephone booth with an intact phone. Book got out and stretched.

"I'll call the boss and then make sure the money goes in our account," Book said, and Clint laid his seat back and closed his eyes. A hotel bed would feel good.

When Book got back in the car, he wasn't smiling.

"So?" Clint asked.

"So, we go back," Book said.

Clint said nothing. He and Book knew how to follow orders. But something bad had happened, or they wouldn't have to go back. In the two years they'd been doing this they'd never had to go back.

"They found the head at the dump," Book explained.

"No way. We buried her parts all over the landfill, Book. No way they found her," Clint said, but then he remembered the dogs. He'd kicked one of them and sent it scrambling, but maybe it came back. Maybe they should have buried the parts deeper. In any case, this was all Book's screwup. He was the one that had insisted on cutting her body into pieces.

Clint had met Book in Iraq, where they were both armored gunners, and they had become fast friends. Spent some time in Afghanistan, too. Clint's original plan was to be career Army. Book, too. But after watching several of their buddies dissected by IEDs—improvised explosive devices—Book had shared an epiphany with Clint. Why get killed for the pennies the Army paid when they could make serious dough as mercenaries?

Clint agreed. They had become very proficient at taking the lives of their country's enemies. What did it matter if they killed someone besides Uncle Sam's enemies? The money was better on the private side.

They were nearing the time to reenlist, so Clint and Book sent a dozen responses to ads in mercenary magazines. They had just deployed from Iraq back to Ft. Hood, Texas, when a letter came addressed to Book. There was no sender's name or address on the envelope, and inside was a single slip of paper with a telephone number typed on it.

Two weeks before their scheduled departure from the Army, they called the number and spoke to a woman with an East Coast accent, who made them an offer they couldn't pass up. The deal was struck, and two weeks later they were on a bus to Trenton, New Jersey, and a career change.

The woman's voice was the only contact with the organization she just called "The Company." It was a simple setup. She gave them their missions, they carried out the orders, and the payment was deposited into their ever-growing bank accounts.

Until now work had been plentiful, monetarily rewarding, and simple. Until Book screwed up, that is. Book had done some messed-up stuff in Afghanistan, too, but that was war. He knew what was wrong with Book. His mind was still stuck in *haji* land.

Clint slumped in the seat, sulking. He knew that going back meant more work for the same amount of money. They were paid by the job, not by the hour. Every day they spent in Evansville would come out of their own pockets, and he had just bought a lakefront cabin and a new bass boat. He sure as hell couldn't afford to lose money.

"We may not be in Evansville more than a day," Book said. "Let's head back to Terre Haute."

"What's the job?" Clint asked, and Book laid it out for him. As Clint listened, the simplicity of the plan made him smile.

CHAPTER NINE

Jack waited for Liddell to shoehorn himself into the passenger side and push the seat all the way back so his knees weren't shoved against the dashboard.

"Put your seat belt on," Jack said.

"Yes, Mother."

"And call dispatch on your cell. I don't want any reporters to come around."

"Yes, Mother."

Jack accelerated out of the parking lot of the morgue, and then slid around the corner at Garvin Street directly in front of a car driven by an elderly gentleman. Liddell pulled his seat belt tighter as the other car came alongside them, blasting its horn, the old man inside giving them the bird.

"Slow down, pod'na! Are we going to a fire?"

"We've got a lead. Murphy's Law says, 'You snooze, you lose,'" Jack said.

"We have to get there first," Liddell said, gripping the dashboard.

Nina Parsons's house was located in the gated community of Eden Village, a subdivision of newer garden homes built in the seventies and now occupied by senior citizens. Hers was a single-story wood-sided home, painted old-fashioned slate blue with dark blue trim, faux-wood vinyl shutters, and a front porch complete with wicker furniture. A single-car garage was attached on the left. Crime-scene SUVs bracketed the driveway of 118 Village Lane, and Jack stopped behind the nearest one to survey the neighborhood.

The lots had just enough room to run a lawn mower between the houses. Across the street an elderly woman was reading a book on her porch, pretending not to notice the police cars.

Sergeant Walker stood on the porch as the two detectives joined him. Walker handed them paper booties and latex gloves. As they put them on, Jack said, "Eric said she lived by herself."

Jack put his face close to the front window and peered through a crack in the curtains, where he could see into the living room and down a hallway that led to a kitchen and one or two bedrooms. Nothing looked out of place.

"We just got here," Walker said. "No sign of forced entry, Jack. We checked the back and we're setting up a perimeter." Walker nodded to one of the techs, and she hurried off with a roll of yellow and black tape.

Jack said, "Eric Manson said he came by earlier. He showed up at the morgue and identified the victim as Nina Parsons."

When the name registered, Walker said, "Nina Parsons? You mean the deputy prosecutor?"

"You know her?"

Walker said he did. He had testified in a couple of the cases she'd prosecuted.

"Eric said she didn't show up to do pre-charges with another employee and he came to check on her welfare." *How could I forget to ask Eric how he knew Nina hadn't come to work today? Or ask if he had a key to her house?*

"Did he go inside her house?" Walker asked.

"He said he did a walk-through," Jack said. "To tell the truth, I didn't ask him a lot of the questions that I should have. He was with the chief."

Liddell interjected, "Jack has a lot on his mind. Eric and Jack's ex are—"

"Drop it, Bigfoot." To Walker, Jack asked, "What do you need, Tony? Do we need to bring Eric out here?"

"It would be nice to know what he touched. What rooms he was in," Walker said.

"We'd better get him over here to show us. I'm assuming he has the key, so we won't have to damage the door."

Liddell gave Jack a questioning look. "You sure that's a good idea?"

"It would be helpful," Walker agreed. "And he's already been inside once."

Jack grinned. "Yeah. Why should we have all the fun?"

CHAPTER TEN

Dr. John Carmodi, known simply as Doc, or Dr. John, was a forensic pathologist by trade, but his hobby was collecting antique ambulances and lovingly restoring them. In his job he took bodies apart to see why they had quit working. He was proud of what he did, but it didn't satisfy his creative spirit like taking apart an old ambulance and bringing it back to life. People thought it strange that a medical examiner would own a hearse, but it was no different from a cop owning a donut shop, as far as he was concerned.

That Sunday morning Dr. John had been looking forward to working on a recently purchased 1962 Pontiac hearse that was first off the line when limo builder Stageway merged with the Armbruster factory in Fort Smith, Arkansas, in 1962 to form Armbruster Stageway. Most people thought of hearses as Cadillacs, Lincolns, or Mercedeses, and all of those were built on a Pontiac body manufactured between 1960 and 1974, so he had a real collector's item. Now he had to find parts, match the original paint and carpeting, a headlight, and it would be ready for the Frog Follies in the next year or so.

He owned two other hearses, and he was driving one of these, a 1963 Pontiac Superior Ambulance, almost identical to the one that transported John F. Kennedy's body after the assassination in Dallas. He hardly noticed the stares he was getting from other traffic as he took the road to Illinois.

He knew he was close to his destination when he drove by a road sign that declared, "Welcome to Harrisburg," and beneath that, "Home to 4,000 nice people and one old grouch." Painted on the sign was a hillbilly with a straw hat, missing teeth, wife-beater shirt, and no shoes, holding a jug of whiskey. It made him think of something Jack Murphy would say: "He's got summer teeth. Summer there, 'n' some ain't."

Although his medical practice was based in Vanderburgh County, Dr. John's job as a forensic pathologist took him to several adjoining counties. This time he was responding to a request from the coroner in Saline County, Illinois. He was just entering Harrisburg when he got the call from Lilly. A woman's dismembered head and an arm, presumably from the same body, awaited him upon his return at the Evansville morgue.

He turned onto Main Street and looked for the coffee shop, which, according to Harrisburg detective Mike Jones, was the only thing in town that was open on Sunday. After the two-hour drive from Evansville, he needed a strong cup of coffee, and Jones had assured him it was strong enough to stand a spoon in.

He had never met Jones, but there was only one customer inside, a man in his forties sporting an old-fashioned brush cut, his hair graying on the sides. He was heavily muscled, as evidenced by his black knit shirt straining at the seams. He reminded Dr. John of the Hulk, only shorter.

"Dr. John," Detective Jones said, extending a hand.

Dr. John took the offered hand and felt the heavy calluses and strength in it.

"Saline County ain't big but it can boast two things, Doc. It's home to the smallest post office and the biggest Kentucky Fried Chicken in the United States," Jones said. "Backwater, USA. But having said that, I've got to show you something."

They ordered their coffee and Jones led Dr. John outside. "We can walk from here," he said, and they hoofed it half a block to a brick building with boarded-up windows and a sign over the door that read FRED'S. Jones had a key to the door and led him inside.

Dr. John checked out the tiny morgue and thought it looked like an old-fashioned meat market, evidenced by the scarred chopping-block table, steel counters and sinks, and the door to a walk-in freezer.

Jones said, "If you're thinking this looks like an old meat market, you'd be right. The county bought it after Fred went out of business. It's not state of the art, but it has what we need."

Jones opened the freezer door and Dr. John's eyes went wide as the detective brought the items out.

Jones put the trays on the butcher block, and despite his training, Dr. John gave an involuntary wince. On the first tray was the head of a female and next to it the head of a male. The male was approximately thirty years old, maybe ten years older than the female. The man's head was intact, but the female's eyes had been carved out of their sockets, and the teeth and lips were smashed and crusted with blood.

This wasn't the first time Harrisburg had requested him to examine decapitated heads. It'd had three others in the last four years. But the level of violence that had been inflicted on the young woman before him was the work of someone truly evil.

"Is the coroner on his way in?" Dr. John asked.

Jones explained, "Les Winters is the coroner now. He was a city councilman, but after Dr. Wilbert passed away he ran for coroner. Just between you and me, I don't expect he'll keep this job. He was at the scene all of one minute before he barfed and said he was going home sick."

"Where exactly did you find the heads?" Dr. John asked.

"We found these side by side on the back steps of the Rent-A-Center. Just down the street a few blocks. A big dumpster was ten feet away from them, so whoever did this didn't try to hide them, or they could have chucked them in the trash."

"The bodies?" Dr. John was thinking of the earlier murders. The police had found the heads of the victims, but no bodies were ever found.

Jones shook his head. "No sign of the bodies. But they weren't killed where they were found. The site was staged. Not much blood. One of our patrol cars spotted them around noon, and I can tell you, the officer damned near messed his drawers. I've put it all in the report." Jones handed Dr. John a big manila envelope. "Near as I can figure, they weren't there before eleven last night, so they were put there sometime between then and noon today."

Dr. John started to take some digital pictures.

"My narcotics guys think they know who did this," Jones said, adding, "and I'm pretty sure I know who these belong to."

Harrisburg was a tiny town, so Jones's remark came as no surprise to Dr. John. But even so, a legal identification would require more than that. Forensic dentistry might be able to identify the remains of the female's mouth and jaws, but the amount of damage done meant he'd have to get DNA to confirm the identities.

"We'll need DNA on both of these if we ever get to court. So, who do you think they are?" Dr. John asked.

"I'm eighty percent sure her name is Hope Dupree. She was in the hospital a few days ago. Domestic violence. Her pimp beat her up."

"And the man?" Dr. John asked.

Jones grinned and pointed at the male's head. "That's her pimp."

"Ahh, of course it is."

As Jones took a sip of his coffee, his eyes searched the doctor's face. "You did the older cases, right?"

Dr. John absentmindedly raked his bottom lip with his teeth as he glanced again at the horrors on the table in front of him.

"It was a field day for the news media back then. Two heads propped up in the middle of Main Street, in a small town. It had news written all over it. But then another head was found two years later. Hell, even the national stations sent crews to cover the discovery. I think it was even given a mention on the *Today* show in New York."

That head had been found behind the same Rent-A-Center. With the rise of drug sales came the proliferation of violence and death. But he had determined the other heads were hacked from the bodies, not cut cleanly like these two. Dr. John added, "Also, those victims weren't beaten after death like this woman."

He looked with foreboding at Jones. "Do you think it's starting again?"

Jones tossed his paper cup in the trash. "Sure as hell hope not, Dr. John. I still have nightmares from that time."

"Let's get these bagged by your crime-scene guys, and I'll take them with me back to Evansville."

"I'm doubling as crime scene today, Doc," Jones said. "Harrisburg PD isn't big enough to have a full-time crime-scene technician on weekends."

Dr. John suspected as much. "By the way," he said, "I've got another one of these severed heads waiting for me at home."

"Seriously?" Jones asked, and when Dr. John nodded, he asked, "Mind if I tag along?"

CHAPTER ELEVEN

The stretch of Interstate 70 running between Indianapolis and Terre Haute was straight, flat, and unremarkable. Clint drove a little over the speed limit, but not too much. To his mind, they had already stayed in Indiana past their comfort zone. Most of their contracts were in-and-out jobs—never an overnighter. He wasn't nervous, but mistakes could happen. He was in this for the money, pure and simple. He wasn't so sure about Book anymore.

Clint grew up on a farm in Wisconsin, so he knew all about slaughtering—if you don't kill, you don't eat. Then in the Army they'd taught him another kind of slaughtering. He killed for his country at first, but then it became easy, like a regular nine-to-five job. He was aware that was a sick comparison, but it helped justify his actions. By the time he had been discharged from the Army and went into business with Book, it was too late to stop. Killing was the only thing he knew, or felt comfortable with. He wasn't that Wisconsin farm boy anymore. That guy was dead as well.

But for Book it was different. When they were in Iraq together, Book told him of growing up in infamous Cabrini-Green on Chicago's north side and being raised by an uncle. Book said that when he was eight years old, his father had been robbed and killed while driving a cab. His mother deserted him a short time later. She just left him sleeping in the hallway of an apartment building one morning with no money, no food, and no options. He was twelve the first time he was arrested.

Book knew firsthand what violence had done to his own family, so why was he so eager to visit this on others? It was a puzzle to Clint. He didn't look forward to the contracts, but Book lived for the next kill. No, Book was in it for other reasons. Maybe he hated all women because of the betrayal of his own mother. Maybe that was the reason Book didn't have sex unless it was violent and depraved.

Clint drove west for over an hour and was almost to Terre Haute when Book sat forward and said, "Take the ramp."

Clint had seen the sign for Hulman International Airport two exits back. He had intended to pull off anyway, but Book liked to be in charge, so Clint said nothing and slowed for the off ramp.

They exited the interstate and cruised the parking lot of the airport until Clint found a Chevy panel van with dark tinted windows that would serve their purposes.

"Let's leave the Taurus here in the long-term lot," Clint suggested.

Book gave him a questioning look. "Don't you think we need the car? What if we need to ditch the van real quick-like? We take them both."

Clint didn't feel like arguing, and two hours after stealing the van he was following Book down Highway 41 to the Flying J truck stop, just across Interstate 64 from Evansville. They left the Taurus in the lot of the Flying J, where cars and trucks were parked, sometimes for days, by over-the-road truckers.

Book got in the van with Clint. "Turn right." He directed Clint westward on a narrow road that ran parallel to the interstate.

"Where we going?" Clint asked.

"Just keep going."

"Turn here," Book said, and Clint obediently turned down a farm road where, nailed to a tree, was a hand-lettered sign that warned, "No Hunting."

Clint continued on across a dry ditch and stopped at the edge of the woods.

"We're here," Book announced, and they both went around to the back and opened the cargo doors.

Both men were sweating and covered in welts from large black mosquitoes by the time they had unlatched the bench seats in the cargo area and tossed them into the woods. The back of the van was windowless. It would make the perfect killing ground.

"When are you going to tell me the plan?" Clint asked.

"Sorry I been so quiet," Book said, and reached his hand out for the keys to the van.

Book started it up, hands gripping the steering wheel. "The job tonight will be easier with the van. When we're done, we go back to the Flying J, trade vehicles, and head back to Indy. From there we go home." Book held out a big fist.

Clint felt his stomach rumble and realized he was starving. He bumped knuckles with Book and said, "Let's eat first."

CHAPTER TWELVE

Eric Manson parked his new black Mercedes-Benz SL in front of the house where the elderly woman sat reading in a cane rocker on the porch. Eric nodded a *good afternoon* to her and pointed the car key back over his shoulder as he walked to Nina's. The car made a chirping sound as it locked.

"Liddell. Jack. Sergeant Walker," Eric said as he stepped onto Nina's porch.

"Did you bring the key?" Jack asked.

"Key?" Eric asked. "I don't have a key. When I was here earlier, the door was unlocked."

With a gloved hand, a tech twisted the doorknob and pushed. It wouldn't budge. "Well, it's locked now."

"I didn't have a key, and I didn't lock it when I left," Eric protested.

Edging the tech aside, Liddell put his shoulder into the door and it gave way.

"Must've been stuck," the tech suggested.

Liddell struck a bodybuilder pose. "You ever seen such muscles on a mere mortal? Who does this remind you of?"

"Congressman Anthony Weiner during the Twitter scandal," the tech said.

"The blonde on *Charlie's Angels*?" Eric offered, and even Jack laughed.

"Why don't you start the walk-through with Walker, Bigfoot? I need to talk to Eric," Jack said.

A tech entered the doorway first, taking digital photos of everything as they made their way inside. Liddell was last through the door, saying "I'll be back" in his best Arnold Schwarzenegger impression.

"Your partner's a funny guy, Jack."

"Yeah," he said, instantly dismissing the distraction. "Tell me again why you were here at Nina's this morning, Eric."

There was very little shade on the porch, so Eric held up his hand to block the sun. "I've already explained this to you—*and your chief*. Is this your idea of a grilling, Jack?" he asked half-jokingly.

"Answer the question."

Eric sighed and moved into a pocket of shade before answering. "Trent got a call from Cindy McCoy this morning." Anticipating Jack's next question, Eric added, "You'll have to ask Cindy how she came about the neighbor's number."

The elderly woman was no longer on her porch, but Jack noticed the curtains twitch in the window. "Go on."

"Anyway," Eric continued, "the neighbor told Cindy she hadn't seen Nina since yesterday morning, and then reported a loud argument at Nina's late last night. Cindy decided to call Trent at home to see if he could get someone else to come in and help because she couldn't reach me. I was at the party. Remember? I had my phone turned off until I saw you head out in a hurry."

Jack had picked up on the most important detail. "This is the first I'm hearing of this argument. Why didn't you tell us about that earlier, at the morgue?"

"Hey!" Eric said, holding his hands up. "Don't shoot the messenger. I'm telling you everything I know."

"You are now."

"I guess I forgot," Eric said, his voice tinged with anger.

Walker stuck his head out the door. "I'm ready for you, Eric."

"Do I get gloves?" Eric asked.

"Just don't touch anything," Walker said, and led him inside.

Jack waited on the porch. He knew that if any obvious clues had been left inside, Walker would already have told him. Awhile later Eric came back out. "I think I should have worn those paper shoe covers," he complained. "Booties or whatever you call them. There's no telling what I dragged in there on my feet."

"Did you step off the paper runner onto the floor?" Jack asked him.

"No. But there's less contamination issues if I'd had the same thing as your guys."

Jack knew Eric was used to being in charge, and he decided to shake his tree a little. "Eric, why were you really here?"

Eric acted offended. "I already told you."

Jack made a point of looking at the old woman's porch. She was gone now, but Eric saw where Jack was looking.

Jack pressed, "Why would you lie to me? Are you hiding something, Eric?"

Eric's gaze involuntarily landed on the porch lamp by the door.

Jack fought a smile as he realized he hadn't looked there for a spare house key. He stretched up and felt a small box of some sort. He pulled out a magnetic case for hiding spare keys. He slid the top back—no key.

Jack extended his palm. Eric's shoulders slumped. He reached into his pocket, pulled out a brass-colored key, and dropped it in Jack's hand.

"Why don't we start again?"

Eric admitted that the door had been locked when he arrived at the house. He claimed he had *found* the key and used it to enter the house to check on Nina. He swore everything else he had said was true. He obstinately denied having past knowledge of where the key was, but he couldn't maintain eye contact when he did so.

"Why did you lie?" Jack asked.

Eric looked embarrassed. "I was afraid you'd think just what you're thinking right now—that we were having an affair. But I assure you I have never been involved with her."

Jack had a fleeting memory of Bill Clinton saying almost those exact words.

"What else haven't you told me?"

Liddell came out onto the porch. "You can still smell some kind of cleaner with pine scent inside. Walker says no fingerprints jump out at him. Plus, here's a weird angle. If she had luggage, it's gone. Not much in the dresser drawers, several empty hangers in the closet. I couldn't find any makeup or medicine bottles. And no car in the garage."

"Well, we know where she ended up. Let's find out where she was before that," Jack said.

"Roger that, pod'na. I'll get her vehicle information and put out a BOLO. We going to call in for help for the neighborhood check?"

"Let's check the nearby neighbors ourselves," Jack suggested. "Mostly retirees, so they should have been home last night."

"You played me, Jack," Eric said suddenly. "No one saw me with the key, did they?"

When Jack regarded him blankly, Eric's face went red. "You don't know anything for sure. Maybe she didn't own luggage. Maybe nothing is missing. Maybe her car is in the shop for repairs."

"Ever know a woman who didn't have luggage? Or makeup?" Jack asked. "Was she seeing someone, Eric?"

"How would I know?" Eric shot back. "If you're accusing me of something, Jack, just say it."

"I'm not accusing you, Eric," Jack lied. "I'm just asking questions. You know how this works."

Eric looked angry enough that if he truly had killed Nina, he was either a great actor, or could lie with impunity. Whoever killed Nina had gone to a lot of effort to eliminate their presence from the house. It would have taken a great amount of time to wipe the house of latent fingerprints, pack her things, and get out—taking Nina's car—without being seen.

And what was the purpose of all this subterfuge? The killer had gone to great lengths to make Nina disappear. Was it supposed to look like Nina had gone on an unexpected trip? Or was her killer simply trying to slow the investigation down?

Eric said the neighbor Cindy McCoy had called heard an argument at Nina's last night. If that was true, Jack assumed the murder took place inside Nina's home.

Jack needed to find the car and locate the neighbor. He had a good idea where to find the neighbor at least.

"Eric, I want access to Nina's office," Jack said.

"Today?"

Jack thought Eric looked uncomfortable. "What have you done, Eric?"

"Look, Jack," Eric began. "As we were leaving the morgue, Chief Pope said something about Nina's job being the reason for her murder. I thought I was helping."

Jack couldn't believe what he was hearing. He knew that if Eric had gone in both Nina's house and her office, he was hunting for something.

"Look, Jack, I didn't find anything, and I didn't move anything. I was just looking for an address book or a calendar—anything to help with the investigation."

Jack had quit listening to the liar. He wished he could take Eric downtown and charge him with interfering or obstruction, but if Eric was involved in Nina's murder, he would gain nothing by talking to Jack. And he was an attorney, so he would know enough to clam up and ask for one.

"We'll talk again," Jack said irritably. "You can leave for now."

Without a word or a backward glance, Eric stormed off for his car.

Liddell watched the retreating figure. "You didn't ask him if he found anything in Nina's office?"

"He'd just tell another lie." Jack held his hand out and dropped the key in Liddell's hand. "A present from—guess who?—Eric."

Liddell took the key and it turned in the front door lock. "We should give it to Walker and have him bag it as evidence."

Liddell went to find Walker and to put the BOLO out on Nina's car.

While Liddell was inside with Walker, Lilly called Jack.

"Dr. John's here," Little Casket said when Jack answered, "and he's brought friends."

Before Jack could ask whom she meant, the line went dead.

CHAPTER THIRTEEN

When Jack and Liddell arrived at the morgue, they saw Dr. John's old ambulance, or hearse, or whatever he wanted to call it, parked in front. A black Crown Vic was backed into the garage entrance, and a middle-aged man was helping Lilly pull Styrofoam coolers from the trunk. The man wore black military BDU pants and a black knit shirt like a modified SWAT uniform. "I didn't know you were having a tailgate party, Lilly," Liddell said as he and Jack approached the open trunk.

"Jack Murphy, Liddell Blanchard," Lilly said. "Meet Mike Jones."

Jack noticed the Harrisburg Police Department shield embroidered on the left breast of the knit shirt. He wasn't wearing a street cop's gun belt with all the nifty tools of the trade, but he was carrying a Smith & Wesson semiautomatic and a pair of federal handcuffs tucked into his waist.

"Detective Jones. Harrisburg PD." He extended a hand to Jack and then Liddell.

"Forty caliber?" Jack asked him.

"Smith & Wesson M&P40, double-action, fifteen-round clip and one in the pipe. It's kickass," Jones said like he was talking about his child just hitting a homerun.

"Introductions over," Lilly said. "Before you ask, yes, Dr. John's here and doing something in his office. Now help me with this." She held out the cooler and Liddell took it.

"Where do you want me to put it?" Liddell asked.

Lilly turned on him, eyes the size of Ping-Pong balls behind her thick lenses, and said, "You don't want me to tell you where to put it, but I will if you keep standing there like a big ape."

She headed off through the garage and into a door in back. Jack led the men after her and entered the autopsy room, where Lilly had already pulled out a steel gurney.

"This is some crazy shit, huh?" Jones said. "You find a body yet?"

"I'm not holding my breath," Jack responded. He'd read the news about the murders in Harrisburg a couple of years back, but he didn't remember if they found the bodies to match the heads. "This isn't Harrisburg's first rodeo, is it?" Jack asked.

"No," Jones said. "We had two heads left smack in the middle of Main Street four years ago. Then, two years ago, a head was found on top of a dumpster. And now these two. Never any bodies, though."

"Any leads?" Jack asked.

Jones said, "We identified the first three victims. They were all meth heads. And I think I know who these two are. The female was a meth head prostitute, and the guy was her pimp and a drug dealer. One of our narcotics guys is verifying that as we speak."

Those are different from ours. "So you think it was a drug thing?"

Jones rubbed the back of his neck. "Looks like it."

"Ours wasn't involved in drugs that we know of. She was a deputy prosecutor here and I don't think she handled any drug cases. She was dumped at the landfill, so not out in public like yours."

"And ours was armed when we found her," Liddell pointed out, and both detectives turned to him. "I mean, we found an arm, too."

"You have anything serious to add, Bigfoot?" Jack asked.

Liddell grinned and said, "Hey! I'm just proud to be allowed to watch two great detectives putting all the leads together."

"You boys done bonding?" Lilly asked, wedging between Jack and the Illinois detective. "Doc's ready."

They made their way to the autopsy room.

"Let's see if we can make some *headway* here," Jones deadpanned, causing Jack to groan and Liddell to grin.

Deputy Chief Richard Dick finished the telephone call, placed the old-fashioned handset back in its cradle, and studied his reflection in the mirror above the table. He was proud of his shape—not a bit of fat, and his features and prominent nose looked like they were chiseled from a block of stone. He was considered to be ruthless in his dealings with his police officers, and he was glad he had that reputation. Getting cooperation was easier if the rank and file feared him.

His wife of thirty years was in the kitchen making lemonade, just the way he liked it, with real lemons and real honest-to-God sugar. He and Barbara had planned to sit on their air-conditioned patio and listen to Eddie Money on the new surround-sound system he'd had installed out there. From down the hall he could hear "Two Tickets to Paradise" was just finishing up. Next would be "Take Me Home Tonight"—his favorite.

"Who was it, honey?" Barbara asked, and he was pleased to hear her slicing another lemon. She was happiest when she was making him happy. And he was happy that she was that way. Their mutual desire for his happiness was what made their marriage work.

"It's nothing to stop you from making that lemonade," he said.

The phone call was from Eric Manson, who was not only the chief deputy to the prosecutor, but also a friend. He called to complain that Murphy had given him a public dressing down, and then had gone as far as to suggest Eric was complicit in a murder. This only cemented Dick's hatred of Jack Murphy and that Cajun-reject partner of his, Liddell. Dick didn't tell Eric that he had also been dressed down this morning. Chief Pope had called him after seeing Dick on television and "reminded" him that the police department had a public information officer to release anything to do with active investigations. "Remind" was a diplomatic way for Pope to order Dick to butt out and go home. As deputy chief, *he* was the titular head of the entire investigations unit and should by all rights be leading this case. Then, to add insult to injury, Pope hadn't even called to tell him when the victim had been identified.

But their attempt at keeping him in the dark hadn't worked. He already knew who the victim was. Detective Jansen had called and filled him in just before he received the call from Eric. The victim was a deputy prosecutor, so this case had taken on a new dimension of importance, both to the police department and the news media.

He felt his face tightening, his jaws clenching, and he deliberately had to make the muscles in them relax. Captain Franklin, Jack Murphy, and Liddell Blanchard worked for him. They owed him some courtesy and respect. *Marlin Pope may protect Murphy now, but when I become chief of police, all that will stop, by God!*

A thought came to him. Jansen had taken it on himself to butt in at the morgue this morning, but if Dick had someone keeping tabs on Murphy, he could stay in the loop. The chief couldn't object to his giving Murphy an extra investigator. He should have thought of this sooner. He could monitor the case, plus score some points with Eric. It never hurt to have a friend in the county prosecutor's office.

He picked up the phone and punched in the cell number for Captain Franklin. When he answered, Dick said, "Captain, I've decided Jack Murphy needs some assistance with this murder case he's on. Yes, the landfill case. Now, here's what I want you to do."

CHAPTER FOURTEEN

Autopsies are a necessary evil in death investigations, but Jack thought the practice barbaric. With all the advances made in technology, he was surprised the medical field hadn't kept up. Maybe in twenty years a detective would merely have to scan the deceased person with his iPhone and a computer would tell the detective everything he needed to know. Maybe Apple would come out with an iAutopsy app.

"Earth to Jack," Liddell said, nudging him.

Jack looked up in time to see Detective Larry Jansen standing in the conference room doorway.

"I didn't know you attended autopsies," Jack said.

"Deputy Chief Dick called me in." The rumpled detective looked around the autopsy room, daring anyone to challenge him.

"I guess *Dick* wants to *double* the detectives on this one," Liddell quipped.

"When is this going to start? I ain't getting any younger here," Jansen said, taking a notebook out of an inner pocket and holding it close to his chest while he scribbled something.

"Not that I don't trust you, Larry," Jack said, taking his cell phone from his pocket. He made a call to Captain Franklin and spoke briefly, then hung up and said, resigned, "The captain says he's working with us."

"Mike Jones, Harrisburg PD," Jones said, and briefly shook Jansen's hand. He sensed the bad blood in the air, but Jack didn't make any attempt to explain.

Lilly poked her head in from the hallway. "Doc's ready."

* * *

Dr. John stepped on the pedal that operated a microphone suspended over the autopsy table and began reciting. Sergeant Walker was on hand to snap digital photos from every angle while Dr. John examined the decapitated head of Nina Parsons. "We have the head and right arm of a white female. Approximately thirty years of age, dark hair about thirty-five centimeters in length, blue eyes, no obvious scars or blemishes. The flesh of the face shows evidence of animal activity with partial skull exposure, the skull itself being intact."

Dr. John washed detritus from the open wounds and continued on in medical speak, but Jack quit paying attention. If Dr. John wanted him to notice something, he would point it out. Until then Jack withdrew into his own thoughts.

He knew who the victim was, but not how she had died, or why, or who had killed her. Because of what she did for a living, the obvious place to start was her job, so he needed to find out what cases she was handling. And even if someone wanted her dead, why did they have to do this to her?

"If you were one of my students, I'd throw an eraser at you," Dr. John said, and Jack zoned back in.

"Sorry, Doc. You were saying . . . ?"

"Cause of death is hard to determine. The hyoid bone is fractured, so strangulation is possible. Removal of the head occurred postmortem."

"She was strangled to death?" Jones asked.

Dr. John shook his head. "Although the fracture of the hyoid bone could have been accomplished after death, say by a heavy blow to the throat with a fist or some other object, I don't see any damage to the surrounding tissue to indicate that. The hyoid's position in the throat doesn't make it susceptible to an easy fracture, and—look here, and here," he said, pointing to some bruising to the left and right side, just under the jawline. "What does that look like to you?"

Jack saw two crescent-shaped contusions just under the jawbone, about three inches apart and one on each side of the throat. "Thumbnails," he said, and Dr. John nodded appreciatively.

"That's exactly what they are, Jack. You see, the killer grabbed her by the throat, thumbs crossed over each other, and dug into the tissue under the jaw with enough pressure to create these half-moon impressions. That would be enough pressure to crush the hyoid, definitely."

Dr. John rolled the head onto its side. "There's a contusion with at least a six-centimeter laceration in the center of it on the back of the head. I'll have to look at the skull underneath to determine exactly what caused it—whether she fell, was struck with something, or, more likely, given the evidence of strangulation, her head was shoved against something hard. In any case, this would have resulted in heavy bleeding." He stopped recording and asked Jack, "Was there a lot of blood anywhere at her house? On a door frame, or a concrete floor, possibly?"

Walker volunteered, "We didn't see anything obvious, doc. I'll have my guys at the house look again."

Jack said, "We don't know where she was killed. Her house was clean, with nothing valuable missing, no signs of a struggle or anything like you're describing. And her car is missing. What you see there is what we have." Jack was embarrassed that he knew so little.

Dr. John started recording again. "The cutting instrument was heavy enough to chop a head off with one blow. There is no evidence of multiple cuts."

He turned the head so that the detectives could see the damage to tissue and bone.

"This is one cut, Jack. The blade went through the trachea just below the thyroid cartilage and then through the fifth and sixth cervical vertebrae without tearing any of the surrounding tissue or muscle."

Dr. John said in a subdued voice, "Not an axe, because there's not enough damage to the surrounding tissue, and in any case, that would have crushed the trachea and vertebrae. This weapon was long, razor-sharp, and wielded with enough strength to sever the head from the body in one stroke. Does that suggest anything to you?"

"I think I know what the weapon is," Detective Jones said. "Our narcotics unit has been investigating rumors of gang drug activity in the Harrisburg area for the last several years. The gang they're hearing about is called La Mara Salvatrucha. That's the official name, but they are known on the street—"

"As MS-13," Jack finished for him, and Jones nodded. Jack said, "I've heard about these guys. Aren't they from El Salvador?"

"That's where they started. Then they spread like cancer to the West and East Coasts and, according to my guys, they've now moved into Tennessee. That's what, two hours southeast of here?"

"If it is MS-13, the deaths are just beginning," Jack said.

Jones went on, "We think they're making a move into Illinois. I'm pretty sure they were behind the first three killings because there was a big jump in the drug traffic during that time. And . . . the weapon of choice for MS-13 is the machete, and they like to take heads." Jones paused to let that sink in.

"La Mara Salvatrucha is known for their violence. They have the other gangs running scared," Jones said. "And there are rumors that they're fronting for Al Qaeda. Of course, everything that goes bump in the night is tied to Al Qaeda these days. But I have to tell you, these guys scare the hell out of me!"

Liddell put his mouth to Jack's ear and whispered, "Do you believe it's gang-related?"

Jack shook his head. The only connection Nina could have had to MS-13 was through her work. Plus, they would have made a public display of her like their other victims. He knew that MS-13 traditionally took over drug operations, or enforced their own territory from other operations by killing everyone who opposed them, and then made a public spectacle of their kills. They were similar to terrorists in that way.

Jack couldn't buy the idea that it was gang-related. The gang-bangers he'd talked to were all numb-nuts—in other words, they thought with their balls. He could make MS-13 possibly for the killings in Harrisburg, but they weren't savvy enough to have cleansed Nina's house of all evidence. That aspect was professional, like someone with a lot of police and court experience.

Dr. John picked up a scalpel. "Let's finish this, and then we need to meet in the conference room. I have something to show you."

Lilly, who had gloved up, held the head facedown on the table while Dr. John made a lateral incision along the base of the skull and lifted the scalp forward until it slipped over the top of the head and then over the face of the victim.

"No evidence of concussion, although we'll have to examine the inside of the skull," Dr. John said, and Jack could see the bruising and gash on the inside of the scalp. "So far it looks like the head was struck against something flat that caused this cut," Dr. John continued, and pointed to the approximately three-inch vertical tear in the inside tissue. "You can see the hair is matted with blood, which is a good indicator that this was caused before she died."

Dr. John held his hands up at shoulder level and mimed choking someone. "The killer grabbed her by the throat and struck her head against something flat and hard. A wall. Maybe a concrete floor. I'll give Walker some of the hair to send off to the lab. Maybe there is trace evidence on it to show what she was struck against."

Jack was already thinking ahead, and he looked at his watch.

"I get the message," Dr. John said, and reached for the bone saw to finish the autopsy.

Twenty minutes later, the detectives and Dr. John retired to the conference room while Lilly packaged the victim's remains and Walker took hair samples and scraped the fingernails of the hand on the arm that was recovered. The arm showed no defensive wounds, so she hadn't tried to protect herself from her killer. *Or wasn't able to.*

The detectives sat around the conference table and looked through photos Dr. John had taken of the Harrisburg victims. Four years ago, the victims were both males in their twenties, one Hispanic, the other white. Two years ago the murder victim was a black male. He spread the victims' photos in order on the table, starting with the oldest cases. "The one thing all these victims have in common is that their heads were removed from their bodies. Can we all agree on that?"

No one objected. "Now for what is different." He moved the three oldest Harrisburg photos in a row across the top, and slid the most recent underneath those. "The first three victims were alive when they were beheaded. The most recent victims were probably dead before it happened."

"So there are at least two different killers?" Jack asked.

"You're the detective," Dr. John said. "All I can tell you is that the edges of the cuts on the most recent three are clean. A very sharp weapon was used." He looked at Jones. "If it was a machete, the person wielding it is extremely proficient."

He knelt down and bowed his head toward the floor. "The first three victims were probably in a kneeling position, and the first blow came from behind the neck. But the multiple cuts and the damage done to the surrounding tissue indicate that the head was hacked from the body. I would say they were most likely alive when the first blow came because they were in a kneeling position."

"Execution style," Jack said.

"Exactly," Dr. John agreed. "The last three victims, including Nina Parsons, were lying on their backs when the deed was done. I'm only guessing here, but I would say they were already dead, or so incapacitated that they didn't move."

"So what killed Nina?" Jack asked.

"Animals caused the damage to her face and scalp. From the size of the bite marks, I'd say it was a dog, or dogs. She probably didn't bleed out from the head wound, but it might have rendered her unconscious. There was no evidence of a concussion or damage to the brain."

"What about the two we found in Harrisburg this morning?" Jones asked.

Dr. John examined the close-up photos on the table. He picked up the photo of the young woman. "The eyes were cut from their sockets by something pointed, sharp, and bigger than a pocket knife. Maybe a hunting knife."

Dr. John continued. "The pock marks in the bone around the orbits might be where the edges of the blade notched the bone when it was thrust into the eye socket." He looked at Jack. "Can you get me some different knives to compare with the injuries?"

"I can do that," Jones said.

"By the way, Larry," Liddell said, "can we compare your knife? And where were you last night?"

"Piss off, Liddell," Jansen said.

Jack wasn't listening to the men squabble. He was thinking about what this new development should tell him. Is this the same killer? Or are the killings even related?

CHAPTER FIFTEEN

The sun was setting when Jack and Liddell parted ways with Detective Jones at the morgue. The temperature seemed to have dropped ten degrees. A short while later they pulled up behind Sergeant Walker's SUV in front of 118 Village Lane. A black-and-white was parked in the driveway with the interior lights lit. Inside the car, Jack could see a uniformed officer reading a book propped against the steering wheel. The neighborhood, Jack noticed, was a virtual ghost town.

"Eat by five p.m. and in bed by dark," Liddell remarked.

"Bigfoot, are you referring to the advanced age of the residents in this community? Shame on you."

"I'm just saying, we haven't seen anyone outside all day except that old lady across the way. Either we're in the beginning of a zombie movie, or it's an old folks' community," Liddell said.

Jack saw the uniformed officer's head come up, and the book disappeared. He exited the car, carrying a clipboard up the steps, a look of boredom unmistakable. "It's been quiet, Jack. You going in?" he asked, and held out the clipboard.

Jack signed the entry log and handed it to Liddell.

"What are you reading?" Jack asked.

"*Plum Island*," the officer said. "Nelson DeMille."

"I'm just glad it's not one of those sissy Nicolas Sparks love stories," Liddell quipped. "Although I can see how you could get mighty lonely sitting all by yourself."

The officer frowned, grabbed the clipboard, and hurried away.

"Don't look now, but your BFD just got here," Liddell said, looking over Jack's shoulder.

Jack gave him a quizzical look, and Liddell explained, "BFD— you know, Best Friend Detective."

A white Chevy Caprice came down the street and parked behind their car. The Caprice was the older model that looked as worn-out as its driver. Detective Larry Jansen exited and shook the wrinkles from his coat before running a hand through his gray hair. He walked up on the porch, complaining, "You lost me in traffic, Jack. You should have told me we were coming back here. I had to call dispatch."

Before Jack could come up with an appropriate response, Walker came outside holding latex gloves in one hand and paper shoe covers in the other. He handed these to the detectives. "I don't know how we missed this. It was right in front of us the whole time."

Jack raised his eyebrows. "Show us?"

"Stay on the paper," Walker cautioned Jansen. To Jack, he said, "We've got blood, and plenty of it."

Donning the protective gear, they entered the living room in a loose row, keeping their feet on the paper runner as they threaded through black Pelican cases full of crime scene equipment.

On the prior visit, Jack had spent merely a few minutes inside the house to get the layout of the place. Now he saw the living room was fully furnished. In the far corner, opposite a brick fireplace was an old-fashioned brown sectional sofa with embroidered doilies lying perfectly centered over the back cushions.

Walker took orange plastic goggles from one case and handed them out.

"It's going to get dark in here, but keep looking at the fireplace." Walker nodded at a tech standing in the front doorway. The tech pulled the curtains and shut the front door. The room was plunged into darkness.

"I'm going to spray a chemical called Luminol on the fireplace," Walker explained. "The chemical reacts with the iron found in hemoglobin. It's not an infallible test, but it is a good indicator where an assault has taken place."

Jack heard the sound of a spray bottle being pumped, then a faint light came on. Walker was holding what looked like a cable with a light glowing on its end. As he played the light over the brick fireplace front, a white/blue vertical smear appeared at eye level and seemed to splash downward onto the hearth, where it pooled into large circular shapes.

"Is that what I think it is?" Jansen asked.

Walker switched off the light and said to one of his people, "Get the lights." To the detectives he said, "You can take the goggles off now."

The lights came on and Walker collected their eyewear.

"We used Hemastix to test the bright areas you saw with the goggles. The presumptive test was positive for blood, Larry. We'll send samples to the state lab to confirm and run DNA."

"So is it her blood or not?" Jansen asked.

Walker patiently said, "I don't know if it's the victim's, but I think it is blood."

Jansen scribbled something in his notebook.

"What do you think happened here, Tony?" Jack asked.

Walker cast a glance at Jansen and hesitated before saying, "I think she was killed here," but stopped when he saw Jansen writing busily in his notebook. "No fingerprints—except for the victim's," he reluctantly added.

Understanding the reason for his hesitation, Jack said, "I'll check with you for updates, Tony," and then to Liddell, "I guess there's no point in taking up Sergeant Walker's time. If he says there's no more evidence, that's good enough for me. Can I see you on the porch, Larry?" Jack asked, and walked out through the front door.

Jansen came out, scowling, and asked, "Aren't we going through the house? If not, I need to start interviewing neighbors."

Jack saw that he would have to lay down the law. "Look. Larry, I know you were assigned to help me with this case by Captain Franklin. But . . ."

Jack knew he should probably feel guilty for what he was about to do, but he didn't. Jansen hadn't worked in Homicide—or even as a real detective—as far back as Jack could remember. Plus, Jansen had a bad ticker, a sick wife, and a propensity to sell information to the news media. If Jansen wasn't kissing Double Dick's ass, he wouldn't even be here.

"But what, Jack? What have I done wrong?" Jansen asked.

"It's not that you've done something wrong, Larry. I'm just not used to working with anyone but Bigfoot. Look, I've got a job for you. You okay with that?"

Color bloomed in Jansen's face and neck. He pushed both hands in the pockets of his nicotine-stained trench coat. "I get it. You're in charge. So, what do you want me to do, b'wana?"

Unfazed by the hostility, Jack wrote a telephone number on a slip of paper. "Go downtown and call Angelina Garcia at that number. Tell her I asked her to come in and help us out. If she says no, call me. If she says yes, wait for her at headquarters and give her all the names we have so far. Get her started running them through the computer. When you're done, I have another job for you."

"Why am I going to headquarters? Can't Angelina just go in and work on that stuff?"

Jack was one step ahead of him. "Larry, you carry more weight as a detective than she does as a civilian employee. It's vital that you look through all the old mug shots, fingerprints, and find connections between any of the people you have in your notes. Recruit some of the girls in Records to help you. They'll do it for you. I know we've had our differences, but you're a good detective, Larry. No one can say any different."

When he wanted someone out of his hair, he could either order the offender to go away, or try to lose him in traffic. Jack had already tried the traffic thing and it hadn't worked out. Besides, the downside of doing it that way was you didn't know where that person was, or when, or where they were going to turn up.

Jack went back inside after Jansen drove away. He found Liddell and Walker talking.

"I heard you out there, you smooth-tongued devil." Liddell said. "Do you want to call Garcia and tell her Jansen's going to call her?"

"No, she'll figure it out." Jack turned his attention to Walker. "What did you want to tell us?"

"I didn't want this on the Channel Six News," Walker said, "but this place has been cleaned, and I mean thoroughly. Anything of evidentiary value has been destroyed. We've got zip. The blood we were lucky enough to find using Luminol on the fireplace has been contaminated with whatever they used to sanitize the place. Probably bleach. You can still smell it. We only have one set of unknown latent fingerprints on the inside and outside front doorknob."

"Those will be Eric's," Jack said, and told Walker about getting the key from Eric.

"Why would he lie about having the key?" Walker asked, annoyed, putting the key in an evidence bag.

"Because he's a dick," Jack wanted to say. "He might have thought he'd be a suspect. He has the upcoming election to worry

about . . . and publicity." He didn't say anything about Eric's engagement to Katie, because everyone at the police department
knew about his tendency to roam toward any and all stray breasts.

"We'll compare the prints on the knob against Eric's," Walker
said.

"What else?" Jack asked.

"Well, besides the missing clothes and luggage, there's only a
small amount of makeup in the bathroom. No medications in the
medicine cabinet. Her purse is gone. There are no towels in the
bathroom. No dirty clothes. No trash. The carpeting in the living
room and two bedrooms show signs they were vacuumed recently,
but I didn't find a vacuum cleaner. There's plenty of food in the refrigerator, including fresh fruit and vegetables."

"Do you think she was killed here?" Jack asked.

"Dr. John said the hyoid bone was broken. That usually means
strangulation, and that may have happened here based on the blood
we found. Maybe her head was knocked into the bricks. One of my
techs found some hair stuck to the mortar."

Jack rubbed his chin, and asked, "Do you remember Lenny
Sturdevant?"

Walker said, "Married policeman, on duty, visits his girlfriend
and beats her to death, then kills her cat and puts both bodies on her
bed and sets the bed on fire. That Lenny Sturdevant?"

Jack had forgotten Walker helped work the case before he transferred to the Crime Scene Unit. "Yeah. He went back to the house
after he killed her and set the bedroom on fire. If he hadn't gone
back, we probably never would have caught him. He had the perfect alibi because he was working—on patrol—and his beat was
clear across town."

"Are you trying to make a comparison with this murder?"

"My point is that he was a policeman. He thought he had committed the perfect crime, but when he didn't hear the fire department being dispatched to his girlfriend's house, he got worried.
Then he started wondering if he had left something behind. His
anxiety made him go back. That's why he was caught."

Walker cocked his head to the side. "Are you thinking Eric did
this?"

"Think about it. It's a fact that most killings are done by someone close to the victim. A husband. A lover. A family member. A

coworker. And Eric's reputation as a skirt chaser has to be considered. We can't prove it yet, but I can think of a handful of motives for him to kill her."

Liddell grinned. "The way I heard it, if you tested the bed sheets of half the women working with Eric, they would test positive for the presence of Eric." Realizing what he'd said, he added, "Sorry, pod'na. That was uncalled for."

Jack waved the comment off. "I don't really think he's capable of it, but he fits the profile. He found the body, he lied about having a key or at least knowing where the key was hidden, he has a reputation of philandering, and he would have the knowledge it would take to sanitize the crime scene."

"But that's assuming Eric and Nina were doing the nasty, which is an unknown," Walker reminded him. "And whoever did this had to cut Nina up and take her body parts to the landfill. I just can't see him doing that."

Jack knew Walker was right. Eric wouldn't have the guts to do all of that. Besides, a first-time killer didn't usually dismember his victim. Like drinking Scotch, dismembering was an acquired taste. Of course, there was always the exception.

No, Eric's a jerk, and maybe he was even Nina's secret lover, but the man is just too prissy to be a killer. That's why I can't imagine what Katie saw in him in the first place—with his tea-sipping, manicured, Ivy League mannerisms.

"I guess we're through here for now, Bigfoot. Tony, you know where to find us," Jack said. Walker nodded and left them on the porch to discuss their next steps.

"Maybe Garcia's computers can turn up something," Liddell said hopefully.

"Maybe. In the meantime, we have a granny to visit."

CHAPTER SIXTEEN

She hailed from a long-ago era, when visitors were still invited to come inside and proper etiquette was observed. True to her upbringing, she insisted the detectives let her serve them tea. They followed her through to the kitchen and Jack noticed the table was already set for three, complete with a steaming teapot. The tray and three tiny spoons were silver, and the cups, saucers, and teapot looked like very old and expensive china. The smell of something baking filled the air.

"Call me Laney," the old woman said, using the end of the apron she wore to dab at the tears brought on by their news of Nina's death. "Poor girl."

"Mrs. Alvarez—Laney—you needn't trouble yourself. We only have a few questions," Jack said.

Laney's features were as delicate as her china, with skin the color and smoothness of porcelain except for the wrinkles beside her eyes. She moved slowly but with grace and poise. Thick white hair spun around the top of her head like cotton candy. Her eyes were dark blue and alert.

She was the lady Jack had seen sitting on her front porch earlier pretending not to notice all the police vehicles. But, as he had suspected then, her shrewd eyes didn't miss a thing. Eric must have thought so, too, or he wouldn't have coughed up the key so easily.

"I'm ninety-three years old tomorrow," she said proudly, and then, shoulders sagging, said, "Please, I need to sit."

The detectives instinctively moved forward, each taking an arm with Jack pulling one of the chairs away from the table, easing her into it.

She folded her hands atop the table, fingers laced tightly, head down, taking slow and deliberate breaths. Then she looked up, unlaced her fingers and announced, "I'm okay. You boys sit. I've made you a fresh batch of cookies. You must be thirsty and hungry."

Jack didn't even have to look at his partner's face. *She had Liddell when she mentioned the cookies.*

"May I pour the tea, Laney?" Jack asked, and was rewarded with a smile.

"I've already sweetened it. I hope you like it sweet," she said.

Jack and Liddell sat down and took a sip of the scalding hot tea. It *was* sweet and strong, and the floral fragrance rising from the cup reminded Jack of his own mother and time spent with her in the kitchen as a child.

Laney sniffed the air and said, "The cookies are ready." She asked Liddell, "Would you take those out of the oven? We wouldn't want them to burn, and my old legs are tired."

"No, ma'am. I wouldn't mind at all," Liddell said, and jumped up. He found a kitchen mitt hanging on the oven door, and when he pulled the baking tray from the oven, the room filled with a mouth-watering smell.

"I don't put them on a cookie rack to cool," she explained, and instructed Liddell to slide the fist-sized oatmeal-raisin-walnut cookies onto a serving tray. "They're much better when they almost burn your mouth."

When Liddell rejoined them, Jack said, "Mrs. Alvarez, thank you for your hospitality, but I'm sure you can understand that we're working and time is important."

"Please, call me Laney," she said. "If you sit with me a spell, Detective Murphy, I'll answer your questions." She added, "On *CSI: Miami*, that nice Lieutenant Caine—he's played by David Caruso, the actor—always takes time with his witnesses."

She took Jack's silence for submission and said to Liddell, "You can have all of the cookies you want. You look like you're starving. I see you're married, Detective Blanchard. You tell that wife of yours to feed you more." She beamed a smile and pushed the tray closer to him.

"She'd kill me, Missus...Laney," Liddell said, and helped himself to several cookies.

She dipped a cookie in her tea and tasted it. "That young woman called, looking for Nina, and you know, I didn't want to get Nina in trouble in case she had overslept. These young people don't appreciate having a job nowadays, but Nina wasn't one of them. I can't imagine her not going to work. Except . . ."

"Except what?" Jack asked.

Laney sat up straight, and locked her hands together in her lap.

"What is it?" Liddell prodded.

"That's not the way you do it. You have to tell me to spit it out." She put her hands on the table and fidgeted with the cookie tray. "Well, I'll spit it out. You don't have to grill me."

Jack and Liddell exchanged a look but remained silent.

"A black Mercedes would come late at night and park at the dark end of the street. Not under the streetlights down at this end. I've complained to the homeowners association about the streetlights, I can tell you."

"Black Mercedes," Jack repeated.

Laney gathered her thoughts and continued, "Yes. One man. Always late at night. He would get out of the car and look up and down the street, then hurry straight to Nina's door and go inside." She leaned in conspiratorially, and said, "Nina keeps a spare key on top of the porch light beside the door."

"Did you ever see the man use a key, or was Nina waiting for him?" Jack asked.

"No," she said. "I don't want to . . . you know. She was a good girl. Always quiet. And kept her yard so nice. We would visit from time to time."

Jack didn't understand where she was going with this and then remembered Mrs. Alvarez had come from a different time, when it was ruinous to a woman's reputation to be seen cavorting with a man.

"This will just be between us three," Jack assured her, and saw her visibly relax.

"He had his own key," she said, and scowled as if she had drunk something bitter. "I saw him walk right up to the door and use it once or twice, but I think most of the time she let him in." She put a hand to her mouth and said with a slight shake of her head, "What respectable person would sneak around in the dark like that? But if something was going on, it was his doing. Not hers."

Liddell forgot the cookies. He got out his notebook and scribbled something. "You're doing good, Laney," he said encouragingly.

She continued. "That went on for several months, but then the man quit coming about awhile back. I didn't see him or that car again until last night."

"Excuse me. What time was it when you saw the car?" Jack asked.

She said without hesitation, "It was a few minutes after ten o'clock. Jay Leno had just come on when I heard the commotion going on at Nina's. My hearing is perfectly fine. Nina's house was the only one that had lights on."

"Can you describe the car?" Jack asked.

"A newer Mercedes. Black. We owned one until six years ago when my husband passed away. Of course, this one was newer than ours," she said. Liddell wrote it all down.

"And you're sure that was the same car last night?" Jack asked.

"As sure as I can be," she said. "But I didn't see him this time," she reminded the detectives.

"Okay. Please tell us what happened last night, Mrs. Alvarez?" Jack said.

"Please call me Laney," she insisted, and Jack remained patient.

"I didn't see him, but I saw his car parked where it always parked when he visited her. I was kind of surprised because it had been so long. Anyway, I was watching Jay on the television and the only reason I noticed was because of the loud voices. I heard Nina and a man. The man was yelling at her and she yelled at him, but I couldn't hear any of the words. They both sounded angry."

"Where were you when you first heard the argument?" Jack asked.

Laney looked at him quizzically. "I was in my house. I told you that," she answered.

"Okay. What drew your attention to the arguing? Where were you when you first heard noticed the arguing? In the living room? Kitchen?"

"I was sitting in the rocker in the living room." She pointed to a wooden rocker facing the television. "My back hurts something terrible when I sit on the sofa. I told Mort—that was my husband's name—I told Mort to get rid of that sofa, but he was so frugal he refused. Then he passed and I didn't have the heart. I just put the rocker in the room." She looked wistfully at the couch.

"Laney," Jack said, drawing her back. "So you were sitting in the rocker and . . ."

"Then I heard voices. They were so loud I could hear them over the television. I cracked the curtains and looked outside, but there was no one. I listened and could tell it was coming from Nina's house.

"The arguing went on for a few minutes and then it just stopped. It was quiet for a long time, and I kept watching, but the man didn't leave, so I assumed they made up, and—you know?"

"And then what happened?" Jack asked.

"It was quite a bit later. I had some hot chocolate and was sitting right here at the table when I heard an engine start up. I went to look out the front, and by the time I got to the window Nina's car was pulling out of her driveway."

"Was the man's car—her visitor's car—parked at the end of the street still?"

"No. It must have left. It's funny that I didn't hear it leave, but then I never heard it arrive either. I didn't see anyone driving, if that's what you were going to ask. And—"

"Are you sure it was Nina's car?" Jack interrupted. "The one you saw leaving?"

She nodded. "She drives a dark green Ford Taurus. It needs a new muffler. My husband used to work on cars, so I know that much."

"Did the car that was leaving Nina's driveway have a loud muffler?" Liddell asked, biting into the last cookie on the tray, and then wiping crumbs from around his mouth and off the front of his shirt.

"Now that you mention it," she said thoughtfully, "I don't think it did."

Jack stood and motioned to Liddell that they should leave.

"You didn't let me finish, Detective Murphy," Laney said.

"I'm sorry," Jack said, and sat back down. "Please continue."

"You asked if I saw the black car at the end of the street when I looked out the second time. I didn't see it. It was gone," she said. "But there was another car parked there. It was a sports car, but I can't tell you what kind. And I've never seen it around here before, or since."

*   *   *

Thirty minutes and many, many cookies later, they left Laney Alvarez behind and headed back downtown. Liddell drove.

"She's single," Jack observed.

"Tempting, but man doesn't live by cookies alone. Besides, Marcie would kill me if she knew I ate so many cookies."

"Or that you have your pocket full of them?" Jack suggested.

Liddell patted his pocket, and said, "Well, Murphy's Law says, 'Waste not, want not.'"

Jack wasn't that interested in the subject, though. "What did she tell us that we didn't know?"

"Well, we confirmed that Cindy McCoy called Laney this morning when Nina didn't show up for work," Liddell said. "And Laney heard loud voices coming from Nina's around ten-fifteen last night. Her hearing seemed pretty good to me."

"Her eyesight is excellent, too. She wasn't wearing glasses and she saw the hunger in your eyes and drool dripping from your slack jaws."

"Wow. That's just mean, pod'na," Liddell said.

"She saw a black newer model Mercedes sedan at the end of her block, so we'll have to check with the neighbors again to see if anyone owns it, or anyone saw it. Several hours after the disturbance she looked out again and the Mercedes was gone, but a silver convertible sports car was parked there, and Nina's car was driving out of her driveway about midnight."

"Nina owns a dark green Mercury Sable," Jack said.

"What do you make of the black Mercedes?

"Eric owns a black Mercedes," Jack said.

"Are you hoping to get rid of the competition?"

Jack shot him an angry look, and said, "She saw a dark sedan that may or may not have been a Mercedes Benz. The man she described sounded a lot like Eric," Jack answered. "And he has a reputation for philandering."

Liddell conceded that Laney's description matched Eric, and the man's reputation wasn't good.

"Are we going to show her a photo lineup?" Liddell asked.

Jack shook his head. "It was dark. Even if we got an ID from her, a defense attorney would eat us up because of her age. Not to mention the shit storm we'd start downtown when politics got involved. And you know Eric would find out. We still don't know who the leak is. Or who they're working for."

Jack thought through what they'd heard, and then raised another point. "She said the man was there several times a week, always about the same time of night, and Nina seemed to be waiting."

"Sounds like a booty call," Liddell suggested, and Jack nodded in agreement.

The man stopped coming about a month ago. That was about the same time Eric and Katie got together.

CHAPTER SEVENTEEN

Book strummed his fingers on the van's dash, his posture stiff and alert as he watched the building entrance. Clint was in the driver's seat, feet on the dash, playing a game of Scrabble against himself on his iPhone.

"Is S-P-L-O-D-E a word?" he asked Book.

"Yeah," Book answered. "Like in 'I'm going to *splode* if you don't shut that damn thing off.'"

"Good one, Book," Clint said absently. He dragged his finger around the iPhone's screen. "Nah, that don't work." He poked a button and the screen went blank.

Clint looked through the tinted side window toward the Fares Avenue strip club where a small trailer held a flashing marquee that read, BUSYBODY. Under that in foot-high red letters were the words *Live Girls*.

"Hey, Book. See that sign?" Clint pointed at the trailer. "If they were dead girls, they wouldn't be dancing, would they?" he said, and Book laughed.

"One of those girls will be dead soon, buddy. Like shooting fish in a barrel," Book muttered.

Soon enough the door to the strip joint opened, and a hammerblast of music accompanied a pretty blond girl outside.

SUX, the shortened name of the chemical compound succinylcholine, causes immediate muscle paralysis. In small amounts it is used during surgery by an anesthesiologist. But Clint knew the dose Book had in mind would stop their breathing altogether.

Book had scored a quantity of SUX from a medical student when they did a job in Chicago last year. In exchange for the drug Book had promised not to kill the rich little bastard. He'd lied. Book had tested the SUX on the medical student. He went limp and then suffocated.

"There's a parking lot behind the strip joint," Book said. "Let's go back there, and the next time the blonde comes out, we get her."

The van was parked in a motel parking lot catty-corner from the Busybody Lounge. Clint moved it to a spot near the back of the lot. He had watched the blonde make several trips up and down the street on the side of the business. Each time she would strut her stuff, then look around to see who was watching. It was obvious to Clint what she was doing. He just hoped she would come out soon, because they couldn't afford to raise suspicion. A few minutes later the blonde appeared on the street.

"Here she comes," Book said. Clint started the van to attract her attention while Book climbed in the cargo area, taking out the syringe loaded with SUX.

She walked along, teasing her hair, and then turned toward the van and smiled at Clint. Book took the cap from the end of the syringe.

She was wearing a low-cut peasant blouse exposing her midriff and a lot of cleavage. Her thick makeup made it hard to determine her age, but she looked delicious in the cut-off jean shorts and cowboy boots. Thick blond hair fell in perfect waves around her face, down onto her shoulders, and accentuated a pair of tits that filled Clint with lust.

Book said from the rear, "Dancing sure has kept her in shape. There ain't a ounce of fat on her." But something about her reminded Clint of the farm girls he grew up with in Iowa. Those girls worked their asses off. They worked alongside the men, from sunup to sundown, then cooked supper and cleaned the dishes before they went to bed, with few exceptions. There wasn't a chance of them gaining weight. Suddenly he didn't want to do this, and the feeling was so strong it shocked him.

Clint twisted in the seat and saw Book was already poised with his hand on the door.

Clint whispered, "Let's skip this one, Book. It don't feel right."

"Just get her around to the cargo doors, Clint!" Book hissed, and gave him an unbelieving look, as if to say, "What's wrong with you?"

Clint turned back just as the young woman walked up to his open window. Her eyes widened when she saw the large fold of cash Clint was holding.

She leaned against the van's door and asked, "Have you been inside?" Clint shook his head. "I didn't think so. I would have noticed you," she said flirtatiously.

Clint felt shame, and it was unlike him. He hoped his face wasn't turning red, but he could tell it was.

The woman started to laugh and said, "Is this your first time?" She reached through the window and her hand found his crotch and began rubbing. "Come on, baby. I'll do you real good."

Clint found his voice again, and said, "I got a hundred dollars."

She looked around the parking lot and Clint thought he'd messed up. Maybe a hundred dollars was too much and she smelled a rat. Maybe she thought he was a cop?

He quickly said, "Of course, it's for the whole night," and this was rewarded with a slight nod of her head.

"I got a place we can go," she said. "Show me."

He held up five twenties to let her see the money.

Clint felt Book nudge him in the back and quickly said, "Why don't we do it right here first? I can't wait till we get to the room."

She twirled a strand of hair around her finger as if thinking his proposition over, then grinned and said, "Hell. Why not?"

"Let me help you," Clint said. Getting out, he led her around to the cargo door and took her by both shoulders as if to kiss her. The door slid open behind her, and she let out a startled squeal as Book wrapped a thick arm around her neck, plunged the needle in her throat, and emptied it. Her eyelids fluttered, she tried to speak, then went limp. Clint helped Book hoist her inside the van.

So much for that farm girl, Clint thought.

CHAPTER EIGHTEEN

Katie had been calling Eric's home and cell phone periodically during the day, but his voice mail picked up each time. Now it was late and she knew she should get some sleep, but she couldn't rest yet because she was concerned.

This morning had been going so well until Jack rushed off, taking Liddell with him. Shortly after, Eric told her he had to do something for Trent, and left her to make his excuses to their friends. She'd masked her disappointment, but here it was almost midnight and he still hadn't called to explain why he'd left.

When she'd been married to Jack, this was a common enough occurrence. He was never off duty. His phone would ring at all hours of the night and day and he would just give her a wry smile, a peck on the cheek, and he was gone. He might be gone for a day, maybe two, and on more than one occasion he had come home with cuts and bruises that he wouldn't talk about. The worst of those times were when he'd been involved in shootings. He would grow pensive and refuse to admit that it affected him, and after a while he really believed that it didn't bother him.

She shuddered at the memory of her own brush with death by a psycho who had kidnapped her and wanted Jack to watch her die. She closed her eyes and unbidden tears ran down her cheeks as she imagined the knife that had been against her throat and the look on Jack's face right before he shot the man. She had cried for months afterward, even sought professional help, but sometimes she would still wake from a nightmare with the smell and feel of the man's blood spattering her face and shoulders.

But not Jack. He was straight-faced, even calm, after what he'd done. She felt guilty having these thoughts because she knew Jack had no other choice than to kill the man.

Jack was a good man. But his job was turning him into a monster.

She hoped life would be different with Eric. She knew lawyers put in long, hard hours, but deputy prosecutors were different. They rarely worked weekends, and until today Eric had never been called away. In fact, he'd spent so much of his time with her over the last few months that she'd given some thought to his suggestion that they move in together before the marriage. It made sense, at least financially. He was still living in an apartment, and she had all this room.

But if he was going to disappear without her knowing what he was doing, she would have to reconsider.

He might be injured somewhere right now, and they wouldn't know to call her. But the idea of Eric being in danger was ridiculous. He was an attorney, for God's sake, not a cop. He didn't carry a gun, and the closest he came to criminals was in a courtroom where they were shackled and under guard by armed deputies.

But still, she had heard Jack talk about the newer, younger prosecutors, and the times he had called some of them to be on hand while he executed a search warrant, or even made a forced entry into the homes of armed criminals. She hadn't thought to ask Jack if the prosecutors went inside. Jack never talked much about his job. She'd had to find out the details from other policemen's wives, and in truth, she was glad Jack hadn't shared his close calls with her. He had always tried to spare her. And she had let him. *What did that say about her?*

He was so different when they had met in college. She was going to teach grade school, and Jack was already on the police department, taking courses for the detective test. He was so full of fun, life, and enthusiasm back then. The future had looked so bright and within their reach. But after they married, and after he'd made detective, he had changed. It was as if he had taken on the weight of the world. He called people "his victims" as if they were his personal charge. And instead of being the fun Jack, he had pulled into himself and was more wary. It was a perfect trait for a policeman on duty, but it played hell with a relationship.

But even with that, he changed back into the old Jack when she announced she was pregnant. He spent more time at home, fixing the spare room into a nursery, planting bushes, and making repairs around the house like he was nesting. He even bought a video camera, and was talking about buying a van because he planned to have a big family. *He would have been a wonderful father.*

They already knew the baby was going to be a girl, and even though Jack had bought things for a boy, he was so happy that he cried. They were going to name her Caitlin, a name shared by Katie's mother and Jack's grandmother.

Tears welled in her eyes when she thought about the day she and Jack had visited the doctor for her thirty-six-week checkup. She was almost full-term, and this would have been one of the last appointments until she delivered.

The doctor had listened to her stomach for an unusually long time and then had the nurse come in. An ultrasound was ordered to physically look for the baby's heart because the doctor was having trouble hearing it. After that it was a blur of activity. She was rushed to the OR, labor induced, and several hours later their daughter was delivered—stillborn. Caitlin had been carried to heaven.

She sat on her bed, chastising herself for dredging up these painful memories.

I should have seen the writing on the wall.

I should have known that Jack would take all the blame for Caitlin's death.

That's who he was. That's who he still is.

But Jack had never let her see him grieve. He never let her share in their loss. He treated her like she was made of glass, and even their sex was gentle, and careful, *and planned.*

He didn't have to say it, but she knew they would never try to have another child. They never spoke about Caitlin, and when she tried, he would say, "It will just upset you." But she knew it was because it upset him, and he was too tough to ever admit that he was hurting. He needed love. He needed another child. But instead he had "his victims" and "his dead bodies," and in the end, that was all he had.

"Poor Jack," she whispered, and turned off the bedside lamp.

CHAPTER NINETEEN

It was midnight when Jack arrived at police headquarters. He parked in a reserved spot for a city councilman, and trudged up the steps to the back entrance. A lone third-shift detective was sitting on the steps of the lineup stage in the squad room. He was smoking a cigar, blowing the smoke up the lineup staircase that led to the old jail. He gave Jack an acknowledging nod and continued puffing.

As Jack wearily settled in behind his desk, his thoughts turned to the new hot tub he'd installed on his deck this year, and how good a soak and a couple inches of Scotch sounded. The thought of Scotch made him think about Eric's remarks at Katie's house that morning, and that reminded him to call Katie and apologize for bailing on her today. Then he looked at the wall clock. It was midnight.

Oh, hell! he thought, and dialed Katie's number.

"Eric?" Katie's voice came over the line, and Jack felt his throat tighten at the mention of the other man's name.

He remained silent for a moment, wanting to hang up, but said, "No. It's me, Katie."

"Jack. Is anything wrong? Is Eric okay?"

No. Eric's not okay. A lot is wrong with him. "I'm sorry for calling so late, but I wanted to apologize for leaving your party without an explanation. I didn't mean to wake you. I'll let you go back to sleep."

He heard a click and imagined she had turned on the small lamp beside her bed. The one she insisted wasn't girly at all, even though it had a frilly pink shade.

"Are you and Eric working the same case?" she asked.

He wondered how to answer her question. He was the detective working the case, and Eric was the . . . what? The suspect? Well, not yet. At least not definitely.

"We must have both been called in about this case," he said. "He was with me earlier. I'm not sure where he is now." *Maybe he's in bed with another coworker.*

"He hasn't contacted me since he left here," she said, and Jack could hear a tiny edge to her voice. "I heard from Moira what you're working on. I'm so sorry, Jack."

This struck an all-too-familiar note, and Jack didn't respond at first. "Well, go back to sleep, Katie," he finally said. "Sorry I woke you."

"I'm glad you did," she said, and he felt tightness in his throat. "Good night, Jack."

He said good night and put the handset back in its cradle. *She said, "I'm glad you did." What did she mean?* But before he had time to analyze the meaning of Katie's words, Garcia called.

"Good news—I think."

"Tell me and then go home," he said. And she told him what she had gleaned from the Internet, which was a lot.

When she was finished, she asked, "Do you think the prosecutor knew about Nina's involvement with MS-13 in North Carolina?"

"Well, you found out just by Googling her name," Jack said. "If they interviewed her before they hired her, I would assume they also knew she was special prosecutor on dozens of those cases. You say she received death threats?"

"That's what the newspaper articles said," Garcia said. "They made it sound like she was a one-woman antidrug campaign."

Jack had to consider how this new revelation affected the investigation.

"Are you going to call Eric and have him check it out? Or should I call Nina's old boss in North Carolina? I can do it first thing in the morning."

He knew he should call Eric, but the prick had lied to him once already. No, he decided. This information should be discussed with the prosecutor himself. Yet it was almost twelve-thirty. Not a good hour to be calling Trent Wethington at home.

"I'll make the call," Jack said to Garcia. "Good job. Now go home."

"I'm leaving, boss. Out the door right now."

Jack had to check in with Captain Franklin, and though the captain sounded annoyed, he agreed that Trent needed to be called right away. "I'll notify Chief Pope and we'll all meet early in the morning."

Jack hung up with the captain and called Central Dispatch. The prosecutor's home number wasn't listed in the telephone directory, but like everyone else in Vanderburgh County, his home address and telephone number were on file.

He dialed the number he was given and it immediately went to voice mail. "This is Trent Wethington, *the* prosecutor for Vanderburgh County."

Jack had heard the message dozens of times because Trent rarely answered his office telephone. He was about to hang up and try again in the morning when the phone was answered by a sleepy voice. "Hullo."

"This is Detective Murphy."

"I know who you are, Jack. For God's sake, do you know what time it is?"

Good. It's the *prosecutor,* Jack thought. "Sir, we need to talk."

Jack heard rustling and then a whisper—"It's okay, honey, go back to sleep"—and then a throat clearing. He imagined Trent putting on a silk smoking jacket and fez, and going to another room where he could talk. He'd never been in the man's house, but knew it was located in a neighborhood of million-dollar homes.

Trent came back on the line with no trace of the earlier drowsiness. "Is this about Nina?"

"Yes, sir," Jack answered. "Can we talk?"

"No!" Trent blurted. "I mean, can't this wait until morning?"

"I'm afraid Captain Franklin said it couldn't. I can come to you if you want."

"That won't do," Trent said. "I'll come to my office. Meet me in twenty minutes, Detective Murphy." The line went dead before Jack could respond.

Why did Trent want to meet face-to-face? He didn't even ask what information I had. Weird!

Jack called Franklin again, and was told to stay put.

The captain and the chief of police are coming in. At one o'clock in the morning, no less. What's wrong with this picture?

* * *

Except for the relaxed mood of Captain Franklin, the prosecutor's office was somber. The men acknowledged each other as they entered with a lowering of the head and quick glances. Jack felt like he had been called into the principal's office as he sat in a hard wooden chair across from Trent Wethington. The county attorney Bob Rothschild flanked Jack on his right, with Marlin Pope on his left. Franklin sat on the window ledge with his legs dangling above the plush carpet.

Jack had merely called Trent to ask if he was aware of Nina's past work on cases involving MS-13. This hastily arranged late-hour meeting seemed like an exaggerated response to that telephone call.

Trent had yet to ask any questions of Jack, and the fact that he called in the county attorney without knowing what Jack had to say smacked of subterfuge. In a normal case, if a suspect refused to answer questions and obtained an attorney, it was considered suspicious behavior that bordered on an admission of guilt.

Of course, these were not ordinary times. Trent was running for governor, and Jack reckoned he was just trying to protect himself.

Trent came to the meeting dressed for work, wearing a pink dress shirt with white collar and cuffs, and his deep blue suit jacket was draped around the back of his chair. Gold and onyx cuff links clacked against the desktop when he placed his hands together. His dyed black hair was slicked back and perfectly in place.

"Jack has updated me," the chief of police said, breaking the silence. "Ask your questions, Jack." He glanced at the county attorney, and Rothschild nodded at Trent to answer.

"How well did you know Nina Parsons?" Jack asked pointedly.

Trent took too long to think about the question. "I'm not sure what you're asking, Detective Murphy."

So, I'm Detective Murphy now? "It's an easy question, *Mr. Prosecutor.*"

"Come on, Jack!" the county attorney chimed in. "There's no need for an attitude. You asked for this meeting and we're here."

Jack sat back in his chair. *Maybe Trent knew Eric was having an affair with Nina, and he is trying to keep his office out of a scandal.* "In the first place, Bob, I didn't ask for this meeting. I called Trent to ask some questions about Nina and he wanted to meet tonight. Second, I don't understand why you're here."

Rothschild cleared his throat. "Well, it seems from the tone of your questions that it's a good thing Trent asked me to be here."

"Are you representing Mr. Wethington?" Jack asked.

"I don't need to be represented, Detective Murphy," Trent said. "You're right. I called this meeting. I did so because I wanted an update on your investigation, and not to be interrogated like a common criminal."

Jack wondered why Trent was being so defensive. "I haven't interrogated you. I think I've asked an appropriate question. As her employer, Trent, you should be able to tell me things about Nina that we haven't discovered during the investigation. I'm only asking what you can tell me about Nina."

"I agree with Jack," Marlin Pope said. "The question was appropriate, and she *was* your employee, after all. Does she have any family, or a significant other, that you can tell us about? Was she involved with anything in her business or personal life that could have resulted in her death? Your office should be bending over backward to cooperate with us."

Jack appreciated Marlin for coming to his defense, but he remembered something his mother told him. *You catch a lot more flies with honey than vinegar.* Of course his father would correct her, by saying, "You catch more flies with honey—and a gun— than with vinegar."

Trent and the county attorney sat stone-faced, arms crossed over their chests, obviously angry with Jack. He swiftly changed gears. "I'm sorry, Trent," he said. "I'm just tired and cranky. Hell, we're all tired. I know you're worried sick about this." He saw the antagonism start to fade, and he continued in that vein. "Hell, the only lead I have is an old lady who saw a silver convertible near Nina's the night she was killed. I'm sorry for not using other channels to contact you, but to be honest, I've always looked to you for guidance, sir."

Jack hoped he wasn't laying it on too thick, but evidently he wasn't. The anger had drained from Trent's expression and he began tugging at his cuffs, looking satisfied that the hired help had finally discovered their place in the grand scheme of things.

"Of course, *Jack*," Trent said. "It's been a long and sad day for all of us. I'll help any way I can."

He then did something that Jack had seen him do a thousand

times for the cameras when he was campaigning. Wethington put two fingers over his right eyebrow, said, "Scout's honor," and gave his dazzling white—albeit phony as a politician's heart—smile, and smartly dropped his hand to the desktop in a little salute. *Clink* went the onyx cufflinks.

Bob Rothschild, the county attorney, spoke up for the first time. "I drive a silver convertible. A BMW Z4, to be exact. Am I a suspect, too?"

Marlin Pope interjected, "No one's making accusations here, Bob. We certainly don't suspect you. Jack is just covering the bases. The prosecutor can appreciate the thoroughness of Jack's work."

Trent nodded and smiled. "Jack's like a hound. Once he gets the scent, he never gives up."

Jack was uncomfortable with praise, even from someone he didn't care much for, and he thought he would throw up just a little in his mouth if it continued. He changed the subject, and the next ten minutes were filled with questions and guarded answers.

Yes, Trent was aware of Nina's involvement with the MS-13 gang, and she had regaled him with these stories when she interviewed for her position with his office. That said, he never saw a case come through his office involving the MS-13 gang. But he had heard of the gang, and now felt this line of investigation merited Jack's full focus. He started to tell a personal story about Nina but stopped, looking at Jack.

"Eric told me you're under the mistaken impression that he had an affair with Nina." It wasn't a question, nor an accusation, but simply a statement without any wiggle room at either end. It was like asking, "Do you still beat your wife, yes or no?"

So, Eric ran crying to his boss.

"Not at all, sir," Jack deadpanned. "I merely wanted to eliminate the possibility. You said it yourself, sir. Nina was an attractive woman and you have to admit, Eric has a reputation. If I didn't ask, someone would."

"That's not how we do things here, detective," Trent scoffed. "I run a tight ship, and I'm unaware of Eric having a *reputation*. You might as well accuse me of having an affair with her." He waved the idea away, then gave Jack a hard look. "Don't you think you're letting your personal feelings get in the way of your investigation?"

Trent hadn't said it maliciously, but Jack took it that way and he could feel the heat creeping into his face. Thankfully, the chief of police answered for him.

"I have every confidence in Jack," Pope said.

With that challenge the prosecutor leaned back and spread his hands in a gesture of peace. "Of course. I meant nothing by it," Trent said. "I'm sure Jack will get to the bottom of this." He turned his attention to Pope and said sternly, "I think this gang thing is your best lead for now, don't you, Marlin? They sound quite capable of committing both the murder here and the ones in Illinois."

When Pope didn't answer, he said, "I can assure you that neither I nor Bob killed Nina."

Meeting over. The men made for the parking lot and home, but Pope pulled Jack aside.

"Just a word of caution," Pope said. "And I'm not saying you should have mentioned Bob Rothschild's unneeded presence, but you had better be careful where you step. Bob is not only the county attorney, but also he's Trent's campaign manager. Trent hired him because he has clout. I don't know from where, but he does have a lot of pull."

"Are you asking me to back off, Chief?"

"No, Jack. I want you to do what you do." He then gave Jack a grave look, and said, "Just be cognizant that the people involved in this are very powerful."

CHAPTER TWENTY

The unfinished deck on the west side of Jack's cabin would eventually wrap all the way around, but since he was doing the work by himself, he would probably need the rest of the summer. He could get it done in a day if he hired a crew, but the idea of a bunch of lowlifes hanging around his cabin didn't appeal to the cop in him.

Cinderella, his mixed-breed dog, lay beside the hot tub on a stack of untreated wooden planks, chewing a piece of rawhide. Jack had hoped it would deter her from destroying any more of his shoes, and that part had worked, but when he'd come in at two a.m. he'd found a pair of his socks shredded across the kitchen floor. She was strong-willed, suspicious, and wouldn't respond to any other name besides the one her previous owner had given her. Cinderella.

Jack had sort of inherited her—sissy name and all—when her owner was murdered and she'd been left injured and homeless. He hadn't wanted a dog. Being an animal owner didn't mix well with his job because of his uncertain hours. But then a redneck police chief in Illinois had wanted to shoot her and he couldn't allow that. He'd taken her to Dr. Brent Branson, a college buddy who ran a veterinary hospital, and had her wounds treated. To his own amazement, he ended up taking her to recuperate in his cabin.

Four months and a thousand bucks later, she was still with him. He thought she would be grateful, but she hated men. She would growl and snap at any man unfortunate to get around her sharp teeth. *Ungrateful mutt! I think I dated a girl like that in high school.*

Cinderella had stopped chewing and lay motionless, with her eyes locked on him, as he stripped and lowered his body into the tub. The water temperature was set to eighty-five for the summer.

He turned the jets to the highest setting, leaned back, and sipped the twelve-year-old Scotch on ice. The day's tension melted. He closed his eyes and let the water jets beat the tensed muscles in his legs, arms, and back.

He was glad he'd moved to this secluded part of the river, where the night sky was clear, the stars were bright, and his nearest neighbor was a mile away. Sleeping had not been a problem out here in the boonies.

His father always said that a cop had to eat and sleep when he could, because he never knew what was around the corner. His dad had been in World War II before becoming a policeman, and he had explained that during the war getting food and sleep was a crapshoot. Soldiers sometimes slept standing up in a foxhole, or opened K-rations to find the contents moldy, but they ate them anyway.

He opened his eyes and glanced at Cinderella. She was sleeping, muzzle down over the half-eaten rawhide chew, paws together. The dog was either deep asleep or ignoring him, but Jack knew two things. Cinderella hated him, *and* no one else would want her. If he took her to an animal shelter she would be put to sleep. He had saved her from the redneck sheriff, and he would never allow her to be hurt. She had protected her owner and Jack respected that. Besides, he was responsible for her now.

"You're my dog. Get used to it," he said.

The water swirled around him, and the three fingers of Scotch were having the desired effect. He thought about the party that morning, and about Katie, and while he was sorting through his feelings about her impending marriage, his eyes closed and soon after, both man and beast were asleep.

Eric Manson had been busy after leaving Nina's house several hours earlier.

It was true that he'd found her key hidden in the front porch light, just like he'd said. But he hadn't told Jack everything. He sat on the side of the bed, the lights in the room dimmed, wondering what the hell he had gotten himself into.

He pulled the initialed nickel and brass key holder from his pocket and tossed it on the mattress. It was hard to believe that something so small could carry with it the power to make or break careers. If Jack had found it first, Eric had no doubt that his life, and several others', would be forever changed. His life had already been altered by the day's events.

He wondered how much Jack had told Katie. He was sure Jack had already talked to her. She regarded Jack as a hero, like he was larger than life. She would never look at him the way she looked at Jack. He'd not spoken to her all day. *How will she interpret my silence? And what has Jack told her? About me? About Nina?*

He pushed the nagging thoughts away. His relationship with Katie, even his engagement, wasn't where his focus should be right now. He'd had his hands full today doing damage control, establishing an alibi for when Jack asked, knowing that it would eventually come down to that. *Damn Nina! Why did she have to die?* It was all so inconvenient. But at least he had someone on the inside. He hoped Deputy Chief Dick would come through for him.

Trent would support the police investigation. How could he not? It was in his best interest to see this case closed quickly. The public would not accept an unsolved attack on a district attorney. They would see it as a weakness of the future governor. That wasn't good for Trent's campaign, or his own future, for that matter.

He was pulled from his thoughts by the ringing telephone.

"Eric," Trent said, "I want you in my office first thing in the morning."

"We shouldn't talk on an open line."

"Oh. Of course," Trent said. "Can you come to my house?"

Eric's thoughts returned to his meeting with Trent. "We decided to meet at the office in the morning," he repeated. "Nothing we can do tonight."

"I just wanted to fill you in," Trent said, and Eric could tell the man was in a panic. Close to tears. But Trent would have to suck it up. A mistake now would ruin everything. Trent was right to be afraid of Jack Murphy.

"I'll see you in the morning. I'm tired," Eric said.

"Bring Nina's files with you. All of them."

Eric found he was gripping the phone for dear life as he placed it back in the cradle. He was used to Trent barking orders. He had worked for the man for almost six years now. But soon, if all went as planned, Trent would become Indiana's governor, and Eric would be the next prosecutor of Vanderburgh County. Eric would be the one calling some other jerk in the middle of the night, barking orders like some alpha dog.

He lay back on the bed without undressing, turned the lights out, and punched up his pillow. Murphy was grabbing at straws. That was his style. He was like a Tasmanian devil. Whirling around like a destructive dervish to see what flew out. But he didn't have any evidence.

He laid his head down and a more pleasant thought came to mind: *Katie. Screw Jack, I'll call her tomorrow.*

CHAPTER TWENTY-ONE

"We made the news, pod'na," Liddell said, and flipped the Evansville newspaper onto Jack's desk.

The front page headlines read, "Deputy Prosecutor Murdered: Cannibalism Suspected." The story claimed unnamed sources "close to the investigation" had reported three human heads were found on Sunday, one in Evansville and two in Harrisburg, Illinois. It went on to report that three other heads had been found in Harrisburg several years ago, and that the bodies had never been recovered. The article then speculated that cannibalism might be the explanation.

The article didn't give the names of the victims. Either they didn't have them, or they were going to use the knowledge to blackmail the police department into giving them an exclusive on the progress of the case.

If they had the victims' names, that meant they had verified the identification with at least two sources. Jack knew the coroner's office would never give that information out without checking with him, so that limited the culprits to other policemen or the prosecutor's office as the leak.

"Has the chief seen this?" Jack asked.

"Who do you think gave the paper to me?" Liddell responded without a trace of his usual humor. "This time the backstabbing weasel has gone too far."

Jack knew the weasel that Liddell was referring to could only be Larry Jansen.

"Jansen was supposed to meet us here this morning. He was in Records until about midnight," Jack said. When Liddell had come to work, Jack immediately caught him up on the meeting in the prosecutor's office last night. Liddell agreed it was odd behavior. "Have you heard from him?"

"No, but I'm not surprised. He's probably at the newspaper collecting his thirty pieces of silver."

Jack wanted to get to the bottom of this leak as bad as anyone, but Jansen was Teflon-coated. No matter what he was caught doing, nothing ever stuck. He had once been suspended for illegally wiretapping the mayor's office. That was a federal offense, but Jansen had never been charged. And later, while he was on sick leave, he shot and killed a newspaper reporter who he claimed attacked him with a hatchet. The kicker was, he was inside the reporter's home—illegally.

Any other cop would be charged with murder, but Larry took a short paid leave while the shooting board investigated the killing, and less than a month later, he was back in his old job, in Missing Persons.

Jack never understood how Jansen could work in the Missing Persons unit when he himself should be reported as a missing person.

"We won't be able to prove it was him, Bigfoot," Jack said. "Let Captain Franklin deal with it. Besides, the cat is out of the bag now."

"Yeah, I know, but I'd still like to see his goose cooked for good."

"Do you ever stop thinking about food, Bigfoot?"

Garcia stuck her head in the door. "The captain wants both of you in his office—twenty minutes ago."

The hand-printed placard she placed on the front of the desk in her new, albeit cramped, office, read, MOIRA CONNELLY, and printed under that, DEPUTY PROSECUTOR.

That morning the secretary had ordered two engraved nameplates. One for the top of Moira's desk, the other for the door to her office.

My office, she thought, and smiled. Three years of eating ramen noodles, cleaning tables, serving drinks, and the long hours of studying had finally paid dividends. Here she was. An attorney. A deputy prosecutor! How great was that?

She heard a rap on her door and saw Abbey Dennis, the deputy prosecutor who would be helping her acclimate to her new duties.

She was the sweetest person Moira had ever met, but she had a reputation for being tough on new employees.

Abbey said, "When you're finished wallowing in your own grandeur, I need you to come to my office and start the orientation."

"I'm not wallowing!" Moira protested.

"You are," Abbey said, but she was grinning now.

Moira held up the paper nameplate. "Yeah, you're right. And I so deserve it."

"Yes, you do. Now let's get this show on the road. Lots to do today."

Moira followed Abbey on a short tour of the office.

A room with a glass wall at the end of the hallway was filled with Formica-topped tables and several upholstered sofas. Abbey stopped at the open door and pointed at a refrigerator. "This is the break room. You can bring lunch, but I wouldn't. After you look in the fridge you'll see what I mean."

Then she introduced Moira to the two investigators who worked for the office. They were both men in their late fifties who had retired from the Sheriff's Department.

Eric Manson came up close behind Abbey.

"Moira, there you are," he said, and rubbed Abbey's shoulders in what Moira thought was a too-familiar fashion.

"Well, where else would I be?"

"I'll finish showing her around," Eric told Abbey.

"I have some things for her to sign in my office when you're through." As Abbey walked away, she glanced back over her shoulder, rolling her eyes and giving an exaggerated shudder. Moira got the point.

"Come on. I have a surprise for my soon to be sister-in-law," Eric said, and reached for her arm.

She involuntarily pulled back, but Eric took her by the wrist, leading her around the corner and down a parallel hallway.

"That's Trent's office at the end," Eric said, pointing to a closed door. "The one on the right is mine."

As they reached the door to Trent's office, she could hear voices coming from inside. Eric's door was open and she could see that it was neatly arranged, with a mahogany desk the size of her current office and bookcases full of legal tomes. The door across from

Eric's was closed and didn't have a nameplate on it. Eric pulled a set of keys from his pocket and put them in Moira's hand.

She looked at him wide-eyed. "You mean this is mine?"

He lowered his voice to barely a whisper. "Listen, Moira. I don't want you to feel bad about getting a nice office. Truth is, no one else wants it."

After a moment his meaning sank in.

"This was *her* office? Nina's?"

Eric nodded.

Moira didn't know what to say. The office she was currently occupying was no bigger than a broom closet. But this was Nina Parsons's office. The woman wasn't even buried and they were already giving her office away. It somehow seemed wrong.

Moira looked at the keys and then at Eric. He was smiling like a mischievous child.

"Geez, Eric. I mean, what can I say?"

"Thank you, Eric," he said. "Go on, open it."

She put the key in the lock and pushed the door open to find the office was the exact opposite of Eric's inside. To say it was a total mess was an understatement. The room and desk were stacked floor to ceiling with folders and overfilled storage boxes. The bookcases were buried under paper.

I smell a rat, Moira thought.

"And I guess you expect me to clean all this up?" she asked.

"Katie said you were quick to catch on."

CHAPTER TWENTY-TWO

Franklin was leaning against the front of his desk, having a conversation with someone, when Jack and Liddell filed in.

Jack spotted Eric in a chair in the corner, listening to the captain and tapping some information into his smart phone.

"I've asked Eric to sit in on this meeting," Franklin said.

Franklin circled around his desk and sat down. "Since Eric was unable to attend the meeting last night, and because of the recent news, I thought we should have a quick meeting."

Eric put the phone away and nodded at Jack and Liddell. "Good morning, gentlemen."

The detectives remained stoic, and an unnatural silence filled the room before Eric cleared his throat and continued.

"Well, Trent and I appreciate being kept informed, and I'm greatly interested to hear what you've discovered thus far. But—"

"But the news media is putting pressure on Trent to release the names of the other victims. Am I right?"

Eric turned to Franklin. "Trent sent me to see what he can release in the news conference this morning. Specifically, anything we need to confirm or deny on our end."

Franklin explained, "The television stations are now calling us unfair for giving Nina's name to the newspaper and not sharing it with them."

"We didn't give this to the newspapers," Liddell said.

The captain shook his head. "No, we didn't. For all we know, this could be drug-related, gang-related, or a personal vendetta against Nina. We don't have evidence supporting or dispelling any of this, but if we don't tell the public something, the media will simply report whatever they hear." He held a copy of the newspaper featuring the cannibalism story. "Like this."

Eric took the newspaper from Franklin and looked at the front page. "Any ideas where this came from?"

Liddell raised his hand, saying, "I know this one. That's a newspaper, Eric. They print those at a newspaper building." Liddell then walked his fingers across his palm. "Then these little guys on bikes deliver them to houses and businesses—"

Jack talked over Liddell, asking, "So, do you want to be updated, or is this a witch hunt?"

Eric glared at Jack. "From what I hear, you don't have anything except an old woman who thinks she saw a mystery sports car."

Jack shot back, "Well if you know everything, why are we bothering with this meeting?"

"The prosecutor is concerned, Jack. We have to put an end to these leaks, gentlemen."

"I agree," Franklin said. "And we're looking into it."

"It's obvious that someone on the inside the investigation is the source of this leak," Eric said defensively. "That makes the police department look bad."

"We're looking into it," Franklin repeated.

Jack said, "Well, maybe you should look closer to home, Eric. I think the leak makes us all look like amateurs, and that includes your office."

"Well, that was all I had," Eric said, and stood to leave.

"Gee, Eric, I guess you've sorted us out. So with turnabout being fair play and all that, I would like to come by and look at Nina's office," Jack said.

Eric stopped with his hand on the doorknob. "I thought you already did that."

"I've been a little busy, and the prosecutor's office isn't exactly open 24/7," Jack shot back. "Do I have access?"

Eric seemed amused. "By all means, Jack. You can walk back with me if you like."

"Let's go," Jack said, not taking his eyes from Eric's. "Are we done here, Captain?"

"News conference is in five minutes. But you needn't be there," Franklin said.

CHAPTER TWENTY-THREE

Things were forever changed on September 11, 2001. Security-mindedness became contagious and everyone looked suspicious until they were photographed, fingerprinted, scanned, patted down, and their identification checked nine ways from Sunday.

Jack emptied his pockets into a plastic basket at a Civic Center security checkpoint. Then he was required to lock his weapon in a gun cabinet before going through the metal detector and entering the judicial areas of the building. Jack thought all the security measures were totally unnecessary. What, a cop was going to charge in and decide he was a terrorist?

"Look, Jack," Eric said, walking through the metal detector. "Can't we just bury the hatchet?" He slipped back into his five-hundred-dollar Italian loafers.

"My partner suggested the same thing, Eric," Jack said. Only he suggested he bury the hatchet in Eric's brain. "Look, I don't have a problem with you. I just want some answers, and the prosecutor is too busy playing politics to take me seriously. What about you, Eric? Should we call the county attorney again? Or can you answer some questions without benefit of counsel?"

Color crept up Eric's neck. "I'm not sure what you mean, Jack. Don't get paranoid on me. If anyone can put this case together, it's you."

"Flattery, and all that," Jack said, thinking he himself had pulled the same manipulative shit on Jansen last night. "You know Trent is more worried about how this murder looks to the public than what happened to Nina Parsons."

"I think you're wrong, Jack. But you're entitled to your opinion, same as everyone else."

If he was hostile, Eric was going to be hostile. Lawyers were like pit bulls, and they would dig in when confronted. Jack decided to take another approach. "Sorry, Eric. I appreciate you cutting the red tape and letting me in," he said, and meant it. About half of the information in Nina's office was confidential, and Eric could have made Jack jump through hoops.

Eric used his key to let them into the foyer of the prosecutor's wing. He waved to the receptionist and, when the door buzzed, led Jack past the break room and around a corner to the hallway that detectives had nicknamed the "Hall of Shame" because it led to Trent Wethington's personal office. That's because the only reason a detective ever came here was to get dressed down by Trent for some faux pas in their investigation, or to take the blame for a prosecuting attorney losing a case.

"Nina's office is down what you guys call the 'Hall of Shame,' " Eric joked.

Jack smiled. He didn't know Eric was aware of what the policemen called the hallway. He imagined Eric knew a lot of other things, too. He'd keep that in mind.

Eric rapped on the door, and when it opened Jack was shocked to see the new occupant of Nina Parsons's office.

Moira, seated behind the desk, smiled as Jack came into the office. Trent Wethington beamed his thousand-dollar smile as he grabbed Jack's hand in both of his own and gave it a vigorous shake.

"Jack! How are you?"

Jack wondered if the D.A. was getting senile. He'd been in Trent's office less than eight hours ago. "I'm fine, Governor," Jack said, and saw Trent's smile slip a little.

"Well, not governor yet."

Moira came around the desk and hugged Jack. "How are you, big brother?"

She had never called him *big brother* before. Jack wondered if she was trying to send a message to the other men, like, "Hands off. My dog bites."

He hoped they hadn't already started hitting on Katie's sister. He never heard anything, good or bad, about Trent Wethington in regard to sexual liaisons. But he had heard plenty about Eric.

"I'm great . . . sis," Jack said. "You getting settled in?"

She held up her paper nameplate. "Moira Connelly," she said, "attorney-at-law."

Jack tried to picture her as an attorney, but saw only the moody teenager that he'd watched grow up. She had always been so defiant of authority. But she *had* grown up and she'd turned out okay.

"I told Jack he could go through Nina's—I mean Nina's *old* office," Eric explained.

Trent's face stiffened for a second, but then he smiled, and said, "Of course."

"Do you want me to give him Nina's files from your office as well?" Eric asked Trent. He'd delivered a stack of Nina's files to Trent earlier.

"Of course, I'll get them," Trent said, and then, smiling at Moira, he added, "She's a great little gal, Jack. She'll fit in perfectly here. Just remember, Moira, I take my coffee black."

Trent left the office, so he didn't see the moue of distaste on Moira's face, but Eric didn't miss it.

"Don't mind him," he said, then lowered his voice to a whisper. "He's old school. He doesn't know we don't make remarks like 'little gal' anymore, and we *all* make coffee for Trent."

Jack said, knowing Moira was capable of fighting her own battles, "Can I get to work?"

Eric looked at his watch. "Yikes! I forgot why we came." He turned to Moira. "We had better go and let the great detective do his stuff."

"Maybe I can help?" she suggested.

Jack wouldn't mind help with this colossal mess. "Maybe so."

Eric's brow furrowed. "Okay, that can be your first assignment. You have to go through this stuff sometime. But nothing leaves this office without telling me first. Understood?"

Jack wearily made a cross over his heart.

Moira playfully punched Jack on the arm after Eric left them alone. "How about that? I'm working with the great Jack Murphy. So, where do we begin?"

Moira was just joking around. She had completed law school at the top of her class. She had been always a conundrum—half tomboy, half juvenile delinquent, and always the champion of the underdog. Katie had once told him a story about Moira when she was in the fifth grade. Moira had hidden in the school bathroom after class, then sneaked into the science and biology lab and freed all the animals from their cages.

Jack picked up a stack of manila folders that were stuffed with forms. "Look for a label that says, 'This is why I was killed,' or maybe, 'Greatest Hits of MS-13.'"

"MS-13?"

"I forgot, you haven't heard about that. Well, I'll give you the nickel tour," he said, and patiently told her the details they had withheld from the news media. He also offered his own opinion that MS-13 had nothing to do with the murders, but he told her to keep an eye out anyway.

"There is a lot we don't know about Nina yet," he said at the end. "Including why someone would be angry enough to kill her and hack her into little pieces."

CHAPTER TWENTY-FOUR

The big truck braked to a slow roll behind the Evansville newspaper offices. The green dumpsters were always filled to overflowing, and bags would undoubtedly be piled on the ground. The driver had had less than four hours' sleep and had deliberately saved this stop for last. He was nursing a terrible hangover, and that's why he was slow to realize that the front of one of the metal containers was smeared with dark red paint. He jammed on the air brakes, jerking him forward and back. The violent motion sent screaming jolts through his aching head.

"Damn kids!" he growled, and swung down from the cab to see if he would need to report the vandalism. If the dumpster just needed hosing down, he could knock on the back door at the loading dock of the newspaper and borrow a hose.

His supervisor was a little dictator, and would have a stroke if they had to bring out another bin. And that would take about three hours because it was a Monday, and the downtown traffic was a bitch to navigate with the big trucks.

Yet as he approached the bin, he saw that it wasn't graffiti, or paint. A shiver ran through him. It looked like blood, and it was smeared all down the front of the bin. Dreading what he might find, he pulled his handkerchief from his back pocket and used it to lift the lid and sling it backward. A swarm of buzzing flies assaulted him. From down inside, he reeled from the miasma of a rotting corpse.

Jack and Moira had plowed through most of the boxes, and hundreds of folders, without finding anything of importance, before

Jack's cell phone buzzed with a message. A few minutes later he and Liddell were driving east on Sycamore over abandoned railroad tracks and into the loading dock area of the Evansville Courier building, where a small crowd of policemen and civilians were separated by yellow caution tape.

So far only a half dozen locals stood at the mouth of the alley, each jockeying for a view of what the police were doing. Jack thought immediately of this morning's meeting, where the leak to the press was discussed. *Shit! There's no way this is staying quiet.* As if on cue, a haggard young man with a camera burst out of the back door of the loading dock and started arguing with a white-clad crime scene officer. Then a Channel Six television van—equipped with an antennae dish—pulled up to the mouth of the alley.

Sergeant Walker, in a white Tyvek suit, complete with a hood and plastic face shield, slapped at flies on his arms as he walked over. "Jack, Liddell." He pointed down the alleyway. "The driver was making collections, and he saw blood all over the front of one of the dumpsters. He looked inside and found a human head. White. Female."

A green trash truck was parked inside the crime scene tape. A skinny middle-aged man wearing a faded yellow wifebeater stood next to it. His face was beet-red and he was rubbing his eyes like he was crying.

"That the driver?" Jack asked.

"He knows squat," Tony said. "Saw the blood, opened the lid, and saw flies buzzing around the head. End of story."

"Is there a body to go with the head?" Jack asked.

"We haven't gone through the dumpsters yet," Walker said, shaking his head. "Nothing at the landfill either. I've had guys out there all night going through acres of trash. I'm calling them off this morning, unless you want us to stay out there."

They were all wondering the same thing. Did Nina's remains start out in a dumpster and were then dumped in the landfill by a less observant driver?

"Any idea how long this one has been in here?" Jack asked.

"The blood was still wet in places. I'd say no longer than last night, but don't hold me to that. We'll see what Dr. John thinks," Walker said.

"I think we should continue at the landfill for now," Jack said. "This is the second dismemberment in two days. Fourth if you count the two in Harrisburg. Has Lilly been called?"

"Been and gone," Walker said. "That's exactly what she said. And she told me to send this one along when it's convenient," he said, referring to the recent remains.

"Is it *our* guy?" Jack asked the other big question.

Walker nodded. "I think so. We haven't had a good look, but yeah, I'd say it's the same type cut."

"Can we take a peek?"

Walker handed them latex gloves and walked with them to the row of four dumpsters. A new painter's cloth had been laid on the ground in front of them. A step stool was pushed up to the front of the blood-covered container.

Jack stepped up and peered inside. In the full sun, the dumpsters were harder to see inside. The flies were a swarm of blackness, and then he spotted hair. Maybe blond. And then he could make out the face. It was a white female, probably in her twenties. Hard to tell. Her eyes were open. The mouth was wide open and looked like a bloody hole in the face. Dr. John would have fun with this one.

"Email me some digitals, Tony," Jack said, and stepped down to let his partner take a look. As Liddell stepped up, the stool groaned under his weight.

"Already have," Walker said. "They should be on your phone."

Jack hadn't looked at his phone since leaving Nina's—check—Moira's office.

"Call me when you collect it?" Jack asked.

"You'll be the first."

Liddell stepped down and moved away to allow crime scene investigators to do their jobs. "You thinking what I'm thinking?" he asked, almost whispering.

They ducked under the tape and headed for their car. A Channel Six reporter approached them with notebook in hand and a cameraman in tow.

Twenty-six years old, Claudine Setera had been promoted to news coanchor after the previous anchor died of cardiac arrest. Today she wore a black skirt and yellow top that emphasized her fabulous figure and long dark hair. She was naturally dark, not tanned. While she was on the air, she sounded like a Harvard graduate, which she was, but off camera her thick Bronx accent came through.

Her dark eyes widened dramatically as she asked, "Detective Murphy, is it the cannibal?"

CHAPTER TWENTY-FIVE

Jack and Liddell decided to grab something to eat while they waited for crime scene to do their thing. Since they weren't involved in searching the dumpsters, they would be in the way. And they couldn't talk to any neighbors since it was an industrial area and the closest inhabitants lived several blocks away.

They went to Milano's, an Italian restaurant, located on the Main Street Walkway in the heart of downtown. The motif was Italian, the owner was Lebanese, and the waitstaff were from various Middle Eastern and Asian countries. It was Katie's favorite place. Candlelit at night, and sounds of Italian music would drift from mounted speakers. Her favorite dish was baked ziti, although she picked at it—as with all her food—like a bird. He never understood how she could stay alive, as little as she ate.

His own appetite seemed to have left him. His plate of spaghetti with meat sauce set untouched while he sipped the mint tea that was forced on him by Kazan, the owner.

"You gonna eat that?" Liddell asked.

Jack pushed his plate across, but kept one of the handmade rolls called garlic knots and began nibbling at it.

"Why did the killer try to bury Nina?" Jack said, not realizing he said it out loud.

"That's easy," Liddell said. "We weren't supposed to find her."

"That's what I thought," Jack said. "So why smear blood all over the front of that dumpster?"

"C'mon, pod'na," Liddell said. "Don't read too much into it. These guys are all nuts." He shoveled what remained on the plate into his mouth, and around the food, said, "Okay, let's play that game. If he did the Harrisburg girl and her pimp, then he left the heads where they would be found. Then he kills Nina and takes her head and puts it in a garbage bag with one of her arms, and then cuts the fence and buries that inside our dump. Some dogs find it and think, "Mmm mmm . . . this looks tasty," and so they drag it out by the fence."

Jack put a hand on Liddell's arm before he could continue. Several people had stopped eating and were staring openmouthed at the two detectives. Jack and Liddell got up, paid their bill to a grateful clerk, and headed outside.

"Sorry, pod'na," Liddell said when they were back on the sidewalk. "They just got entertained for free. Better than an episode of *NCIS*."

"So go ahead and finish your theory," Jack said. He was interested to hear Liddell's perspective.

Liddell pulled a napkin from his pocket and dabbed his mouth. "Okay. So he kills Nina and buries her head and her arm in the landfill—maybe the rest of her is buried there as well. Why doesn't he put her in a dumpster like the other ones. Why does he clean up the scene at Nina's house to make it look like she has left town. The answer is obvious to a trained detective like me."

This wasn't the first time Liddell had used a dramatic pause, and Jack took the bait. "So what's your explanation?"

"The killer knows her. He may be a boyfriend we haven't found out about, or an ex-husband. Or someone she prosecuted that's pissed."

"Wow!" Jack said. "You came up with all that?"

"No. It was the secret surprise in a box of Cracker Jacks."

Jack could see the sense in what he said, up to a point. "There's a hole in your theory, Bigfoot. If it's a revenge or jealousy killing, why kill the other women? The guy who dismembered Nina and decapitated this new victim has killed before. Most first-timers don't chop heads off. Whoever this is, he isn't squeamish."

"I didn't say it was *the* answer, pod'na. I was just offering an explanation. So, what do you think?"

Jack just shrugged. Something Liddell said struck a chord, but the thought was buried in the back of his mind, just outside of his grasp.

* * *

Jennifer Mangold, secretary to the chief of police, hurried toward Jack and Liddell as they were crossing the street in front of the police department.

"The chief wants you," she said, a little out of breath. She was forty going on fifty, with a constant dark tan, and deep lines around her mouth from years of chain-smoking. But she knew how to keep a secret, and that had kept her in a job through three administrations.

"Hey, Jennifer," Liddell said as they entered the building. "Does the Pope shit in the woods?" This was a regular routine between them.

"No, he doesn't. But there's a steaming pile of it waiting for you in there." She pointed at the chief's door.

Jack was about to knock on the chief's door when Jennifer put a hand on his arm.

"Jack, I need to tell you something before you go in there."

"We're all ears," Liddell said, pulling his ears forward.

She pulled a piece of notepaper from her desk drawer and handed it to Jack. He spied two names with phone numbers, and one of them he recognized. "Karen Compton is the receptionist at the prosecutor's office, isn't she?"

"She is," Jennifer said. "And Sylvia Jennings is the receptionist for Juvenile Court."

Liddell grinned. "Are you selling tickets to the Receptionist Ball?"

"Can you be serious for one minute, please?" she said. "The reason I'm giving you these names is they both overheard a terrible argument two days before Nina was killed."

Liddell immediately sobered, and they listened to her story.

"Once a week we three meet for lunch, and we got together today. We were talking about Nina's murder, and I mentioned that Nina seemed like a very nice person. Both Sylvia and Karen disagreed. They both thought she was a real . . . Well, you know what they thought. Anyway, I asked why they thought that, and they both said they had overheard a very heated argument recently. Nina and Bob Rothschild were arguing—yelling at each other really—on the side of the building."

"Did they know what the argument was about?" Jack asked.

Jennifer shook her head. "But they overheard Bob scream at Nina that if she kept doing something, he'd make her wish she were dead."

Jack and Liddell traded a long look.

"Bob Rothschild the county attorney?" Jack clarified.

"Yes. I hope I did the right thing telling you," Jennifer said. "I just thought it might be important. I don't want to get anyone in trouble. Even that little snake in the grass."

"You did exactly the right thing, Jennifer," Jack said. "But I will have to talk to Karen and Sylvia."

"I already talked to them and told them I was going to tell you first chance. They understand and will talk to you."

"Thanks," Jack said. *That will have to be checked out,* he thought as he knocked on Marlin Pope's door. Inside, he could hear a raised voice, and it wasn't the chief's.

"Come," Pope ordered, and they went inside.

"It's about time!" Trent Wethington said and stood up.

Jack ignored the big show of indignation. "You wanted us, Chief?"

"Have a seat."

Eric Manson looked uncomfortable, and Bob Rothschild was staring at his feet. Trent had his shirtsleeves rolled up on another pink shirt with white collar and cuffs, and his deep blue tie was loosened.

"Cooperation, gentlemen," Trent said. "That's the name of the game. Cooperation is what clears cases. *Clear* and *timely* communication clears cases. I hope I'm clear on that?"

"I'm sorry, Trent," Jack said. He had witnessed the prosecutor's "take no prisoner" stance before, and he didn't want to waste time. "It's my fault. There's no excuse."

This mea culpa seemed to quell Trent's emotional tirade. He regarded Jack like a forgiving father. "I know you've got your hands full, Jack. But you must keep me apprised of any progress in future."

Jack risked a look at Marlin Pope, who rolled his eyes. "Will do," Jack said.

Trent turned to the police chief. "Are we any closer to finding that leak on your department?"

Pope's eyes narrowed. "*We,*" he said, "haven't determined that the leak came from my department."

Trent cleared his throat. "Of course. I misspoke, Marlin."

Pope continued. "But *when* we identify the person, I'll be bringing charges against them. I trust your office will pursue criminal charges this time." Jack knew he was referring to the past leaks of Larry Jansen and Deputy Chief Richard Dick that had gone unprosecuted.

This shut Trent down. Pope knew the prosecutor would never file charges if the person involved were an employee of either Trent's office or the police department. It was tantamount to washing city laundry in public. In effect, Pope had just issued a challenge to put up or shut up.

"We'll discuss it," Trent said, and turned to Rothschild. "I suppose we're done here, Bob." The county attorney, who had not uttered a word, followed the prosecutor out of the office.

Eric Manson stood to leave as well, but Jack stopped him.

"Eric, I want to ask a favor. Do you mind looking up to see if Nina ever prosecuted Hope Dupree? You know, the victim in Harrisburg?"

"Cooperation is the name of the game, gentlemen," Eric said in a voice mimicking that of his boss. "Or is it communication? I'm so confused."

"Good one," Liddell chimed in. "I didn't think Trent allowed you to have a sense of humor."

"I usually keep it in my desk," Eric said.

Liddell said into Jack's ear, "Should we corral Bob now?"

Jack shook his head. "Let's talk to the women first."

CHAPTER TWENTY-SIX

Moira leaned back in her chair in frustration. "Where would I put important files in this *mess*?" Every flat surface in her new office was covered with paperwork, some of it loose, some in stacks, some in manila folders or in banker's boxes that lined the walls. At first glance, the job of sorting and filing all of this had seemed an insurmountable task, but Moira soon settled into a rhythm and, like a marathon runner, found her pace. In the two hours after Jack hurried away, she had three-fourths of the task completed. At the very least she had divided active cases from closed ones.

Eric said he would have a temp worker take the boxes to their storage room in the basement. He had already taken Nina's current caseload with plans to divide these among more senior people. That would allow Moira to start fresh after she was trained.

Eric also made the note that Nina was a pack rat, and Moira had to agree. In going through this stuff she had found cases going back twenty years or more. The Indiana statutes of limitations restricted the length of time the state has to prosecute someone for a crime. These lengths generally depended on the type of crime, and the terms on all of these cases had expired. Moira couldn't imagine why Nina would keep these cases around.

She stepped into the hallway, intending to find more bankers' boxes. *Maybe her death has nothing to do with her job. Maybe Nina was a target of opportunity.*

"Would you come in my office, please?" Trent said, startling her.

He was leaning out of his doorway. She entered his office and he shut the door. He walked behind his desk, indicating for her to take a seat. He remained standing and turned to look out of his window. "You're helping Jack look through Nina's files."

Moira didn't know if he was asking a question. "Is that what you want me to do?"

He flashed a brief smile and his eyes bored into hers. Moira imagined that was the look he gave opposing counsel during trials, calculated to break a suspect on the witness stand. She prided herself on being self-confident, but she wilted under Trent's blazing stare.

"It's exactly what you should be doing, Moira." He took her hand and put one of his business cards on her palm. Yet he continued to hold her hand, longer than necessary and making her uncomfortable. She extricated her hand at last, and he said, "My home and cell phone numbers are on the back."

Moira glanced at the card, and he continued, "I know you and Jack are already family, but *we* are your family now. Me. Everyone in the prosecutor's office."

Moira wasn't sure what he was getting at, but she nodded agreement with his statement.

He moved to the door, indicating that the discussion, or whatever it was, was over. She stood up, intending to get back to work, but Trent braced an arm against the door and moved closer to her, saying, almost in a whisper, "The police have someone leaking information to the news media."

Jack had told her about the leak, but she didn't see the significance. The police were always having leaks. So did every other government agency, be it city, county, or state. What she did know was that she was uncomfortable with Trent's closeness, and being in his office with the door shut. But he was her boss.

"What can I do, sir?"

"Please, when we're alone, you may call me Trent," he said in a tone that was anything but fatherly.

"Yes, sir . . . Trent."

"The point I'm making, Moira, is that you owe as much loyalty to your working family as you do to your kin." He let his words to sink in. "If you, or Jack, find anything . . . I want to be the first to hear about it. You understand?"

"Yes, sir," she said, and then remembered, "I mean, Trent. You will be the first."

He gave her a toothy smile and took his arm from the door.

"You take care of us, and we'll take care of you." Putting two fingers beside his right brow, he added his tagline, "Scout's honor."

She escaped down the hallway, but not back to her office. He had creeped her out and she needed to get outside for a smoke. Then she would have to spray herself with Febreze so Katie wouldn't smell it when she got home. She'd quit smoking later—after she got used to the way people acted in this place.

CHAPTER TWENTY-SEVEN

The call from the Narcotics Unit was brief and uninformative. Jack guessed that could be expected from someone working in that unit for twenty years, as Sergeant Kim Hammond had. Jack and Liddell left the morgue and drove to headquarters, where they took the stairs to the basement.

Their latest victim was as yet unidentified, but the manner of her death had an unexplained detail. Dr. John thought she might have been injected with something, because he found a needle mark in her neck. He was putting a rush on the toxicology, but Jack wasn't holding his breath for a quick turnaround.

In the basement, they passed the indoor pistol range, the Crime Scene Unit, and then forged deep into the recesses where the Narcotics officers dwelled. Jack had never had any desire to work narcotics because their field investigators tended to be as quirky as the suspects.

Outside the door where they stopped, Jack noticed something taped to the wall. It was a crayon stick drawing of a person with a long and pointy object in one hand. Under the drawing, scribbled in red crayon, were the words, *Runs with Scissors*.

Jack put a hand on Liddell's arm. "You said something earlier about Nina's death that's been bugging me. Both she and Hope— and the pimp—were killed the same night and the same way. What are the odds of that? And now this one is killed, maybe injected with something, and her head is left where it would get the most attention—the newspaper offices."

"So?" Liddell asked.

Jack searched for the right words and then said, "This one matches some particulars from Harrisburg and some of ours. So far none of ours had been left out in the open." He kept spinning the idea out. "Nina is the center of this. I'm sure of it. She's the only one the killer tried to hide. We haven't found any of the kill locations, but at Nina's house we found a lot of blood. That's the only time he screwed up. I've been asking myself why, and the answer I keep getting is that the killer knew Nina. She was special."

"So you're saying the killer is trying to make us think these are gang killings? That it's drug-related? But it's not. It's about Nina."

"I'm not sure yet." Yet he did think of the lies Eric told them. *Maybe he deserves a closer look. Garcia can check with the police in Pennsylvania. Why did he leave that place, anyway?*

Liddell pushed the door open and said loudly, "Knock, knock."

"What's the code word?" inquired a female voice from somewhere inside the dark maze.

Kim Hammond had adapted to her job well. Years of working undercover left her with numerous tattoos, high blood pressure from poor sleeping and eating habits, and a lifetime of chain-smoking, not always tobacco. She was short, sturdily built, with a youthful appearance for a woman nearing fifty years old. But she smelled like a doobie.

"You still smoking devil weed?" Liddell asked.

"You know it, Big Mon," Kim said. "A bag a day keeps the doctor away."

Kim was in charge of the narcotics unit evidence room. Being in there for any amount of time left a person smelling like cannabis.

"What have you got for us, Kim?" Jack asked. He could see a small tic at the corner of her mouth.

"Hope Dupree was mine," she said, and rubbed her face. "She was my snitch."

CHAPTER TWENTY-EIGHT

"Did Mike Jones know Hope was your snitch?" Jack asked.

"Why didn't you tell us before about Hope?" Liddell added.

Sergeant Kim Hammond motioned toward several empty desks. She remained standing while the men sat.

"I don't have to tell you about keeping confidences," she began. "Dupree was involved with some pretty heavy stuff. Major players!"

"And I don't have to tell you that I'm working a double homicide," Jack countered.

Liddell leaned his chair back against the wall. "Okay. What *can* you tell us?"

"This isn't my first rodeo, guys. I'll give you what I can, but some things I would have to clear with the chief." She waited for them to nod in understanding, and then continued. "I'm part of a bigger task force. I can't tell you details about our investigation because you don't have clearance, but I can tell you that Detective Mike Jones didn't know Hope was working for us."

Jack momentarily wondered why that would be, but then again, they hadn't told him or Liddell either.

Kim leaned forward lowering her voice, more out of habit than fear of being overheard. "Eric and Trent are on the task force. I've heard through the grapevine that Eric's the one who identified Nina."

"We were at the landfill still recovering the remains when Eric contacted the chief directly and showed up at the morgue with him. He identified her for us."

"You mean Eric Manson didn't tell you?" she asked, looking from Liddell to Jack. "Eric got her charges dismissed a couple of months ago so we could keep her in play. Maybe he thought that detail wasn't important."

Jack felt his jaw clenching. He would deal with Eric later.

"Then the dumb broad got hooked on crack cocaine. I thought I was going to have to arrest her myself, but then she got killed," Kim said.

"Is MS-13 involved?" Jack asked.

"Nah," she said. "They aren't interested in Harrisburg."

"Do you know Detective Mike Jones from Harrisburg PD is working the murders of Hope Dupree and her pimp, Dick Longest?"

"Yeah." A tic started at the corner of her mouth.

Jack and Liddell exchanged a look. Jack said, "He's working several similar killings. He's the one that told us about Hope Dupree and Dick Longest."

Kim paced a bit, no doubt deciding how she could tell.

"Between us?" she asked, and both men nodded.

"Jones would have you believe these killings are the work of a drug gang. If you ask me, he's using them as a convenient excuse for not catching the real killer. It's common knowledge that one of their county councilman's kids is involved in those earlier murders."

"So, why doesn't Jones know about Dupree?" Liddell asked.

She looked around out of pure habit before answering. "This goes to the grave with you, okay? There's dirty stuff going on in Saline County. A lot of big people are involved. Judges. A couple of cops. A state representative. Someone higher up, maybe. Dupree was our mole."

"*Our*, meaning you? Or you and the Feds?" Jack asked.

She didn't answer his question, and that was all the answer that was needed. Instead she said, "That's why it's being kept quiet, Jack. We couldn't risk a leak. We wouldn't have brought Eric in on this, but we needed our prosecutor to drop the charges against her."

"Is Jones dirty, too?" Jack asked.

Kim screwed up her lips, considering what to say. "Truth? We just don't know. That was part of Dupree's assignment. She was inside."

"Your best guess, Kim?" Jack asked. "Do you think Hope's death has anything to do with our cases?"

She gave an exaggerated shrug. "You're the big-shot detective. You tell me."

Back in the main hallway Liddell dug deep in his pockets and came up empty. "You got some change, pod'na?"

Jack gave him what he had, which was mostly nickels, and mulled over the new information while Liddell plunked the change into the slot and punched some buttons.

"You going to talk to Eric?" Liddell asked. The snack machine whirred, but the candy bar didn't drop. Annoyed like a hungry bear, Liddell shook the machine until it wobbled on its metal feet.

"You mean, am I going to ask an attorney why he lied? No, thanks. If his lips are moving . . ." Jack replied. "Besides, it doesn't get us anywhere."

Jack watched Liddell shake the candy machine.

"Damn machine."

"Hey, it's the A-Team." Larry Jansen said. It was cool in the basement and Jansen wore his rumpled trench coat over a suit and tie that looked like it was discarded by a thrift shop. He was smiling and rubbing his hands together as he approached them. "I got something for you."

"Your, uh," Liddell said, directing his gaze down at Jansen's crotch.

Jansen reached for his zipper, to find it was pulled up.

"Gotcha," Liddell said. "You got any change?"

"Go to hell, big shot," Jansen said to Liddell. "I guess you've got bigger things to worry about than a missing exotic dancer."

"What did you say?" Jack asked. He had checked and there were no recent missing person reports.

Jansen grinned and shoved his hands in the pockets of his trench coat. "It's my case. I took the report this morning. I only mentioned it because . . ."

He didn't get the chance to finish. Liddell grabbed huge fistfuls of Jansen's trench coat and began shaking him only a little less vigorously than he'd shaken the machine. "If you don't tell us right now, I'll drag your sorry ass into the chief's office!"

"Okay! Okay! Jack . . . you know I was just kidding. Right?" By now Jansen's back was against the cinder block wall, his face nearly buried in Liddell's chest.

"Who is she?" Jack asked, and Liddell leaned his weight forward.

"I can't breathe," Jansen complained, looking up at Liddell's towering figure.

"Yeah?" Liddell said. "Well then, you don't want to waste any breath."

Jansen swallowed hard. "We trade. I get to clear my missing person case, and you get the name."

Jack didn't care about clearing a missing-person case. "I'm listening," he said, and Jansen began to talk.

"One for the A-Team, zero for Colombo," Liddell said as Jansen disappeared down the hallway.

"You can bet he's already on the phone with Claudine Setera," Jack said.

"Yeah," Liddell said. "She didn't press us at the scene for a statement, so she has Jansen on speed dial."

They pushed through the doors to the detective squad, where Garcia was sitting behind Jack's desk in an animated telephone conversation.

"You'd better. *You* owe *me*, buster," Garcia said, and hung up as they approached her.

Garcia was all of a hundred pounds, but she had a fierce temper. Jack felt sorry for whomever she was talking to.

"What up . . . An-gel-eena?" Liddell said, his skillet-sized hands making gang signs in the air, then reaching out to bump knuckles with her.

Her expression went from pinched to amused. "Shut up," she said to Liddell, then to Jack, "I've got something. Maybe."

"Okay," Jack said, "go ahead. Then I need you to do something for me."

Garcia checked her notes. "In a nutshell, Nina Parsons never had much to do with MS-13 when she worked for the prosecutor in Raleigh. The closest she came was reviewing some cases before they were filed in court. No reason for MS-13 to have her in their sights."

That was awfully curious. Jack remembered Trent Wethington telling about Nina's involvement with MS-13 in North Carolina.

Trent said she had bragged about it. *So either Trent was lying, or Garcia's information was wrong.* Garcia was seldom wrong.

"I agree with you about MS-13," Jack said, realizing that this information was further confirmation of what he'd suspected before. "Now pull up anything you can find on this woman," Jack said, handing her a slip of paper with the name Jansen had given them.

"Is your password still 'JackMurphy' with an exclamation mark?" she asked.

"This month," Jack said. "Until those pencil heads in IT decide to change them again."

She logged in to Jack's computer with Jack's password and typed the name into Google. The screen changed and a list of possible matches came up. She scrolled to one and clicked the mouse.

The picture of a pretty young woman's smiling face filled the screen.

Garcia read off what she had found. "Samantha Steele. 'Sammi' to her friends. Dancer by profession. She's got over three hundred friends on her Facebook page, Jack. She also has a Twitter account, and a MySpace. Who the hell uses MySpace anymore?" Garcia asked. "So, what about her?"

CHAPTER TWENTY-NINE

Jarrod Poiles had reported his girlfriend missing about three o'clock that morning. Jack got his name by running Samantha Steele through the computer for addresses and associates. He wasn't surprised that Jansen hadn't filed a missing person report even now.

Jack and Liddell went to the address on the computer readout and knocked loudly, but no one answered.

"That's his pickup truck in back," Liddell noted.

"Maybe he went out," Jack said, but it wasn't likely. The people who hung out at the Busy Body Lounge were late risers. They stayed up all night partying, then slept until they were conscious and/or sober, and did it all over again.

Jarrod Poiles was known on the street as J Rod. He worked as a bouncer for the Busy Body Lounge when he wasn't stealing and selling food stamps.

"I'll knock," Liddell said, and using the side of his closed fist, he hammered the door until the front windows rattled. He kept on banging for several minutes before a voice from inside said, "What? This better be important."

The door flew open and a man about thirty years old, tall, overweight, his long hair braided Jamaican-style, appeared in the opening. He wore a dirty gold wifebeater and a heavy gold chain around his neck—and nothing else.

When the man saw Liddell's size, he lost the attitude and yanked the end of his shirt over his turgid member.

"Are you a Gold Member?" Liddell asked, and Jack stifled a laugh.

"Jarrod Poiles?" Jack asked.

"Who're you?" the man asked, looking from one detective to

the other. His face took on the numb expression Jack had seen on many a suspect.

"We're from the blind pole dancers association and wondered if you'd care to make a donation?" Liddell deadpanned.

"You're cops," Poiles said.

Jack and Liddell showed him their credentials, and he stepped back from the doorway. "You want to come in?"

"No, but we have to ask you some questions about your girlfriend," Jack replied. "Then we have to take you somewhere. Get dressed."

They followed J Rod into the front room of a shotgun-style shack where every flat surface was covered with empty fast food wrappers, boxes, and beer cans. J Rod found a filthy pair of jeans and pulled them on.

"What's this about?" he asked. "Where is Sammi? She in trouble?"

When pressed, Jarod provided some useful information. He and Samantha Steele—her real name—met at the strip club a year ago, hit it off, and moved in together. She paid the rent, bought the drugs, they ate out three times a day, and fornicated like rabbits. It was a match made in heaven.

But what she liked to do when she wasn't wrapping her naked body around a pole—while sweaty drunks masturbated into napkins and stuffed money into her G-string—was what caught Jack's attention.

Jarrod said he found that Sammi had a God-given talent for oral sex, and so he acted as her "manager." When she finished dancing for the night, she would meet clients he had lined up while she danced, or troll the parking lots around the Busy Body for customers.

Most nights, Jarrod kept an eye on her. But last night he got lucky with one of the other dancers, and when he got home he figured she'd done the same. When Jack told J Rod they needed him to come to the morgue, his expression froze, and he tried to work up some tears. They didn't come.

Jansen opened the door of Duffy's Tavern and the smell of stale beer and burned grease washed over him. The occasional raised voice followed by hooting laughter made him want to turn around and leave. But he had a meeting inside.

Internal Affairs caught Dick in the act, right where Jansen told them they'd be. Chief Pope wanted to fire Dick, but the mayor nixed that plan. So Dick was given a paid vacation and warned to keep quiet or Pope promised to bust him in rank and suspend him without pay.

Jansen told Pope about Dick's "secret" meetings with Maureen Sinclair at La Sombra Coffee Shop. He told him that the leaks were coming from Dick and he resented like hell being suspected of something he didn't do. Pope already knew that Dick had assigned Jansen to Murphy's case, so it wasn't a great leap of logic to figure out that Dick was the leak. Jansen resisted telling on Dick just enough to sell it, and it had worked.

Marlin Pope and Trent Wethington had someone's head on a pike for the leaks. The pressure was off. Now it was time to make some real money.

Jansen smoothed the wrinkles in his coat, made sure his shirt was tucked in, and stepped into the gloom inside.

CHAPTER THIRTY

On the way from J Rod's apartment, Jack busied himself on his cell phone while Liddell drove toward headquarters.

"Where to now, pod'na?" Liddell asked.

"Head downtown to the old courthouse building."

When he provided no further information, Liddell followed up with, "Are you going to tell me who we're going to see, or is it a surprise party for me?"

"Bob Rothschild."

"It's about time," Liddell said, and sped up. "Are you gonna be the good cop or the bad one?"

"I'll do the questioning, Bigfoot," Jack said. "No point in both of us getting in trouble with the politicians."

"That's why I love you, pod'na. Always protecting me."

The sarcastic tone didn't sit well with him. "Do you want to question him, Bigfoot? I'll be more than happy to wait in the car."

"No, no, you do it," Liddell said, sounding like Jack had offered to scald him with hot water. "I just wanted to complain a little so you wouldn't think I was unwilling."

They parked and walked across the street to a tall building. Inside, the lobby was decorated with stone pillars, polished marble floors, and brass fixtures at every turn. Liddell found the office number for Bob Rothschild, walked to the elevator, and punched the up button.

"He's in 12A," Liddell said. "Ever been here before?"

Jack shook his head. "Me neither," Liddell said. "Some building, huh?"

"Big ego, big office," Jack commented.

The elevator arrived, and when the doors opened, both detectives were surprised to find a small black man in a red uniform, complete with a red/gold embroidered cap, operating the elevator.

"What floor?"

"Twelve," Liddell said, then whispered in Jack's ear, "Do we tip him?"

"Nah, suh," the man said. "I get paid well."

Jack shot Liddell a scathing look, and Liddell's face went red.

When they stepped off the elevator, Jack said, "If he's got a secretary, you stay with her and see what she knows about Nina and Bob's involvement."

"You don't want me to go in with you?"

"Like I said. No sense in both of us getting called in to the chief's office."

They reached 12A and Liddell asked, "Ready?"

"As I'll ever be," Jack said, and they entered the office.

Bob Rothschild was not part of a firm, but to look at his grand office space you would think he was the senior partner of Wee, Cheatem & Howe Law Firm.

They showed their credentials to a knockout redhead who was obviously hired for her skills. Liddell had made himself comfortable on a leather sofa, while Jack was buzzed into Rothschild's inner sanctum.

Fifteen minutes later Jack came out of the office and made eye contact with Liddell.

Liddell grinned. They thanked the secretary and walked back to the elevator.

"She said she wants me," Liddell said.

"She couldn't afford to feed you."

Liddell punched the down button on the elevator and heard the hum of a motor somewhere. "Yeah. You're right. But she gave me a lot of information. And she's not a secretary. She's an administrative assistant to Bob."

The elevator opened and this time the operator was a young woman. Same uniform, same cap, same expression on her face as the other one. "Floor please?"

At the car Liddell slid in behind the wheel. "Did you get anything from Bob?"

Jack summarized what he had learned. "I asked him what he did for Trent and he asked why it was any of my business. When I asked why he had been at our last few meetings with Trent he said he was on Trent's election committee and was wondering how the scandal of these murders would affect the campaign. Then he asked me to leave."

Liddell raised an eyebrow. "But you didn't, and . . ."

"I asked him if he knew Nina Parsons on a personal level, and he lied. Then I asked what they were arguing about."

"And *then* he threw you out," Liddell said.

Jack nodded, and asked, "So, what did you get?"

Liddell pulled his notebook out. "The secretary—excuse me, administrative assistant—is Bob's niece. She's finishing her last year of college and going to IU in Bloomington next year for legal studies. Bob has her lined up to intern for a Superior Court judge when she's home on break."

He flipped the page. "Nina has been a visitor to Bob's office many times over the last year because—like Bob—she was on Trent's election committee for his run for governor. Bob is the chairman and treasurer of the committee, and Trent's campaign manager. Nina's job was to find dirt on Trent's opponents and de-tractors. Her other job was to assist Bob.

"Bob's niece said she arranged rooms and travel for Nina and Bob when they were required to go out of town to campaign. Nina and Bob traveled a lot together. She said about a month ago Nina suddenly quit the committee. Bob told his niece that Nina quit be-cause of her increased caseload."

"Anything else?" Jack asked.

"She's a Scorpio and her favorite color is green. She likes long walks along the riverfront and holding hands in the rain."

Jack ignored that crack, thinking about the information they had. Now he understood what Bob probably meant when he told Nina if she kept doing something her life was over. He was refer-ring to her life in politics.

In the meantime, Liddell was looking at his iPhone. "You won't believe this," he said soberly.

CHAPTER THIRTY-ONE

Alaina Kusta was a civil lawyer. Her office was the front room of her tiny house near Garvin Park. She owned a red Mazda Miata with vanity plates that read: SOSUEME. *A civil attorney with a sense of humor,* Jack thought as he and Liddell watched the little red sports car being loaded onto the back of a flatbed wrecker.

The killing was macabre. Doubly so because Alaina was murdered in the middle of a busy shopping mall parking lot, and in broad daylight. Despite all the people walking to and from their cars, no one had witnessed the vicious attack—at least, no one willing to stick around and talk to police. Nor did the video cameras that covered every inch of space inside Eastland Mall prove of any help. They posted very few cameras outside, and not a one covered the parking lot where the murder had taken place.

Blood was smeared down the driver's side of the car, and a small amount had pooled on the parking lot. Dumped unceremoniously beside the car was the naked body of the woman. Long, deep gashes and cuts covered almost every square inch of her flesh. Her throat was cut so deeply, it almost severed her head from her body. The registration in the car matched the driver's license in the purse near the body. Alaina Kusta had purchases from JC Penney, Foot-Smart, and Macy's, still in their bags, some in the front seat, some on the ground beside the body.

The young security guard who had found the body was so shocked by the sight that an ambulance had to be called. Jack had tried to talk to him, but he was goofy from the tranquilizers the EMTs had administered.

"She was attacked beside her car," Sergeant Walker said, "but she didn't get those injuries there."

"What do you think?" Liddell asked.

Sergeant Walker pointed at the pool of blood. "We found cast-off blood patterns on the driver's window of the car, so she was attacked right here. But there isn't enough blood on the ground to explain all the wounds on the body."

He turned in a circle. "I think she was struck once or twice," he said, mimicking the attacker wielding a blade over his head and striking downward. "She was stunned, reached out to her car, and slid to the ground. The killer must have put her in a vehicle or something to finish the job. When she was dead, he dumped her corpse beside her car."

"A vehicle where he could finish cutting her up. Maybe a trailer or a van," Jack offered.

"Yeah," Walker said. "That would explain the blood here." He pointed the flashlight. "This looks like blood was dripping straight down from the side of something. See how it's almost in a straight line. If we're right, there's one hell of a mess inside that vehicle."

Jack eyed the sprawled body, obscene in its nakedness. "Where are her clothes?" he asked. "Anything taken from her car?"

"We haven't found her clothes," Walker said.

"I'll run her license plate and have a uniformed car secure her house."

Walker rubbed the back of his neck, and his face was gray with weariness. "What the hell is going on here, Jack?"

The clerk in the Records Unit took Jack's call and handed the phone to Jansen.

"Larry, I need you to find anything you can on a woman named Alaina Kusta. She was an attorney."

"Was?" Jansen asked.

"She's the body that was found at Eastland Mall," Jack explained.

"Call you right back," Jansen said, and broke the connection.

"Jansen?" Liddell asked when Jack hit the end button.

"He's still working with us. He's in Records."

"I guess Internal Affairs couldn't pin anything on him. But they got his evil master," Liddell said. "With Double Dick gone, Larry doesn't have any protection."

Five minutes later, Jack's phone rang.

Jansen reported: "Alaina Kusta was fifty-three years old. Her eighty-three-year-old mother is in a nursing home. Alaina received a parking ticket a month ago for double-parking outside the Pine Haven facility. So I called Pine Haven," he explained. "I found out she visited her mother yesterday, but she didn't come today. The nursing staff said she came every day at five o'clock."

Larry didn't have much else. As a civil lawyer, she had worked on money disputes and custody and divorce, so she had made lots of enemies. People can become murderous when they lose money or their kids. So that added a couple hundred suspects to the list.

Kusta also had a daughter, also a lawyer and living in Indianapolis. Jansen was trying to get her contact information and would call her. He had gotten her address from the dispatcher and sent two cars to secure it. Kusta's address for her home and office were the same. North Main Street—a block before it ended at Garvin Park.

Jack grew up less than a mile away from the park and knew the area well. When he was a kid, there was a meatpacking facility catty-corner from Kusta's place. It was equipped with pens, cattle fences, and the chutes they would run the cattle through to slaughter them. Cows and pigs were brought in by cattle trucks, processed, and shipped out in refrigerated trucks. Like most kids, he had been fascinated with the gory stories some of the older boys told at school, but when he went to see for himself, he was sickened by the reality and couldn't eat meat for weeks. It was ironic that he'd never been able to kill an animal, but he had killed several men. The difference, he guessed, was the men deserved it.

Jack and Liddell parked and got out on the street in front of the victim's home/office. The color of the house was bright green faded to chalky olive. A gravel parking lot separated her house from a condemned building that had once been a family-run tavern that Jack remembered having the best BBQ in Evansville. Directly across the street was an auto body shop, whose yard, driveway, and street were strewn with cars and trucks with mix and match paint jobs.

It was past eight o'clock, and the nighttime streets were already filling with kids, riding bikes or skateboards, and wannabe gangbangers clutching their sagging pants. Old folks sat on the porches of houses with nothing but window fans for air conditioning, trying to catch a breeze. The overpowering smell of sewer gas permeated the air.

Jack had played basketball just down the street in Garvin Park when he was a kid. He and his younger brother, Kevin, went to St. Anthony's grade school a mile away, but the park was the closest place to find a game of pickup basketball, or maybe a fistfight, or maybe both. The neighborhood hadn't seemed so poor back then, but the kids were tougher than today's crop and more capable of controlling their violence.

"Smell that?" Liddell asked.

"Do you mean the hopeless desperation of a forgotten community?"

Jack knew Liddell could relate to the surroundings. He had once told Jack that he grew up in a similar neighborhood, and if not for the neighborhood cop taking an interest in him, life would have turned out much different.

"No. I wasn't referring to the obvious breakdown of the social contract between government and its citizens."

Jack smiled at his partner. "I love it when you talk all intelligent and stuff."

A familiar black Mercedes-Benz turned the corner at Garvin Park and came in their direction. It stopped in the street, looking for a place to park, then the driver spotted Jack and rolled down a window.

"We need a search warrant," Jack said.

"This is the victim's house and office?" Eric asked, looking around uneasily.

No doubt worrying about leaving his car on the street in this neighborhood, Jack thought.

"Who cares?" Liddell remarked. "We gotta search something. This house will do."

"Okay, I get your point," Manson said. "I'll go back to the office and start the papers."

Jack stopped him. "Actually, I had you come here because I was hoping you would get the search warrant from here. I want you to go through the place with us."

Eric raised an eyebrow. "Care to tell me why?"

It's not because I like your company, Jack thought, but said,

"The truth? Your boss wants to be kept in the loop, and I don't have the time to call him every five minutes. Plus, you can be on hand in case we need legal help."

Eric laughed. "You mean, in case she comes back and catches you roaming through her underwear drawers and confidential legal files?"

"She's not coming back, Eric," Jack said solemnly. "She's dead."

Manson walked to the curb, talking into his cell phone. When he finished he walked up the wooden handicap ramp onto the porch where Jack, Liddell, and Walker waited.

"What's the verdict?" Jack asked.

"Someone's on their way with a warrant," Eric said. "They just have to stop by a judge's for a signature and then we can go in."

"Did you tell Trent?"

Eric held his cell phone up. "That's who I was just talking to."

Jack noticed Eric rubbing his thumb and forefinger together and recognized this as Eric's thought process. Everyone had a different way of focusing mental energy on solving a problem. Liddell would become chatty. Garcia was a visual thinker. Jack wasn't sure what he did. Scotch maybe.

"This is the second attorney killed in as many days," Jack said.

That got Eric's attention. "What are you suggesting, Jack?"

Jack didn't really know what, if anything, he was suggesting. If lawyers were being targeted because of some criminal activity on their part, Jack wanted to be sure he found the evidence legally. And finding it with Eric—the chief deputy prosecutor—would eliminate any questions about how it was found or if it was planted by the police just to discredit some political bastard.

"I'm not suggesting anything, Eric. Just making an observation," Jack said.

A uniformed officer came down the sidewalk, talking animatedly on his walkie-talkie. "We found her clothes strewn along Stockwell Road at Vogel," he said when he got close.

"How do you know they're Ms. Kusta's?" Eric asked.

The officer grinned. "Well, counselor, these were women's clothes and they were blood soaked and cut to rags." To Jack he said, "No weapon."

"Have them check the businesses along Stockwell," Jack said. "Roofs, sewer drains, trash, anywhere outside someone could throw a weapon."

He knew it was an exercise in futility, but it had to be done.

The officer hurried off and Eric looked down the street. "The warrant's here."

To his dismay, Jack recognized the ten-year-old red Camaro. The car pulled to the curb, and Moira walked up to the men.

"What are *you* doing here?" Jack asked.

She flashed him a kid-sister smile. "I've got the search warrant." She handed the stapled papers to her boss, Eric.

"I mean you, why are you here? If Katie finds out I let you get involved, there will be hell to pay."

Moira gave Jack a defiant look. "You're not the boss of me. And for that matter, neither is my sister."

"She's right, Jack," Eric said, examining the warrant. "It's good experience for her. Jump right in, that sort of thing. If you want to be mad at someone, be mad at me. I asked her to bring it."

Jack's tried to bite the words back, but they came out anyway: "You think this is a game, Eric?"

He did this just to piss me off.

"She could be in danger just being seen with us. No disrespect meant, Moira, but a lot of people have died because of this monster."

"You mean being seen with you, Jack?" Eric asked. "You do attract a lot of crazies. I'll give you that. But Moira is a deputy prosecutor, and while she is working for us, that trumps being your sister-in-law. She's assisting me, and I'm assisting you." He seemed to consider the matter closed, and held the papers out to Jack.

You don't know Katie at all, Jack thought, not without a twinge of pleasure. Wait until Katie found out.

Liddell, who had watched this exchange, took the papers from Eric and headed to the front door with two crime scene techs in tow.

Crime scene techs used a pry bar to yank open the front door, and a uniformed officer made entry first. As he passed through the door, he yelled, "Police. Is anyone in here?" He repeated this announcement as he and another officer moved through the house. They came back and one officer said to Jack, "Windows are locked.

Back door is dead bolted and the chain is on. We didn't see anything out of place, Jack."

Jack nodded and the officer left to guard the front door.

Walker and one crime scene tech went in next and were gone only a few minutes before returning.

"It's all yours," Walker said, and he advised his people they could leave. "I'll stay here just in case," he told Jack, and held out latex gloves.

Eric took two pairs and handed one pair to Moira.

Jack's phone rang. He talked for a moment and then hung up.

"They find something in her car?" Liddell asked.

Jack shook his head. "That was Sherman Price, the manager at the landfill."

Three blocks down the street, a cargo van pulled away from the curb and turned east toward Governor Street before turning its headlights on.

CHAPTER THIRTY-TWO

Sherman Price stood beside his work truck, wringing his big hands, as Jack and Liddell arrived at the landfill. Sergeant Walker was tied up at Alaina Kusta's house, so Corporal Kim Booker was the ranking officer at the scene.

"Hey, guys," she said, approaching the detectives. "We found something." Without further ado, she led the two detectives and the landfill foreman back in the direction she had just come from.

They gingerly stepped around bits of broken glass, shards of metal, and other hazards poking through the scrim. Two white-clad CSU technicians stood beside one of the monster compacting tractors, and looked down at a mangled trash bag whose contents were spilled out near the chopping blades.

"Don't this just beat all!" Price said.

Ten feet away, a human leg with the foot still attached lay next to a female torso. Where the head and arms should have been were only bloody wounds. The chest was crushed and eviscerated, most likely by the compactor blades. Price's stomach lurched and he walked away.

"The other remains were in the same type of bags," Corporal Booker remarked.

"It would have taken someone very strong and very determined to haul all these bags out here," Jack speculated. The cut in the fence was over two hundred yards away.

"No way he could do it in one trip," Liddell added.

Unless the killer has an accomplice, or a partner, Jack thought.

"He didn't dig very deep." Liddell pointed at the shallow impressions where the recent bags lay.

"Interesting point," Jack said. "Maybe the compactors were supposed to mix the body parts in with the rest of the garbage."

"We must have walked right over this spot yesterday," Booker said.

Jack cast his gaze out over the sprawling mounds of trash. *Now what? It will take an army to search this whole place. No guarantee of finding anything else.*

"GPR," Corporal Booker said. Both Jack and Liddell turned, and she explained. "Ground-penetrating radar."

Jack had heard of it, but had never seen it used before. The principle was the same as radar used by the Navy. "Do you have one in your pocket?"

She laughed out loud and said, "Smartass. We had one donated by the city engineer's office. They got a new one that actually works and gave us their crap, like usual."

"Have you used one?"

She put her hands on her hips and scowled. "What? You don't think a woman can program a remote for a television, do you? Maybe I should get a man to come and run the damn thing."

"Slow down, girl," Liddell said.

She dropped her hands to her sides. "Sorry, guys. I'm not a feminazi, just a little touchy when someone questions my work."

"I just meant if you had experience," Jack said.

"I'll call Walker and get permission to use it. We can cover a large area in less than an hour. But," she pointed out, "with this ground being full of all kinds of stuff, we might not be able to penetrate the ground more than eighteen inches."

"That's as deep as these were buried, right?" Jack asked, and she nodded. "Sherman, can you have your guys take a break?"

Price kept his gaze pinned on his feet. "Sure. Whatever you say, detective."

A brown Ford Taurus was backed up to the recycling bins near St. Joseph Avenue, with one man in the driver's side. The passenger was putting a soda can in the bin. Neither man's eyes left the group of policemen on top of the landfill.

"Those are the ones," Clint noted as he came back to the car, "we have to watch."

* * *

Eric Manson was waiting for the detectives in their office at police headquarters when they returned. Liddell went to the coffeemaker and filled paper cups for each of them. Jack filled in Eric on the recent discovery at the landfill.

Eric said, "Do we have any idea who the leak is?"

Jack wondered what that question had to do with the information he'd just given him.

"It's not a tough question," Eric said. When Jack still didn't respond, he added, "I've been informed that you aren't considering MS-13 a viable suspect anymore. Is that correct?"

Jack wasn't sure what the hostile tone was all about. "You tell me, counselor. You seem to know everything. In light of what I just told you about Nina, I think we can safely say her killer wasn't from a gang."

Eric then delivered his salvo. "I just got off the phone with Claudine Setera. That little Channel Six girl. Trent wasn't pleased to hear about this from a reporter instead of the investigators."

Claudine would eat Eric for breakfast if she heard him describe her as "that little Channel Six girl," Jack thought wryly.

Eric was on a roll. "She knows the names of the victims. All of them! She already knows you found more body parts at the landfill. And she knew about MS-13, that you aren't considering them as suspects," Eric said. "These leaks have to stop!"

Jack now knew why Eric was so steamed. Claudine Setera no doubt got the information from Jansen.

Liddell put the cups on the desk in front of Jack and Eric. "Coffee?"

Eric took the cup of steaming black liquid and sipped, grimacing at the bitterness. "I'm sorry, guys, but the prosecutor is beside himself."

"You mean like an out-of-body experience, where he's floating and looking down at his body?" Liddell said.

Eric ignored him. "Trent's talking about having the state police take the investigation over."

"He can't do that," Liddell protested, suddenly serious.

As prosecutor, Trent had the authority to request the state police investigate any case, and in turn, they had jurisdiction anywhere inside the state. Since Trent was running for governor, it was a perfect opportunity for him to kiss up to them. And they would jump at the chance to show off for their prospective boss.

"Be my guest," Jack said, knowing that if the state police took over and were unsuccessful, people would question why Trent had changed horses midstream. Trent probably had considered the same thing or he would have just made the change.

Eric couldn't believe Jack was being so nonchalant. "You're a royal pain in the ass, Jack."

"Thanks, Eric. You, too."

"But you're a good detective, and that's all that's saving you."

He wasn't going to be patronized by this jerk. "Eric, I can see you're stuck between a rock and a hard place. If you don't back Trent, he can pull his support of your ascension to the top. If you do back him—and he's wrong—then the public won't elect you. Is that about it?"

Eric evaded the question. "So what are you going to do now?"

Honestly, Jack didn't know. When an investigation was stalled, no matter how hard he pushed, no matter how many people you talk to, no matter how many rocks you turn over, there's nothing to be found. It was too late at night to call Sylvia Jennings and Karen Compton, the witnesses to the argument between Rothschild and Nina. That would be a good place to start in the morning.

"Now we all go home and hope no one is murdered tonight," Jack said.

CHAPTER THIRTY-THREE

Katie and Moira had the much sought-after window seats at La Sombra Coffee Shop on the downtown walkway. Katie ordered orange juice and Egg Beaters. In front of Moira was set a platter with two eggs over easy, four strips of bacon, hash browns, toast and blackberry jam, and a carafe of coffee.

"You sure you have time to eat all of that?" Katie asked.

Moira pulled a twenty-dollar bill out of her purse and laid it on the table. "I've got the time, and I even have money."

"How generous of you, considering I've cooked for you for the last week." Despite what she said, she was glad Moira had suggested they go downtown for breakfast before they both went to work. If not, she would already be at Harwood Middle School, grading papers before her sixth grade class began.

Katie took a sip of orange juice and noticed Moira was picking at her food. "Is everything all right?"

"There's nothing wrong," Moira said, none too convincingly, and then in true Moira style, her mood changed to excitement. "Can you believe I'm working with Eric *and* Jack?"

Katie had never desired to get involved in Jack's work, and Eric deliberately kept his job and political life out of their conversations, unless he wanted her to attend a fund-raiser. And Eric hadn't called since Sunday's party. So she wasn't sure how to answer the question. She did recognize, however, the glow on Moira's face. She couldn't remember when she'd seen her sister so excited.

"So, how is your new office coming along?" Katie had a feeling that things would be different between her and her little sister from now on. The acne-challenged monster she grew up with had turned into a smart and beautiful woman. In fact, Katie felt a small measure of jealousy. Moira was young, vibrant, and thrived on excitement. She was a lot like Jack and Eric in that way.

Not for the first time, Katie wondered what Eric saw in her. She was almost middle-aged. A sixth-grade teacher. The most exciting thing that happened during her day was a fight between kids during lunch, and none of them—thank God—ended with more than a bruise, or at worst a black eye.

"Eric is taking care of me. I guess," Moira said, dragging Katie back from her thoughts. "Eric gave me a big office. It's right next to Trent's."

"And that's a bad thing?" Katie asked.

"Yeah, I'm really being punished," she said and rolled her eyes. "New job. Great office. Lots of money."

"So what's the problem?"

Moira leaned forward and said in a low whisper, "It's just that Trent's creepy."

Katie's eyes grew wide. She had met Trent at several fund-raisers. She knew he could be a little touchy-feely, but she never had the impression Trent harassed his employees.

"I can't put my finger on anything, sis. Just the way he makes me feel when he stands near me." Moira laughed suddenly and sat up straighter. "Maybe I'm being silly. He's old and happily married and someday he'll be governor. That can't hurt my résumé."

"Just remember, Jack is always there for you," Katie said. "He wouldn't let anyone abuse you."

"Yeah, Jack's a good guy, sis," Moira said, but then remembered how he had treated her last night. He sure wasn't happy to see her show up with the warrant.

Katie said, "Did I tell you Jack called to apologize for leaving the party?" She didn't add that Eric had not called. He was probably busy putting political fires out.

"He's still got a thing for you," Moira teased, and Katie's face reddened. "I'm serious, sis. He lights up when he gets around you. He isn't that way around any other women."

"Quit being the matchmaker," Katie said, though she didn't mind thinking she still had Jack on a string.

"You're the same way when you're around him. Do you think . . . ?"

Katie held her palm up. "Stop right there. I'm engaged to Eric. Remember?"

"Yeah," Moira sighed.

CHAPTER THIRTY-FOUR

Jack's sleep had been filled with nightmares, and his T-shirt was soaked with sweat when he jerked awake at four a.m. He dressed and went back to headquarters. He was sitting at his desk, starting his third cup of coffee, when Liddell showed up with a white paper bag in one hand and a maple honey bun in the other.

"Jansen's really stepped in it this time!" Liddell said, and devoured the donut in one bite.

"Your donut will get caught in your lungs if you inhale it," Jack said.

His phone rang and he snatched it up. "Murphy."

It was Little Casket. "I hope you're happy. You used up my entire year's budget making Dr. John stay all night."

"Take it up with the coroner," Jack said brusquely. He was tiring of her constant bitching about money. "What has Dr. John got for us?"

"Am I your secretary?" she said. "Here . . ." and the line went quiet while she handed it off.

"Jack?" Dr. John said.

"Just give me the high points. I'm putting you on speakerphone. Liddell's with me."

"Well, good morning to you, too," Dr. John said. "Okay, there was no sign of trauma to the torso you found at the landfill, so I feel a little safer saying the cause of death was manual strangulation. We still have to wait for the DNA match, but the cuts on the neck of the head and arms match those of the torso," Dr. John said. "And before you ask why I said arms, I'll tell you. Walker found the other arm after you and Liddell left. He said to tell you he was sorry for not calling, but you wouldn't be surprised."

"He's right about that."

"And a gold ring with a garnet stone was found on the forefinger of the arm Walker found at the landfill last night," Dr. John said. "Garnet is the birthstone for January—and that's Nina's birth month."

"What can you tell me about the one from Eastland Mall? Did she have a needle mark?"

"I've sent off samples for toxicology, and no, there wasn't a sign of a needle mark on this victim's neck. It's going to be a while."

"So what was her cause of death?"

"This one's easy. Kusta died of exsanguination—loss of blood—due to assault with a cutting instrument. If it matters, she died within minutes of the onslaught," Dr. John said. "And by that I mean the blade cut through her neck just behind the point of her jaw and was pulled forward, severing the jugular vein, carotid artery, and the trachea. The other cuts were totally unnecessary, Jack. She would have bled out even if she was in a fully ready surgery room. The other cuts on the body were postmortem or close to that. Thirty-three cuts in all."

Jack thanked him and they hung up.

"What have we got here?" Liddell asked. "He goes from leaving just the heads to dumping an entire carved-up body. What kind of person could do that?"

Instead of starting a guessing contest, Jack wanted to get back to what his partner had said earlier. "Who stepped in what?" Jack asked.

"Let me tell you why I'm late first," Liddell said, digging another donut from the bag.

"I can see why you're late. You're wearing the excuse around your mouth."

Liddell did not dignify that comment with an answer. "Anyway, I stopped by Juvenile Court and the prosecutor's office and talked to Sylvia Jennings and Karen Compton. They told basically the same story we heard from Jennifer, but they didn't make the argument sound so sinister. They both said Bob was angry and yelling, but they said that Nina was just as angry and just as loud. All they heard Nina saying was something like, "You tell him I know everything." To which Bob yelled, quote, "If you do this, your life was over. We'll make you wish you were dead.""

"We?" Jack asked.

"Yeah. That's what both women said and I interviewed them separately. I can only assume he was talking about himself and maybe Trent or someone else on the committee. I'm trying to get a list of committee members as we speak."

"Good work, Bigfoot. That sort of makes up for making me interview Rothschild alone."

Liddell grinned. "Hey, I didn't make you do anything, pod'na. You saddled that horse all by yourself."

Jack asked, "Now tell me who stepped in what?"

"Oh, yeah. I just talked to Coin," Liddell said. Coin was one of Liddell's street people. He usually had good information, but he was known to sell the same information to a dozen investigation agencies for a little coin, hence the nickname. No one knew his real name and Coin had probably forgotten it himself.

"Coin was hanging around Duffy's bar yesterday," Liddell continued. "And guess who he saw being all chummy in a booth?"

"Jansen and Miss Setera," Jack answered.

"How'd you know?" Liddell was unable to hide his surprise.

Jack didn't know, he was just guessing. But it was the first thing that came to mind.

Captain Franklin stuck his head in the door. "Jack. Liddell. Chief's office. Now."

"He's expecting you," Jennifer Mangold said, and whispered, "Did you talk to Rothschild?"

"I capped him with my nine," Jack said, pretending to hold a gun gangster style, and then blew the smoke from the barrel.

"Forget it," she said. "You'd better get in there."

Jack followed Liddell into the office to find the chief sitting on the front of his desk. Captain Franklin was seated in the corner. The chief was dressed in a dark suit and tie instead of his usual police uniform dress blues. The flat-panel television mounted over the credenza was tuned to Channel Six and Claudine Setera's perfect face filled the screen. She was wrapping up a news report.

"Take a seat," Chief Pope said. The camera angle changed to allow the viewers to be reeled in. Claudine turned to look in the camera. *"To date, The Cannibal has claimed five victims, one male and four females. Three of the victims' bodies have not been found.*

Police have been unable to establish a connection between any of the victims."

"Chief, I think my partner has something you both will want to hear," Jack said.

Their attention turned to Liddell.

"We can't go to court with this, but I think I can prove Jansen gave all this to Claudine Setera," he said.

"Walk with me," Pope said.

They discussed Liddell's information as they made their way downstairs to the classroom where the news media were set up and waiting.

"I knew Coin when I was still a rookie cop on motor patrol," Pope said, and chuckled at his detectives' look of surprise. "Of course, he was a lot cheaper back then."

"His information has always been good, Chief," Jack said.

Captain Franklin held up at the bottom of the steps, his hand on the doorknob. "I believe Jansen did give us up. I just don't think the information is enough without Claudine Setera or Jansen admitting that he gave her the information. And I don't see that happening, do you?"

Liddell ground a huge fist into his palm. "Give me ten minutes alone with him, Chief."

Pope said, "I don't want to suspend Jansen. I want to fire him! *And* press criminal charges of obstruction of justice!"

He straightened his tie and made his back ramrod straight. "First the deputy chief goes to the newspaper," he said, "and now this. Sometimes I wish I was back on patrol."

Franklin looked at his watch and said, "It's time, Chief." He opened the door so they could go face the stirred-up media horde.

CHAPTER THIRTY-FIVE

The two men had met at the Rescue Mission this last winter. Despite the vast difference in their ages they had become steadfast friends.

Norman was nearing seventy-five. His wife's long illness had eaten up their meager savings, and the year after she passed away, his job had been outsourced. He had lost his wife, his life savings, and his job in less than year, so being homeless wasn't much of a hardship for him. He had survived the next twelve years doing odd jobs. There wasn't much call for a sixty-something tool and die man. His hair was thinner now, but it was still there, unlike his teeth. He had rheumatism in his right hip, and his toes felt numb most of the time—he blamed all that on too-tight shoes and old age. Everything he had would fit in a small garbage bag, and though it wasn't much, it was enough. He didn't take handouts, except for the use of a bed at the mission.

Norman's buddy, Tom, was barely twenty-three, tall and muscular with a scarred face and forehead that looked like he'd survived a fire. He was home from Iraq—ex-military—and had been staying at the Rescue Mission for the best part of a year, but he wouldn't talk about his past. In fact, he didn't talk much at all. Norman suspected his hitch in the Army had messed him up in the head. But Tom had a good heart, and would work sunup to sundown.

They had spent the winter helping out around the shelter, doing what work they could find downtown—shoveling snow, hauling trash—whatever it took to get by. But when summer came Norman did what he had done his whole life. Fish. Today was the first time he'd asked Tom to go with him.

Norman kept a small wooden skiff hidden near the Pigeon Creek overpass on Maryland Street. Early this morning, before the sun came up, Norman and Tom had made their way on foot the mile or so from downtown to the creek. Norman was relieved to see the skiff hadn't been destroyed or stolen.

They dragged it from where the man-high weeds had camouflaged it, and gave it a good shake to make sure no snakes were in the bottom. Together, they dragged it to the edge of the creek and slid it partway into the water.

Hours passed in the most enjoyable way Norman could imagine. The sun would be overhead soon, and they needed to get their lines pulled in and reset for tomorrow's catch.

Norman sat in the skiff's stern, nursing a cold can of beer in a foam Koozie imprinted on the side with the slogan, *Beer . . . It's whut's fer breakfast.*

"What the heck is this? It's tough as a steel cable." Tom tugged at the floating trotline.

Norman squinted at what Tom was holding up. Even though they were less than four feet apart his eyes weren't so good anymore, especially with the sun reflecting off the water and right into his old eyes. "What's it say on that spool down there by your feet, idjit?"

Tom picked up the spool of fishing line. "S-U-F-I-X," he answered.

"Sufix. Ha! That's the best fishing line in the world, son!" Norman said. "Eighty pound test line. Man, I tell you what. That stuff could pull the Loch Ness monster out of the sea!"

"I don't like it. It's too stiff to work with, old man."

"I got somethin' stiff you can work with," Norman answered, and cackled through a toothless grin.

"In your dreams, old man," Tom said, and began pulling the trotline into the boat.

The portion of Pigeon Creek under the Maryland Street overpass was Norman's favorite place to put his trotlines down. The creek fed into the Ohio River about a mile downstream. Fish, particularly young catfish, came upstream from the river. More fish meant more money. He'd caught enough last year to put some change back and help feed the shelter for most of the winter.

Tom grunted and yelled, "Hoo-hah! Got me a big one!" He held up the catfish. "Two pounds, I bet!"

"Hmmpf. That's a baby. We got bigger fish to fry," Norman said, then snickered and said it again, "Fish to fry." He began working the line at his end of the boat and felt a thrill at a sudden tightening in the line. He pulled in several feet, but then it refused to budge. *Damn thing is snagged.*

Norman pulled harder, but not too hard. The baited line was eighty-pound test line, but whatever was hooked to it was way more than eighty pounds. *Maybe a tree root. Or worse, an alligator!* He shivered at the thought. He heard about people bringing baby alligators up from Florida and turning them loose in sewers and such.

"Come down here and help me!" Norman yelled. "And get the gloves out of that box there." He pointed under Tom's seat to a cardboard shoebox.

Gloves were found and both men began working the line out of the water. Soon they were sweating with the effort.

"It's come loose, old man!" Tom said, feeling whatever was on the other end of the fishing line move slightly. They redoubled their efforts, pulling in several feet of line, and then it stopped. This time both men rained expletives down across the water.

Without letting go of the line, Norman said, "Get me the hook!"

The floor of the boat was littered with beer cans and fast food wrappers, but Tom found the broom handle the old man had rigged with a garden hook on one end. He worked it from under the bench seats and went back to help Norman.

"Water's deep here, remember," Tom cautioned.

"You swim, don't you?"

"I never learned how," Tom said.

"Well, it's not that I don't care, but I ain't losing my hooks!" Norman yelled. "Now grab it!"

Tom crouched and reluctantly shoved the homemade contraption over the side with one hand, holding on with the other. When the boat canted, he almost fell into the water, and would have if Norman hadn't grabbed his belt.

"Thanks, Norm."

Tom got settled on his knees and tried again. His arm was submerged all the way up to his shoulder in smelly creek water. While

Tom moved the hook around, Norman kept the fishing line taut. Whatever was down there was heavy.

Tom suddenly stopped.

"You got it hooked?" Norman asked.

Tom said, smiling, "I felt the hook bite into something."

Jack stood, hands in his pockets, looking down the bank at what the two fishermen had pulled from the water. The body appeared to be that of a young woman, now lying gray-skinned and headless on the mud-crusted blue tarp that had been her burial shroud. Eric was with him when he had received the call and insisted on driving separately while Jack picked up his partner.

Eric Manson stood on the muddy creek bank nearby—his five-hundred-dollar Italian loafers ruined in the green mud—and watched the fire department's water rescue diver slip back into the water. Responding police and fire department vehicles were parked a hundred yards from the creek, but any tracks near the creek bank had already been covered by dozens of others.

Jack and Liddell had interviewed the first arriving officers and were told the fishermen said they had "hooked" into "it" directly under the overpass. When they pulled "it" up to the side of the boat, they saw a blue tarp wrapped with chains. They were so shocked they almost turned the boat over. The old man had paddled to the creek bank while the young one held on to the gaff. They had both dragged it—and the concrete blocks that were tied to each end— out of the water. Then they called the police.

"Do you think it's the dancer?" Eric asked as another diver splashed into the muddy creek water.

"Samantha Steele was five-two," Liddell remarked. "The girl from Harrisburg was taller than that, wasn't she?" He checked his notebook. "Hope Dupree was five-five."

"It could be either of them. Or neither of them," Jack said. It was difficult to accurately estimate a person's height when the head was missing.

Eric remarked gloomily, "We have a serial killer on our hands."

Walker came toward them, his boots making a sucking sound each time one would dislodge from the mud. "This one has a tattoo of a butterfly on her left ankle. I've got close-ups."

"Can you send all these photos to Detective Jones in Harrisburg?" Jack asked.

"Will do," Walker said.

Eric lifted one shoe out of the mud with a sucking sound. "No reason for me to stay here. I'll call Trent."

"Good thinking," Jack said, glad to dismiss him. Had Eric just realized this was a serial murderer case?

He examined the body. No defensive wounds on the hands. Tattoos—ivy vines—climbed around the left arm from elbow to shoulder. A butterfly on her ankle stood out in the filmy mud on her skin. No other visible wounds or lacerations on the torso or extremities. So, maybe it wasn't Hope Dupree. Most meth addicts lived a rough life. He would expect her body to be more emaciated, and somehow damaged. This body was not anorexic.

"Liddell, can you get someone to find the dancer's boyfriend?"

"Way ahead of you, pod'na. He's going to meet us at the morgue."

"Where are the witnesses?" Jack asked one of the uniformed officers.

"Over there." The officer pointed toward a skate park just east of their location. "And that," he added, pointing to a bow sticking out of the head-high brush twenty feet away, "is their skiff. We checked. There's nothing in it."

"Let's look anyway," Jack said to his partner.

"That's why we get the big bucks, pod'na."

The skiff was made up of rotted planks that were sealed, here and there, with what looked like roofing tar and cut strips of rubber inner tube material. A cardboard shoebox was open on its side in the bottom of the boat. Fishing line, fishing hooks, red and white floats, and a pair of rusty pliers were strewn on the floor with dozens of empty beer cans. A mop or broom or rake handle had a large metal hook wired to one end, and the contraption lay on the ground by the skiff.

One of the rescue divers surfaced in the creek and shouted to get Jack's attention. He raised two fingers and pointed into the water.

"Aww! What the . . . ? Oh shit!" Jack said.

Divers brought up two more blue tarp–wrapped bundles identical to the one the fishermen had snagged with a homemade gaff.

Both were weighted with cinder blocks, and one was tied with the kind of chains used on a swing set. That one contained the body of an adult white male, fully clothed, covered in what could best be described as prison tats: one a dragon, another some kind of Celtic knots, others too faded from age to make out, and some scars that might have been old knife wounds. F-U-C-K Y-O-U was tattooed on the fingers, most likely not by his mother. The right nipple was missing, but it looked to be an old wound and had healed completely.

The other body was that of a young white female, early twenties or younger. Her legs looked strong and were absent of body art. She was unclad, except for a pair of skimpy panties. Her navel was pierced with a diamond stud. *This is the dancer.*

"I'll call Jones and tell him to expect the photos," Jack said.

Walker went to help his beleaguered techs. "I'm going to need more help. I've sent all the photos to Detective Jones."

Jack's phone buzzed in his pocket and he answered.

"The pictures just came through," Jones said. "Keep this up and you'll be even with me on murders."

"Recognize anything from the pictures?" Jack asked.

"Yep. That's Hope Dupree. I recognize the tats. She has a butterfly tattoo on the left ankle and an ivy vine on the upper left arm. We have medical records if you need them."

Jack walked over to the corpse that was found by the fishermen. The body had a butterfly tattoo on the left ankle. "So you can make a tentative identification on the female?"

"Yeah. And I'm pretty sure the body of the male is Dick Longest. He always went for the biker look. He had been stabbed in the back and stomach in prison and had one of his tits cut off in a bar fight."

"Okay," Jack said. "We still have a jurisdiction problem." Until they found the exact locations where the victims were killed, the jurisdiction usually went to the place where the body was found. The problem was, body parts were found in two jurisdictions. Heads in Harrisburg, bodies in Evansville. Jack doubted if Harrisburg's chief of police wanted to add two more unsolved homicides to his record.

Jones said, "Hey, they're all yours. And good riddance."

"Will you have your chief call my chief to make it all legal?"

Jack asked, not trusting Jones at his word. After all, the man was on EDP Narcotics and the Fed's radar. Personally, he thought both were full of shit. Jones seemed like a solid cop. But still . . .

Jones chuckled. "Yeah, I'll do that. And then we can do lunch."

"Jack," Walker said, walking up to the detectives. "I think we've identified the second female's body."

"That was quick," Jack said. "Did you see it in your crystal ball?"

"Better than that. She has 'Sammi loves Cliff' tattooed on the back of her shoulder."

CHAPTER THIRTY-SIX

Moira came home from work, fixed a salad and a generous pour of Chablis, and took the meal to her room. It had been a long and strange day. She didn't want to tell Katie that she was worried that maybe she'd gone into the wrong line of work.

When Eric asked her to get the search warrant for Alaina Kusta's house, she'd jumped at the chance to become more involved. True, Eric hadn't told her to bring the warrant in person, but she couldn't resist the chance to see firsthand what they would do with it. She didn't plan on being one of those prosecutors she always heard Jack complaining about: "They sit on their asses and never get their hands dirty." But he didn't seem to like it any better when she got off her ass.

When they let her go inside the victim's house, the hairs initially stood up on her forearms. But in the end the walk-through had been anticlimatic, and truthfully, a little sad. Seeing how little Alaina Kusta had to show for fifty-three years on this earth scared her into wondering if, someday, that might be her life. A few diplomas on the wall, and ending a lonely solitary existence with no one to remember you or mourn your passing.

Watching Jack and Liddell process the scene was less dramatic than she had imagined. On television the detectives always find a clue that sheds light on the case. Her experience today was more like walking through a museum of a person's uneventful past.

She pushed the remains of the salad around the plate, her appetite gone, and then made up her mind. She grabbed her car keys.

"Hi, Nova. Remember me?" Moira asked the Civic Center's night man.

Nova looked like he was in his late sixties, but hands twisted into arthritic claws and the exaggerated stoop to his walk suggested he was much older. His thick gray hair was pulled into a ponytail. The faded gray shirt and pants and heavy gray beard gave him the appearance of a shadow in the doorway.

Rheumy eyes widened behind corrective lenses while he studied her face, and then recognition illuminated his eyes, lending truth to his name: Nova, which means "suddenly brightening star."

"Moira. You're Jack Murphy's friend."

"You have a great memory."

"I'm old. Not stupid," Nova said. "We're closed, you know? Forget something, did you?"

"I need to get in my office, Nova. Jack said you would help me."

At the mention of Murphy's name the old man became cooperative. "Well, I guess it won't do no harm." He unlocked the door and pushed it just wide enough for her to step through.

"I got a master key," Nova said. "Do you need your office unlocked, too?"

Moira held up her key, thanked him, and he shuffled off into the gloom. Once she reached her office, though, she found the door open and the lights on, revealing the stacks of boxes. She was glad to see that at least someone had the forethought to bring empty bankers boxes while she was gone.

Stacks of heavy-looking boxes leaned against the walls. She closed her door and hoisted the nearest box with great effort. It was heavier than she had imagined and slipped from her grasp and hit the floor. The box split down the sides, and spilled files and loose documents across the floor and under the desk.

"Just great!" she said, dropping to her hands and knees to crawl under the desk. She was reaching for the files when she noticed a small square of plastic taped to the underside of the desktop. She pulled it free, and leaving the splayed folders, squirmed backward until she could stand.

She peeled the cellophane tape from the item and felt a thrill of excitement at what she had found. In her palm was a computer flash drive.

She eyed the mess of files that still lay scattered on the floor. She would leave it until tomorrow. *But what about the flash drive?* she thought, gripping it tightly. She was dying of curiosity. What did it have on it? Should she take a look? Should she share her discovery with Trent—or Eric now? At this hour? Both men had made her promise that if she found anything that she would come to them right away. She was a new employee, and disobeying her supervisors was grounds for dismissal. In any case she couldn't leave it in the office. Too many people—even Nova—had keys to her office.

She made up her mind to give it to Eric in the morning. Hurrying slightly, so she could go home to see what was on the flash drive, she turned her lights off and stepped into the hallway. She was pulling the door shut when someone grabbed her from behind.

Moira screamed and twisted her arm away. She continued screaming as she ran down the hallway.

"Moira! It's me!" came a familiar voice.

Heart pounding, Moira stopped to see Eric Manson standing beside her office. The folders he'd been carrying were scattered across the floor.

"You scared me to death!" Moira said, walking back. "I'm sorry, Eric, but you startled me." She held up her hands and showed him that they were shaking.

"What are you doing here?" Eric asked.

"Why are you still here?"

"I had to pick something up and I heard noise coming from your office." He pointed to her closed hand. "What have you got there?"

Maybe it was the angry look on his face, or maybe she just didn't like the tone of his voice, but she lied. "It's mine, Eric," she said matter-of-factly, and pocketed the device.

Eric stepped in close. "Did Jack send you to snoop around?"

She felt her face burn as shock of being grabbed from behind was replaced by anger at his insinuation.

She had never seen him angry and it wasn't a good look on him. His mouth was set in a grim line. Redness crept into his clamped jaws, and his hands were crushed into fists.

"I don't snoop, Eric," she said, icily, refusing to back down from his angry stare. "I was working. And on my own time, I might add."

"Working on what?" he demanded to know. "You haven't been assigned any cases yet."

His caustic words stung her. Until now she had only heard what a valued employee she was. How they were a family.

In that moment she decided to give the flash drive to Jack. It would serve Eric right. And, besides, if she gave up the flash drive now, it would only prove to Eric that she had been snooping—and she had found it by accident.

"I was working on those boxes of files," she said, and that much was true. "I thought you would appreciate my hard work."

His expression softened. He pushed her door open and saw the floor was littered with files. A broken box lay nearby. Suddenly he became the old Eric, the one engaged to her sister.

"Sorry, Moira. I guess we scared each other," he said, giving her a sheepish grin. "Did you find anything?"

"Uh, no," she lied.

He glanced at the pocket where she had put the flash drive, but then put a hand on her shoulder, saying, "Let me walk you out."

CHAPTER THIRTY-SEVEN

Jack sped west on Diamond Avenue, turned north onto Heidelbach, and floored it.

"Want me to drive?" Liddell asked.

Captain Franklin's call had put Jack in a dark mood.

"Moira is Eric's employee," Jack said, barely slowing for a stop sign at Louisiana Street. "I didn't send her to snoop around their offices. Why would Eric think that? What's he got to hide? And why would he call Franklin and ask if I sent her?"

"Get it out. That's good. Let's talk about it, pod'na."

Jack gripped the wheel tighter and the Crown Vic's tires squealed around the corner onto Maryland Street.

"C'mon, Jack. She was just doing what you would have done," Liddell said. "You have to give her some credit."

"She's in a dead woman's office at night! By herself! Snooping around!" Anger tinged Jack's every word.

Liddell punched Jack on the arm. "So, who's that remind you of?"

"Shut up," Jack said. But he knew Liddell was right. She was just doing what he would have done, given the circumstances. He should have seen it coming.

"So, your plan is to go over there and yell at her. Am I right?" Liddell asked.

"I'm not going to yell at her."

"Yeah, you are."

Jack slowed down and pulled to the curb. "I'm going to reason with her," he clarified.

"Uh-huh. Good luck with that."

Jack was in no mood for smart aleck remarks. "Okay, Bigfoot. What would you do if Marcie got involved in one of your cases?"

Without hesitation Liddell said, "I'd yell at her."

Jack huffed in victory, but Liddell added, "Course, she's not a deputy prosecutor whose job it is to ensure cases are thoroughly investigated and tried in a court of law."

Jack ran his hands through his hair in a new burst of frustration. "You want to drive?"

"Nah. You're doing great. Let's go to Donut Bank. Tell you what, you can yell at me if it makes you feel better." Liddell leaned back in the seat.

Jack was about to pull away from the curb when his phone rang.

Moira said, "Jack. You've got to come over right away!"

"You want me to come in with you?" Liddell asked. "Or would you like to be alone?" he said with a big grin.

"Moira said she has something to show us," Jack said. "I might need you to stop me from yelling."

As they walked onto the porch, the door opened. A soft light framed Katie as she stood in the doorway. Jack had a pleasant flash of memory. Back when they were first married, Katie would be waiting for him when he came home. She would greet him at the door in just the same manner. *Less clothes, maybe.*

"Hi, Katie," Liddell said, and wrapped her in a bear hug. "Congratulations." He mouthed the word at her so Jack wouldn't hear.

She stood on tiptoes to peck Liddell on the cheek, then turned to Jack and said, "If you're here for Moira, she's upstairs."

Jack recognized the look on Katie's face. It said that Moira was in a mood and he should tread lightly. "I'm not here to yell at her. *She* called *me*," he said defensively, and headed for the stairs.

Liddell put an arm around Katie's shoulders and led her toward the kitchen. "Do you have something to eat in there? Jack never eats, you know."

Moira was sitting with her back to the bedroom doorway, and the glow from her laptop monitor was the only light in the room. This had been the nursery once upon a time, and Jack felt a twinge of unease at seeing a twin bed, a small dresser and a desk crowded into the room. He wondered if it would have looked like this if Caitlin had survived. She would be seven next month.

Noticing his presence, Moira jumped up and pulled him into the room. Her words came out in a torrent. "I went to the office to do some work and found this taped to the underside of Nina's desk. It has to be Nina's. Don't you think? It must be important or she wouldn't have tried to hide it. And then I thought I should give it to Eric or Trent, but it was late and I decided to take it home and give it to them in the morning, and then Eric grabbed me from behind when I stepped out of the office and accused me of snooping. So here," she said, and dropped the flash drive into his palm.

Jack's gaze moved slowly from the flash drive in his hand up to her face.

She realized her mistake. "I'm so sorry, Jack. I shouldn't have touched it, should I? I mean, fingerprints and whatnot?"

"It's okay, Moira," he said. But what he wanted to say was, "What were you thinking?"

"I guess I shouldn't have opened the files either," she said, but he could tell she wasn't sorry at all.

"Let's see what's on it," he said, handing the drive back to her.

She snapped it into a port on the computer and then tapped a few keys on the keyboard. The screen saver was replaced with two icons whose titles were strings of numbers. She double-clicked the icon on the left and a list appeared. The list was composed of three columns. The first column was a long set of numbers and capital letters. The second column was dates, and the third column was sequential numbers beginning at zero-one.

"What is this?" Jack asked.

"I think the first column of numbers might be internally assigned numbers for cases. The prosecutor's office uses these to track assignments," she explained. "The middle column might be dates and times. The last column might be how many cases are included in the folder. I'm not sure."

Jack raised his eyebrows. "And why would Nina have this?"

Moira grinned and said, "I found out a little about her today from my training supervisor, Abbey. One of Nina's jobs was to create spreadsheets of each deputy prosecutor's caseload. Trent apparently tries to keep the case assignments spread evenly among the attorneys."

Jack was familiar with the concept, but he also knew that if the prosecutor's office was anything like the police department, that kind of system wouldn't work. Some people worked hard and others did the bare minimum.

He toted up about two dozen numbers on the list. "Surely these aren't all of the cases that were assigned," he pointed out. "Can we find out what these cases are? Whom they were assigned to?"

Moira excitedly clicked that folder closed and double-clicked the other icon. This one was a list of picture files. He noticed that the numbers for some of these were the same as the string of numbers and letters on the first set of files.

Moira opened one of the photo files and it revealed a scanned copy of a newspaper article from 1983. The headline read "Police Raid Massage Parlor." The story dealt with prostitution, drug issues, and hinted at police corruption. Jack scanned down the page, but the material meant little to him. He recognized one or two of the names, but the article was pretty generic, and he had been in high school when it was written.

Moira clicked on the next file and another newspaper article appeared. This one was of a similar nature, dated a year earlier than the first.

"Who knows you have this?" Jack asked.

"No one," Moira answered.

"You're sure."

"Yes," she said. "Do you think it's important?"

"Like you said. Why else would Nina hide it? Moira, are you absolutely sure no one saw you with this?"

She shook her head, but then she thought about Eric. "When I was at the office, I ran into Eric. He asked me about it."

Jack wondered what Eric was doing at the office that time of night. "Do you think he saw it?"

Moira looked deflated and said, "I told him it was mine."

Jack told her about the call from the captain. "We will need to investigate this, but we are going to start, right this minute, giving you as much cover as possible."

CHAPTER THIRTY-EIGHT

The strip mall in Owensboro, Kentucky, was less than a twenty-minute drive from their room, and only twenty more minutes to Evansville. It was late and very few cars were parked in front. It reminded Clint of some of the towns where he grew up, with upscale shopping malls and sprawling homes on one side of the city—ghetto housing, bars, and pawnshops on the other. The haves and have nots, both white and black and Hispanic. He thought that maybe he'd go home for a visit when this job was finished. He hadn't been home for a while.

He found a pay phone in front of Radio Shack and called the boss while Book went to find coffee. When he finished the call, he spotted Book at a patio table in front of Tacos To Go. Two young ladies sitting in the front window of The Yogurt Shack had his full attention, sucking on sodas, casting furtive glances at Book and giggling behind their hands.

"They been watching me since I set down," Book said.

Clint checked the ladies out. They were about fourteen. Book liked young girls; they were always good for some fun. But they wouldn't be good for much else when Book was through with them.

"What did the boss say?" Book asked.

"I told her Murphy and his partner were on television," Clint said. "She already knew. She said the client was nervous."

"The client is nervous?" Book asked.

"Yeah. Nervous. The police found the bodies in the creek," Clint said.

Book sipped his coffee. "So we're done. It's over."

Clint shook his head. "She wants us to stay. Gave me addresses for the two cops. Wants us to stick close to them."

Book cast one last glance toward the girls and let out a deep sigh. "Does she want us to kill the cops?"

"She didn't say."

"So how we gonna know what to do? We can't be calling her every five minutes," Book said.

"I took care of that. I bought a disposable cell phone at Radio Shack. We can use that instead of a pay phone. I gave her the number so she can call us," Clint said.

"We never needed a cell phone before. This should be over by now."

Back at their car, Book asked, "I wonder who the client is? I mean, why is he so important?"

Clint was wondering the same thing. "Maybe she wants us here in case the client needs to be whacked?"

"That'd be okay with me. I say let's get it done with."

They walked to the van and Clint's pocket started vibrating. He looked at the screen and the caller was blocked. "Hello."

"Rush job," the feminine voice said. "Write this address down."

Clint dug in his pockets for a pen and Book gave him a scrap of paper. He listened and wrote, and then disconnected the call.

"What?" Book asked.

He showed the slip of paper to Book, saying, "We go to this address and recover a computer flash drive. Murphy and his partner are there with some girl. The girl has the drive. The boss says it's a priority."

Book slammed a fist into his palm. "About time."

They arrived twenty minutes later at the two-story colonial set at the end of a cul-de-sac. The lawn was perfect and the railed porch had huge wooden flower boxes full of flowering vines. From what the boss told him the house belonged to Murphy's ex-wife. Women were always decorating, Clint thought. It was in their DNA.

He spotted Murphy's Crown Vic in the driveway, and picked a surveillance spot under a huge oak tree whose limbs hung precariously out over the street. He was positioned at a cross street so as to not attract attention if they had to follow the detective. The van was almost invisible in the dark.

"So what's the plan?" Book asked.

"The plan is we wait until he splits. Then we go in and mess with them."

CHAPTER THIRTY-NINE

"Thanks for coming to talk to her," Katie said.

"She's hardheaded. I want you to know that I didn't intend for her to get involved in any of this."

She gave Jack a hug and a peck on the cheek—something she hadn't done for a while. It felt both affectionate and strictly arm's-length at the same time. "She's my sister. I know how she is."

"Okay, I'll get him out of here," he said, hooking a thumb over his shoulder at Liddell, "before he gets hungry again."

Moira appeared in the doorway. "Thanks for coming so quickly. I really didn't know what to do."

Jack patted his pocket. "Thank you for saving this for me," he said. "I'll give it to you first thing in the morning and you can turn it over to Eric. Have you thought of an excuse for lying to him?"

She feigned a hurt look and said, "I'm an attorney, Jack. I don't lie. I just tell the truth the way it's most convenient."

Jack shook his head. When Trent Wethington found out she'd taken evidence out of the office, she might not have a job.

CHAPTER FORTY

Jack pulled in behind police headquarters and parked next to Liddell's unmarked police car. "Is this close enough for your poor tired feet and your growing waistline?"

"I'll bet you say that to all the girls," Liddell said, and winked.

They got out and looked at the night sky. The moon was full and surrounded by clouds the color of blood. That seemed appropriate for the season Jack had been having.

"Native Americans called it Hunter's Moon, and sometimes Blood Moon," Liddell said. "It's rumored to have mystical powers to draw prey out in the open. Maybe it'll work in our favor, pod'na."

Or maybe not. "Go home, Bigfoot. Tell that wife of yours to call Katie sometime. I think she would like to talk about something else besides work."

"Will do. How about letting me take a look at that gizmo?" Liddell said, surprising Jack.

Jack dug in his pocket and handed over the flash drive.

"Knock yourself out," he said. "Just be sure to get your beauty sleep. The autopsy on Hope Dupree is scheduled for eight in the morning. We have to get Garcia to make a copy of that thingamajig and give it back to Moira before the autopsy."

"Gotcha."

As Liddell slid into his car and drove out of the parking lot, Jack looked skyward. It was the third night of a full moon, and the superstition attached to the full moon had so far proven itself. All hell *had* broken loose. All he wanted now was three fingers of Glenmorangie single malt Scotch poured over lots of ice, and some sleep. In that order.

* * *

Clint had parked in the Superior Court building, just on the other side of a tall hedge from where the two detectives were talking. He heard them discussing the flash drive. He didn't think they were going to take it into the police station, but he secretly hoped they would. That would be that. Maybe he could get the hell out of Evansville then. But then he heard the one called Liddell take the flash drive from his partner and take it home with him. He headed back to the van.

Liddell's tan Crown Vic drove down Sycamore and went straight. Clint started the van and headed for Walnut Street, where he could get ahead of the Crown Vic heading east on Lloyd Expressway.

"You got the address for that one, right?" Book asked with an edge of excitement to his voice.

"Yeah, the boss gave it to me. His name is—"

"I don't care give a crap what his name is," Book snarled. "Just keep driving while I punch the address into the GPS. He's going to have a surprise when he gets home."

Clint followed directions until the voice on the GPS announced, "You have arrived at your destination." He found a space and had just backed the van into it when the Crown Vic came down the street. The driver seemed to be in no hurry to get out of the car.

"Showtime," Book said. They exited the van carrying aluminum baseball bats and wearing holstered Beretta 9mm handguns—just in case. Pounding the hell out of an unsuspecting person should be a piece of cake, but this was a cop. Kind of scary. Kind of fun.

CHAPTER FORTY-ONE

The red Camaro came to a screeching halt in front of the emergency entrance at St. Mary's Hospital, and Katie and Moira rushed through the doors. A half dozen uniformed officers were milling around the waiting room, and another came to his feet from behind the security desk as the startled receptionist looked up. Katie and Moira disregarded them and pushed through the double doors into the treatment room.

"You can't go back there," the receptionist called out, but not one of the uniformed officers made a move to stop them.

An armed officer did move to block the upcoming doorway, then recognized Katie and his features softened. "I'm really sorry, Mrs. Murphy, but you can't come in yet. Doctor's orders, ma'am."

"Let them in, Bobby," a familiar voice said from inside.

Katie and Moira entered the room and found a curtain drawn around a hospital bed. When a nurse parted the curtain, Moira's hand went to her mouth.

"Oh, my God!" she said, seeing the unconscious bloody shape on the bed.

A young ER doctor was standing to one side while a nurse took vitals and monitors beeped and IV bags dripped into flaccid arms.

"Is he . . . is he . . . ?" Katie tried to get the words out, but she couldn't breathe.

From a chair in the corner Jack said, "He's alive."

Marcie refused to leave her husband's side, but an orderly led Jack, Katie, and Moira to a small room down the hallway where they could wait. Jack told them what he knew.

He had dropped Liddell off behind headquarters and was on

Highway 41 heading home when his phone rang. The caller ID showed it was Liddell, so he picked up expecting to hear a bad joke.

"Jack! Oh, God, help me, Jack! He's dying!"

The voice was so shrill, he didn't realize at first that it was Marcie. Despite all his training and experience, he didn't react. Couldn't move. Then he slewed the Crown Vic across the grass median and stomped the gas all the way to the floor. He struggled to hear Marcie over the roar of the big engine.

"I shot him! Oh, God, he's not moving!"

Her words weren't making sense. Who had she shot? Liddell? "Where are you?"

"At home. I shot one of them! They were wearing masks. They kept hitting him, and— Oh, God, Jack! He's not moving! He's so bloody!"

"Stay on the line, Marcie. Don't hang up. I'm getting help," he said, and grabbed his radio mic. "Marcie. Don't hang up."

He called police dispatch and had to yell at the call taker to shut up and listen.

The call taker said, "We've already dispatched officers to that address reference a shots fired call. I'll dispatch an ambulance." Then he heard the call for AMR.

From Marcie's end he heard sirens coming. Ambulance and police units were arriving. He himself was less than a mile away. He arrived to a symphony of red and blue flashing lights and found Marcie on her front porch. A third shift officer named Rodriguez was standing with her. A Glock .45 was stuck under his gun belt in the back of his pants, and he explained that he had taken it from Marcie after a few anxious moments of her refusing to give it up. The gun had been fired. He'd checked the clip. Empty.

Jack thought the gun was the one Liddell had bought for home security. He remembered Liddell said he was giving Marcie shooting lessons. Marcie said on the telephone that she shot one of the suspects. He hoped she had killed him, but he didn't see any bodies, so they must have gotten away.

"What happened, Marcie?"

"I was in bed and I heard him yelling," she said. "I've never heard him like that. From the window I saw two men standing over him. I must have grabbed the gun when I came outside. I don't remember. But the two of them were big. Both big guys. Wearing masks. And they had bats! Baseball bats, Jack! And they kept hitting him and hitting him and he wasn't moving."

Liddell had been loaded into the back of an ambulance and the paramedics were closing the doors.

"Please! I need to be with him," Marcie cried.

"Hey!" Jack yelled at the ambulance crew. "Hold up a second."

He put an arm around her shoulders and led her to the ambulance. He helped her into the back and asked, "Did you see what they were driving?"

Tears were streaming down her face. "I didn't warn them. I just pulled the trigger. I heard one of them scream. Then they ran to the van . . ."

"That's good, Marcie. That's good. Now, what color was the van?"

"White. I think. I'm not sure. I kept pulling the trigger until it wouldn't shoot anymore."

"We've got to go," a paramedic said, and shut the door.

The ambulance pulled away with his partner inside, fighting for his life. Part of him wanted to follow the ambulance, but he had to make sure a few vital steps were being taken here.

Jack found Officer Rodriguez. "Be sure to fill out a chain of custody on that," he said, referring to the gun Marcie had used. "Give it to no one but crime scene."

Rodriguez looked chagrined, then embarrassed. "Guess I got my prints all over it, huh?"

"Don't worry about it. Just find out who called in the shots fired, and get a detective out here. I'll call Captain Franklin."

He left for the hospital and had dispatch put out a BOLO. The descriptions were thin. A white van. Two men. Armed with baseball bats. No direction of travel. Nothing.

His hands clenched the steering wheel.

He didn't have much to go on, but he knew he would find them. And when he did, he would kill them.

CHAPTER FORTY-TWO

As Book drove the two-lane road running north, they bounced around a blind curve. Clint's hand went to his side and came away bloody.

"We should have killed that crazy bitch!" he said, gritting his teeth.

"Quit whining. You just got a scratch. Now let me concentrate on where we're going."

"You're not the one who got shot, Book. Slow down," Clint said angrily. Yet he knew Book was right to hurry. They had to get rid of the van pronto.

It had all been going as planned. He and Book had gotten out of the van quietly and walked across the street with baseball bats. The big cop got out of his car, his back to them. Made to order.

Book hit him first, across the back, and the guy just stood there, so Clint hit him across the lower back, around the area of his kidneys. No matter how big you were, if your kidney got crushed, you went down. But the guy just grunted, and put his hand on his back. And then both he and Book started swinging for a home run. It sounded like someone beating a rug. *Whop. Whop. Whop.*

The cop was tough. Clint would give him that. He'd taken eight blows to the back and chest before he became angry and made a grab for his gun. Clint swung the bat at the cop's arm with all the force he could put behind it, and he hurt the guy because he at least let go of his gun. But then he started to get up. Book finally smashed him in the back of the head and he dropped like a rock.

Clint took the cop's gun from his holster and then rifled through his pockets for the drive. Unbelievably, the cop grabbed Clint's hand. By that time Clint had had enough. They couldn't stop beating him.

Book hit the guy one last time in the stomach, and that's when it all went to hell.

Clint felt a bullet slice across his ribs before he heard the gunshot. If they had worn ski masks, he knew Book would have wanted to stay there and shoot it out with the crazy bitch. But they didn't. Instead they ran to their van and got the hell out of there. But not before he heard bullets punching through the back doors. One smashed into the dashboard; another went through the windshield—missing his head by mere inches.

He'd been in firefights in Afghanistan and knew that it wasn't like in movies, where guys would spray bullets around and hope they hit something. Adrenaline, fear, and anger all affected muscle control, the fine motor skills needed to control a weapon. Even if a person took his time and aimed, it was a crapshoot whether he hit what he was aiming at. This woman was Annie Oakley on crack.

"What was she firing at us?" Book asked as they passed cornstalks illuminated in the headlights.

"Felt like a sledgehammer, Book," Clint said, and leaned against the passenger door.

Book laughed, but there was no humor in it. The fact was the broad had shot their asses up. Book wasn't worked up about being shot at. He was pissed that he had been made to run like a coward.

"We should have been told about the woman," Clint said. "We got bushwhacked."

"Yeah," Book muttered. "How could we know someone would come out shooting? It's that cop's fault for yelling. The big pussy."

Clint remembered how the cop stood up to their blows. "He wasn't a pussy."

Book said, grudgingly, "Yeah, you're right." He smiled. "But we gave him something to remember us by, didn't we?"

Clint twisted in his seat and dug in his pants pocket. "At least we got it." He opened his fist and revealed the flash drive.

"You done good, Clint."

"You know, I been thinking about that guy. The one who was waiting for us to come and get the first body."

"So what about him? We got the flash drive. We call the boss, then we leave."

"What if we were set up?" Clint asked.

Book's voice filled with uncertainty. "You think the boss set us up?"

"Maybe that broad back there wasn't just some woman. Maybe it was another cop. Maybe she was supposed to take us out," Clint said.

Book fell silent, brooding. The van headlights illuminated a cutout that led west into a pasture. Book took the turn and drove across hard-packed earth and saw grass for several hundred yards. The track ended at a clearing in the middle of which was a barn. Their rented Taurus was parked along with several large pieces of farm machinery.

Book pulled the van into high grass and continued onto a small rise. He stopped and cut the headlights. Both men walked to the back of the van, and Book let out a soft whistle.

Clint took a penlight from his pocket and examined his own damage. Blood soaked the right side of his T-shirt, and his hands were covered with it. He lifted the shirt and breathed a sigh of relief. Book was right about it being a scratch. The bullet had cut a six-inch path, front to back. The wound should receive stitches and a good cleaning, but going to a hospital was out of the question. He twisted gently, testing, and took in a sharp breath. The bullet must have hit a rib. He'd have to let Book sew him up, and forget about the rib. Even if it was broken—and it felt like it was—it would have to heal on its own. *Shit!*

Clint dropped his shirt back over his wound and watched Book count the bullet holes in the back of the van.

"Seven hits, Clint," Book said almost proudly. "Three in the left door and four in the right." He covered the three holes in the left side with his palm. "That's some damn fine shooting."

"Yeah," Clint agreed, and emptied his pockets on the ground. "There's about twenty dollars and change, a wallet with a badge, the flash drive, a half candy bar, and"—Clint pulled a pistol from under his shirt—"his gun."

".45 Glock," Book said.

Clint felt the weight of the gun and lined up the tritium sights. "Think I'll keep it."

"Too hot," Book warned. "The serial numbers will be in their computer in no time. You get caught with that thing, they'll put you away for good."

Book picked up the loose change and handed it to Clint. "You keep the money. That's for getting shot."

Clint stuck the money in his pocket. "What do we do with the rest of this stuff?"

Book took the baseball bats and the cop's wallet and gun to the edge of the lake, where he tossed them in.

Clint held the flash drive out to Book. "The boss said to destroy it."

Before Book could take it, though, Clint changed his mind. He closed his hand and stuck the flash drive in his pocket. "The boss isn't here," he said. "I say we see what's worth all this. It may be our ace in the hole in case they *were* trying to set us up."

Book didn't seem to think that was a good idea, but he didn't say a word.

"Think the water's deep enough?" Clint asked, pointing out over the water.

Book picked up a piece of wood and got back in the van. "Only one way to find out," he said, backed it up fifty feet, put the gearshift in drive, and wedged the stick against the gas pedal.

CHAPTER FORTY-THREE

"He's stable now," the young emergency room doctor said. Anticipating the rush, he stood with his back blocking the door. "He can't have visitors until we see the MRI results. He's completely awake and alert and demanding to go home. Just to be safe, I'm going to keep him in hospital overnight."

"Has he said anything?" Jack asked.

The doctor shook his head. "You're Detective Murphy, aren't you?" Without waiting for Jack to answer, he touched the scar that ran down the right side of Jack's face and disappeared inside his collar. "That healed rather well."

Jack recognized him at last. "You're the doctor who took care of me when I was cut."

"You and your partner live a dangerous life," the doctor remarked, and left the room.

"You're a legend, Jack," Moira said.

"Yeah, I'm a man ahead of his mind," Jack said, and opened the door to the hallway.

"Where are you going?" Moira asked.

"To see my partner."

Moira started to go after him, but Katie stopped her. "Let him go, sis."

Captain Franklin stood in the ER driveway, and in between drags on his cigarette he spoke on his cell phone to a sleepy Trent Wethington.

"Mugging? How could this have happened to one of your detectives?" the prosecutor asked.

Franklin wondered why every time Trent spoke, it sounded like an indictment of the police department.

"We don't know it was a mugging. They're keeping him overnight, Trent," Franklin responded. "I'll express your sympathy to his wife."

"Oh, yes. Sorry, Charles. I didn't mean to sound insensitive," Trent said. "Tell her that if she needs anything, anything at all, to call my office. We take care of our own."

Franklin wasn't sure who the prosecutor considered "his own," but there was no benefit in arguing with the man. He dropped his cigarette onto the pavement and crushed it underfoot. "Thanks, Trent. I'll tell her. I'm going to see Jack now." He started to end the call, but Trent wasn't finished.

"Captain, I have to say something."

"Yes, sir."

"I don't have to remind you how sensitive this case is. You need to take Murphy off the case. He's too close to this. I mean, with what has happened to Detective Blanchard . . ."

Franklin pulled the phone from his ear and stared at it. Trent was still speaking, but Franklin had stopped listening. *Why did he keep wanting the department's best homicide detective off this case?*

In the treatment room Marcie was talking with a nurse who was taking Liddell's pulse. Liddell was sitting up in bed, dangling his bare legs and feet over the side. He was sporting raccoon eyes. He tried to smile when Jack entered, but with his face so swollen it came out a leer.

The nurse turned toward Jack in irritation. "You're his partner," she said. "Tell him he should stay at least one night."

Jack recognized her face. Her name was Julie something-or-other. She'd been at a couple of Christmas parties. Some older cop's daughter.

"You should listen to Julie, Bigfoot. You look like hell."

"I'm going to get you some slippers," the nurse said to Liddell. "And you're going to let me put you in a room, mister. That's an order."

Liddell gave a grunt of disagreement. His words came out stiff and slurred. "Gang up on me, why don't you? Do I have a choice?"

"Looks like you're outvoted," Jack said, and as the nurse passed him to get Liddell admitted, she whispered in Jack's ear, "My Prince Charming." She touched Jack's arm in a familiar way and was gone.

He stared at her retreating figure, feeling the stirrings of a memory. He had drunk a lot at the last Christmas party. He hoped he hadn't done anything inappropriate, but the smirk on Liddell's face told another story. "Shut up," he mouthed at Liddell, then for Marcie's benefit, "You gave us all quite a scare."

Liddell scooted to the edge of the gurney, but when his feet touched the floor he cried out in pain. Both Jack and Marcie needed all their strength to help him back into bed.

Marcie felt his face and neck. "Do you need something for pain, honey?" she asked. A thin sheen of sweat covered his skin and his color had gone pale.

"I'll get the nurse," Jack said, and hurried out of the room.

Liddell's condition improved quickly after he had taken two Percocet. When he was docile, he was moved to a private room.

"I'll give you two a few minutes to talk, and then the doctor says he needs to rest," Marcie said. "I'll go see the girls." Her expression softened and she gave him a hug. "I don't know what I would have done without you tonight."

"Captain Franklin was in ER. He's putting a security detail outside the room."

Marcie looked concerned. "Do you think they'll come back?"

Jack's fists clenched. He really hoped they would. "They'd be crazy to try. I'm going to stay for a while."

Marcie's look of relief made his heart ache. Once she left the room, he turned to his partner. Liddell's eyes were lidded and he was trying not to nod off. Jack had a million questions to ask, but he would settle for a few.

"Feel like talking?"

The drugs were working their magic. "Tell Marcie—go home. Get sleep . . ."

Jack saw tears forming in the corners of Liddell's eyes. That was a side effect of Percocet. It helped with the pain, but it heightened emotional responses, such as anger, fear, or remorse. He'd been down in that valley himself not too long ago.

He fingered the thick scar that ran beside his own ear, down his neck and chest and ended just beside his nipple. A year ago he had lain in a bed at this hospital, on this same floor. Liddell had saved his life.

"I'll take care of her," Jack said, and was surprised when Liddell reached out and grasped Jack's arm.

"Hit me from behind," Liddell said, and a look of anger flickered across his features. "Kept hitting me. Tried to get my gun." His voice was a labored whisper.

"Who tried to get your gun?" Jack asked. He hadn't checked with anyone at the scene whether or not they had recovered another Glock.

"Me," Liddell said. He vaguely patted for a holster he was no longer wearing, and then lifted his right hand close to his face. With weird intensity he examined the purplish bruise that covered his hand and wrist. "I heard gunshots. Was that me?"

Jack felt a tower of rage building inside. *Cowardly bastards!* They blindsided him. That brought another question to mind. *Why didn't they kill him?* They could have easily. But according to the doctors, he had only been struck in the back of the head once. You don't attack an armed policeman—especially not one the size of Bigfoot—with baseball bats. The way Marcie described the beating, it was just that—a beating. Was this some personal vendetta?

Liddell had given in finally to the painkillers and was lightly snoring. Jack pulled the covers up and said softly, "I got you, partner. I got you."

Moira and Katie had gone, Marcie was curled up in a recliner, and Jack sat in a chair against the wall. He stared out across the parking lot. The nurse had brought Liddell's personal belongings and put them in the cabinet, and Jack had gone through this while Marcie and Liddell slept.

Jack uncovered his shirt, pants, belt, and holster, but his gun was missing. Jack called everyone who would have been involved with collecting the weapon, and no one had seen it. They all thought Jack had it.

Liddell's pants pockets were empty. His police wallet, badge, money, and credit cards were gone. He could see why the responding officers had assumed it was a robbery. Yet if it was a simple street robbery, why pick on someone Liddell's size? Plus, they took his keys, so why not steal his car? True, carjackings were rare in Evansville, but so were attacks on policemen.

On the other hand, if it was personal, they would know Liddell was a policeman and armed. Why bring bats to a gunfight? The kicker was, the flash drive was taken. Jack didn't believe in coincidence. Who would know that Liddell had the flash drive? Only a handful of people even knew it existed, and he had given it to Liddell minutes before the attack.

"You look like shit," a raspy voice said from across the room.

Liddell's eyes were open, and the nasal cannula dangled from his skillet-sized fist.

"Welcome back, partner," Jack whispered, and pulled the chair closer to the bed. "You're the one who looks hammered like you-know-what."

"You should see the other guy, pod'na," Liddell said through dry lips. His tongue made a feeble effort. "Need a drink."

Liddell tried to pull himself up, but Jack gently kept him in place. "Whoa, big guy. You don't move until I get a nurse."

"Water first," Liddell rasped, licking his dry lips.

Jack maneuvered the straw to his lips and Liddell drank thirstily, then closed his eyes and moaned.

"What's wrong?" Jack asked, and stood to get help.

"Brain freeze," Liddell said, and tried to smile, but ended up wincing in pain.

"I'm going to get the nurse," Jack said, punching the button next to the bed that summoned the nurse's desk.

Marcie woke up in a bleary panic. "What's happening? Is he awake?"

"You still with me, partner?" Jack asked, but there was no reply.

Liddell had only come up for air.

CHAPTER FORTY-FOUR

Chief of Police Marlin Pope had already fielded a dozen voice mails—most wanting a statement about the attack on one of his detectives. He knew he couldn't hold them off forever. He would have to make some statement.

His intercom buzzed, and he gave a sigh. He preferred to be at the hospital, where he had an injured man, but his job was here, running the department. He was also expecting a visit from Trent Wethington. Franklin had prepared him as to what the prosecutor wanted to talk to him about.

Jennifer Mangold, the chief's secretary, buzzed his phone again. "He's here."

The door opened and Trent Wethington came in, followed closely by Eric Manson and county attorney Bob Rothschild. Unlike Pope, all of them looked well rested.

"Trent, gentlemen," Pope said, and motioned for them to take seats.

"We won't take much of your time, Marlin," Trent said, and they remained standing in front of his desk.

Pope stayed in his seat, resigned to what he knew was coming. "Okay."

"I'll get right to the point, Marlin," Trent said, and leaned forward, his hands on the chief's desk. "I've contacted the State Police and suggested they take control of these investigations. I want Detective Murphy to stand down."

"I understand, Trent," Pope said to a surprised audience.

Trent straightened, a smile tugging the corners of his mouth. He adjusted the onyx cufflinks in his starched pink shirt. "I'm glad you understand, Marlin. We have discussed this at great length, and we believe it is the best course of action."

Trent started to turn toward the door—mission accomplished—but stopped when the chief of police said, "I understand, *but* I'm not taking Jack off the case."

Trent grew rigidly stiff. "I thought you would agree with me, Marlin. I'm disappointed you can't see the downside of having a loose cannon like Jack Murphy running around out there."

"I guess I'm not real smart," Pope said, pretending humility. "But don't worry, Trent. Jack will play nice with the state investigators. And I'll remind you—you're not governor yet. You still have a responsibility to Evansville. Jack's the best we've got and you know it." Pope didn't add that the state police investigators didn't have a tenth of Murphy's experience and skill.

"You won't be convinced?" Trent asked, recovering from the shock of someone countermanding what he said.

Marlin read the comment as a threat, knowing Trent would go to the mayor—Pope's boss—and have him ordered to take Murphy off the case. And the mayor would do just that. But in this case, he would have to refuse.

Pope kept eye contact but didn't reply, and Trent shook his head. "Well, I guess there's nothing else to say."

"I guess not."

The prosecutor and his men filed out of the room.

Pope stood and took his hat off the credenza. He straightened his uniform and walked into the outer office.

"Jennifer," he said, "I'm going to the hospital. Need to know, okay."

That was code for her to tell no one where he was. He was going to the hospital to see Liddell and show respect to Liddell's wife. If the mayor didn't like it, well . . . he was tired of being chief of police anyway.

CHAPTER FORTY-FIVE

"Does that mean I can finally go home and get something to eat?" Liddell groused. When his breakfast had come, even Jack thought the portions were small.

The nurse smiled at him and left the room without commenting.

Liddell's clothing and personal items had been thrown into a large plastic bag with ST. MARY'S HOSPITAL embossed on the side. Marcie began going through the bag, folding his bloody shirt and pants, and then held out his size fourteen triple-E shoes. "Is this is why you call him Bigfoot?"

"It was that or Swamp Thing," Jack said, glad to see her smile.

"Hey!" Liddell protested. "I'm in the room, you know."

She stuffed his socks inside the shoes and slid the empty holster from his belt, then suddenly realized: "His gun is missing. So is his wallet and money and keys."

Jack and Liddell exchanged a knowing look.

"I'm checking into it," Jack said.

"Checking into what," said the chief from the doorway.

Marcie went to Pope and bussed his cheek politely. "Thank you for coming, Marlin."

"I just wanted to come by . . ." Pope began, but seeing the condition Liddell was in, he was at a loss for the right comforting remark.

"Thanks, Chief," Liddell said. "They're sending me home. I'm ready to get back to work."

"I think going home will be up to your doctor," Pope answered, examining him more closely. "As far as coming back to work— we'll see."

"While you're here, Chief, I was just getting ready to call the captain to see if they found Liddell's gun. Can we talk in the hall?" Jack asked.

"I want to talk to you, too." Pope spoke to Liddell for a moment, and assured Marcie they would be protected until this was over. "Walk with me, Jack," he said, and they left the room.

In the hallway Jack told him about the flash drive.

Pope asked, "Is anything else missing?"

Jack didn't want to feed into the idea that what happened last night was a mugging, although it did look like a robbery. "His wallet, badge and ID, cash, and his gun, too."

"It wasn't a robbery. Someone went to a lot of trouble, and a lot of risk, to get that flash drive."

Jack couldn't hide his surprise that the chief was agreeing with him.

Pope said, "Don't look at me that way. I used to be a detective before I lost my mind and tested for rank." Then he told Jack about Trent's announcement that state police investigators were being called in.

"I'll cooperate with them completely," Jack lied.

Pope nodded, knowing that Jack would stonewall the state investigators as much as possible. In fact, he was counting on Jack's insubordination.

"So I'm still on the case?" Jack asked.

"Like your partner is so fond of saying, 'Does the Pope shit in the woods?'" the chief replied.

Jack looked sheepish. "You know about that, huh?"

"Oh, the things that I know." Pope grinned and walked away.

As Jack walked back to Liddell's room, two things occurred to him. First, the chief had said nothing about Marcie shooting at someone last night. Second, the chief didn't act surprised about the existence of the flash drive.

He turned and ran to catch up with the chief.

CHAPTER FORTY-SIX

The conversation with the boss took a turn Clint wasn't expecting.

"We found the item you told me about. The big cop had it. Not Murphy," Clint explained. "We had to hurt him to get it, but I don't think he's dead."

The response was dead silence. Clint continued quickly, "We tried to make it look like a street robbery, but some woman came out of the house with a gun and started shooting."

The line remained silent. Clint debated telling her about his being shot, but decided against it.

"I know about the cop. He's in the hospital. The woman was his wife. I have two questions for you." She paused and Clint imagined she could see his nervousness. "Did you destroy the thing I asked you to?"

With no hesitation he answered, "Yeah. I found it in the cop's pocket. I smashed it with a rock and threw it in a farm pond." He didn't know why he was lying about destroying the flash drive, but his gut told him that if it was important enough to grab, it might be a good bargaining chip if all this went to shit—like it was threatening to.

The voice that came through the phone receiver was barely controlled. "Can the woman identify either of you or the vehicle?"

Clint heard the skepticism in her voice. Unless the client was a cop—and he didn't believe that for one minute—the boss had someone close to the case in her pocket. That made him nervous. He felt the telephone grow sweaty against his ear.

"We sank the vehicle in the farm pond. No one will find it for a long time. And we didn't leave anything in it to lead anywhere."

"Are you sure?"

"Yeah! I'm sure," Clint said a little too forcefully, but she was making him mad. He would probably regret it, but he asked, "Why is that flash drive so important?" Then he realized his mistake and said, "I mean, why *was* it so important?"

She said, "Here's your new instructions."

Her men had performed well—considering they had to improvise. If she'd been told about the problem sooner, she could have come up with a better plan.

She was curious how the client could have let things get so out of hand. After all, he had an inside track. His continuing needs, along with all the changes of plans, made her look bad to her superiors.

The company she worked for didn't know about the client's multitude of problems. If they *had* known, they wouldn't have made the deal. But it was too late now.

She turned her thoughts to the problem at hand. Book and Clint were good at what they did, but she'd never used them for a job like this one. She wondered if they would be able to keep it together much longer. Clint was starting to ask questions.

Jobs were compartmentalized. She told them what they needed to know and nothing more. She planned, they executed. She could tell them to clean up the mess, and that would mean killing everyone involved. If the client weren't so valuable, she would have Book put a bullet in his head. Make it look like a guilt-ridden suicide. Problem solved.

In any case, she would have to make a decision about this cop Murphy. If he was as good as the client said he was, he might get onto her crew, and that would lead to a lot of questions, and possibly back to her.

She didn't want to retire her men early, but then again, *c'est la vie.* She'd heard about a couple of ex–Navy SEALs who were looking for work. Her primary job was to protect the company.

CHAPTER FORTY-SEVEN

Eric sat at the kitchen table with Katie, sipping coffee while managing to look both overworked and apologetic. Moira had left for the office. It was the first time she and Eric had talked—much less been alone together—since their interrupted engagement party. She didn't honestly know how she felt about his absence.

"You know I'll have to talk to Moira about taking evidence home, don't you?"

Katie had made it clear that she didn't want to talk about Moira, but he still was pushing the issue. Putting her coffee down, she said, "Is that the only reason you came by? She's my sister, Eric. I'm not her mother."

He turned his face away, but not before she saw his annoyance.

"Look, Eric, she lives with me, but Moira's a grown woman. She has a strong sense of loyalty, and family."

"Hardheaded is more like it," he groused. "I'm sorry, Katie. I just don't want you to be mad at me over this."

She thought, *You have enough fences to mend here to worry about work*, but she said nothing.

He took her silence for agreement and reached across the table, putting a hand over her. "I love you, Katie Connelly."

Since she'd met him, he'd refused to call her by her married name of Murphy.

She squeezed his hand and then pulled it back to pick up her coffee. "Me too," she said.

"I was surprised you were home when I called this morning," he said, wanting to keep the conversation light. "Don't you have classes?"

They had been dating off and on for nine months, seriously for the last six, and sometimes she thought the only thing they shared was great sex. At times like this she realized they really didn't know each other at all.

"I go in early on Monday and Friday," she explained once again. "We had breakfast here last Wednesday morning, Eric," she reminded him.

His look softened and he said, "What can I do to make you feel better?" He reached across the table and began rubbing her arms.

She recognized the look on his face, and was horrified to see that he was thinking of sex.

She stood up and pushed her chair in. "Shouldn't you be going to work?"

"You're right," he said, getting up from the table. "I guess I had better go." He took his suit jacket from the back of the chair and left the kitchen.

She felt guilty at the look of rejection on his face, but he still hadn't explained why he hadn't called. As the front door shut behind Eric, she wondered what was the matter. This definitely wasn't the way a couple should behave if they were in love. And she did love Eric. Didn't she?

She would make it up to him tonight. She had at least two hours before she had to be at school. She could go to the store and buy something for a nice meal. Maybe some flowers to brighten the table.

Then she thought about Marcie alone at the hospital, and her mood darkened. *Marcie must be going crazy! And poor Jack. You would think he was the one who was beaten, given the look on his face last night.*

She grabbed her keys off the peg by the back door and hurried to her car.

"Katie," Marcie said with a surprised smile. "You're just in time. He's being released."

"They're trying to starve me to death," Liddell said from the hospital bed. "You just missed Jack. He had to get ready for work."

Katie gave Liddell a hug. "How are you this morning? Still in a lot of pain?"

"I've been worse," he answered, and pulled Marcie close.

"I don't want to make a habit of doing this," she said.

"What do you say we get together for a crawfish boil when this is over?" Liddell asked.

Marcie's eyes were sunken with dark circles beneath, and she was still wearing her slippers from home. Then Katie noticed Marcie's pajamas were stained with blood.

What kind of friend am I? Katie thought. *I should have come here right away.* "Have *you* had any rest?"

Marcie looked down at herself and cringed. "I must be a sight."

"I should have brought you a change of clothes," Katie said, putting her arms around her friend.

"I'll be fine. But I'm ready to get home. A hot shower and some clean clothes would be nice."

Katie smiled at her. Marcie and Liddell were perfect together, and Liddell was such a good man; it hurt her heart to see him like this.

Marcie surprised her, saying, "Have you talked to Eric?"

Katie's face showed embarrassment. "I wasn't very nice to him this morning."

CHAPTER FORTY-EIGHT

The nurse came in every hour during the night to perform neuro checks—that is, check his pupil size and reactivity to light, level of consciousness and grip-strength equality. If Liddell wasn't brain damaged, the hourly tests would make him so. Jack had woken up for each of the visits, so he wasn't faring much better.

All in all, it was a truly shitty night, and the morning didn't get any better. When Jack went home to get ready for work, he found the present Cinderella had left in his new shoes. It was a smelly and wet reminder that she couldn't be left unattended for such a long period.

When he arrived at the morgue, three vehicles were parked in the front lot. One was Dr. John's pet project, a 1963 rust-colored Ford Falcon, complete with rusted quarter panels and bald tires that could have been the original Firestone radials. Little Casket's Suburban was parked next to Dr. John's. Jack didn't recognize the third vehicle, a new black Dodge Charger. He parked next to the Charger, with its unblemished paint and barely legal dark-tinted windows, gleaming in the morning sun. In comparison, his five-year-old Crown Vic looked like a black washed-out wreck. The Charger either belonged to a cop or a drug dealer, but it wasn't likely that a drug dealer would be at the morgue unless they were there as the guest cadaver.

He first made his way to the conference room, but it was empty, so he checked the autopsy room and found it empty as well. Then he heard someone talking in back by the coolers.

An attractive woman of about thirty came out of the refrigerated room and held the door open for Little Casket and Dr. John, who were pushing a gurney occupied by a sheet-covered corpse. An arm was hanging over the side, and Jack spied a tattoo of an ivy vine curling up from the wrist and disappearing under the sheet. *Hope Dupree*. The girl from Harrisburg.

Jack and the newcomer looked each other up and down, trying to assess friend or foe. Despite her looks he pegged her as a cop.

"Well, don't just stand there gawking. Help me get her on the table," Lilly said to Jack, and pushed the gurney alongside the steel autopsy table.

"I thought we were doing the male from Harrisburg first." Jack looked at the clock and saw it was eight o'clock. He wondered how long the autopsies on all the bodies would take.

"I just do what I'm told," Lilly said.

"I'm afraid I'm to blame," the new woman said, and motioned for Jack to help her slide the body onto the autopsy table. They each took hold and slid the body over in one practiced move.

"You must be Detective Murphy."

"Why's that?" he asked, and saw a flicker of a smile.

"It's your sparkling personality, Jack," Lilly answered.

"Your reputation as a smart-ass precedes you?" Dr. John offered.

"I *am* armed," Jack pointed out.

"Lilly could take you in about two seconds," the woman whispered in Jack's ear.

"And you are?" Jack asked her.

"Brooke," she said, and extended a hand.

Jack noticed that she didn't wear jewelry, and her nails were cut short and practical for doing police work. Her red hair was worn shoulder length, stylishly cut, and loose about her face, not tied back into the tight buns that some female law enforcement officers preferred.

He took her hand and was surprised at the strength in her grip. She was a few inches shorter than him, even in two-inch heels—apparently her one concession to her gender. She wasn't wearing a gun. Tight-fitting tan slacks—too tight to conceal an ankle holster—and a blue short-sleeve shirt with the State of Indiana logo emblazoned over the left pocket completed the picture. All in all, she was a very attractive woman.

The Great Seal of Indiana had a picture of a guy with an axe chasing a buffalo through the woods. Jack had never seen a buffalo until he took a kayaking trip in Montana, but he guessed buffalo must have roamed in Indiana at one time. Guys with axes must have chased them all out of the state.

"Indiana State Police?"

"Is my traffic ticket book showing?" she asked, and smiled. "Special Investigations Unit. On loan from Indianapolis."

Jack was surprised by her last remark. Chief Pope said the state police were being called in, but Trent must have called her in even before the attack on Liddell. The man-who-would-be-governor hadn't wasted any time.

"Long drive from Indy," he remarked. "You must be tired. Why don't you freshen up and I'll take care of things here?"

She laughed, not taking offense. "Actually, I was just about to suggest the same thing. I thought you would want to be with your partner, Liddell, and his wife, Marcie."

Jack's eyes narrowed at their mention. Brooke had done her homework. This whole arrangement reminded Jack of a spaghetti western, where one of the gunfighters would say, "There ain't enough room in this town for the both of us." And then the other would say in a menacing tone, "Draw, partner."

"If you two are done sparring, I need to get this body ready," Lilly said, stepping in between them.

Brooke promptly pulled on latex gloves. "What can I do to help?"

"Both of you can get out of the way," Lilly sighed. She began washing the body down with a length of garden hose attached to one of the faucets of the double stainless steel sink.

Dr. John slipped into a surgical gown, complete with hood and plastic visor. He pulled on a pair of mint-green latex gloves and approached the table as Lilly finished removing the mud caked to the pale body. A foot pedal operated a microphone suspended above the table, and Dr. John stepped on this and began the examination.

In the next hour, he collected the samples of liver, stomach content, heart, and lungs that would be saved or sent for toxicology.

With the physical part of the postmortem completed, Lilly pushed the remainder of the organs back into the body cavity and stitched the T-shaped opening shut with coarse twine. Then she pulled a sheet over the body.

Jack kept an eye on the state detective's face. She had turned a little green around the gills during the removal of the internal organs, but if she had never attended an autopsy before, she hid it well. He knew veteran street cops who had thrown up or passed out under similar circumstances.

"So, no sign of sexual interference?" Brooke asked.

Dr. John pulled the facemask and hood off, wiping away the accumulated sweat. "The rape kit will tell for certain, but off the record, I would say she was not the recipient of a paramour's attention."

Brooke didn't respond to the pathologist's attempt at humor.

"No obvious sign of sexual activity," Dr. John confirmed. "But that doesn't mean the lab won't find something."

"I'll get the lab to put a rush on the samples."

"You buying?" Lilly asked. She hoped the state would absorb the cost of all the tests that would be needed.

"How can I say no?" Brooke said.

"Well then . . ." Lilly said, her mouth twisting into a smirk, "how about those tests we asked for on the other victims? Any chance of getting those expedited?"

"I can get things done," Brooke said, and gave Jack a challenging look.

Afterward, Jack went outside to make a call. He had to shove his cell phone hard against his ear to hear over the sound of heavy truck traffic lumbering past on the Lloyd Expressway.

"What'd you find out, pod'na?" Liddell asked.

Jack wanted to tell him to forget about the case and rest, but he knew that was pointless. Staying involved was how cops survived.

"Brooke is rushing the toxicology and DNA results on the bodies the fishermen found in the creek. With her connections I'm hoping she gets the tests back pronto."

"Brooke?" Liddell asked.

Jack was sorry he'd slipped out with the name. He didn't feel like telling Liddell about the political backlash that had wormed its way into their case. He glanced at the open garage doors to see if anyone was listening. "Brooke is with the state police," Jack said. "Special Investigations Unit from Indianapolis. Ever heard of them?"

"Sure," Liddell said. "Special Investigators, as in, they wear bicycle helmets and ride the short bus?" Jack was glad to hear his partner joking around again.

"She's driving a smoking hot black Charger, Bigfoot." And she's smokin' hot herself.

"Interesting," Liddell noted. "Is she cute?"

Jack didn't want to get into that subject. "So, when are you going to quit stealing sick time from the city and come back to work?" He secretly hoped the Liddell would take a few days off.

"I see my doctor tomorrow. Captain Franklin won't let me come back without a medical release." Liddell didn't sound pleased.

"Oh? That's too bad," Jack lied. "But I guess it proves what I've always said. You are the most hardheaded person I've ever known. Anyone else would be in the hospital for a month."

"Listen, pod'na. Katie was at the hospital this morning, and I think she was hoping you'd be there. Is there any chance?"

Jack was glad Katie was there for Liddell and Marcie. "Any chance I'll be at the hospital?" Jack asked, as if he were confused by the question.

"You know what I mean, pod'na."

"How is Marcie?" Jack asked. He knew where Liddell was going with this, and he wanted to stop him before it got started. Katie was engaged to someone else.

"The doctor took his sweet time discharging me, so Katie got Marcie some hospital scrubs to wear home. They have little animals all over them. They're kind of *hot*."

"You are one sick man, Bigfoot," Jack said. Then he smelled cigarette smoke. "Gotta go. Someone's coming."

He hung up just as Brooke came out of the garage. She was startled to see Jack there.

"Those things will kill you," Jack said, nodding at her cigarette.

"So will a head-on collision at high speeds, but I still drive fast."

He gave her a grudging smile, and she offered him one back.

"I don't smoke," Jack said, and started back inside.

"Maybe we got off to a rocky start, Detective Murphy," Brooke said before he could get away.

Hearing the signs of a truce, he carefully chose his words. Nothing was ever as simple as it looked, nor as innocent. The prosecutor had called her in for one reason, and that was to get Trent off the hook politically. Therefore, her interest in the case was tainted. She might be a great detective. But he didn't trust her.

"I promised my chief I would cooperate. You're welcome to look through my case files, but I don't have the time to catch you up to speed without slowing down the progress of the investigation."

"What progress?" she said testily. "You don't have a motive. You don't have a suspect. In fact, you don't have any evidence except a bunch of bodies in the morgue's freezer."

Jack didn't have to put up with sidelines calls. He was turning his back when Brooke put a hand on his arm. "We should work together."

He pointedly looked at her hand until she removed it.

"We are working together," he said. "And when I catch these guys, you can have all the credit, *Brooke*."

She feigned a disinterested look, but he could tell his remark hit a nerve. The last thing he needed was another agency meddling in the case. She might be pissed off, but that was okay as long as she kept her distance.

CHAPTER FORTY-NINE

Seeing yet another press conference being held at police headquarters, Jack climbed the back stairs that led to the squad room. When he opened his office door he found Moira perched on the edge of his desk. Smiling, she held out a CD-ROM.

"What's this?" he asked.

"I talked to Marcie this morning. She said the flash drive was stolen."

Jack raised an eyebrow as he took the silver disc.

"That's a backup of the flash drive," Moira explained. "I copied it to my laptop before you came over last night. And before you give me a lecture, you already know I'm not going to stay out of this. I can't. It's my job."

Jack didn't know whether to be angry or hug her. "Come with me," he said, and led her down to the basement, carefully avoiding any newspeople. After several twists and turns Jack led her into an office where a sign on the outside of the door said VICE UNIT.

Inside, a woman a few inches shorter but not much older than Moira sat behind a desk covered with computer equipment and two laptops. Her flawless skin was the color of yellow coal, with dark hair pulled back into a ponytail, and even darker eyes that bordered on black.

Jack made the introductions. "Moira, meet Angelina Garcia. Angelina, this is deputy *prosecutor* Moira Connelly."

Garcia smiled and reached across the desk. "I was wondering when I'd get to meet you."

Moira took her hand and said, "Me, too. Jack says you are the genius behind their work."

Garcia's dark eyes grew wide at the compliment. "Funny, he never tells me that."

Jack handed Garcia the disc. "This is a copy of the flash drive I told you about. Moira found the thumb drive in Nina Parsons's office, and this is the only copy. It doesn't exist. Understood?" After what had happened with Liddell last night, he didn't want to take any chances, and he didn't want to get Moira into worse trouble for not turning the copy over to Eric first.

"Sure thing, boss. I'll get right on it," Garcia said. She lowered her voice to a whisper and asked, "Is Detective Jansen still on this?"

Good question. Jack hadn't seen or talked to Jansen since Tuesday, when Liddell had forced him to give them the name of the dancer, Samantha Steele.

"I'll find out, but my guess would be no, he's not working with us anymore," Jack said.

Garcia inserted the disc and started scanning files. "If you've got a minute, I think I can give you something. This doesn't look too difficult."

Jack and Moira traded a look. They had both been stumped last night.

He asked Moira, "Did you get in trouble for taking the flash drive home?"

Moira's face flushed at the memory of the dressing down she had received from Eric Manson in front of half the office. She had to wonder if Katie had seen this side of him.

"Eric's being at the office last night is kind of odd now that I think about it. He accused me of snooping, but wouldn't say what he was doing there so late. And when I first got there, I found my office door open and I'm sure I closed and locked it when I left work earlier. He and Trent both gave me the loyalty speech, about how we're one big family, and if I come across anything in Nina's office I should let them know immediately. Why do you think that is, Jack?"

"Maybe Eric was in the office late working?" Jack suggested.

Moira made a face at him. "Not dressed like a roadie for Lynyrd Skynyrd he wasn't. You should have seen him, Jack. I had the feeling I surprised him when I came out. He gave me an ugly look, and insisted on walking me out. Which makes me wonder how he knew I had found the flash drive in there. I said it was *my* flash drive."

Jack had the sheepish answer for that. "It's my fault he found out. I'm sorry. I told Captain Franklin about you and the flash drive last night, and I'm sure he told Eric."

"It's okay," she said. "I should have told him myself."

She was right, but he was still glad Moira had given him the flash drive first. If Eric or Trent had known about it, they might have held it back until they were sure there was nothing embarrassing on it or, worse yet, given it to Brooke.

"Any idea who the two guys were who attacked Liddell?" Moira asked. "Or why?"

Jack shook his head. "Liddell didn't see it coming. He remembers getting out of his car. He vaguely recalls the beating and then waking up in the hospital. He didn't even hear the gunshots."

Moira's voice dropped to a whisper. "Did Marcie really shoot one of them?"

"There was a lot of blood in the gravel, but Liddell did take quite a beating."

Moira's innocent question flipped a switch in Jack's brain. He'd been so worried about Liddell and Marcie, and dealing with the prosecutor's interference, that he hadn't really concentrated on his questions from this morning.

If the motive for the attack was to obtain the flash drive, how did they know about its existence? How did they know Liddell had it? And how did they know where Liddell lived? They must have been waiting at Liddell's. So, it was an ambush. And that brought up a new thought.

If the recent killings in Harrisburg were connected to Evansville's, there had to be more than one person involved. How could a lone killer subdue and dismember both Hope Dupree and her pimp? And how was Nina's body carried through the fence and buried in pieces in the landfill? That was almost impossible for one man to accomplish. Just the fact that all that had been accomplished over a seven- or eight-hour period made the scenario of two or more killers involved more likely.

In light of all that, the attack on Liddell by two men armed with only baseball bats didn't make sense. The other victims were killed with a cutting instrument. They could easily have killed Liddell before Marcie came out, but they didn't. Why not? Was it really a robbery gone wrong? Was the flash drive taken by coincidence? Or did the two guys who "moved like a military team" have something else in mind? *These guys are too good to be pulling street robberies. They went after Liddell and the only thing he had was the flash drive.*

The thumb drive was the key. He didn't know what all those numbers meant, but he had learned to trust his instincts.

"Done," Garcia said, pulling him out of his thoughts.

"Most of these are Vanderburgh County Superior Court files. Drug and prostitution cases. Others are from counties where a special prosecutor was requested. I've sorted the cases into local ones and those that are from other jurisdictions." She switched to another laptop and punched up another set of files. "These are the cases from other counties." Garcia gave Jack a significant look. "All the cases from other counties had a special prosecutor from Vanderburgh County assigned to them."

"How can you tell that?" Moira said, awed.

Garcia pointed at a letter at the end of the case file number. "This column has the cases where a special prosecutor was assigned to another county. This number here tells me who the prosecutor was. Trent Wethington tried all the cases until about five years ago. After that, Eric Manson was special prosecutor on everything."

She indicated another set of numbers. "This column of numbers all represents cases within Vanderburgh County. Once again, Trent did the older cases, and Eric took over about five years ago. And the last two cases show Nina as the prosecutor."

"Is there any way to get a list of the defendants and victims in those cases?" Jack asked.

"The Indiana statute code is part of the case number. Here," she said, pointing at a list of numbers. "I can't tell from this who the victim and suspect were, but I can tell you that all these cases were drug or prostitution cases." She asked, knowing what Jack would say, "You want me to give you a list of names?"

"Drugs, prostitution, and Eric and Trent," Jack said. That didn't tell him anything.

"Maybe Nina was doing some research for Trent?" Moira suggested.

Jack shook his head. "So why tape the flash drive to the underside of her desk? And why just Trent, Eric, and herself?"

Moira shook her head. "Maybe there was some special way these cases were handled. Eric or Trent assign all the cases, so the two that Nina had were given to her by one, or both, of them."

"I've heard Trent doesn't take cases to court unless it's a high-profile defendant," Moira said. "Eric's the same way. Eric does most of the case assignments. Trent spends most of his time with Bob Rothschild. It's a joke around the office that Eric is the real prosecutor and Trent just works on his campaign for governor."

"Angelina, get the names from those cases," Jack said. "Let me know what you find."

"What am I looking for?" she asked.

"You're the computer genius," he said with a smile. "Sort them and call me."

"I have your permission to hack the court database?" she asked.

Jack thought about using Moira's computer authority, but he didn't want her to get any more involved. If her name came up flagged, she would be in deep shit.

"Use my name and password. I'll take the heat."

Before Jack even finished speaking, she had typed in some commands. She snapped her fingers and said, "Okay, you're in."

Moira looked surprised. "You already got in the court database?"

"Not me. Him." After a few more keystrokes she sat back.

"These local cases"—she pointed at the monitor—"were dismissed, had a finding of not guilty, or were pleaded out to probation," she said. "Drug charges. Prostitution and a smattering of theft cases. It's just the kind of mix you would expect from drug addicts. The common denominator is that all the cases involved female plaintiffs. Eric or Trent were involved in about all of them."

"What about the cases where a special prosecutor was involved?" Jack asked.

"The same. Drugs, prostitution. All women defendants. All were pleaded out or dismissed."

"Maybe these women were confidential informants?" Moira suggested.

"Any of our victims listed in there?" Jack asked, and Garcia shook her head.

Female confidential informants. Was that what Nina was looking into? Could she have known Hope Dupree or any of the others? She and Eric had only served with the prosecutor's office for five or six years, and some of these cases went back almost twenty years. Eric's philandering wasn't likely a connection to all of them. And Trent? Not much chance.

But if Eric or Trent were involved with any cases involving Hope Dupree, or Sammi Steele, Garcia would have found out. The records check on both women didn't show any arrests for prostitution or drugs, but Hope was well-known in Harrisburg for drugs and prostitution, and Sammi could have moved here from somewhere else. If that was the case, why didn't Jansen find anything? Of course, if they were confidential informants, maybe the records were sealed. That would explain the lack of information.

"Can you print out a list of the names of all the women on the disc? Then call Kim Hammond in Narcotics. See how many of them are working as CIs for the narcotics unit."

Moira was very pleased. "You mean you think I'm right?"

CHAPTER FIFTY

The police upper brass had a small parking area behind the police department. Not much more than a carport, it was a gathering place for the high-ranking smokers. Captain Franklin was just lighting Brooke's cigarette when they spotted Jack exiting the building.

"There's your new partner," Franklin said. "Looks like you've tracked down your prey."

Jack was beginning to feel like prey after having gone out of his way to escape from the building unseen, and yet here Brooke was. He had to give her credit for tenacity.

"Don't look so surprised, Detective Murphy," she said. The end of her cigarette glowed as she took a long pull. Small curls of smoke escaped her mouth and nose and curled around her face as she spoke. She squinted one eye closed and waved at the smoke before continuing.

"I think your face is on fire," Jack said, puzzled as always by why someone would willingly ingest toxic hot air into her lungs. "How did you get out here so quickly? You must tell me your secret."

"So, you've already met Special Investigator Wethington," Captain Franklin said.

Wethington? Jack's cheeks flushed and his eyes locked on hers. Brooke stared back defiantly.

"Yes, Jack. Trent is my uncle," she admitted. "It's not relevant."

Jack couldn't believe this. "It sure as hell *is* relevant! The prosecutor—your uncle—wants to pull me off a case because my partner got beat up. But then he gives the case to his own niece? How's that work?"

She stood her ground. "I was under the impression we were working this case together."

"She's right, Jack. This case is too important to squabble over jurisdiction," Franklin said, stepping in to settle the dispute. "And it sounds as if her assistance will be a blessing."

Franklin was right about that, Jack had to admit. Things that would take his own people weeks to accomplish, Brooke could get the state lab to do at lightning speed. But he didn't like the fact that he hadn't been informed that Trent was her uncle. Now her first loyalty would be to family and not to the investigation.

"Were you going somewhere in particular?" she asked.

"It'll wait until I bring you up to speed," Jack grumbled. "Walk with me."

When they had pulled a certain distance away, he said, "I'm going to trust you with something, Brooke, but you have to keep it between us." She looked doubtful, so he added, "Just for the time being."

"It depends on what it is."

"I'm going to come clean with you about the investigation. But in return I want your word none of this will get back to your uncle."

"I don't work for the prosecutor, Jack. I work for the State Police. But again, it depends on what you tell me," Brooke answered.

"Take a ride with me?"

She shrugged and said, "Lead on."

Soon they were headed east on the expressway. He pulled out his cell phone and made a call. Brooke listened to Jack's side of the conversation.

"I'm bringing someone to see you. Yeah. I'll be there in a few minutes." A slight pause and then, "Will do." He hung up.

"Do I have to call you if I want to know where we're going?"

"Sorry, I had to prepare them. Marcie is family. I don't know how all of this has affected her," Jack explained.

"I thought your partner went home from the hospital."

"I guess I can give you the nickel version since we'll be there in a few minutes," Jack said, and began his story. He began with Moira's finding the flash drive in Nina's old office. Brooke already knew about the flash drive's existence from talking to Eric and

Trent this morning, but she thought it was lost when Liddell was attacked.

Jack said, "This is the part I want you to keep to yourself—for just a bit." Brooke didn't reply, so Jack took that for a yes.

"Moira made a copy of the flash drive and gave it to me this morning. I had my computer analyst review it. There are two sets of files. The first set were Superior and Circuit Court cases. Most were recent, with some going back twenty years. All of them were from Indiana, and most were local. Only three people from the prosecutor's office were involved in every case that was listed on the flash drive."

He looked over to see if she was following, and she was paying full attention. "All of the cases involved women, drugs, prostitution, and most of them were given a pass by the prosecutor's office in exchange for becoming confidential informants." He didn't tell Brooke his suspicion that Eric was involved in this all the way up to his curlies.

"So you think what was on the flash drive is connected to the recent murders?"

Jack couldn't tell by her expression if she was taking him seriously or blowing his theory off. "And by association, you think it has something to do with the prosecutor's office."

Jack nodded.

"You say there are three prosecutors named?"

Jack had expected the question, and that was where his theory was weakest. "Yes," he admitted.

"And you say some of the cases go back twenty years?"

Jack nodded, and said, "Yes. So the only thing those have in common with the newer cases is that Trent was the prosecutor during the entire time." He saw the hostile look she gave him, and he added quickly, "But I'm not suspecting Trent."

Brooke didn't respond right away. He had to imagine she didn't like the implications involving her uncle. "How do you know that the flash drive belonged to Nina? And if it did, how do you know she wasn't doing something legitimate?"

Jack explained, "Moira found it taped to the underside of Nina's desk. What's that tell you?"

"Again, how can you prove it was Nina's? Were her prints on it?"

"Come on, Brooke. Even if the flash drive wasn't stolen, the prints would have been ruined by Moira, you know that."

"Okay. So what? Is that all you've got?"

Jack told her his other theory—that there were two or more killers involved in these slayings—and to his surprise she didn't laugh at the idea.

"I can see there being more than one person doing the killings, but that would mean they were working as a team, and that's not very common," she said. "But how can you prove the same guys who beat up your partner and stole the flash drive are involved in the murder of Nina Parsons? You have to admit that's a stretch."

Jack agreed. "That's why we're going to Liddell's house. I'm going to let you question his wife. Maybe she remembers something new."

Brooke looked straight ahead, her face unreadable. "You sure you don't want to blindfold me?"

"Great idea. But it would mess up your hair."

"Is that a sexist remark?"

Jack glanced at her. "Yes."

"Okay. Just so we're clear."

He wound through upscale homes with ornate fences and landscaping that would require a crew of gardeners. Liddell lived on the far side of this neighborhood in an older subdivision where the yards were only separated by courtesy and the neighbors often helped each other with the yard work, or to drink a beer, or come over for a spur-of-the-moment cookout.

Jack pulled to the curb behind a black-and-white. A uniformed officer the size of a house walked out of Liddell's front door with a sandwich in one hand and a Coke in the other.

"That's Floyd," Jack said, and Floyd nodded at them. "Floyd, this is Indiana State Police Special Investigator Brooke Wethington."

Floyd looked her over and, unimpressed, muttered, "He's expecting you," and went back to his car.

Without knocking, Jack opened the front door and motioned for Brooke to go in first.

A woman's voice came from down the hall: "We're in the kitchen, Jack."

Liddell sat on a stool behind the kitchen island. His right arm—covered from knuckles to elbow with a cast—was propped on a small pillow on top of the marble countertop. He was wearing an unbuttoned short-sleeve shirt. His exposed chest and stomach were covered with bruises. The sleeves had been removed from the shirt, and a rip ran halfway down the right side. Above the cast, from elbow to shoulder, was covered in purple bruises. His face was fading from purple to yellow, with both eyes black and swollen almost shut. *Raccoon eyes. It feels worse than it looks,* Jack remembered from experience. The way Liddell was sitting, with the ripped shirt and all, he looked like the Hulk—only purple.

"This must be Brooke," Liddell said, and raised his uninjured arm to take her hand.

"Detective Brooke Wethington," she said. "Indiana State Police, Special Investigations Unit."

"Wow!" Liddell said with a grin. "That's a mouthful! Are you related to Trent Wethington?"

"He's my uncle," she said. "My dad's a retired state trooper, and no, my mom wasn't a state trooper."

"So this is what an Indiana State Police Special Investigator looks like in person."

"Don't start picking on her," Marcie said, and playfully tapped him on the leg.

"Before now you were just an urban legend among the other police departments. It's like finding out Santa Claus is really coming to town." He winced in pain, his hand going to his jaw.

He noticed Brooke was trying not to stare and said with a grin, "It's okay. By the end of the week I'll look like a rainbow. Then I'm going to San Francisco and march in the Dorothy Parade."

Jack said, "Ignore him. He's on a lot of pain medication. And even when he's not, he isn't always right in the head."

Brooke smiled and turned her attention to Marcie. "Jack said you didn't see the suspects' faces. But we wondered if you remembered anything later."

Jack nodded that she could answer.

"No," Marcie said. "Only . . ."

"What is it, Marcie?" Jack asked.

She looked embarrassed. "You'll think this is silly, Jack." She reached for Liddell's hand and squeezed it. "It's just that when the guys were running away, they did it like—well, like the way I've seen the police practice when you're shooting and running." She paused, thinking about that image. "Like a team."

Jack thought, *Cops?*

"You think they were cops?" Brooke asked.

Marcie shook her head. "That's not what I said. Look, it's just my opinion, but they weren't running like ordinary criminals. These guys ran like a team. Like they had done this before."

"Soldiers," Liddell suggested.

"Yeah!" Marcie almost shouted the word. "Like those film clips on CNN where they show soldiers in battle. They ran like that."

They were depending on surprise, but what they got was an angry woman with a gun. Jack was glad Captain Franklin had assigned an officer to guard Liddell and Marcie.

"The flash drive is the key to this," Jack murmured.

"I'm sorry I lost it, Jack," Liddell said.

"Don't worry about it. Moira made a copy."

Liddell's gaze moved to Brooke. "Is Moira in trouble?"

"She doesn't work for me," Brooke said. "I found out about the flash drive this morning. And I just found out about the copy and what was on it a few minutes ago."

"For argument's sake, let's say these guys were after the flash drive," Liddell said. "How could they have known about it? And how did they know I had it? And, best for last, how did they know where I live, and that I was coming home?"

"Eric knew," Jack said. "Eric called Franklin and complained. He accused me of sending Moira into the office to snoop around. He knew about the drive before I did." He didn't have to say that Eric also could find out where Liddell lived.

"But how did they know that I had the thing?" Liddell persisted. "You were carrying it until we got to headquarters. And again, how did they know that it wasn't at Katie's? I mean, I'm glad they didn't go there, but still. Do you think someone was outside the house and then the police station listening?"

"That's pretty far-fetched," Brooke said. "I know. The government has a bug on your car, Jack."

Jack could tell by Brooke's stiff posture that she didn't believe the attackers had targeted Liddell because of the flash drive, and honestly, he didn't care if she believed it or not. This was his case. She was just along for the ride.

Jack sauntered over to give Liddell's medical getup a closer look. "You didn't spend enough of my tax money already," he said to change the topic. "You had to get a cast, too?"

"Two casts, pod'na," Liddell said.

Jack and Brooke walked around the kitchen island and saw another cast on his lower left leg.

"They only come in white," Liddell complained. "I wanted fluorescent orange."

Marcie put in, "He has a hairline fracture. They didn't find it when they brought him in because he was in and out of consciousness. We discovered the injury to his leg the hard way this morning when I was helping the nurse get him dressed to leave."

"Yeah, boy!" Liddell exclaimed. "I'd been on a bedpan because they didn't want me to get up. But when I tried to get up to get dressed, I fell flat on my face."

Marcie leaned over and hugged him. "He's so big he pulled me and the nurse down with him."

Liddell waggled his eyebrows at Jack. "Threesome," he said before Marcie could clap a hand over his mouth.

Jack chuckled, but he'd had enough of Liddell's foolery. He had gotten what he had come for: a further clue about his mystery duo.

"Okay, well, you figure out that. I have to go. Unlike some people out on medical leave, I have a case to solve."

CHAPTER FIFTY-ONE

"So, what aren't you telling me?" Brooke asked Jack when they were driving back to headquarters.

"What makes you say that?"

"Oh, I don't know. Maybe because of the looks you and your partner kept giving each other when you thought I wasn't watching. Maybe because I'm an experienced investigator. Maybe just because I'm a woman and I can always tell when a man is lying. And yes, that's a sexist remark."

Jack had a simple answer. "You're Trent's niece. You might not want to know what I'm thinking."

"I'm also your partner on this," she said, sounding aggrieved. "I'm sorry you don't have Liddell, but you're stuck with me. We have a better chance of catching the killer, or killers, if we're honest with each other. I can't say or do anything to make you trust me, Jack. That's up to you," Brooke said, her arms held tight across her chest.

"Okay, we'll call a truce. Let's get coffee and donuts." He knew just the place.

Penny Lane Coffee & Cigar Shop was located in an economically depressed area of the city. Churches of all denominations were scattered like Starbucks, popping up on every corner, selling salvation by the pound. The area, known as Rosedale, had once been the most prosperous part of the city, with ornate three-story mansions and English cottages that had been left to decay over the last forty years. Those grand old homes were now overrun with the homeless and the helpless.

Jack pulled to the curb in front of their destination. The two-story brick structure had housed many tenants over the years. It started out as a corner grocery, then a music store, then an antique store, and then an immigrant named Penny Landowskiwicz bought it and renamed it Penny Lane—a shortened version of her name.

The inside of the building hadn't changed much with each new owner. They entered a large seating area lined by tall windows, with a small kitchen behind a long counter. Penny lived upstairs. She had tried to serve fancy gourmet drinks, but the neighborhood wouldn't have it. Now she served coffee, tea, cigars, and privacy. There were none of those sissy drinks like lattes or frappes or skinnies or imitation flavors or colors made from bugs. The only thing that frothed in Penny Lane was the table of old codgers that complained about the world's ills in their daily coffee clutch. They were curiously absent today. Maybe the battle was won or they had declared armistice.

A woman behind the counter was taking plates and mugs from a double sink and stacking them on trays to dry. Upon seeing Jack, she filled two mugs with steaming coffee and placed them on the counter. "Coffee in a dirty mug. Hot and black, the way you like your women, right, Jack?"

Jack grinned and handed one coffee to Brooke. "Penny, this is Brooke."

Penny was mid-forties, very blond, and very beautiful with high cheekbones and piercing blue eyes. She reached a callused hand across and Brooke shook it.

"You better watch out for this one," Penny said, and returned to her task.

They found a table by the window, and Jack noticed two men sitting at an outside table; one old, one maybe in his twenties. The older man was wearing a suit and looked hot and tired. The youngster wore shorts and a tank top with a slogan on the front that said, "Kill them all. Let God separate them." His Oakland Raiders baseball cap was worn backward, and he appeared to be interviewing with the older man for a job.

"What do you think of the military angle?" Jack asked.

"It's pretty thin," she said, "but it would explain the propensity for violence."

Jack had known a lot of ex-GIs, many of them hired by the police department after serving time in various places such as Iraq,

Afghanistan, or, if they were lucky, some vacation spot like Hawaii or Germany. The department had their share of veteran old-timers, too, and they could tell some humdinger stories about Vietnam, but the ones who saw real fighting rarely spoke about it.

Brooke was right in her remark about the tendency to violence. The guys, and gals, that served their country seemed desensitized to it. The lack of shock at the violence going on around them helped on one hand, because they handled themselves better in combat situations. But it could also rob them of human emotions, any sharing of compassion or validation of the victims' feelings. They were hardwired to do whatever it took to stay alive, and the military failed to switch them off before sending them home.

"Were you in the service?" Jack asked, and the question seemed to surprise her.

"Three years. Air Force. MP for two years, investigator the last year. I could have made a career but figured I was needed here," she said. "You?"

"Army for three years. Intelligence, then a psychological warfare unit. Then college and the police academy, where I met my wife. My ex-wife."

Brooke said, straight-faced, "Military intelligence is an oxymoron."

Jack passed over the tired old joke. "I agree the military angle is thin," he said, "but it could be important if we come up against these guys. Would you rather fight a couple of jokers who like to kill, or trained soldiers who are good at it but predictable?"

"Speaking of that, I've heard some things about you, too," she said.

"Oh, goody," he said. "I'm a legend, for starters."

"Aren't you a little bit interested in what I've heard?"

"Shoot," he said, and added, "I mean that figuratively, of course."

Brooke bored in on him. "Well, I heard that your ex-wife is engaged to Eric Manson. And I've heard that there is a betting pool on when—not if—you shoot him."

Jack laughed out loud. "I guess it wouldn't be fair if I placed a bet?"

"I'm sorry," she said. "That was very rude of me."

"That's the way I like my women—rude and heavily armed."

Jack was no stranger to violence. Or killing for that matter. But he'd never killed anyone who didn't need it. He remained silent, waiting to see where this was going. He was curious about her as well. For example, why didn't she like to carry a weapon? He noticed her hand nervously adjusting her holster constantly as she talked. It was as if she was bothered by its presence.

She changed the subject. "Okay, let's talk about what you haven't been telling me."

CHAPTER FIFTY-TWO

Clint ended the call with the boss and dialed the number for the bank in the Caymans. The money was there. He placed the handset in the cradle and exited the phone booth. The boss had doubled their pay, but it wasn't for free.

They had their final target. And this time they were told to kill anyone who got in the way. Clint would keep that in mind, but he decided not to tell Book.

New Harmony, Indiana, with its one traffic light and smattering of little shops, couldn't be considered a city, but it was close to Evansville and two miles from the Illinois state line should the need arise for a hasty retreat. They had come here to call the boss, eat, and maybe find a new place to stay. They could accomplish two of these, but finding a room was a problem. There was only one place to stay—The Red Geranium. It was too busy and too fancy to not attract undue attention when they paid with cash. Even the bed-and-breakfasts were too pimped out.

On the way into town, Clint had spotted a tiny café on Main Street that looked like their style, and there was a coffee shop at the intersection.

While Clint made the call, Book had been waiting for him in a small park next to the town library. Clint came back and filled him in.

"Let's go in the library and see if they have a computer," Clint said.

"We know who the client is, Clint. What are you hoping to find?" Book said, and remained seated on a park bench. "We do this job, then we're outta here. Just throw that thing in a trash can. You need to get to a doctor and we can't do that here."

Clint ached all over. He knew Book was right, but he was curious. "Ten minutes."

"Okay. Ten minutes. Then we go find some food."

Inside, the library was the size of a large living room with books lining every square inch of available space. He hadn't been in a library since he was a kid, but he remembered the dry smell that was both pleasant and cloying. In the back of the room was the sole librarian, a wizened old man with a twist of white hair rising straight up from the top of his otherwise bald head.

In the center of the room, a long wooden table held two desktop computers, the old-fashioned kind with a tower and separate monitor. Clint sat at one of those, and he became aware of a feverish sweat covering his forehead and upper lip. The pain in his side was getting worse. He had had Book change the dressing in a pull-off just outside town, and the area around the stitches was bright red, oozing pus, and it smelled of infection.

He pushed the flash drive into a bus port on the tower and used the mouse to open the files. The computer screen showed some newspaper articles without photos, and lists of numbers that didn't mean anything.

"The stories are all about illegal massage parlors and court stuff." He turned his head and looked at his partner. "You think that girl in Illinois was a prostitute? Or a druggie?" he asked.

Book shrugged and said in a low voice, "How the hell would I know?"

"Well, a bunch of these stories are about drug addicts and prostitutes. We're wasting our time with this, Book. None of these names mean anything."

"I told you it was a waste of time," Book complained. "Let's get something to eat and get back to our room."

Clint unhooked the flash drive and put it in his pocket. It had been half a day since they'd eaten. Everything in Indiana seemed to be fried or overcooked, and the thought of anything fried made his stomach queasy.

"Listen, Book. No matter what happens, the boss can never know we've still got this thing."

"Why didn't we destroy it, Clint?"

"Just trust me," Clint said. "It's like insurance."

Book wasn't going to let it go, however. "If she finds out we still got it, she'll send someone to kill us. She won't quit until we're dead."

Clint tried to smile, but he was feeling dizzy. He leaned against the table for support. "That's exactly why we're keeping it. If she tries anything, we'll send it to the FBI. It must have some damning information, but I'll be damned if I can find it."

"You really don't look so good, Clint," Book said. "Let's go to the coffee shop on the corner. Maybe they can make us a sandwich."

They walked past the park and back to the coffee shop, where Book tried the front door. It was locked. Then they saw a small arm reach out and switch the open sign off. He could see a small woman inside and knocked on the door as she hurried out of view. A voice yelled from inside, "We're closed."

"What the . . . ?" Clint said, looking at the deserted business. He looked at his watch. "Who closes at four-thirty" He leaned unsteadily against the faded brick façade.

Book nudged him and pointed down the street to a business in the middle of the block. The sign over the door said, CRAIG'S PHARMACY. A man in a white jacket was standing in front smoking a cigarette.

"What are you thinking, Book?"

"I'm thinking you need some medicine, my friend," Book said with a broad smile. "You go on to the car. I'll be right there."

"I'm going with you," Clint said, not trusting that look. "I got your back."

CHAPTER FIFTY-THREE

"This is off the record," Jack said after Penny refilled their coffee and left them alone.

"You know I can't promise you that, Jack," Brooke said. "But if it isn't evidence, I'll try to keep it to myself. Best I can do."

That promise wasn't exactly what he wanted, but it would do for now. "Eric Manson lied to me about knowing Hope Dupree." Brooke didn't seem surprised, and he continued, "He was the prosecutor who had her drug charges dismissed so she could continue to work for narcotics as a CI."

"So, he lied." Brooke said. "You never had an attorney lie before?"

"Wait, there's more." Jack paused, thinking about how to fill out the story.

"The first murder—even before we knew who was killed—Eric called Marlin Pope. How did he know it was Nina we found at the landfill? Then I find out he'd already been inside her house that morning. He was still at his engagement party when I got the call from dispatch that morning. He claims he was worrying about her not showing up for work. But how did he get involved so fast?"

Brooke remained neutral, and Jack expected her to just get up and leave at any moment.

"Just hear me out," he said. "Our crime scene didn't find his fingerprints inside Nina's house. He said he walked all the way through the house looking for her. How did he do that without touching anything? *And* he lied to me about having a key. That's not to mention, Eric has a reputation for extracurricular activity with his employees."

Brooke's eyebrows rose at last. Jack had her attention.

"I'm telling you, Brooke, this has Eric's stink all over it."

Then Brooke said something that made Jack's blood run hot.

"Are you sure you're not making too much of Eric's involvement? I mean, Eric *is* engaged to your ex-wife and you obviously disapprove of him."

"I don't know, Brooke," he said. "Are you sure you're not making light of this because Eric works for your uncle? I mean, having a killer on the payroll couldn't be good for Trent's career plans."

If she'd been cool before, that made her turn positively frosty. In the tense silence that ensued, Jack's cell phone played a jingle. It was Garcia. He listened to what she had to say and then hung up.

"That was Garcia," he said, "Hope Dupree is one of the cases listed on the flash drive."

Brooke took the news in but said nothing.

"Hope Dupree was listed in the court records as a confidential informant. Garcia was able to trace it back to a narcotics case and we just confirmed it. Eric Manson and Nina Parsons were the prosecutors who handled that case. Plus, Nina recently dismissed charges against Hope in another drug case. There's our connection between Nina and Hope." And Eric, he thought.

"What about Hope's pimp?" Brooke asked. "Or Alaina Kusta, or Samantha Steele? How do they fit in?"

Or two killers who ran like soldiers, Jack thought. Brooke was right. As much as he liked Eric for Nina, he still had major pieces that were not fitting into this puzzle.

CHAPTER FIFTY-FOUR

Moira's day had thus far consisted of running errands and filing paperwork for the more senior deputy prosecutors. The work was mind-numbing and exactly what she had hoped to avoid as an attorney. But she needed experience before she considered going into private practice, and that meant starting at the bottom somewhere.

As the other attorneys' demand for her services lessened, she returned to her own desk and booted up her computer. Unlike the other government offices in the Civic Center, the prosecutor's database was housed on its own server. Even the police department didn't have the ability to access it, although she had access to the police database as well as IDACS, or Indiana Data and Communications System, and NCIC, the FBI's National Crime Information Center, and all of the court systems including civil matters.

With so much information at her fingertips she decided to be nosy. Entering the police records database, she typed in the name Hope Dupree and received four matches. She scrolled through these and found they all matched the same person. The first three files involved juvenile entries: runaway, missing person, minor in possession. The last one reported what Angelina had already told them about.

She checked the list of defendants through the state and federal databases, as well as local and court systems. She was reading charging information for one of the older cases when she heard a knock on her door. Trent Wethington strolled in, came around her desk, and placed his hands on her shoulders.

"I just came to see how you're settling in. I can see you're busy," he said, eyeing the computer screen.

"Just trying to get prepared for tomorrow morning," she lied.

"I'm reading some charging information forms so I can help Abbey prepare them." She wasn't doing anything wrong, but if he thought she was snooping around again, he would be angry.

"That's Billie Mastison," he said, and she felt his grip tighten on her shoulders. "She was one of my cases many years ago. Why are you looking at this?"

"Oh, is that right? I thought it would give me the correct wording for a charging affidavit. It was really one of yours? Wow! You have a good memory. You must have worked thousands of cases."

He didn't look flattered. "That's the old form. We don't use that one now, so you need to find the proper one, young lady."

He leaned across her and pulled up a new charging information form. "That's the one we use these days. You might want to save it on your desktop so you don't have to go hunting around in the computer files."

"Thanks," she said, trying her best to hide the burn showing on her cheeks.

He left without saying anything else, but she had the feeling that his last remark was a veiled warning.

Trent had barely left when Eric knocked and came into her office. She sighed inwardly, wondered if her day would be like this until she went home. That thought led to wondering if she was being singled out as someone to keep an eye on. She decided to ask.

"Eric, I know I was wrong to take the flash drive home. Am I still in trouble?"

He came around her desk, just as Trent had done, to check her computer screen. Luckily, the new charging information form was still up.

"As a matter of fact, that's why I came over," Eric said, and put his hands firmly on her shoulders. She hoped everyone who worked here wasn't touchy-feely because she hated it.

"Oh?" she asked, and swiveled her chair sideways to face him.

"I know you want to make up for your mistake, and I want to help you do that. You seem keen for extra work, so I'm allowing you some overtime. What are you planning tonight?"

"Eric, I have dinner plans with Jack," Moira protested, before she remembered what she had just said about taking the flash drive home. "But if it will get me back in good graces, I'll call Jack and cancel."

Eric's smile widened. "Yes, it would make a great difference. I'll tell Trent you volunteered for overtime. That will impress him." He picked up her legal pad and wrote some notes on it. "These are the cases I want you to pull. Have them on my desk in the morning."

As Eric headed out, Moira picked up her desk phone to break her dinner plans. Eric turned back and said, "Don't bother calling Jack. I'm seeing him in a bit and I'll be sure to tell him."

She frowned at this intrusion into her private affairs, and he added, "Don't worry. Jack will understand."

Moira picked up the legal pad and looked at Eric's instructions.

Christ, this will take all night. These cases are probably in storage in the basement.

CHAPTER FIFTY-FIVE

Brooke was silent during the drive to police headquarters. Once there, she got out and said, "I promised, so I won't tell anyone what you suspect. But, Jack, you need to be very sure before you accuse the next prosecutor of Vanderburgh County of murder."

"I'm not accusing Eric," Jack said, "but you have to admit, he's the best suspect we have."

Brooke did not look convinced in the slightest. "You said yourself, there are two killers. So who is Eric working with? Trent? Or maybe Moira?" she added with a sarcastic tinge. "She came back to Evansville just before this started. Maybe she was making an opening for herself by killing Nina. Or maybe I'm one of the killers and secretly married to Eric. I could go on and on."

"Hey, cut that out," Jack said.

Brooke leaned in the door and said, "I'm just grasping for suspects. Like you."

"You've made your point," Jack said sullenly.

She slammed the car door and headed to her own car.

Just then a detective approached Jack's window. "Scotty, in New Harmony, wants you to call him right away. He said he doesn't want to put anything over the radio. Call his cell phone, he said. Have you got that number?"

Jack nodded that he did. Scotty Champlin kept a thirty-foot outboard at Two Jakes Marina. He had retired from the Mt. Vernon police department years ago and planned to spend his golden years fishing, but the economy started to tank, so he took the job as town marshal in New Harmony. He and Jack were fishing buddies off and on.

Jack honked his horn and Brooke looked up. He motioned for

her to come back to the car and dialed Scotty's cell phone. He listened to what he had to say and asked, "You have video? I'll be right there."

He disconnected the call as Brooke approached his door. Before she could make another smart remark, he said, "Get in. There's been another murder."

The sleepy village of New Harmony, set along the Wabash River where it divided Indiana from Illinois, had been founded in the mid 1800s, and the population had remained at about eight hundred people, mostly farmers and such. The lack of crime in New Harmony made the town marshal's position almost honorary, but if Scotty wasn't exaggerating, all that was about to change.

Jack found a parking place in the post office lot, and they walked up the steps at the rear of the town hall. Scotty Champlin was waiting for them at the back door. He had retired at the mandatory age of sixty-five. He was nearer seventy now, but his lean and muscular physique belied his age.

Scotty ushered them inside a small room filled to overflowing with filing cabinets and boxes of old paperwork. From a small refrigerator set atop one filing cabinet he handed out bottles of ice-cold water.

"Welcome to small-town USA," he said. "Let me show you what I've got."

He led them behind a row of filing cabinets where he had folding chairs pushed in front of a cheap black-and-white television/VCR combo that played VHS tapes.

"I think it's those two guys you're looking for. The ones who beat Liddell up."

Jack's heart raced, thinking this might be the break he'd been waiting for. He wasn't surprised that Scotty had put this together so quickly. He had been—still was—a good cop, and when anyone attacked a cop, every lawman in a hundred-mile radius was out for blood.

"When did this happen?" Jack asked, taking a seat.

"Bob was just closing," Scotty said, and punched the rewind button on the old-fashioned television-VCR combo. "Bob Craig is the owner of the pharmacy. This happened at four-thirty today." He hit the play button and the small screen came to life.

The place had two cameras, one behind the pharmacy counter and pointing toward the front door, the other camera in a corner over the door and pointing to the back of the store where the pharmacy counter could be seen. Jack watched the split screen.

"Sorry for the quality of the video," Scotty said. "Bob must have used the same three tapes over a hundred times."

Jack waved the comment off. "At least the video displays a time and date."

"I checked and it's accurate. Bob always goes out for a smoke before he closes," Scotty said. The tape showed four-twenty-eight p.m. exactly. "He comes back in right here." The screen switched to the camera looking into the store. A man wearing a white coat was walking down the aisle toward the pharmacy counter.

"Here's where they show up," Scotty said.

Bob turned around as if someone had come into the store. He began to walk back toward the front door, stopped, and then put his hands up in the air. He was saying something.

"No audio?" Brooke asked. Scotty shook his head.

Bob Craig stood with his arms over his head just like in the old movies where someone had yelled "hands up!" A large figure wearing a dark jacket and jeans with a balaclava covering his head and face moved toward him with a handgun pointed at Bob.

"Beretta nine millimeter," Brooke observed.

Jack agreed. It looked like the military issue, model 92S. Jack owned one.

The view changed to the camera looking toward the front of the store. "Cameras switch every ten seconds," Scotty explained. On the video the robber was placing the gun against Craig's head.

"Can you pause it, Scotty?" Jack said, and Scotty punched a button on the television. The screen froze at the point where the robber was using the barrel of the pistol to push Craig toward the pharmacy.

In the background, visible in the front doorway, was another figure. He, too, was wearing dark clothing and a balaclava and held something down by his side. The second subject was big, but the guy holding a gun on the pharmacist was bigger.

Jack noticed these guys didn't have the jerky hurriedness of junkies out to score some prescription drugs. They moved like a team. One man took control, the other covered him. Even without sound Jack could tell that the robbers said nothing, their actions were practiced. Scotty was right. These were the guys who beat Liddell.

"Can we get better shots of these guys?" Jack asked. The pictures would be grainy to the point of useless when they tried to print them.

"Yeah," Scotty said. "They both go behind the counter near the end. Hold on." He hit play again.

"Look at their hands, Scotty. Not wearing gloves. And the bigger guy is black," Jack said.

The robber took Bob Craig behind the counter and pushed him against the wall. Then he began scanning the shelves and pocketing certain items. The video wasn't good enough to see what he was taking, but they could at least see where he was taking them from.

"Do you know what he took?" Jack asked.

Scotty paused the video to answer. "He took stuff from the shelf where they keep the painkillers," he said. "But I don't think they were after drugs because they took a bunch of antibiotics, too. Or at least that's what we think. The assistant pharmacist thinks it was Keflex. We'll know for sure when they check the inventory." Scotty hit the play button.

The camera angle changed, and each time the man in the doorway moved closer to the counter, his arm rising, a Beretta 92S at shoulder level. The camera switched back to the counter, and Bob Craig reached for something under the counter. The man searching the shelves didn't see the move.

Then Craig's head exploded. It came apart like a busted melon, and his body fell straight down, beyond the view of the camera.

The man who was searching the shelves jerked around, his mouth moving, and he pointed the gun downward and fired repeatedly. Jack counted fourteen.

The other man leaned over the counter with both hands—his right hand still holding the gun—looking down.

"Stop it there!" Jack said, and Scotty froze the picture. "Now back it up to where that guy comes to the counter and play it forward again."

Scotty froze the screen at the spot where the man leaned against the counter with both hands.

Brooke said. "I'll get my people out here."

"I already called the state police," Scotty said. He hit the slow forward button.

The gunman at the counter brought his right hand down and held it to his right rib area. When he finally turned around, his hand remained pressed against his side.

"Marcie said she shot one of them," Jack said.

Brooke mouthed the words, "Not Eric."

Jack scowled. It wasn't Eric. "Let's play it real slow. I want a good look at their faces."

CHAPTER FIFTY-SIX

For most of the Vanderburgh County Prosecutor's Office employees the workday was over. Moira's wouldn't be over until late in the evening. The basement of the Civic Center building was cool, if not downright cold, and smelled of damp paper and small creatures Moira didn't want to think of. The concrete floors were painted battleship gray, as were the walls, made of heavy gauge steel. Fluorescent light fixtures hung from the open ceiling and butted against long tubes of ventilation ducts, scattering the uneven light. Doors on her left and right were marked for their various purposes, but some were merely designated by a number. She was up to number seven, and she was looking for twenty-four, which, of course, was at the far end of the hallway, past the elevator.

Finding the door to room twenty-four locked, she used her office key, and was grateful to feel the tumblers give. The door swung inward and she stepped into a pitch-black space. She felt around for a light switch. Her hand closed over a plastic box and lights sputtered into life. *Motion sensor.*

The room was mammoth. Steel-wired cages separated the storage space into two rooms, each the size of a small house, and each divided by a dozen rows of metal shelving eight feet tall, each shelf lined with banker's boxes. An aluminum stepladder leaned against the wall of the nearest cage.

"Heard you down here," a voice said from behind her.

Feeling a slight start, she whipped around to find the night maintenance man, Nova, standing beside a cart loaded with tools. "I'll be working down here for a few hours," she said, not knowing why she was justifying herself to the old guy.

"Well, you won't be doing much without these," he said, and used a set of small brass keys to unlock the doors to the steel cages.

"They didn't tell me I needed keys," she admitted, and felt foolish. Of course she would need keys to access sensitive documents.

"There's a light switch down the hall," he said, jerking a thumb in the direction she had come from. "The lights out here go off in about an hour, but you can turn the hall light on if you ain't left by then. These lights in here are on a motion sensor, so if you find yourself in the dark, just wave and they'll come back on." He left without another word.

She perused the list of files Eric had written down and then checked the labels on the shelves. All the files she needed appeared to be on top. *Just my luck.* She dragged the ladder into the cage and opened it under one of the boxes she needed.

As she climbed toward the top, she had the feeling of being exposed. She glanced downward, just to make sure no one was there. But of course there wasn't. It was a trick of heights, knowing it was a long way down. Who in the world would show up late at night in the basement of the Civic Center? No one, she thought gloomily, except me.

CHAPTER FIFTY-SEVEN

"This isn't going to work," Jack said, viewing the picture he'd just taken with his iPhone. He wanted to have a photo to show Marcie, but he kept getting his thumb in the picture. Brooke took his iPhone from him, did something, and handed it back to him.

"It's set to take video now. Start the VHS tape where you want," Brooke said, and Jack rewound the tape to where the pharmacist turned to see who had come in and hit pause.

Brooke pointed at a red button at the bottom of his cell phone screen. "Start the tape and touch the red button on your phone. It will start recording. When you get what you want, hit the red button again and it stops."

Jack hit the play button on the VHS and then touched the red light on his phone. He let the video play through to where the second gunman was approaching the counter and touched the red button again. *No need for Marcie to see what happened after that.*

Brooke showed him how to play it back on his telephone and said, "I'll have several copies of the VHS tape burned onto CDs."

"Can you get still photos enhanced? We need to put them out to law enforcement."

"Is the Pope Catholic?"

He looked at her in surprise, thinking that was what Liddell would say.

"What's the matter?" Brooke asked.

"Nothing." The parallel with Liddell made him realize that she'd been very helpful on this lead. "Hey, thanks for doing this, Brooke," he said. "Maybe bringing you into this wasn't such a stupid idea after all," he wanted to say, but said instead, "I'm glad you're working with me."

"So what do you want to do with the video? Besides show Marcie, I mean?" she asked.

Jack checked with Scotty, not wanting him to feel that his authority had been usurped, but Scotty raised his hands and said, "This is way above my pay grade. It's a state police show, not mine."

"I'll show what I've got to Marcie," Jack said. "If she identifies these as the guys, we may want to hold up on showing the pictures to the news media."

"On the other hand," Brooke said, "these guys might be local talent. If we put the video on the news and show it around the tristate area, maybe someone will come forward."

"Or maybe the bad guys will see themselves and disappear on us," Jack countered.

"Either way, they're wearing masks. What do you want to do?"

They had come full circle. It was a call that would ultimately be made by someone higher up the food chain, but for now they agreed to hold back the video until Jack showed it to Marcie.

"Better to ask forgiveness than permission," Brooke said.

This town's not big enough for both of us, Jack thought.

When Jack returned to Evansville, he stopped at a K-Land gas station to fill up. The city was getting raped on gas prices, but they had a fuel contract with K-Land. It was like the Army paying four hundred dollars for a hammer. Why should the Army have the patent on wasting tax dollars?

While at the pump he called Liddell and explained about the video.

"Do me a favor, pod'na," Liddell said. "Marcie has been through enough. I don't want to scare her. Can she be kept out of this for now?"

Jack thought about the times he'd kept case developments from Katie. At the time he thought he was keeping her safe by not bringing his job home. But after the divorce, she told him how disconnected she had felt.

"Absolutely. But she'll find out from somewhere. You should tell her. Or let her choose if she wants to hear it."

"Yes, O Wise One," Liddell said. "Okay, come on over, but let me see it first."

Jack hung up and dialed Moira's cell phone to cancel their dinner plans. Moira's phone rang for a good while and went to voice mail. He hung up without leaving a message and started to dial Katie's cell phone, but then hung up. *What if Eric's with her? What if she doesn't know anything about Moira asking me to dinner?*

Moira would call him when he didn't show. She'd be mad, but it was her own fault for not answering her phone.

Katie looked in the refrigerator. She was glad to have her sister's company, but groceries didn't last long with Moira around, and she found she was spending a fortune on food that she didn't even like or eat. She shut the refrigerator door and picked up her car keys. Moira was planning on cooking for Jack tonight, so that meant Katie would be expected to help. She didn't mind, but they had nothing to cook in the house, unless Jack liked frozen TV dinners or avocado sandwiches.

If she was honest with herself, she was glad Jack was coming over for dinner. She had become friends with Susan Summers, his last girlfriend. It had been a bit awkward at first, but Susan was good for Jack. Since she was the chief parole officer for the state, she understood Jack's passion for the job. It was silly, but when Jack started dating Susan exclusively, Katie felt jealous. When they had broken up, she had truly felt sad for both of them, though relieved that he hadn't married again. But by then she had started dating Eric, and Jack threw himself into his work, just like he always did to avoid facing his emotions.

She made a mental list of groceries she would need. Absorbed in planning, she opened the door—and staggered back when she found herself inches away from a figure standing there.

"My, my! You Connelly girls are jumpy!" Eric said. "Aren't you going to invite me in?"

"You should have called, Eric," she said, immediately regretting her choice of words, but he had scared her. "I mean . . . I didn't know you were coming. Sorry. Of course you can come in, but I was just on my way to the grocery store. Moira invited Jack for dinner, and of course she didn't bother to go shopping for something to eat."

He waved her words away. "Moira will have to learn how to plan ahead next time. Listen, instead of buying food and cooking, how about I take you out somewhere nice to eat? You see, I want to make amends for the way I've been acting lately." Katie was still hesitant, not able to shift gears right away. "Moira and Jack will just go out to eat," Eric said. "They'll be fine."

Katie was catching up to the new idea by now. Eric was right. *Moira invited Jack without asking me.* It would serve her right to have to cook on her own.

"Sounds wonderful, Eric," she said.

"Great! I've made reservations at Bone Fish. You love that place."

Yet Katie still held back, feeling responsible for her sister—and Jack—even if Moira was being thoughtless as usual.

"Here," he said, taking one of his business cards from his suit coat, "use the back of my card. Leave them a note if that makes you feel better. Here's a pen."

That settled the matter. Katie took the items and wrote a note.

Moira, With Eric at Bone Fish, be home soon.

Eric took the note and read it before sticking it in the doorjamb, where it would be visible. "Home soon?" he remarked. "Who's the big sister?"

She didn't like him making remarks about them. He had no idea how much they shared. "She won't be here forever, Eric. She needs me."

His expression turned serious. "I need you, too. I love you, Katie. "

"You've told me that," she replied.

CHAPTER FIFTY-EIGHT

Brooke Wethington prided herself on multitasking, but her uncle had put her in a difficult position by demanding that she drop everything and meet with him. She needed to be monitoring the crime scene in New Harmony, staying on top of the lab, keeping in touch with Jack Murphy. But Trent had prevailed over all of her arguments, and now, here they were, in a fancy restaurant on Evansville's east side. She found herself wishing her cell phone would ring and give her an excuse to leave.

Her uncle uncharacteristically ordered a double of Maker's Mark bourbon, neat, and belted it down.

"So, what do you think of Jack Murphy?" He was dressed immaculately, blue blazer carefully folded over the chair beside him at the bar, wearing a blue shirt with white collar and cuffs.

Brooke felt uncomfortable as he stared at her. She always had. Trent was her uncle, but, first and foremost, he was a powerful man. He had been the prosecutor for this county for almost as long as she had been alive, and he would likely be the next governor of Indiana.

"Answer, please," Trent commanded.

"He's very capable, sir," she said, and her uncle's expression darkened. He hated it when she called him *sir* when they were alone. "Uncle Trent."

"But is he getting anywhere, Brooke?"

She wasn't sure how to answer. She had told him what she was doing in New Harmony and that they now had video of the killers, but he still had insisted on meeting with her.

"So this is gang- and drug-related," Trent said. "Should I call DEA for assistance?"

"It's definitely not gang-related," she said quickly. The last thing she needed was Drug Enforcement Agents breathing down her neck. "We're considering ex-military. These guys are too smooth to be gang members."

He took the news calmly, but she had the feeling he was disappointed that it wasn't gang-related. *Why was that?*

Trent ordered another double, but his eyes never left hers. "We're family, Brooke. This is important to me. That's why I had you put on this and not someone else."

She replied indignantly, "You asked for me personally?"

Trent squeezed her hand and favored her with his most gracious smile. "Okay, partly because you're family, but mostly because you're the best investigator the state police has, Brooke. You always were a smart girl."

Brooke smiled at the compliment. *He's right. I am the best. That means I'm too good to be his family lap dog.*

CHAPTER FIFTY-NINE

It was dark when Jack finished gassing up. He was replaying the video in his mind when his car radio came to life. "One David fifty-four," the dispatcher called.

Jack pulled the radio mic from the holder and pressed the transmit key. "One David fifty-four."

"One David fifty-four. Vanderburgh County, Unit three, Deputy Waligura, is requesting you at the Ridley Farm."

"Has he got a cow in the road?" Jack wanted to ask, but he refrained. "What has he got?"

"One David fifty-four. He advised there is a van submerged in a pond. Fire rescue divers and a wrecker are on scene. He thinks it might be the white van you put the BOLO on."

Jack had no clue where the Ridley Farm was, but the dispatcher gave him decent directions. Ten minutes later, he was standing beside Deputy Sheriff David Waligura at the edge of a pond. A flatbed tow truck and a fire rescue truck were parked on the grass nearby with spotlights trained on the pond.

Jack shook hands with the deputy.

"There's two rescue divers in the water," Waligura said.

Three teenagers were lounging against the deputy's cruiser and Waligura yelled at them. "Get off my car! But don't go anywhere."

The boys stared at him defiantly, but sat down on the grassy hill, nudging each other and smirking. They were soaking wet.

"Buncha little pukes," Waligura muttered.

"I take it those are the kids who found the van?" Jack asked.

Waligura sighed. "You won't get much out of them. Bunch of juvenile delinquents. Troublemakers."

"At least they called it in," Jack offered, and Waligura laughed out loud. He seemed to have a history with these kids.

A diver surfaced and gave the wrecker driver the thumbs-up sign. A winch powered up, and soon a van slowly emerged from the pond by the front end. Cloudy green water gushed out of the open windows. When the van cleared the bank and was pulled to the rear of the flatbed, Jack and Waligura walked around to the back of it.

Streams of muddy water spurted out of holes that pocked the back cargo doors. *She hit it,* Jack thought, checking the number of holes in the back doors. *Nice pattern. Good for you, Marcie!*

The deputy whistled admiringly. "You say a cop's wife did that?"

Jack nodded.

"That's why I didn't teach my old lady how to shoot."

"I'd like to get my crime scene guys here, if that's all right with you," Jack said to the deputy. "I'll do the tow ticket."

Waligura was more than happy to let the city boys take over. The county was huge and he was one of two deputies covering the entire north side tonight.

"Be my guest," he said, and then halfheartedly offered to stick around. He was delighted when Jack declined. "I'll just send the little darlings over to lean against *your* car," he said, and strode toward the teens.

"Is this far enough?" the wrecker driver called out to Jack.

"That's fine," Jack said. "After my guys get here, they'll tell you where to take it."

The driver shut off the engine and settled in for the wait.

Jack called Captain Franklin, told him the details, and was assured crime scene and a detective were headed his way.

Jack also called Eric Manson. He really didn't need a search warrant, but he didn't want to be accused of keeping secrets from the almighty prosecutor's office. Eric didn't answer, so he left a voice mail.

The last call he made was to his new BFF with the state police. Brooke answered on the first ring and sounded glad to hear from him.

"Guess what I've got?" Jack asked.

"I don't care. Where are you?"

Once Brooke hung up, she turned to Trent and said in an apolo-

getic voice, "I've got to go. We've found the van, and I need some-
one to type up a search warrant," she said, leaving out the fact that
Jack Murphy was involved. She took a twenty out of her wallet, but
Trent waved it away.

"Go," Trent said, and stood to get her chair as she rose. "I'll get
someone in to the office."

She beat a hasty retreat. As she headed north in her car, she
thought, *First the video and now the van.* Murphy was having an in-
credibly lucky day. Then again, these killers were very busy boys.

The boys jeered at the retreating deputy as Jack approached
them. One of them said, "Up yours, Walleye"—obviously a play on
the name Waligura—and the others made halfhearted gang signs.

The one Jack took for the leader was a head taller than his two
friends. He was almost as tall as Jack, and at fourteen or fifteen, he
was a few years older as well. The boy turned his back to Jack and
pulled the tail of his wet shirt over something.

"You a cop?" one of the boys asked. This one was scrawny and
was probably the youngest one. The other kid was short and chubby
and had a double chin already.

Jack made a show of letting them see the badge on his belt and
the gun on his hip as he walked past the two smaller ones and put a
hand on the leader's shoulder.

"What have you got there, son?" he asked, and turned the boy
around. The light from the rescue diver's truck barely reached
them, but it was enough to cause Jack's pulse to beat harder. The
grip of a semiautomatic pistol stuck out of the kid's waistband.

"Isn't that Trent?" Katie asked, while Eric informed the hostess
they had a reservation.

He followed her gaze and saw Trent sitting at a table inside
Bone Fish Restaurant, and a woman getting to her feet and leaving
in a hurry.

"Don't look," Eric whispered in Katie's ear. "I don't want to get
stuck at their table."

Katie knew for sure the woman wasn't Trent's wife, because
she'd met her at several official functions. "Who was that with
him?"

Eric took her by the arm, leading her past the front behind their waiter. "She's Jack's replacement," he said with what Katie thought was great satisfaction. "State police special investigator."

They were shown to a table on the other side of the huge room, and as she sat down Katie noticed the woman leaving the restaurant looked harried.

"Does he always take young attractive investigators out to eat?" she asked, and Eric laughed.

"Would it bother you if that were me?" he teased.

The waiter handed them menus and she pretended to study it, even though she already knew what she would get. The bang-bang shrimp were was to die for.

"In answer to your question," Eric said, "that's Brooke Wethington. Trent's her uncle. So no, he doesn't take other women out. Nor do I, Katie. I love you."

Katie smiled and focused on her menu.

CHAPTER SIXTY

The handgun was caked with mud, but Jack recognized it as a Glock .45 semiauto. With a five-and-a-half pound trigger pull, even a skinny fifteen-year-old could pull the trigger. The kid held the gun out, and Jack took it by the checkered pistol grips using his thumb and forefinger. Of course, the kids' prints were probably all over it by now.

The gun was heavy. *Still loaded.*

"I found it," the kid said obstinately, "and possession is nine tenths of the law. So I get to keep it, right?"

"Where did you hear that?"

The kid looked at his friends and bragged, "I done time. That's how I know."

"Where did you find it?" Jack demanded. But his authority didn't faze the kid.

"I know my rights," the boy said. "You can't question me without my guardian present. And you have to give me fifteen minutes to talk to them alone to decide if I'll talk to you or not."

Jack wanted to throw the kid back in the lake. Instead he took a deep breath and said, "You're not under arrest. So you don't get an attorney or a guardian."

The kid rolled his eyes and turned his head away. "Whatever."

"I'm investigating the attempted murder of a police officer, so I'm going to overlook the fact that you were in possibly in possession of his gun."

"So, I'm kind of like a witness for the state?" the kid said, sounding a lot younger.

Jack nodded. "That's right. You're a key witness. So where did you find this gun?"

* * *

Once he started, it was impossible to shut him up. Dakota, or Dak, as he liked to be called, had found the submerged van. He had also found the pistol on the bottom of the lake near the van. "Me and my crew decided to chill for a while." Jack sized up the two other boys with Dak. They had *spoiled rich brat* written all over them. Dak might well become a criminal, but the other two were just playing.

"Explain it to me again," Jack said. Dak described everything with skinny arms outstretched, hands and fingers making gang signs.

"Like I said. We were swimming, and Bobo—that's him there," he said, pointing to the scrawny kid, "felt something under his feet."

Bobo nodded his head like a bobble-head toy.

"Was the gun in the van? Did you or your friends get in the van?" Jack asked.

"That's crazy talk," Dak said, slinging out an arm for emphasis. "I seen a movie once where they got in a car underwater and got stuck inside."

"Okay, so where was the gun? How did you find that?"

Dak wrapped his arms tight across his chest defiantly, and said, "Do I get to keep the gun if it don't belong to that cop?"

Waligura was right. They are pukes. "So how and where did you find the gun?" Jack asked again.

"Well, we dove down and found what Bobo hit with his feet. It was some kind of van. I figured it was ditched there after a drug hit. You know, maybe some dead bangers inside."

Jack fought the urge to laugh, but maintained eye contact and waited.

"My crew, they got out the water," Dak said, and then made diving motions with his arms. "But I kep' on diving, feeling all around in the mud and shit. I musta gone down a dozen times before I found it."

Once the other members of the "crew" saw Dak cooperating, they all wanted to add their own animated descriptions, but Jack stilled them with an outstretched palm, promising them all a trip to police headquarters, where they could tell a detective.

Crime scene arrived first and began working their magic, and then a second shift detective arrived, loaded up the youngsters—sagging pants and all—in his car.

"You need statements?" the detective asked.

"Yeah. Especially the tall skinny one."

As the detective turned toward his car, Jack stopped him. "And you better pat them down before they get in your car. They'll understand that. I'm looking for a flash drive, a thumb drive, about so big," and he held his fingers apart again. The detective nodded in understanding and went to shake the kids down.

Jack stopped one of the crime scene techs and showed them the weapon he'd taken from Dak.

"Looks like one of ours."

"Yeah, I want to verify this is Liddell's."

Jack and Liddell had been issued their Glocks at the same time about five years ago when the police department switched over from the Smith & Wesson 9mm pistols. Since the department bought the pistols in one huge batch, two hundred sequential serial numbers had been issued.

"Can you hold a light on here?" Jack said, and pulled his own pistol. While the tech held a flashlight, Jack compared the serial numbers on both weapons. His was one number higher than the one they had just recovered. It was probably Liddell's gun.

The tech gloved up and took the gun from Jack, dropping the clip, and ejected the live round from the chamber. "Silvertip forty-five ammo like we carry. It hasn't been fired, Jack. Latent fingerprints are a crapshoot after it's been in the mud and handled by those kids. I'll run it through if you want."

Jack shook his head. "I'm going to give it back to Liddell," he said. "Can you just take a few pictures and document that I'm keeping it?"

The tech did what was asked and continued on his way over to the recovered van. Jack made his way through the weeds to the water and washed most of the mud from the pistol, reloaded it, and shoved it in his back pocket.

"Is that a gun in your pocket, or are you just happy to see me?" a female voice said behind him.

Jack turned and found Brooke standing by his car door, smiling.

CHAPTER SIXTY-ONE

To Jack's displeasure, Brooke pulled a major crime scene no-no and lit up a filtered Camel while they examined the recovered van. Halogen work lamps played over the vehicle, creating a dome of light in the darkness.

"Backseats have been stripped out," Brooke said, pointing out the obvious.

"I can see those things haven't killed too many brain cells," he said wryly. "Still think these aren't our guys?"

"Okay, you were right," she said, "Happy?" She deftly flicked the cigarette into the water.

"Damn right," Jack said. "The killers are starting to make mistakes. You take the van, I'll take the gun."

"Why don't I take both?" she asked, holding a hand out for the pistol.

"I'm giving this back to my partner. That's why."

"I could probably take you in a fair fight," she said with a straight face, "but I heard you don't fight fair."

Jack wasn't sure who was filling her in, but he merely said, "A few people taking a dirt nap would agree with you."

"Okay. You keep the gun. So what now?"

"I'm going to have dinner," he said, and when she raised her eyebrows, he added, "Call me if you get anything."

He still needed to show the video to Marcie and Liddell, but he was worried about Moira. She hadn't answered her cell phone, her office phone, or Katie's home phone. He thought about calling Katie, but if everything was okay, she would worry needlessly.

He drove down the dirt access road and punched in Moira's phone number but got her voice mail again. *She had better damn well be home.* He stepped on the accelerator as he pulled onto Highway 41 and headed south. One of the benefits of being a cop was getting to drive fast. Katie wouldn't be home or she would have answered the phone. But why wasn't Moira answering her phone? He called Liddell and explained that he would be a while. He had to go check on Moira. It wasn't like her to not call at least.

He drove down a series of twisty side streets and came out in front of Katie's house. The lights were off inside. He checked his watch again. Almost eight. Maybe they'd given up waiting for him and gone out to eat.

He went to the front door and knocked, and, not getting an answer, walked to the back, where he found Eric's business card stuck in the door.

> *Moira,*
> *With Eric at Bone Fish*
> *Be home soon*

It was Katie's handwriting. *So she went to eat with lover boy,* Jack thought. *That's why Eric didn't answer his phone.* But that was an hour ago. How long did it take to eat? And where was Moira? Why hadn't she left a note for him?

"Crap!" he said, and got back in his car.

Moira brushed a stand of hair back and checked the next item on Eric's list. He wanted all these files on his desk in the morning? It would take hours to find them, and she hadn't eaten. Plus, she was tired from climbing up and down the ladder. She eyed the stack of file folders she'd placed near the door and groaned inwardly at the thought of carrying armloads of them up the basement stairs. Now she wished she hadn't told Eric that she would stay. At least he had told Jack why she had had to cancel their dinner plans.

The building was creepy when it was empty, and she was glad Nova had left the basement hallway lights on. By the time she was finished, the entire first floor would be dark. She would have to feel her way down the hall to her office unless she could find Nova. Maybe he had a cart she could borrow. Or just maybe he would help her.

CHAPTER SIXTY-TWO

The Taurus sat in the school bus parking lot down the street from the Civic Center building. Clint watched a lone female walk down Main Street. "She shouldn't be out alone," he commented.

"Yeah, there are some seriously dangerous assholes out here," Book said, and they both laughed. "You know, I've been thinking. The boss didn't say we had to take it easy this time. She wants this one dead, but she didn't say how."

"What have you got in mind?" Clint asked warily.

"Maybe we can have a little fun. She'll be dead. She won't care."

Clint remembered the full clip Book had unloaded into the drugstore owner. No point arguing with a man who could lose it like that. He looked at his watch. "It's time."

Both men pulled Nomex balaclavas over their heads and adjusted them. Book checked the action of the Beretta 9mm pistol and holstered it. He pulled a hunting knife from the sheath on his belt and held it up. The fifteen-inch blade ended in a wicked point, making it the perfect killing weapon. The serrated edge opened a cut that was almost always fatal.

"I'm gonna gut her like a catfish!" Book said. "But I'm gonna have my fun first."

"Let's just get this done, Book," Clint said.

The two men moved stealthily from their car and into the bushes at the side entrance of the Civic Center. A pair of headlights turned onto the street a ways down. In a minute it would be alongside them.

They sidled onto the landing. Book peered through the glass doors while Clint kept an eye on the approaching vehicle.

"Clear," Book said, and opened the door with the key the client had left in the bushes for them. They moved inside fast and crouched in the darkness until the car passed. To their right was the door to the stairway. They headed down, deeper into the darkness.

CHAPTER SIXTY-THREE

Moira checked the wall clock outside the cage and cursed under her breath. Jack's going to kill me, she thought. But there was nothing she could do about it.

Several of the files were stored in flimsy boxes on the very top shelf, and she wasn't strong enough to lift them down. That meant standing on the top rung of the ladder, bracing herself with one hand, while rummaging through the boxes for the files she needed. It was almost eight-thirty when she was through pulling the files Eric wanted.

She looked at the sheer volume of files she had collected. "No way I'm taking all that in one trip, even if I get a cart."

Now I'm talking to myself! Good grief! I hope Eric doesn't expect me to put these back, or I might have to quit.

She knew Nova was probably somewhere close by, so she pushed the stacks of files against the wall to keep them from toppling over and walked down the hallway toward the elevators. It was almost completely dark in the basement, and she couldn't find the light switch. She remembered seeing Maintenance Room 1 on a door on the way to the storage room, so she felt her way down the hall, trying doorknobs along the way, until one door opened. The lights were on inside and as she looked around, she saw that she had found the workshop. Tools and machinery filled the space.

"Nova," she called out.

Book had learned the hard way not to trust intelligence he hadn't gathered himself. Their target was supposed to be in a room on the right about halfway down the basement hallway. He put a hand on Clint's shoulder and whispered in his ear.

"I'll go back up the stairs. Come down from the main hallway." That way they would push her toward each other. Clint drew his knife and retreated in the direction they had come from.

The door to the stairway closed with a soft snick and Clint was gone. They were a team. He would give Clint several minutes to get in position. But then a noise came from farther down the hallway ahead of him. *Too soon to be Clint. Could be the target.*

The noise grew steady and louder, and he could make out footsteps. Book strained to see into the dark, and a shape began forming. He moved against the wall and slipped his knife from his belt.

The figure was on top of him now, and Book could see the person had long hair pulled back in a ponytail, and the noise came from a wheeled cart.

Book remained motionless, ready to kill silently, and then the figure passed him, continuing down the hall. Book heard a door opening and the cart rattling.

Can't let him stay behind me. He turned and moved toward the noise.

CHAPTER SIXTY-FOUR

Jack's headlights played across the Civic Center Building. He had thought he saw some movement by the doors, but he seemed to be mistaken. He turned the Crown Vic into the front drive and watched the windows of the prosecutor's office as he drove slowly by. No lights. The parking spaces in front were all vacant except for a red Camaro. Moira's car. Then he remembered thinking he saw the side door close—the one that led to "Smokers' Corner." Moira had probably snuck out for a smoke.

He parked in front of the police station and used his magnetic key fob to enter. At the Records Room counter he got the key that led from the police station into the Civic Center, and then dialed Liddell's cell. It was getting late, but he knew Liddell would hit the panic button if he didn't show up like he said.

"Where you at?" Liddell asked. "I had a pizza waiting about thirty minutes ago."

"You have my permission to eat my half," Jack said. "I'm probably not going to make it out there tonight." He then promised to call as soon as he found Moira.

"You going to yell at her?" Liddell asked.

Jack promised to be good, hung up, and headed down the hallway. Why hadn't Moira called him? She had probably been roped into pulling some extra work. Or she was still snooping around despite him telling her to desist. He decided he wouldn't yell at her. He would see if she had eaten yet. He was starving. If he couldn't threaten her, he would coax her away from work with food.

* * *

Book moved quickly but not fast enough. He heard a door click shut just in front of him. With one hand on the hilt of his hunting knife, he tested the door handle. It was locked.

"Shit," he said softly. It was probably a janitor. Clint would be at the other end of the hall in less than a minute. Then they had to find the woman and kill her. He didn't think the person with the cart would be a problem, but a feeling of unease came over him. Nothing had gone right for them ever since the landfill. Maybe Clint was right. Maybe they should pull out now. Just call it quits and go.

But he knew he wouldn't leave without completing what they'd come for. The boss would only send another team to do the job, and he and Clint would become the next targets. Besides, there was no way he was letting a girl, or a janitor, or anyone else screw up this last job.

"C'mon, Clint," he said under his breath as he snuck back down the hallway, toward the target. Clint said she'd never see it coming, but he was wrong. Book was going to make sure she saw it coming.

Clint had his own problems. He had made it to the top of the stairs and down the hall to the elevator only to find the door to the stairway was stuck. It wasn't locked, because the handle turned and he could feel the mechanism working. It was tight. He hoped it wouldn't squeal when he forced it.

He put his shoulder to the door and pressed with all his two hundred thirty pounds until it suddenly gave. The squeal of metal on metal shrieked in the cavernous silence. He stood motionless for several heartbeats, then heard a door opening nearby. Footsteps. Coming his direction.

He stepped through and shut the door behind him. It squealed loudly again, and he cursed. He clicked on a small flashlight and headed down the stairs, taking them two at a time. He didn't have the time to let his night vision kick in.

The footsteps stopped just outside the door above him. *Shit! Someone must have heard me.*

Clint jumped the last four steps to the bottom of the first landing just as he heard the door above him squeal. He heard a man's voice yell, "Hey!" And then, "Police! Stop!" Then he heard someone charging down after him in a big damn hurry.

* * *

Jack had intended to go straight down the hallway to the prosecutors' offices, but to his left around a corner he heard a metal squeal that he recognized as the downstairs door near the elevators. He knew Nova would never use the stairs because he had a bad hip. *Maybe it's Moira?* He hurried around the corner and was about to call out her name when he heard the door slam shut with a groan. When he opened the door to the stairway he saw a large masked figure shining a flashlight and dressed all in black. And then the man ran.

"Hey!" Jack yelled, drawing his pistol. He took the stairs two at a time and yelled, "Police! Stop!"

The retreating figure took the light with it, and Jack was plunged into total darkness near the bottom of the first landing. He slipped on the last step and collided with the wall, letting out a curse before plunging down the last flight of stairs. At the bottom of the stairs, though, his innate caution kicked in. He stopped at the door, trying to recall what he'd seen. Had the man been armed? He didn't remember.

He stood to one side of the door, his back against the concrete block wall. Reaching across, he tried the door handle. With a loud blast a bullet punched through the steel door where Jack's face should have been. The bullet ricocheted off the steps and bounced around the concrete walls. The steel door had muffled the blast, but Jack's ears still rang.

He flung the door wide and dove through the opening. Spread-eagled across the floor, his pistol barrel pointed straight ahead, he watched and listened carefully, but whoever it was had moved on.

Jack had one advantage. Whoever shot at him had ruined their night vision with the muzzle blast of their gun, while Jack had remained in the darkness. He heard the soft pad of someone moving away from him. He couldn't risk firing blindly. He still didn't know where Moira was, but her car was here, so it was a good bet she was somewhere in the building.

He heard the slap of shoes on concrete again. The sound was retreating toward the far end of the hallway, where a door led back upstairs.

He rose to his feet, risking another bullet, and ran toward the sound. The shooter was going up to the prosecutor's floor. If Moira was upstairs, she was in danger of walking right into the killer's path. The leather soles of his shoes made a clacking sound on the concrete floor, giving his exact position away.

Jack heard the bullets whizzing by his head—and saw the bright muzzle flashes—almost at the same instant. He dropped to the floor and crawled back toward the elevators. He knew that pursuing the shooter in that direction was insanity. He would be a sitting duck both in the hall and on the stairway at the other end. Which left him with one choice. He had to reach the upstairs hallway before the shooter came out by the exit doors of the first floor. There was no one in the Civic Center this time of night, and thick concrete and steel walls separated it from the police station. No one could possibly have heard the gunshots.

Moira was in a maintenance room looking for Nova when she heard someone shout and a door slam. At first she thought it was Nova, but why would he be yelling and slamming doors? She was just about to go into the hall and see what it was when she heard what sounded like a gunshot. Very loud. Very close. She instantly flipped the lights off and crouched in the darkness, heart racing.

The door slammed again, even louder this time. She crab-walked back a few steps, but it was so dark. She didn't remember the room layout, and she couldn't risk turning the lights on. She had a cell phone and a cigarette lighter, but they were upstairs in her office.

Her mind raced. Had she seen a telephone in this room? Surely there was one, but it was so dark she couldn't see her hand in front of her face. She felt around and touched the metal frame of the doorway. She grabbed the door handle. *God, please get me out of here!* Then she heard more gunshots and instinctively crouched again.

She waited for agonizing seconds, but staying in the dark room wasn't an option. Without thinking, she flung the door wide and ran headlong for the stairway door directly across from the maintenance room. She yanked it open and ran up the steps as fast as her legs would carry her. When she reached the top landing, she burst out into the dimly lit upper floor.

A strong arm wrapped around her throat and a hand slammed over her mouth, effectively smothering her scream.

* * *

Book heard the first gunshot and saw a muzzle flash down the hallway about where Clint should have come down. He retreated to the stairway and up to the first floor. They had discussed this contingency. If the plan went to hell they would split up and meet back at the car. Book resisted the urge to wait for Clint, and once outside, he fled into the darkness.

Jack retreated to the stairway door by the elevators and, not worrying about making noise any longer, ran up the steps. He made it through the upstairs door when he heard another crash and loud footsteps coming up behind him.

His throat tightened. He knew they worked as a pair. Had he allowed them to trap him between them? Was the other one waiting for him to step into the open and gun him down? His only chance was to surprise the one coming up the stairs. He stepped to one side of the door, gun gripped tightly against his chest. When Moira came bursting through the doorway, he grabbed her and put a hand over her mouth to keep her from screaming.

She struggled violently, but he held on and whispered fiercely in her ear, "Moira. It's Jack. It's Jack!"

She stopped struggling, but he kept his hand over her mouth. "Don't make any sound, they may be up here." When she stopped struggling he released her and motioned for her to get behind him, but she was shaking violently and clung to him.

"You're safe now, Moira," Jack said to calm her. In fact, they were in mortal danger, but she didn't need to know that. Two guns against one weren't good odds.

When she stopped shaking, Jack peeked around the corner. When no one shot at him, he guessed the way was clear. "Let's get out of here," he said, and led her down the hall to the police wing.

CHAPTER SIXTY-FIVE

In the microsecond that he had seen Murphy at the top of the stairs, Clint recognized him from the news. Clint had bolted downstairs and through the door. He turned off the light clipped to the bottom of his pistol and positioned himself directly across from the door. He pointed the Beretta at chest level. If he could get Murphy off his tail, all he had to do was turn right, and run in a straight line to escape out of the other end of the building. He hoped Book saw the flashlight or heard the shout and realized something had gone wrong. Book was probably already clearing out, but just in case, he'd give his pursuer a little present.

When he heard the door handle turn, he fired a bullet into the center of the door. He turned and ran full-steam down the hall. He had about two hundred feet to the other stairway, and he was sure he'd make it. Then everything went wonky.

In his headlong flight, he didn't hear the door that had opened ahead of him or see that something was in his path. Suddenly he was flung head over heels, with metal objects crashing all around him, and he heard someone cry out. He scrambled to his feet and felt a sharp pain in his leg.

He could stand, but his right leg wasn't cooperating. In fierce pain he hobbled up the stairs to the top landing and in the muted light discovered why. A large screwdriver protruded from just above his right knee. He pulled the blade out and dropped it down the stairs. The clatter it made felt like the last straw.

He hurt like hell, but he had to get to the car before Book cleared out. He didn't think Book would leave him behind—at least alive—but this wasn't the Army.

With his gimpy leg and screaming ribs, he crossed the street and ran behind some bushes, along a fence, and then turned into a dark side alley where on the other side of where the school buses were parked. He gave a sigh of relief when he spotted the Taurus coming at him.

CHAPTER SIXTY-SIX

The police response was immediate, but Jack already knew it was too little, too late. He put out a BOLO, but these guys were long gone. The only description he could give the dispatcher was of the one he'd seen very briefly. He added that the man was possibly in the company of another male subject. Both were possibly in dark clothing, and both were possibly armed. But the suspects would have to be idiots to still be wearing balaclavas and walking around the street with guns.

Jack and another detective, Sam Smith, entered the basement from one end, while uniformed officers came down the stairs on the Locust Street side. Other police cars were blocking the more likely streets that could be used to escape. Yet the killers could have fled anywhere in a few minutes' time.

Detective Smith put the tip of his little finger over the bullet hole in the metal door. "You almost bought the farm!"

Jack found the spent bullet on the floor of the stairwell. It had penetrated the metal door and then flattened on the staircase. Another officer found the ejected shell casing in the hallway: a 9mm Parabellum. That was the ammunition used in a Beretta model 92S, like the gunmen in New Harmony had used to kill the pharmacist.

An officer yelled from the end of the hallway. "Down here."

Jack saw a metal cart was turned over—wheels up—and an assortment of tools lay helter-skelter across the floor. The officer was holding the stairwell door open and pointed at the base of the stairs, where a large screwdriver lay. The long blade was coated with blood and a trail of droplets led up the stairs.

"Someone got hurt," the officer said.

"Let's hope it was the right someone," Jack replied.

Jack heard a soft moan coming from behind them. He took a few steps back and pulled a door open. Nova was lying in a heap on the floor, a terrible gash across his forehead.

Jack crouched down and checked his injuries "Call for an ambulance."

The screwdriver and blood specimens were collected, to be sent to the state police lab. In blood, on the handle of the screwdriver, was a clear set of prints. The tech said they were from a right hand—all four fingers and a thumb—and the prints were good enough for comparison. The tech promised to put them through the databases ASAP.

Jack told the tech to send the bullet and shell casing to the state police lab right away for comparison with the ammunition used in New Harmony. "Tell the lab that Brooke Wethington said to put a rush on these." The tech grinned and left with the samples.

In Jack's considerable experience, he'd never made a criminal case on fingerprints. Not because they weren't good evidence, but because people seldom left perfect prints behind. But now they had blood, fingerprints, bullets, shell casings, and the video from New Harmony. The noose was tightening.

He headed back to the detective squad room, where he had left Moira in his office. When he looked in, he was surprised to find Brooke sitting with Moira, with one arm around her shoulders. Moira's complexion was pale. Her makeup was smudged from crying.

"How is the old guy doing?" Brooke asked.

Jack wondered how Brooke had arrived so quickly, but he didn't ask. "Nova's on his way to the hospital."

"Did he get shot?" Moira asked, and Jack shook his head.

"The killer ran right into his equipment cart. Nova was knocked down, and has a cut on his forehead, but he'll be fine. He's a tough old bird," Jack lied.

Moira was already shaken up. She didn't need to know Nova was still unconscious when paramedics arrived and they suspected a concussion.

"Do you feel like talking?" he asked her.

Her voice trembled and she was on the verge of fresh tears, but she nodded. "Eric asked me to get some files from the basement. I told him I had plans with you, but he said he would tell you that I had to stay. I'm sorry I just didn't go home and cook for you, Jack."

He lightly tapped his stomach. "If it makes you feel any better, I wish you had cooked for me, too."

Moira tried to smile, but the gesture was pathetic.

"It's all over. You're safe," he assured her. No thanks to Eric. But it wasn't all Eric's fault. He was angry with himself that he hadn't thought to protect Moira. He should have known that if the killers were after the flash drive, they wouldn't stop with Liddell. He hadn't thought that through, and she could have been killed.

Captain Franklin walked in. The only indication he'd gone home was that his tie was loosened slightly. He went straight to Moira. "Are you okay?"

"I've been better," she said. "If not for Jack . . ." Tears pooled in her eyes and she couldn't finish.

"Everything's going to be okay," Franklin said, and gave Jack a questioning look.

Jack shrugged. "They're gone, but I'm sure they were the same guys that attacked Liddell."

"The two guys from New Harmony?"

"I only saw one of them," Jack admitted. And he wasn't sure which one, "But if one of them was here, they both were." His ears were still ringing from the gunshot in the stairwell.

Brooke added. "Preliminary reports from our weapons expert state that the bullets and casings from New Harmony were fired by a Beretta nine millimeter. Per Jack's request, I've asked the lab for a rush on the comparison. It's nine millimeter ammunition, but until they can examine the bullet, they won't be able to nail down the weapon. It'll take a few hours."

"Anything on the van yet?" Franklin asked.

Brooke took this question. "The tarp we found in the cargo bay had traces of blood and . . ." She paused, wondering how much more Moira could stand to hear after the night she'd just had, but she no longer seemed to be listening.

"Crime scene techs collected bits and pieces of tissue, skin, and other cast-offs from the murder weapon. They must have killed at least one of the victims right there—in the van. I've got a lab crew working overtime."

Jack held up the evidence bag with the bloody screwdriver. "One of them might have been injured with this. A maintenance man works nights here and he was found unconscious next to an overturned tool cart. The guy who shot at me was running toward the stairwell where this was found."

"Could the blood be the maintenance man's?" Brooke asked.

Jack shook his head.

"Can you have the screwdriver rushed through, Brooke?" Franklin asked. "We can get a comparison sample from Nova, the maintenance man, to eliminate him."

"Of course."

"And have them run it through the DNA databases," Jack said.

Now that they had so much evidence in hand, Brooke was being really great. Expediting all this material would help out a lot. Yet in the next moment Jack remembered why she had been assigned the case in the first place. "I guess you'll be calling Trent now?"

"Good idea," she said, and, taking her phone from her pocket, she started for the door to make the call in private. As she approached the doorway, without turning around, she raised her left hand and then her middle finger for Jack to see.

"In your dreams," Jack muttered, but he had to admire her style.

Franklin remarked, "I see you two have become friends."

Moira also had been watching the exchange. "Jack has a way with people," she said, smiling for the first time.

CHAPTER SIXTY-SEVEN

Clint sat on the edge of the bed at the Sleepy Lodge while Book applied a makeshift field dressing. The wound in his leg was deep. An angry red circle surrounded the puncture.

"I think the screwdriver hit the bone," Clint moaned.

"I'm going to patch it. Then we got to go," Book said, and wrapped a strip of white T-shirt around Clint's leg and tied it tight.

They'd learned that lesson in the field. Never stay in one place for long. Especially after a fight. If you got comfortable, that was when *haji* would come out of nowhere, with rifles, rocket-propelled grenades, or other makeshift weapons. And they always came for blood. Revenge was the dish of the day, the screw du jour. If you killed one of theirs, the whole family would come for you. Cops weren't much different, in Clint's opinion.

Still, he was injured. His ribs were on fire, and he wasn't sure he could put weight on his leg. He wanted nothing more than to put his head down. Just for a few minutes. But they had to find a safe telephone. Check in with the boss. Tell her of yet another failure.

With a fighter's determination he pulled himself to his feet, stretched the sore muscles in his back, and limped around on the leg. The pain wasn't as bad as he thought. He picked up the car keys from the dresser. "Let's go," he said—and then his leg buckled.

Book had to help him back onto the bed. He took the keys and said, "I'll be back in an hour. Get some rest, but be ready to leave."

Clint, finally able to close his eyes, was out in a few seconds.

CHAPTER SIXTY-EIGHT

Garcia was running the fingerprints from the handle of the screwdriver through the database known as the Automated Fingerprint Information Systems, maintained by the FBI. She had already checked the Evansville police records filing cabinets to be sure they didn't have fingerprint cards that hadn't yet been entered into the system, and then double-checked with the State Police crime lab. They, too, had followed all the steps. Yet even AFIS pulled up a big zero.

Garcia didn't see how someone could commit these types of atrocities and not be in some agency's files. Her own fingerprints were on file with both the local and state authorities, and she was only a civilian government employee. Surely someone who killed like this had been arrested or fingerprinted at some point in his life.

Then she recalled that Jack mentioned the killers might be former military members. She wondered if the military had an automated system in place. Did the military fingerprint soldiers? She wasn't sure, but she knew someone who would know.

She took her cell phone from her purse and dialed a number, and although it was almost midnight, she knew he would answer if he saw her name pop up on his caller ID.

"Hey, baby girl. What up?" the sleepy male voice said.

She smiled. "I need you to check something for me."

"Anything for you, darlin'. You know that." She heard him tell someone to go back to sleep. Lucius Starling was never alone.

"I need you to get into the military database. Fingerprints," she said. "I've scanned the prints and I'm emailing them to you right now."

"Whoa, girl. Slow down. That's not something you say on an unsecured line." Muffled in the background, she heard a female asking whom he was talking to. She heard Lucius answer, "It's my sister. Just go back to sleep." Then he came back on the line. "Sorry, baby girl. She can't get enough of me. But I've always got some left for you."

"I'm not going to sleep with you, Lucius. No means no." At one time she had played with the idea—Lucius was built like a weight lifter without any of the wilt up front—but two factors kept her from doing it. First, his desire for her gave her a negotiating chip. Men were always more pliable when they were after something. Second, she had met Mark Crowley, chief deputy sheriff of Dubois County, and it was love at first sight.

"Who says we're going to sleep?" Lucius said playfully. She remained silent and he sighed. "Okay, just a minute." Moments later, "What am I looking for?"

"Just check your email."

She could hear him slapping the keys on his computer, and when he said he had the email, she filled him in—as much as he needed to know—and then turned him loose to do his thing. He didn't really need to hack the computer, because his job as a senior consulting computer analyst for the Department of Justice carried some perks. Lucius wasn't the typical muscle head. He was almost as good with computers as Garcia.

He could run what she needed as a "test of the system," and no one would be the wiser. Whereas, if she hacked into the system—and she was perfectly capable of doing so—it would set off all kinds of alarms and begin a search that might lead back to her computer.

"Five minutes," Lucius said, and the line went dead.

CHAPTER SIXTY-NINE

The meal at Bone Fish was fantastic, and expensive, but the atmosphere was subdued and tense. Eric blamed the dull mood on his boss. Trent had not only spotted them upon Brooke's hasty exit, but he also decided to join them at their table.

Katie picked at her food and spoke very little, and then only to answer questions put to her by Trent. Eric didn't blame her for being a little testy because it did feel like Trent was interrogating her about Jack, Moira, and the case.

He had to remind Trent—twice actually—that Katie and Jack were no longer married, and she didn't know anything about what Jack was doing. Then Katie embarrassed him when she said if Trent had questions, he should ask Jack or Moira.

As Eric turned the Mercedes down her street, his plans for the rest of the evening disintegrated before his eyes. Not just because of Katie's mood, but by what was parked in her driveway: Jack's car. Two marked police cars were lined up on the street.

Eric pulled in behind one of the police cars and nodded at the two heavily armed SWAT officers standing on Katie's porch. Katie pushed through the front door and ran into the living room, shouting, "Moira! Moira? Where are you?"

Jack stepped out of the kitchen with a steaming mug of coffee in each hand. "She's in there, Katie," he said calmly. "Just a little excitement at work tonight. She's fine."

Realizing the situation was serious, Katie put a hand on Jack's arm and mouthed the words, "Thank you." She entered the kitchen and found Moira sitting at the kitchen table, a lit cigarette between her fingers. Jack left the sisters to talk and carried the coffees out to the front porch for the officers. He wanted them to stay awake. He promised them relief in a couple of hours.

Eric was standing by the front steps with a scowl on his perfect face. The two officers accept the proffered coffee, and then moved away a respectful distance to allow Jack and Eric to talk. As they passed Eric, one officer remarked to the other, "Three to one on Jack." The other asked, "Killing or just wounding?" The rest of their conversation was lost to ambient city noises.

"Once again I've been left out in the cold," Eric said accusingly.

Jack wasn't sure if Eric was referring to the fact that he didn't know what had happened at the Civic Center, or if he was upset because he wouldn't be spending the night with Katie. It hardly mattered, because Jack was furious with him.

"Where the hell have you been?" Jack asked.

"Where have I been?" Eric asked. "I have to hear from these two goons of yours what happened. That's what you call cooperation?"

"Well, counselor, first of all they're not my 'goons,' they are SWAT officers. Second, if you'd turn your phone on, maybe someone could find you."

Eric wasn't having any of that. "You knew where we were. Katie left a note for you. You could have sent a car to the restaurant to let me know."

"And you would have come running because Moira missed our dinner plans?" Jack was right in his face. "You promised her you would tell me she had to work late. Once again you've lied. You're a piece of work, you know that?"

"I'm a piece of work?" Eric yelled, then lowered his voice when he noticed the SWAT officers looking their direction.

"I was a little busy—getting shot at!" Jack said as Eric stomped off the porch. "Sorry if I upset your plans for the evening, lover boy."

"Up yours," Eric called after him, and saw the SWAT officers were smirking.

Eric made it halfway to his car and stopped. He took some deep breaths to clear his mind. He would like nothing better than to wipe the smirks off those goons' faces, and when he became the prosecutor . . . well, things would be much different.

But more than that, he wanted to go back and make things right with Katie—and Moira, too. No matter how hard he tried, they resented him. It was always "Jack this" and "Jack that."

But he was here now, and Jack would be leaving. He loved Katie and they *were* engaged, so Jack should be the one leaving. He shook off his anger. "That's right." He put a look on his face that was both serious and supportive. "Okay, here we go," he said softly, and walked back to the house.

He walked onto the porch and tried the front door. It was locked.

The officers laughed openly as Eric stomped off again.

CHAPTER SEVENTY

Book was in search of new wheels. The Taurus might have been seen leaving the school bus parking lot. He had almost run down a prostitute and her client or pimp or whatever when he pulled onto the street. People like that were paid by the police to keep an eye out. He couldn't take the chance that they were giving Murphy a description of the car right now.

A billboard on Interstate 64 read, THE OLD BARN RESTAURANT—an appropriate name for a restaurant surrounded by bean and cornfields. Book slowed at the exit ramp and saw a building with sun-bleached planks in the shape of a barn with a red tin roof and a covered porch that was supposed to be inviting. The parking lot in front had a few possibilities, but as he entered the exit lane he spotted two police cars parked side by side in the lot across the street.

Book sped up and passed the exit. The next town ahead was just a dot on the map called Griffin, Indiana. The clock on the Taurus's dashboard read two o'clock. He didn't know where the boss was, or what time it was for her. He guessed it didn't matter, because the boss never sounded like she had been sleeping whatever time he called. If he found a phone in Griffin, he'd make the call.

He took the off-ramp for Griffin. He liked the idea that the town was close to the interstate. They might have need of the Taurus, and this way it would be easy to retrieve. He drove through cornfields so tall his headlights created a tunnel through the darkness. Just when he thought he would never find the town, the cornfields turned to soybeans and then to open fields. Soon he drew up at an intersection with a café shaped like an old-time train station.

He pulled into the cinder parking lot, where he killed the engine and shut his headlights off. A closed sign was in the window, but he didn't need to go in. A pay phone hung on the outside wall.

He sat in the car and scouted his surroundings. Two dozen one- and two-story homes lined one side of the road for two blocks before cornfields closed in again. Everything was dark and closed up tight as a drum. All of the houses had shiny pickup trucks parked either in front or in their weed-strewn gravel driveways. It was a hillbilly's dream.

A half dozen old cars and pickups were clumped together at the other end of the parking area. If he was lucky, the vehicles belonged to over-the-road truckers. If so, no one would report their vehicle missing for a while, and he only needed it for a day.

As he stepped out of the Taurus, he noticed the front of his shirt and pants. Even though his clothes were black, the fabric betrayed smears and streaks where Clint's blood had soaked into the material. Thinking of Clint getting shot pissed him off. They had been to war and neither one was ever hurt this bad. Now, in the matter of two days, Clint had been shot, stabbed in the leg, and if that guy in the drugstore had reached that gun one of them would be dead. He didn't need to wonder who that would have been.

He mounted the wooden steps to the café and picked up the phone. He wouldn't tell the boss what had happened tonight—he was sure the client had already heard the news and was burning up the telephone. It didn't matter what the boss thought. The fact was, they had failed to finish a job. Book was mad at himself for the botched attempt, and he wasn't going to take any shit from anyone.

He always suspected the boss was somewhere on the East Coast. The guy that had recruited them in the bar in Baltimore had a thick Bronx accent. He was loud and laughed a lot, like everything was a friggin' joke. The boss had the same accent, but her voice was softer, more controlled. She had absolutely no sense of humor.

He dialed the old rotary-dial phone on the wall of the café, and when the line was answered, he nervously said, "It's me."

"You let me down, Book," she said. "We have to change the plan . . . again." Her voice was measured, in total control.

"I want a lot more money," Book said before the woman could finish her thought. "We deserve more money."

The line stayed silent, and Book wondered if she had hung up, but then he heard her clear her throat. "Let's see if I have this correct. You messed up, *and* you want more money?"

"I know who the client is, boss. We seen him on television. Clint and me want more money. Double's not enough." He let the veiled threat hang.

The line remained silent, so he continued, "We've got expenses. And Clint's hurt."

"How bad?" she asked.

"He got stabbed in the leg. It's pretty bad."

"Clint let a girl stab him, and you both let her get away?"

"The girl didn't stab him," he said defensively. "Murphy showed up, like someone tipped him off that we was there. Clint had to hightail it and he ran into something in the dark," he said, but he knew it made them sound pretty lame.

The line was quiet for some time, and he was afraid the boss might want him to kill Clint. That wasn't going to happen.

"Here's what I want you to do," the boss said, and gave Book his final instructions.

When she finished, he said, "However this ends, we're out of here. Wire all the money to our accounts now. I'll be checking. If you don't, I'll kill the client and let the police figure it out."

Book hung up, proud of himself for standing his ground. They were getting a half-mil each to finish this, and the best part was, he got the green light to do something he'd wanted to do for a long time now. Kill Murphy.

He made the boss promise to leave them alone for at least a month. He needed a vacation. Clint needed the time to heal. And by using the threat to kill the client, he had ensured the boss wouldn't send anyone after them. The boss knew Book would never turn the man over to the authorities because that would implicate him and Clint, too. But he wouldn't hesitate to kill the client.

It was a shame that when this was over, they would have to find other employment, but that shouldn't be too hard to do. America was one of the most violent countries in the world.

He walked over to the parked cars and trucks and spotted an old junk pickup truck that he was sure he could hotwire. The café's lot would be a good place to leave the Taurus for the time being. It blended in with the other cars.

When Clint was on his feet, they could switch cars again. By then the job would be over. Murphy would be dead. The girl would be dead. Anyone who got in their way would be dead.

That was fine with Book. But in exchange for the concessions the boss made, Book had promised not to kill the client. The more he thought about it, the more he thought that was a mistake.

The client had seen their faces. If he was caught, he would sell them out. So he had to die.

CHAPTER SEVENTY-ONE

He *was lying in his old bed watching Katie sleep. It was dark, but he could see her red hair spilling across the side of her face and the smooth curve of her neck. He could hear the sound of her soft breathing, and his heart swelled. He was home, and somehow he knew everything would be okay.*

A baby was crying. It was coming from Caitlyn's room. He had to go and rock her back to sleep. Maybe she was wet. He started to get up but something wasn't right. She had stopped crying. He felt a chill come over him at the thought of Caitlyn.

His sense of joy quickly became an impending fear of loss, and he felt tears welling into his eyes. Katie stirred and took his hand, pulling him close against her. He instantly felt the cares of the world, and all his fear, melting away. All that mattered was holding her, keeping her close, keeping her safe.

Then he heard loud footsteps. His gun suddenly appeared in his hand and he was moving toward the door when two big men burst into the room. They had guns in their hands and were dressed in dark clothing, their faces hidden behind ski masks.

Katie! The baby! He felt panic rise like bile in his throat as he dove across the bed and rolled Katie onto the floor. He covered her with his body but knew it was futile.

Bullets tore through the mattress, and he heard Katie scream. Bullets struck him like hammer blows in the back and legs. He was going to die. He couldn't save her. Couldn't save the baby.

Katie . . .

Jack woke drenched with sweat, jaw clenched tight, tears in his eyes. He took a deep breath, unclenched his hands, and sat up in bed. His T-shirt was ringed with sweat, his hair damp. Morning sunlight filtered around the sides of the window blinds. He started to get up when he saw Cinderella lying at the bottom of the bed, head down on her paws, her black eyes fixed on his face. A keening sound came from her as if she sensed his nightmare.

Without thinking he reached down to pet the dog.

Cinderella bared her teeth, slipped off the bed, and padded out of the room.

"Ungrateful mutt."

Thirty minutes later, he was dressed, black coffee in hand, and on his way to Liddell's house before he went to work.

He called Garcia, and she assured him she was working on the fingerprints recovered from the murder in New Harmony. She also was keeping an eye on the reports of the Indiana State Police lab.

"Brooke found the owner of the van," she said.

Jack put his cell on speaker phone. "And?"

"It was stolen. But you already knew that," she said. "It was parked at the airport in Terre Haute. The owner flew back in yesterday and thought it had been towed."

"Okay," Jack said.

"Crime scene found bits of flesh in the back cargo area. Brooke is getting a rush on DNA comparison with our victims. And they dug some bullets out of the dash. I've had them check ballistics with the gun you took from Marcie. It's a match."

"Keep that kind of work up, and I'll have to promote you to detective."

"Don't do me any favors," she said, and laughed. They disconnected.

Jack pulled into the drive at Liddell's, waved at the uniformed policeman in a black-and-white parked in front of the house, and called Brooke's cell.

"Where are you?" he asked when she answered.

"Look up."

She was standing in the front door, holding a mug of coffee. Today she was wearing tight-fitting dark blue pants with a short-sleeve see-through light blue top worn over a camisole. She noticed

Jack checking her out, and pointed to her right side to show him she was wearing her weapon.

"What are you doing here?"

"Nice to see you, too. Would you believe I came to see Liddell and wish him a speedy recovery?"

"No," Jack said.

"Okay. I wanted to show the pharmacy film to Marcie. You didn't get around to it last night."

"Yeah, I had some late-night activities."

"Yeah, you did. Too bad you didn't get a better look at the guy you chased."

He shrugged. "Too busy dodging bullets."

She rolled her eyes. "One bullet, Jack. Big deal." Then she smiled, showing she was kidding. "I haven't shown the video to Marcie yet. I was waiting for you."

Marcie came up behind Brooke and said, "He wants you to come in. I have coffee and some cherry turnovers—if you-know-who hasn't eaten them already."

Jack had forgotten to eat breakfast and his stomach was reminding him. He motioned for the ladies to go first and followed them to the kitchen. He was surprised to see Liddell sitting at the table watching a video on a Kindle on the table in front of him.

Jack shot a questioning look at Brooke.

"What? I said I hadn't shown it to Marcie. I didn't say anything about Bigfoot."

"Bigfoot?" Jack asked, and Liddell looked up and smiled.

"I downloaded some of the video to my Kindle," Brooke said.

"Coffee, Jack? Brooke?" Marcie asked.

"Hey, hon, after you get their coffee, I'll take another turnover. Would you warm it for me?" Liddell asked.

Jack turned the Kindle so he could see the screen. "How do you make it start over?" he asked Brooke, and she touched the screen a few times.

Brooke spooned some sugar in her coffee and said, "I was on the phone with the lab before you called," she said. "We have a possible match on the latent fingerprints from the screwdriver and the prints from New Harmony."

As Marcie brought Jack's coffee, he caught her arm and pulled her toward a seat. "Marcie, forget all that. Come here and look at this."

Brooke set up the Kindle for a slide show of the still pictures taken from the video and played this for Marcie first. After viewing a dozen still pictures taken of the men from various angles, Marcie said, "I wish I could help more, but it was dark and they were wearing those things covering their faces. They're dressed the same, but I can't tell anything about their size from these pictures."

Brooke stopped the slide show. "I'm going to show you a video now. I'll shut it off anytime you say, okay, Marcie?"

Marcie took one of Liddell's huge hands in hers, then nodded.

Brooke began the video, and Marcie's hand went to her throat. "Oh! They have guns."

Brooke and Jack traded a look. "Marcie, were they wearing guns that night?"

"I don't know . . . I'm not sure. But I'm so used to seeing guns all the time, I may not have paid much attention. The clothes look the same. The guys are about the same build."

The video played on and Jack thought about the nightmare he'd had this morning. Two big men. Dark clothing that looked like SWAT BDUs. The style was favored by a lot of police organizations, as well as the military, not to mention civilian "military equipment" outlets sold it. There were three stores in Evansville alone, and probably a hundred within a fifty-mile radius.

"Where was this taken?" Marcie asked.

Jack had hoped to spare Marcie, but she had a right to know what she and Liddell were up against. After all, their lives might be on the line. He had already made that mistake with Moira. They would all have around-the-clock police protection now, but they needed to be alert and prepared.

"They shot a pharmacist in New Harmony yesterday," Jack said.

"Was that them?" Marcie asked, and looked closer at the pictures. "I haven't been able to bring myself to watch the news, but I heard the officers out front talking about it when I brought them breakfast."

Liddell gave Jack an angry look. "They just had a shift change," he said. To Marcie he said, "No more going outside alone."

She squeezed his hand and he pulled her close.

"The officers said his wife found him," Marcie said sadly.

Jack put a hand on Brooke's shoulder. For some reason she seemed shaken as well.

"You okay?" he asked.

"Of course I am," she snapped at him. "Sorry," she said, seeing the look on everyone's face. "I was thinking about the case," she said, but Jack could tell she was lying.

"Okay," Jack said at the front door. "I'm going to make sure you have extra security until this is over."

"You don't have to do that, Jack. I've got a gun and the princess warrior," Liddell said, and gave Marcie a squeeze.

"You two get a room," Jack said.

"Exactly what I was thinking," Liddell quipped

Marcie shooed Jack and Brooke out the door and followed them onto the porch. "You two get back to work. We'll be just fine." Marcie pulled Jack to the side. "Are we still in danger?"

"Marcie, you've got a full-grown yeti living in your house. What do you think?"

Marcie turned to Brooke. "Keep Jack out of trouble."

Outside, Jack walked Brooke to her car. She stopped at the trunk and nearly threw her weapon inside.

"Thanks for getting the lab results and stuff so quickly," Jack said.

"A compliment from Jack Murphy," she said, "Wow!"

Unlike the day before, that came out friendly, and Jack grinned. "Don't let it go to your head. It's like a complimentary breakfast at a hotel." She didn't seem to get the comparison, so he explained. "The food is put out there, whether you want it or not. It's nothing personal."

"You're such a romantic, Jack." She remained smiling, as though she had decided overnight that she liked him. "I'll keep checking on the DNA. It takes a little while. But I'm sure your little computer gal has told you all that."

"If Angelina Garcia heard you call her my 'little computer gal,' you would need your gun."

"You're a good friend to the people you trust, aren't you, Jack? I hope at some point during all of this you will realize that I'm not your enemy."

He said nothing. She was right, of course. She hadn't earned his trust yet. But she was making definite inroads.

CHAPTER SEVENTY-TWO

"Clint Hallard," Garcia said over the phone. "H-A-L-L-A-R-D. That's what I got off the prints from the screwdriver, Jack."

"Can we put this out to the troops?" he asked, wondering why Brooke's people hadn't found that.

As she knew very well, he was really asking if she had obtained the information legally. If not, they would need to "discover" the name some other way.

"Yeah, it's clean," she said, and yawned. "It had better be or my contact is in deep doo-doo."

She told Jack about Lucius in the Defense Department. She had emailed him the prints and he had called her back ten minutes ago. When he called he was excited and insisted that she come to his apartment or he wouldn't give up the name. They had quibbled for ten minutes before she was able to negotiate a more open meeting place.

They finally agreed on the Tennessean downtown, and she had paid for and watched him shovel down breakfast before he finally took a napkin and wrote two names on it. Clint Hallard and Trafford Book. That's who the fingerprints matched.

"We might have a picture of his partner, too," she said. "I got a driver's license from Idaho on Clint Hallard, and I just found an Illinois license on Trafford Book. They don't exist in any law enforcement records, and the licenses were issued two years ago."

"Angelina," Jack said. "Before I grow old, please."

"Sorry, Jack. Let me tell it my way, before I forget." And she began with the job description of an Army mechanized infantryman, an MOS of 11 Bravo.

Jack knew basically what the job of an infantryman was, and assumed the mechanized infantryman was one that rode in a tank or other heavily armed vehicle.

"In a nutshell, Clint Hallard was a gunner on a tank in Iraq and later in Afghanistan. He reenlisted twice, both three-year hitches, and moved up a grade in rank. He was an E4, like a corporal in rank, when he left the Army. And there's more." She told him about Clint's friend, Trafford Book.

Book grew up in a Chicago project called Cabrini-Green. He probably learned to fight before he learned his ABCs. Trafford had enlisted during the first push into Iraq and volunteered for an extra hitch to boot. He also served in Afghanistan, where he was promoted to sergeant, and as far as Garcia was able to ascertain, he served at the same times and locations as Clint Hallard. The 1st Battalion, 22nd Infantry redeployed from Iraq to Fort Hood, Texas, in December 2006, and Trafford Book and Clint Hallard ended their service there in June of 2008.

"Both men's records are sealed," she said.

"If the records are sealed, how did your friend get them?"

"My friend is a computer programmer for the DoD. He can basically get into anything he wants. He said their files contained some interesting details, but he couldn't give it to me. He suggested we subpoena their military records, so I need you to call whoever you think will have some pull. Maybe someone in the governor's office can get these guys' records faster and we won't need a subpoena. I have pictures from the driver's licenses, but Lucius hinted that we wouldn't get anywhere. He said, quote, 'These two are ghosts.'"

"I'll call Captain Franklin and ask him to make a call. It will look better coming from someone with higher rank."

"I've got their dates of birth, last known addresses, that kind of stuff off their licenses, but again I don't think the information is any good. No police record, not even a parking ticket, and the military went to great lengths to make these guys invisible. I can't even find birth certificates."

Jack didn't have to ask if she were churning all that info through the system. She was the best intel analyst he'd ever seen. "No one else is to know about this until we have those military records. Okay?"

* * *

They now had pictures and names to go with the fingerprints. With any luck, they would soon have the killers. He didn't think they would leave because their job wasn't finished. Moira was still alive.

The attack on Liddell was planned and executed like a military maneuver, and was successful because they had taken the flash drive. Attacking a cop was a risky move, but exactly the type of boldness you would expect from a soldier.

They had been expecting to find Moira in the basement of the Civic Center, alone, defenseless. It explained their hasty retreat when Jack showed up. The fact that they brought guns told Jack that they intended to kill her. The only reason she would be a threat was because she had seen the flash drive. But then, so had Jack. *They were eliminating anyone with connection to that thing.*

He dialed a number. "Garcia got the names of the killers, Captain," he said. He then passed on the names of the two killers that Garcia had sent to his phone. He ended with, "And I think this should stay between you, me, and the chief for the time being."

Franklin didn't ask why. That wasn't good. "What is it, Captain?"

"Chief Pope was just in my office. He is going to summon Garcia. He said she had been making some unusual inquiries, and he suspected she was committing computer crimes. Something about hacking a secure military database. Since I'm her direct supervisor, he told me as a courtesy."

"What!" Jack said. "How did he find that out?"

"I don't know," Franklin answered.

Jack couldn't believe this. Garcia had said that her friend at the Defense Department had just called her ten minutes ago.

"I'm going to see the chief myself," Jack said. "Garcia has just helped crack this case wide open."

Jack hurried toward the chief's complex, hoping he hadn't done something stupid, like firing Garcia. As he passed into the chief's outer office, the secretary, Jennifer Mangold, said, "He's expecting you."

He knocked on the chief's door, trying not to make too much thunder, even though he was incensed.

"Come in," said the harried voice.

Jack did, but he remained near the door. He didn't plan on staying. "What's this I hear about Garcia?"

Pope looked tired. "Homeland Security is investigating her. I had to send Garcia home, and quite frankly, that may be the best place for her right now. I don't think I can help her if the Feds file charges against her."

Pope shook his head wearily and looked up at the ceiling, as if for divine help.

"She got the information on my orders, chief," Jack said. "I guess they'll have to charge me along with her if it comes to that. But I think I know a way to fix all this."

Pope looked dismayed at the challenge in Jack's voice. "You don't want me to break into the Pentagon?"

Jack asked, "Do you still have an in with Senator Lugar?"

"Yes."

"Care to take a walk?"

CHAPTER SEVENTY-THREE

Senator Lugar's office was located inside the Federal Building, directly across the street from the police station. While they walked, Pope filled Jack in on the situation with Garcia.

"Army CID discovered that someone had retrieved sensitive information from their secure computer databases. The information was traced to one of their senior analysts, who then gave up Garcia. The information she obtained required a top-secret security clearance, and the Army was curious why one of our civilian employees would want it."

Jack couldn't believe their bad luck.

"Wait, it gets worse. Homeland Security is involved. These killers are soldiers who were involved in some sensitive missions. The Army doesn't like the idea of the public seeing them as anything but decorated soldiers. It wouldn't improve public perception to see that two of the Army's finest have turned mercenary and are killing American citizens."

"So what exactly is Garcia's status?" Jack asked.

"I told her she wasn't fired, or suspended. She's going to work out of Liddell's house. That partner of yours has been making a pest of himself with Captain Franklin. This way he'll be involved, but we can keep him safe." Pope sighed. "If you and your team keep going on this way, we'll have to open a substation just to keep you out of sight."

Jack and Chief Pope entered the Winfield K. Denton Federal Building and passed through the metal detectors. They took the elevator to the third floor, where a fashionably dressed secretary took their names and disappeared into the senator's office. She came back and said, "You can go in now."

* * *

The visit to the senator's office resulted in unexpected benefits. With one phone call the senior senator from Indiana took care of Garcia's worries about being prosecuted by the federal government. Jack, who had total disdain for politicians, couldn't help but be impressed with Senator Dick Lugar.

With the requested documents and photos in hand, Jack left the chief of police in the senator's office. As he walked back across the street, he dug his cell phone out of his pocket and called Garcia.

"Am I fired?" she asked, answering her phone.

"I don't want you to come back to the office until this is over. You're safer there with Bigfoot," Jack said. "Also, I found out who ratted you out."

"I know," she said. "It was my friend Lucius. He called to say he was sorry that he gave me up. The files he accessed were classified material that Homeland Security had flagged. He said they came down on his apartment like a SWAT team and threatened to rain hell down on him if he didn't tell what he did with the information. Scared him half to death. I'm sorry for all the trouble, Jack."

"Not your fault." Yet all the while he was thinking that he had seen nothing in the copy of the files he was holding to merit that type of response by the Department of Defense. Maybe Chief Pope was right. Maybe the Army didn't want to be embarrassed? Or maybe something more sinister was at play here.

As he headed for the back entrance to the police station, he flipped through Clint Hallard's file. His military folder was pretty thin for someone who had been in the Army for six years. The initial term of service was three years, and he had reenlisted for three years. There was no record of any psychological testing, or even a debriefing before he left the service. He was decorated twice, but there was no mention of what he did to earn the decorations. *Is that it?*

He considered going back to ask the senator for another look. But his father always told him, "Never look a gift horse in the mouth." Jack assumed that meant because the horse might bite your fool head off.

Back in his office, he meticulously combed through the two ex-soldiers' files. He didn't find any more than he had gleaned while crossing the street. The folder jackets were thin to begin with, and the information contained in them even thinner. He guessed that any sensitive material had been taken out.

Jack just hoped that whatever they had deleted from those files didn't cause another innocent person to die.

CHAPTER SEVENTY-FOUR

Garcia had created a flyer of sorts that was being handed out or emailed to every law enforcement agency, every coffee shop, hotel, motel, flophouse, or B and B within a hundred miles of Evansville. The banks would get the flyer, too, plus photos that they could put into their state-of-the-art facial recognition systems. The hospitals and the airport had the same video security system.

By the time Garcia was done, Clint Hallard and Trafford Book wouldn't be able to rent a room, or even buy a hamburger, without someone pointing them out. At least, that was the idea.

The drawback was that once the killers' identities were released to the public, the two men would run. That was good for Evansville, bad for anyone who confronted them on their way out. Still, it would allow them to take the killers down at a place and time chosen by law enforcement.

Jack sat at the kitchen table, where Liddell and Garcia had set up a temporary office, and studied glossy five-by-seven photos of the men who had killed at least four women and a man, *and* almost beat Liddell to death, *and* had gone after Moira.

He had read the job descriptions for each of the men's military service, and if the records were accurate, Trafford Book was the leader, Clint Hallard the grunt. Hallard seemed to go along with whatever Book did. Book had turned down promotion twice. He'd also turned down Officer Candidate School. Jack thought it was because Book liked what he was doing.

Jack had never tested for promotion for the same reason. If he was a sergeant, he would have to stop being a street detective. He believed in the saying among the troops, "For each promotion you get, they suck eight percent of your brain out."

But there were exceptions, like Charles Franklin, Marlin Pope, and some others. Jack often wondered how they had resisted the zombie mind-suck.

He put that thought aside as his attention returned to the photos. The reason he didn't want to be promoted was because he liked catching criminals. The reason this Trafford Book hadn't wanted promotion? If his killing spree was any indication, he must have developed his lethal tastes overseas.

CHAPTER SEVENTY-FIVE

A police cruiser was parked just outside Harwood School's sixth-grade classroom. Katie pulled the blinds to keep the children from gaping out the window, but one of the officers, a big burly guy whose name tag read Bolin, came to her classroom and advised her—per Jack's orders—that "if they didn't keep her in view, Jack would hunt them down and kill them." Officer Bolin asked politely that she leave the blinds open and that she not leave without letting them follow her home. He handed her a card with both officers' cell phone numbers on it.

She couldn't help but smile as she opened the blinds. She wondered how Moira was making out. For some reason Moira didn't understand the danger was real, even after last night's narrow escape. But Katie knew different. She had witnessed mayhem firsthand.

Eric had assured her he would keep an eye on Moira at work, but, no reflection on Eric, she would feel better knowing Jack was involved. She hesitated a moment and then took her cell phone from her purse, slipped into the hallway, and punched in Jack's number.

"Sorry for any embarrassment," Jack said, guessing why Katie was calling. He was sitting in his office, lights out, waiting for something to happen. Katie's call wasn't unexpected. It had a feeling of déjà vu. The people he loved were put in harm's way because of his job—because of him.

He knew Murphy's Law: Anything that can go wrong will go wrong. He preferred his own law: If someone threatens your family or friends, you take them apart.

"Are you okay? How's Liddell?" Katie asked.

Jack was grateful that Katie's voice carried none of the deep concern he heard the night Liddell was hurt. She was a strong woman in many ways. *But, then, she's had to put up with me.*

"Garcia got into trouble getting the killers' names for me," he told her. "But Chief Pope sent her to Liddell's house to work on the case. He thought it would be therapy for Bigfoot and keep Garcia out of the path of any hard-charging Feds."

"Is Liddell up to it? I mean, he just got home yesterday morning."

"The captain said Liddell was calling for updates every five minutes." They shared a chuckle at that. "So yeah, he's good. He wants to come back to work, but I think he should stay home with Marcie for a while."

"Stay out of your way, you mean," Katie said. "You've got something, don't you, Jack? Will this be over soon?"

"I know who they are. It's just a matter of time now," he said, then decided to get off the subject. Katie knew him too well and she knew he liked to work alone when the hunt was on.

"I'm glad you called, Katie. Listen, I talked to Marcie and she wants you to stay over there for a while," Jack said, although he was sure Katie would refuse, and he hadn't asked Marcie yet.

"What about Moira?"

Jack was surprised Katie would even considering going, so he forged ahead. "I'm going to babysit Moira, and officers are already assigned to Liddell's house. If you want to pick up some things after work, the officers outside the school will accompany you home and then take you to Bigfoot's. Marcie could use the support."

"Actually, I was calling you about Moira," Katie admitted. "I wanted to ask you to keep an eye on her, so if it would make it easier on you for me to go to Marcie's, then I'll do what you ask."

Jack hesitated telling her the rest of his concern, but he had already made a mistake by not considering Moira a target, so . . .

"Katie, have you heard from Eric?"

"Not since we were at the restaurant," she said. "Why?"

"I'm going to ask you something that you won't like, but believe me, it really is for your own good."

"What is it, Jack?" she asked, concern creeping back into her voice.

"Can you avoid him?" Jack asked, and hurriedly added, "Just for a little while?"

Her answer came quickly, surprising him. "I don't think that's a problem," she said. "I've seen little to nothing of him since this began. He's like you."

Jack didn't think that he and Eric were anything alike, but he felt a sense of relief mixed with a small measure of guilt that Eric was probably right about Jack bringing problems to everyone around him. But the important thing was Katie would be safe.

"I promise to explain later, okay?" he asked.

CHAPTER SEVENTY-SIX

Moira was safe in her office during working hours, and Jack would take over after work. She was the bait in the trap. He didn't like to think of it that way, but she had insisted on going into the office.

He gave photos of the killers to Civic Center security, and the Sheriff's deputies working the metal detector, and last year the city had installed a new camera system that included facial recognition. *Nothing is too expensive to safeguard our mayor.*

The expensive camera systems had done their job the night Jack and Moira did their little dance with the killers. Unfortunately, the cameras captured photos of black-clad figures wearing balaclavas over their entire heads. At least they were able to verify that there were two intruders, both men by their size and muscle mass, and to follow most of their movements after they entered the building. Jack had watched the film several times, and each time the purposeful movement of each man struck him. Without any words being spoken, they moved with military precision toward the room where they thought Moira was. *If Nova hadn't picked that exact moment to exit with the cart? If Jack hadn't picked the exact time to enter the Civic Center looking for Moira?*

Captain Franklin had posted two plainclothes officers near the exits from the prosecutors' offices, so Moira couldn't even sneak out for a smoke without being watched. He had talked to the plainclothes and asked them to watch Eric as well, and write down when he came and went. They didn't even ask why.

By five o'clock, it appeared Jack had overreacted. The killers had probably run. They had made no further attempts on Moira or Liddell overnight and thankfully committed no new killings.

Brooke took a batch of flyers from Garcia and Liddell and distributed them throughout her own network, and had given them to the FBI, who promised to interview the suspects' friends and family for background information. Short of a house-to-house search within a hundred-mile radius of Evansville, there was nothing else to be done.

So he sat, staring at his phone, willing it to ring. Someone would call with information that would bring this drama to a close. But, of course, that didn't happen. Instead, a familiar redhead peeped around his door.

"Moira," Jack said. "Heading home?"

She shook her head. "I owe you a dinner." She came in and sat on the edge of his desk. "I owe you a bunch of dinners, in fact. Trent told me I could leave."

"And you shall pay dearly. Trust me," Jack said, and smiled. He noticed her pulling a long face at the sight of Liddell's empty desk and said, "He's fine. He's probably eating a whole roast pig and washing it down with a gallon of BBQ sauce."

"I feel kind of responsible for him getting hurt."

"Listen to me, Moira, he didn't get attacked because of you."

Her expression said she thought differently. She picked up the two pictures Jack had lying on the desk in front of him. "Are these the guys?"

He wanted to make sure she understood the boundaries. "Not your problem. Okay?"

"I got it. I got it."

"I'm serious, Moira. You stay out of this! These guys aren't messing around."

She protested, "But I can help, Jack. I don't have to go after them with a gun. I want to go after them with the law."

Trying to peacefully arrest these two would be like taking a prayer book to the O.K. Corral. Clint Hallard and Trafford Book weren't worried about the law. And now Jack wasn't either.

"How about dinner?" he asked.

She cocked her head at him, considering, and said, "Walk me to my office and I'll close up for the day."

Moira's shadow was a detective named Brad Evrard, who resembled a young Brad Pitt, and he was none too pleased with Jack saying that he was relieved for the rest of the day. Not that Jack could blame the man. Moira was an attractive young woman and they were about the same age.

"Them's the breaks, dude."

"I have to show you something before we go," Moira said.

"As long as it has nothing to do with these killers, I'll look," he said firmly. "You are hereby ordered to cease and desist your meddling."

As they walked past the police records room and turned left into the narrow passage that led into the Civic Center, Moira glanced back at Evrard and remarked, "He was kind of cute."

"I don't know what you're talking about."

"The guy you put at the other end of the hall is old and grumpy," she added.

Busted.

When they neared the elevators, Jack couldn't help but think that he'd walked through here hundreds, maybe thousands of times before, but it would never feel the same. Last night the doors and hallways were pitch-black as he'd pushed Moira toward the police station, the whole time feeling like a duck in a shooting gallery, expecting to be gunned down at any moment. He wondered how Moira was coping with the near-death experience.

"How are you doing?" he asked, draping an arm around her shoulders. She was taller than her sister, by several inches, but she was much thinner than he remembered.

"You were the one who got shot at," she pointed out. "How you doin'?" she asked, mimicking a wiseguy.

Jack bent his right arm up and made a muscle. "Hard as steel, twice as strong," he said, and got a giggle from her.

They didn't speak as they were frisked and wanded at the security checkpoint, but once they had retrieved their pocket change, the deputy gave Jack his weapon back. "You might need it," the deputy said, and buzzed them through the door.

"They changed security measures," Moira commented, and they were buzzed through another door into the foyer of the prosecutors' offices. Jack nodded a greeting at the secretary that had buzzed them in, and then they were headed toward Moira's office.

"What are you doing here, Jack? Coming to see me?" Eric Manson was standing in the doorway of one of the conference rooms.

He pulled the door shut behind him, but not before Jack spotted Trent, Bob Rothschild, and Brooke Wethington inside.

"Is Brooke tattling on me?" Jack wanted to ask. Yet he maintained an easy attitude. "Thought I'd take Moira to eat. Someplace nice. Someplace very public."

He looked Eric over closely. The man's color wasn't good and dark rings spread under his eyes.

"Good work, by the way," Eric said, but his stiff expression belied his words. "At least we know the who, just not the why."

"Well, they obviously hate women attorneys," Moira offered.

Eric scoffed, and seeing that she was not joking, he said, "I think it's more than that, Moira."

"Would you and Katie care to join us, Eric?" Jack asked, and not just to be polite. He wondered how Katie had left things with Eric.

"No offense, Jack. But I think it would be better for Katie to keep her distance from all of this."

Jack could take offense, but in this case, Eric was right. The security detail that was watching Katie was the best. And Jack had inside knowledge that she would be keeping clear of Eric. He had asked the officers to call him if Eric came near her.

"How is Katie holding up?" Jack asked.

"To be honest, she's ready for this to be over."

"I promise you, Eric, it *will* be over soon."

Eric shoved his hands in his pockets, but not before Jack saw the fingers curl into fists. He was about to reply when Trent opened the door and stepped into the hallway.

"Eric, can you take over the meeting? I need to talk to Jack alone for a minute."

Eric was relieved. "Sure thing, Trent. He's all yours."

"My office?" Trent asked.

"I'll only be a minute, Moira," Jack promised. "Why don't you wait in your office? I won't leave without you."

"I'm starving," Moira said, and tugged on Jack's arm. "Don't be too long."

Trent led the way into his office and took a seat behind his desk. "Shut the door so we can talk," he said.

Jack complied, though he remained standing.

Trent announced, "I wanted to clear something up, and I hope you'll keep what I tell you between us."

Jack nodded, and Trent put his hands on top of his desk in an open gesture. "I know all about the argument between Nina and Bob Rothschild a few days before her death."

Jack had been expecting this, but not an admission to the argument. He thought someone would conveniently show up as a witness that the argument never happened or that it was nothing important. He said nothing, waiting to see where Trent was going with this.

"None of us wanted to disparage Nina's reputation. She was a fine attorney. One of the best. But, to put it bluntly, she could be a real bitch."

Jack was taken aback. He didn't know Trent even knew the word *bitch,* much less utter it. "What was the argument about?"

Trent was in his deal-cutting element. "This is where I need your discretion. It would serve no purpose for this to come out. It would only make people think poorly of Nina."

Jack wanted to be the judge of that, so he merely nodded.

"She was leaking information to my competitor."

He said this as if she had been solely responsible for the genocide of the Jews.

Jack's bullshit alarm was going off. "How?" he asked simply.

Trent seemed to have anticipated this question and answered much too quickly.

"I'm not sure exactly how she did it, but it was happening frequently and Bob set up a sting and caught her. That's why he confronted her. It was a poor judgment call on his part to confront her outside in public, but it was unavoidable."

"And you know all of this how?" Jack's bullshit detector needle was now buried in the red. If he said Bob was his only source, Jack would be tempted to yank Bob out of the meeting down the hall and grill him.

"I spoke directly to Nina," Trent said, getting Jack's full attention.

"Go on," Jack said.

Trent recounted Bob's involvement and then his own. He said that Nina was sharing campaign manager duties with Bob, and things went fine for a month. Then private tidbits—things that he'd only discussed with Nina and Bob—began being released to the press by

Jon Parkhurst, his competitor. He trusted Bob implicitly, but Nina was a question mark. Trent had put her on the campaign only because she had pestered him incessantly.

"She was very helpful, at first," Trent said, "but then I shared some information with her and Bob in a closed-door meeting. The next thing we knew Parkhurst planned to release the information. It was a lie, and he finally caught it and stopped its release to the press."

Trent sat back in the chair and smirked. "He even had the gall to call *me* and ask what I thought I was up to. Can you imagine?"

Jack made a show of shaking his head in agreement, but was wondering if Trent knew how bad all this looked for him. *How convenient for you, Trent. Nina was out to destroy you and she is suddenly killed and dismembered.*

"I only have one question, Trent. What do you know of the exchange between Bob and Nina? Can you tell me what was said?"

Trent looked incredulous, so Jack rephrased that. "Not the exact words. But did Bob or Nina tell you what was said, in general?"

Trent locked eyes with Jack, and his face displayed an earnest look. "Bob said he told her he knew she was the leak. She denied it and then said she was going to the media with her lies to ruin my chances at becoming governor. Bob thought she had been promised a job with the governor's office if Parkhurst won the election."

"What about Nina?"

Trent again showed his discomfort, presumably of speaking ill of the dead. "She was such a disappointment to me. She said Bob had threatened to ruin her career. She said he told her, 'Your life is over. You're dead.' But I assure you, Jack, he was just angry over her betrayal. Those two guys, Hallard and Book, are your guys. Let it end there. You're a great detective, Jack. And I apologize for my calling the state police, but I was truly trying to help. I feel like a foolish old man now."

Jack had one more question. "What lies was Nina going to tell?"

Trent seemed to catch his breath but recovered like a pro. "You know I can't tell you that, Jack. Trust me, they didn't have any substance, or anything to do with her murder. She was just in the wrong place at the wrong time."

That bland sentiment set Jack to thinking. Nina wasn't in the wrong place at the wrong time. She was in her house. Alaina Kusta was shopping. Hope Dupree was in Illinois. Sammi Steele was trolling an alley. All these murders seemingly unrelated. The only ones who knew why they died were the victims. He knew he couldn't let all the burden of guilt rest with Hallard and Book. What was it that Garcia said? "They are invisible." They had no motive. They came from nowhere. This case smelled of mercenaries. He wondered if he was focusing on this case in the wrong fashion. Maybe the murders had nothing to do with each other. Maybe only one of the murders was the crux.

When Jack's meeting with Trent ended, he found a seat in Moira's office, which wasn't easy, since every flat surface, including some of the floor space, was still covered with file folders. Jack noticed a tall stack of files in the center of her desk. The dates on the folders were over twenty years old. He intuited that these were the cases that Moira had retrieved from the basement last night. They didn't look like anything to risk a life for. If Eric was so keen on getting them, why were they still stacked on Moira's desk?

"I don't trust him, Jack!" Moira whispered, and shut the door. "I've combed through this stuff all day, and it is all unrelated. They have nothing in common to serve as research value. But I think I found something interesting."

CHAPTER SEVENTY-SEVEN

In Afghanistan, he and Book had holed up in a burned-out building for two days. The bullet-riddled bodies of seven U.S. soldiers were spread around them like puppets with their strings cut. Nine men had gone on this operation. He and Book were the only two who stayed alive.

He hoped he was up to the task tonight. His whole body hurt like hell. He couldn't even lean over to tie his bootlaces. But he was a soldier. Book needed him. He wouldn't complain.

Clint slid on a Kevlar vest and cinched the Velcro straps tight at the waist and chest. The pressure on his ribs hurt and felt good at the same time. He had dressed in black BDU pants, with a T-shirt under the vest. He pulled a loose-fitting Under Armor shirt over it all and the layering of shirts hid the vest well.

Book pulled a Pelican hard-sided case from under the bed, dropped it on the mattress, and flicked the locks open. Nestled inside was a MP5SFA3 semiautomatic carbine made by German firearm manufacturer Heckler & Koch. The assault rifle was equipped with a hundred-round drum-type magazine, an under-barrel flashlight, holographic sights, and was capable of expending eight hundred rounds per minute. On full auto it was accurate to fifty yards.

"Same as the Navy SEALs carry," Book said, admiring the weapon. "Full auto, extra drums of ammo. We got us some kick-ass toys, bro."

"Some broad starts shooting this time, I'm turning her into Swiss cheese," Clint said. The hole in his leg had stopped bleeding, but he still felt hot, feverish, like he had the flu.

Book pulled another smaller case from under the bed. "You get the UMP, buddy," he said, lifting the shorter submachine gun from the case. "Twenty-five round clip." He slammed a loaded clip home.

"Selector switch for full auto or single fire. Loaded with forty-five-caliber Hydra-Shok ammo."

Clint's weapon weighed half of what Book's did, but both weapons were capable of firing several hundred subsonic rounds a minute.

"You know, I can make this last run alone," Book said.

Clint seated a round in the breach of his submachine gun, and said, "*Guns* don't kill people. *Loaded guns* kill people," and they both laughed. They were born for this.

Book zipped open a nylon messenger bag, put extra ammo for both weapons inside, and slung it crossways around his neck. He slid a pair of dark sunglasses on and gave Clint a deadly look, saying, "I'll be back."

"Arnold wasn't no black dude, Book," Clint pointed out.

"He should have been, man. It would have been more realistic. Besides, I'm better looking, better built, and indestructible."

They carried their gear and weapons to the truck. Book stood his rifle against the bench seat between him and Clint with the barrel pointed to the ceiling. Clint's lay across his lap.

Book leaned down, twisted some wires together under the dash, and the engine started. He looked across at Clint. "We're gonna have some fun tonight."

Clint couldn't agree more. It was definitely time for some payback.

CHAPTER SEVENTY-EIGHT

Moira's stomach grumbled, but first she had to show Jack what she found.

"Pull a chair around here," she said. "I did some digging in NCIC—"

"Wait a minute," Jack interrupted. "You got into the FBI database?" The FBI jealously guarded NCIC, or National Crime Information Center. Anyone logging into that computer system had to take a class, pass a test, be certified that they worked for the justice system, and then the computer they used had to be in a secure location and approved by NCIC.

"Moira, you've been here a week. How on earth did you get permission to log into a federal database?"

"I tried to log in with my username and password, but it rejected me. So I found Nina's username and password in her desk and used her login."

Jack couldn't believe what he was hearing. If NCIC found out Moira had used a dead woman's information to gain access, they would shit a brick. Maybe even take the system privileges from the entire prosecutor's office. Or file charges of computer tampering. He had just gotten Garcia out of trouble for the same thing, and now Moira might be in deep shit.

"You taught me that it's better to ask forgiveness than permission. Isn't that right?"

Jack kept his voice level. "Get approved. And don't use it again until you do."

She promised, but he knew she didn't mean it.

"Can I finish now?" she asked, and Jack nodded.

"NCIC didn't have a lot to connect these cases. Or IDACS."

Jack raised his eyebrows. IDACS was another system she should not be able to access. But what the hell. He let her go on.

"So I used her login to get into her personal drive on the office computer," she said. "And guess what I found?" She waited for Jack to ask, but he didn't. "I found this," she said, and handed Jack a stack of paper. She pulled the last page from the stack and said, "She kept a work diary of sorts on her hard drive. Read this one first."

Jack read the journal entry, and then read it again.

"Is this what I think it is?" he asked.

Jack had lied to Eric about taking Moira to a fancy restaurant. Fake left, run right. He and Moira were headed for Two Jakes.

Nina had kept a journal on her computer, going back to the day she started work with the prosecutor's office in Evansville. The entries were dated, and while some went on for pages, some were only two or three sentences. Moira had printed off twenty pages of the last entries and Jack read all of it before they left. Although she didn't name anyone, the entries matched what Nina's neighbor told him about the man who had visited Nina late at night and had then stopped coming around.

Nina Parsons was seeing someone from the prosecutor's office. It had started four months ago, ended a month ago, and the last entry in the journal was bone-chilling.

> *I thought Hope was just another junky out to smear some-one she blamed for her bad life choices. But the more she talked, the more things she told me, about him, about her . . . I knew she was telling the truth.*
>
> *I had suspected as much, but after talking to Hope I knew how corrupt and degenerate he was. Hope wasn't the only one he had used. There were many others known only by street names or first names. Like her, they had all been in trouble with the law. They had all been offered a way out of their conviction of a felony. They had all been given confiden-tial informant status in exchange for sexual favors. He's a pig. And a liar of the worst sort.*
>
> *Going through the files, I found eleven of the women Hope named, and there were twice that many when I searched the archives. Hope said she told him she was pregnant in an at-*

tempt to get money, but she wasn't. He must have believed her lie because he offered to pay for the abortion and then laughed when she said she wanted to keep it. Her behavior doesn't excuse his.

The sight of him sickens me now. Each time I see him at work I'm reminded of what he did to them. Did to me. And to think, I fell for his charm, listened to and believed his lies—let him have me. In a way, I guess, I'll be his last.

The journal ended. Nina didn't explain what she had meant by "I'll be his last." None of the entries named anyone, but the remark "They had all been in trouble with the law" alluded to the list of names on the flash drive. The perpetrator was someone Nina had daily contact with. Another deputy prosecutor? Or maybe a defense attorney, or even a judge. But the journal entry pointed to the reason for Nina's death. She knew too much. She had made a lot of connections. And she was going to do something to right what she saw as a wrong. She was killed to shut her up, and Hope Dupree was killed because she had told Nina. But who would know that?

"Who do you think Nina was talking about?" Moira asked.

Jack was watching the windswept stalks of corn passing by the window, swaying to music that only nature could hear. He was thinking that the computer entry could be challenged in court even if Nina had named her late-night suitor. Maybe the journal would continue with "Tonight I'll see Eric," or maybe it would say, "Tonight I'll wash my hair and read a book." It didn't matter now.

He decided not to answer her question. He had promised Katie that he would protect Moira.

"Honestly, I don't know," he said, and pulled back on the river road.

Eric had lied about knowing Hope Dupree. He lied about how he entered Nina Parsons's house, and how he knew the key was in a magnetic box hidden on top of her porch light. He gave up the key because he thought the old neighbor woman had seen him. Eric drove a dark sedan, like the one the neighbor saw visiting Nina's for several months, and then the visits ended about a month ago. According to Moira, that was about when Eric had proposed to Katie. His fingerprints were found on the outside and inside of the front doorknob at Nina's, but those were conveniently explained away by his being called by Trent, who was called by Cindy McCoy, and all this verified by the three of them. Jack had nothing on Eric except a gut feeling that he was guilty of something.

Maybe Eric was trying to protect his reputation by all the lies he had told. He was going to be Trent's successor and it wouldn't look good if he was tied to a murder victim. But it was Eric's reputation that had fueled Jack's suspicion in the first place. In any case, Eric was a womanizer, and he definitely wasn't husband material for Katie. But was he a stone-cold killer, or maybe had hired these guys?

And then there was Eric's alibi. During the time that Alaina Kusta was killed, Eric was schmoozing some big money people in a campaign meeting at the Convention Center. Jack had checked with a friend who also attended. And he definitely wasn't one of the men on the video from New Harmony or the one from the Civic Center. But he could be pulling their strings.

And then there's Trent's running for governor and Eric moving into the post vacated by Trent. If some impropriety, or, given Eric's past affairs with ladies in his last job, if there were some sexual connotation made with all the cases on Nina's flash drive, it would sink any election chance either man had.

Alaina Kusta, Dick Longest, or Samantha Steele weren't connected in any way to the list of cases on the flash drive. Hope Dupree's pimp, Dick Longest, might have been collateral damage, but the dancer, Samantha Steele, or the civil attorney, Alaina Kusta . . . what could they have done to put them in the killers' sights? Were they collateral damage as well?

Eric had lied to Moira the night she was targeted in the Civic Center. He was the one who gave her the assignment in the basement that kept her working late in the evening. And he had lied to her about telling Jack that she wouldn't be able to meet for dinner. Instead, Eric had taken Katie out to eat. If Moira had been killed, who would know that he lied?

In any case, Eric couldn't afford to have Moira snooping around anymore. If Eric was behind the killings, and he found out Moira had picked up where Nina left off, then he would have no choice but to put Moira on their "still-to-do list."

"Come on, Jack," Moira protested. "What are you thinking?"

"I'm thinking I'm hungry and you're buying."

"Besides that, I mean. Do you think these two ex-military types are carrying out contract killings for someone in the prosecutor's office? I can't put it all together. Help me out."

"I think you're on to something," Jack said. "Trent and Eric are the killers. They beat Liddell up and robbed the pharmacy in New Harmony, and they tried to kill us last night. Marcie shot one of them, probably Trent. Good job, Moira."

Moira twisted in her seat and gave him an incredulous look. "I don't know why I bother talking to you. You haven't heard a word I've said. The flash drive is the clue. Who had a reason to obtain it? And Nina's journal. How do you explain that?"

She was silent and pouting, and Jack was sorry he couldn't discuss the case with her. But it was for her own good, and besides, who would believe that the two top guys in the prosecutor's office were involved in all of these murders?

They drove on in silence.

"Are we going to Two Jakes?" Moira asked.

"Not anymore. I've got a better place in mind," he said.

CHAPTER SEVENTY-NINE

"Perfect," Jack said.

Moira had insisted on cooking, so he had let her put the frozen pizza in the oven. They sat at the kitchen table, where he could keep an eye on the front and back doors. Cinderella had stationed herself near the table, one ear up, the other down, keeping a close eye on the pizza and licking her chops with anticipation.

"Katie told me you had a dog," Moira said around a mouthful of crust.

"That's going a bit far, calling the mutt a dog," Jack said, and tossed a small bit of pizza toward the dog. Cinderella snapped it up midair and inhaled it.

"Poor baby," Moira said, making sad eyes at Cinderella. The dog responded by coming to Moira, sitting up on her haunches, and putting a paw up to shake.

"Oh, please!" Jack said, but he was smiling. He had never seen her do that trick before. In fact, he had never seen her do any trick, unless he considered peeing in his shoes a trick.

"You're a good dog, aren't you, Cinderella?" Moira said in baby talk.

"Don't encourage her, Moira. She already thinks she's a princess. Did I tell you what she does to my . . . ?"

"C'mon, Jack. I'm eating," Moira said, cutting him off.

She tore a big chunk of pizza off for her new friend, and continued the cooing baby talk.

Jack's mind disengaged from the bonding between ex-sister-in-law and dog, and went to work on their present situation. Police cruisers with two officers were stationed at Katie's and Liddell's.

He was guarding Moira, and no one knew where they had gone. He'd lied to Eric about his intention to take Moira somewhere very public for dinner. Unless these guys were clairvoyant, it was all good.

But just in case, his Mossberg riot shotgun leaned against the side of the table near the wall. He had cut the barrel down to an illegal length, and cut the stock off to a pistol grip. Then he took the wooden pin out of the ammunition feeder tube so it would hold six magnum loads instead of three. The magnum shells were loaded with extra powder and double-aught buck, and would take a door off its hinges at a distance of six feet. He hoped it would stop the man mountain, Trafford Book.

The other one, Clint Hallard, was also huge. If he was right in his assessment of the evidence, Clint was injured bad enough that he might be out of the fight. But Jack never underestimated an enemy.

"Penny for your thoughts," Moira said.

Jack saw Cinderella cleaning pizza sauce from her fingers and licking her arms and face.

Jack cocked an eyebrow, and said, "Do you know where that tongue has been?"

When Moira looked at her hands, he laughed, and said, "I'm fresh out of holy water."

"No wonder she doesn't like you," Moira said, and went to the sink to wash. Cinderella followed her, but suddenly the dog's head jerked up and she ran to the front door. She muzzled the door, sniffing, and then backed away, head down, body tensed, and began growling menacingly.

Moira looked out the kitchen window. "Your neighbors are coming."

Jack jumped up, knocking the table out of the way, and lunged for the kitchen light switch. He grabbed the shotgun and yelled at Moira, "Get over here!"

Moira seemed to be frozen in indecision. Jack grabbed her around the waist and began dragging her to the back door.

"We have to go." He hoped the killers wouldn't expect them to abandon the cabin.

"Stay down and stay with me," Jack said. When he cracked the back door open to see if there was someone covering the back, Cinderella pushed through and rushed outside. He could hear her barking. She was going toward the front of the cabin.

"Stay right behind me," he said, and put Moira's hand against his belt. She grabbed on and he dragged her through the door, off the steps, and toward his Jeep. He heard a gunshot, a yelp, and the barking ceased. There was nothing they could do but run. He pulled Moira past the Crown Vic and then between it and his Jeep.

It was the fourth night of the full moon. Clouds blocked most of the light, and Jack was glad for the darkness. He whispered in Moira's ear. "When I open the door, you to jump across to the passenger side and pull your legs in. I'll be right behind you. Okay?"

He yanked the door hard and she dove across the seats. Jack jumped in and he had started the Jeep when the roof and hood popped, and the driver's side window exploded inward. He felt a dozen bee stings on the side of his face and neck. He yanked the transmission into drive, and the passenger side window exploded. Gravel plumed behind the Jeep as it shot forward. The sudden acceleration slammed his door shut with a bang. The front wheels hit something and as the Jeep bounced in the air, the back windshield imploded peppering them both with glass shrapnel.

He shifted into four-wheel drive. The tires found purchase and Jack's teeth cracked together as the rear tires bounded over something. Another hail of bullets struck the Jeep. This time they tore through the cab, and struck the dash and steering wheel.

"Get my phone," he yelled, but Moira didn't react. "My phone. In my pocket," he yelled. She still didn't move. He risked a glance at her and saw her left hand against her face, with blood seeping between her fingers in a steady stream.

The Jeep slewed off the gravel road and tore across the farm field, blinding him with cornstalks battering the windshield. He yanked the wheel hard to the left and bounced up onto the gravel again, fishtailing down the drive, all the while bullets were striking the back of the Jeep and the gravel around them, flying up in miniexplosions of rock. He switched on his headlights and spied the blacktop of the main road up ahead. He slid around a curve and onto the blacktop heading west. The firing stopped.

Jack shifted the Jeep out of four-wheel drive, and slowed to check Moira's condition. She was dazed and cradling the left side of her jaw with a bloody hand. He pulled her hand away from her face and saw that something had cut a trench across her jawline. The bone wasn't exposed, and she didn't appear to be hit anywhere else. It was nasty, but she'd live.

"Keep pressure on it," he said, speeding up to negotiate a sharp turn. Moira wasn't screaming. She wasn't moving. She sat up straight and stared ahead. He had to get her to a hospital before she went completely into shock.

He hit Lynn Road too fast and bounced up the small incline, the front end of the Jeep came down hard, knocking them around. He cut the wheel sharply to the left, and headed toward Highway 41. Another mile and there would be traffic, maybe even a state trooper patrolling the highway. He began to regret his decision to bring Moira with him, knowing he could have easily left her someplace surrounded by policemen, but he had promised Katie that he would see to her.

He began to think they would make it to Highway 41 and safety when he was slammed back against the seat by a vicious impact. The Jeep listed to the right and almost veered off the narrow road. He corrected the wheel and the Jeep swayed left and right, and before he could straighten out, they were struck again and went airborne.

Book twisted the steering wheel hard to the right, bringing the pickup truck's bumper into contact with the back left-side bumper of the Jeep. It was his version of the "pit maneuver" police used to force a vehicle over, or off the road. It had worked perfectly. Murphy's Jeep slewed to the right and would have flipped, but Murphy corrected the skid. Book stomped the gas pedal and struck the Jeep again. It veered off the right side of the road, but Book hadn't slowed fast enough after hitting the Jeep and his headlights shot past them. He slammed on the brakes and skidded to a stop.

"Where are they?" he yelled at Clint.

The stolen truck wasn't equipped with seat belts, and the impact had shot Clint forward into the dash and windshield. He was rattled and squinted into the darkness, but couldn't see any other lights in the field. There was nothing. Either Murphy had cut the headlights, or the Jeep had dropped into a ditch.

"I don't see anything, Book. Back up."

Book backed up a hundred feet, with Clint leaning out of the passenger window searching for tire marks where the Jeep left the road.

Book backed slowly.

"Shit, Book," Clint said. "There's dozens of skid marks along here. Just stop and I'll walk it."

Clint got out and rubbed his forehead. It felt like someone had put him in a duffel bag and beat him with a stick.

The Jeep was airborne. The front slammed into the farm field like it had been dropped from a bridge. Jack and Moira were thrown around inside like rag dolls, but the Jeep held together.

The impact of hitting the ground jarred Moira out of her stupor and she scrabbled at Jack's pocket and dug his cell phone out.

Jack cut the headlights while the Jeep created a path through the brush. They rolled forward, unable to see, making their way over the rough ground and heading north. Jack prayed there were no ditches or sinkholes in their path.

"Find the shotgun," Jack said. He hadn't believed the killers could catch up with them so quickly when they'd fled the cabin. He'd never been up against a military-trained force. He wouldn't make that mistake again.

Moira felt something under her feet. "Here it is."

"Call 911 and then give me the phone," Jack said, but she was already punching in the numbers.

He heard Moira say, "No, I don't know where we are. I've been shot and some guys are trying to kill us." After a beat she said, "Look, lady, I'm with Detective Murphy . . . yeah, Murphy . . . listen, we're in a field—east of Highway 41, I think."

Jack spoke to her, "Tell them we're headed for Interstate 164."

Before Moira could repeat the information, the engine made a loud rattling sound, and a cloud of steam rose from the hood.

Moira shouted Jack's instructions into the cell. Then he heard her saying, "Hello. Hello!"

She punched some buttons and then looked helplessly at Jack. "The phone's not working."

"Do you have your phone?" he asked.

"Back at the cabin," she said.

"We've got to move," Jack said as the Jeep rolled to a stop. "We're going to head west."

He jacked a round into the shotgun's breech. "I think we're close to the interstate. We can flag someone down. Use their phone."

Jack could barely make out Moira's face in the dark. He was worried whether Moira was up for this—both physically and mentally.

"How do you feel?"

"Like I've been shot in the face," she said, "that's how I feel. What do you think?"

Anger was good.

Moira pulled the handle but her door wouldn't open. Jack pulled her out his side.

"Don't let go of my hand," he whispered.

She gripped his hand and they headed west. He looked back. The full moon was behind clouds and it was pitch-black. The killers could be five feet away and he wouldn't see them. It was at least a mile to the interstate. All of the land around them was in the floodplain, but it was a dry summer and the ground was hard beneath their feet, which was good and bad. Good because it made walking faster, bad because everything was dry and each step made a crackling, crunching noise.

They set off north. The going was slower than he wanted. Blackberry-bush thorns tore at their clothing and skin as they waded across the uneven terrain and after a short time he could tell Moira was beginning to tire. With each step he could feel her grip lessening on his hand. He would have to get her somewhere safe soon.

He tried to remember the topography of the area. He had driven through here a zillion times, but had never paid much attention to things outside the car. The blackberry bushes on their left were probably growing along the edge of a drainage ditch. Checking the stars for direction were no good with the heavy cloud cover, but he spotted a faint light on the horizon ahead of them and to their left. If that was Evansville, that meant they were going in the right direction. He was about to point it out to Moira, to give her some hope, but before he could she spotted the top of a gabled roof not far ahead.

"A house," she said excitedly. "Maybe they have a phone."

Jack didn't think anyone lived out here, but they headed in that direction. As they moved toward the structure, the clouds broke up and the moon peeked through enough to dash Moira's hope. What she thought was a house turned into a broken-down farmer's shed.

The rotted building faced east. The doors were gone along with most of the roof and slats that made up the sides. What they had mistaken for a gabled roof were the bare trusses.

Moira let go of his hand and slumped to the ground against an inside wall. As quietly as he could, Jack eased the slide back to eject a shell to check that it hadn't been damaged in the wreck. Satisfied, he loaded the shell back in the feeder tube.

"We'll rest inside," Jack said.

"Do you think the police dispatcher heard me?" Moira asked.

"You did good back there," Jack said. He didn't want to lie to her about their chances, but he didn't want her to give up. The initial adrenaline rush had worn off and for her a mental and muscular fatigue had taken its place. He didn't fool himself that he and Moira had been able to move as fast as two trained infantry soldiers. He wasn't sure they were still being pursued, but if they didn't keep moving, they would find out the hard way.

Moira was sluggish and she could barely hold her head up. He didn't want to leave her behind, but she would have a better chance if he did. He looked around the inside of the shed. Most of the wall slats were missing. The place looked like it would fall down at any moment. He had to make a choice.

"Moira, I want you to stay here," he said, and then heard a noise coming toward them.

"Okay, change of plan. Let's go," he said. He tightened his grip on the shotgun. He pulled her to the back of the shed, and they squeezed between some slats and ran.

Behind them, the roar of a heavy submachine gun fire was deafening and it pushed them harder. In just a few minutes they were stepping over the steel guardrails of the interstate.

"Shut the hell up!" Book hissed.

"But I don't think they came this way," Clint complained. He was feeling feverish again. His head was bleeding where he'd struck the windshield. Murphy was probably armed, and Book might have been wrong about Murphy and the girl heading in this direction.

They came to a wooden structure, and Book signaled for Clint to get down.

"There's something in there," Book said, and brought his weapon up. He didn't waste any time. He rushed the shed, chopping it to shreds with automatic rifle fire, while Clint stood back, prepared to engage any targets that emerged.

Nothing moved. They advanced carefully, Book from the left, Clint from the right. Risking the flashlight, they saw it was empty.

"Let's get back to the truck. Murphy might have called for help," Book said.

Clint would be glad to get back in the truck and not put any more weight on his injured leg.

On the way back they encountered Murphy's abandoned Jeep, and Book lost his temper.

"Shit! Shit! Shit!" He emptied a full drum of ammo, spraying the Jeep from front to back with his MP5 carbine. When the hammer clicked on empty, he started kicking the door.

"We better go," Clint said, and Book screamed in a rage that made Clint groan inwardly. They weren't in the middle of *haji* land, where they could do anything they liked. They were operating in a world where people might be cowards, but they had cell phones.

Two cars drove past without slowing as Jack stood dangerously out in the lane. He held his badge out in one hand, the shotgun in the other. As their headlights washed over him, the cars put on more speed.

Moira sat on the guardrail, one hand to her face, the front of her clothes a bloody mess.

"One of them is on their cell phone calling in about a crazy man with shotgun and a bloody woman," she said.

The way she said it made him laugh. And that brought a half-hearted chuckle from Moira.

"Most likely," he said. But the cynic in him said it was just as possible that the drivers were rushing home to put their experience on their Facebook page. The world had changed.

A car's headlights dawned in the west, and Jack could hear the engine slowing.

The killers had somehow gotten back to their vehicle and guessed where Jack and Moira were headed. He lifted Moira from the guardrail, knowing there was no chance of escaping. He shoved her into a crouched position behind the rail and then stepped out in the open, the shotgun's barrel lined up with the approaching car's windshield.

"Come on, you bastards!" he screamed.

CHAPTER EIGHTY

As the car got closer Jack recognized it and lowered the shotgun.

"Get in. I'm taking you two to the hospital," Brooke insisted.

"The hell you are!" Jack said. "These guys aren't that lucky. Someone's feeding them information. Telling them every move we make. If they weren't after me, how did they know Moira was with me? How in the hell did they get my address?"

He wasn't listed in the phone book, and no address or sign was posted at the end of his gravel lane. Liddell's house hadn't been listed either. But these guys had found them both.

"So what's the plan?" Brooke asked. "There are a dozen state, county, and city police units out here now. These guys are halfway across the state."

Jack was tired, and Moira was completely wrung out. "When they've been caught, we'll go to the hospital," he said. He knew he was in no shape to protect Moira, and he sure as hell didn't trust anyone else. Including Brooke.

"Cinderella," Moira mumbled.

"She can take care of herself," he assured her, but he knew the dog was dead. He heard the gunshot that had killed her. He felt a lump in his throat. Damn dog . . . saved our lives.

Brooke reached for the radio mic. "Who's Cinderella?"

"Cinderella is my dog," Jack said. "She went after the guys when we ran out the back of the cabin."

"You named a dog Cinderella?"

"I didn't name the dog," Jack said.

Moira was sobbing. Through her tears she said, "She was so brave. We wouldn't have made it if—"

"I'll tell the troops to keep an eye out for *Cinderella,*" Brooke said, and picked up the radio mic to call dispatch, but Jack stopped her.

"Tell dispatch that we're okay," Jack said. "Give them the location where you picked us up and tell them these guys are heavily armed. At least one of them has a machine gun. They may be doubling back to the river, back toward my cabin. They're driving an old yellow pickup. It's probably torn up in the front. *Do not* tell them where we're at—or where we're going."

"What? Do you think they have a police radio?" Brooke asked.

"Just do it," Jack said, and Brooke relayed what Jack told her to say and added a description of the pooch given by Moira. She clipped the mic back into its holder. "Okay?"

Jack nodded and leaned against the door. He couldn't afford to rest, but his body wasn't listening to him. Strangely enough, he thought about Katie. And then he thought about how she would kill him when she found out he'd let Moira get hurt.

"By the way, where *are* we going?" Brooke asked.

"Just keep driving," Jack said.

Brooke headed onto Interstate 164 heading east. The road was elevated above river bottomland that was bare, flat, and dark, except for yellow sodium vapor lights along the highway.

Both Jack and Moira were a bloody mess. She didn't know how much of the blood on Jack was Moira's or his own. "I need to take you both to a hospital."

"Just keep driving," Jack said.

"Yes, sir. Are we going all the way to Chicago? Or can I make a suggestion?"

"No hospitals."

"We can use my place."

"I don't think a hotel will work," he said. Probably Eric and Trent both knew where she was staying, and it would be the first place the killers would look when they realized that they hadn't gone to police headquarters. He hated to admit it, but the reason he wasn't going to headquarters was because that would mean they got away. He didn't want it to be over like that. He wanted a chance to thank the killers properly.

Brooke braked sharply and turned east onto Boonville New Harmony Road.

"I grew up around here. My dad left his lake cabin to me," she said. She turned onto a narrow road, then a quick right onto a dirt track that wound around the edge of a small lake lined with pine trees. She stopped the car alongside a squat cabin. It was badly in need of paint, but looked solid. Although it overlooked a lake and not a river, it reminded him of his own place.

"I'm not much of a housekeeper, so don't complain. It's got power and running water."

Jack discovered Moira was fast asleep. "We're here, Moira," he said.

Brooke unlocked the cabin, and as they entered, Jack was impressed. From the outside it appeared to be like any basic fishing cabin, squat, flat-roofed, weather-faded, and unpainted. Overhanging shingles acted as a gutter. The windows were covered with heavy wooden shutters. The door was solid wood. A newer wooden outhouse was visible behind the cabin.

But inside, it was as nice and comfortable as any hotel room with a sofa, two leather recliners, liquor cabinet, fireplace, and a big-screen television. He spied a fully equipped kitchen off to the left. And to the right was a door that probably entered the bedroom. A closed door was in the back of the kitchen.

"Is that the back door?" he asked Brooke.

She saw where he was looking. "No. It would have led to a bathroom. My dad had got as far as framing and hanging the door when he passed away. The door is nailed shut from the outside. I've never had a chance to finish the cabin."

Jack nodded. It was a six-panel inside door, made of pine, but it wasn't as thick as the front door. It may be nailed shut, but it was the weakest point in the rear. He could force it if he had to. So could the killers.

Moira sat down on the sofa while Jack checked out the cabin. She leaned back with her eyes closed, both hands in her lap. When Brooke switched on the front room lights, Moira's wound didn't look as bad as he had thought. Her front was covered with blood, but she didn't exhibit any signs of shock. He just wanted to make sure she didn't go to sleep.

"I'll get the first aid kit," Brooke offered. Jack nodded and she went back outside. Every police car was equipped with a basic first aid kit.

He woke Moira and helped her into the kitchen. He pulled up a chair for her near the sink, turned on the water, and heard a pump come on under the sink. He twisted the hot tap all the way open and looked around for clean towels. He found several dish towels under the sink and put one under the water. It was still cold.

"No hot water," Brooke said, coming back in with the kit. "On my to-do list."

"Can I have a drink?" Moira asked.

"The water's okay," Brooke said. "Just tastes like iron. It's from a well." She opened a cabinet that revealed a couple of red plastic picnic cups. She filled one and handed it to Moira, who drank thirstily and asked for another.

Jack tried to hand the wetted dish towel to Brooke, who declined, saying, "What makes you think I know how to clean a wound? Just because I'm a woman?"

Moira grinned slightly, and her hand went back to her face. "Brooke, could you please? Thank you, Jack."

Brooke relented and ran the water and dabbed Moira's face, washing the blood away.

Jack went to the front and opened a window, then the shutter, and had a view of the lake and the dirt drive approaching them. He looked back toward the kitchen and made eye contact with Brooke.

"It's not too bad," Brooke said. "You'll need this examined, but maybe there won't be a scar."

"I hope not," Moira said.

Brooke expertly applied a bandage over the laceration and taped it in place. "There. That will hold for a short while."

"I think I'll lay down for a minute," Moira said, and Brooke led her to the bedroom and pulled the door shut. She walked over and stood beside Jack, looking out the window.

"Were you hit?" she asked.

Jack looked down and noticed blood dripping from his hand

onto the hardwood floor. He lifted his sleeve and saw a hole on both sides of his bicep.

"Come in the kitchen and we'll get you patched up, too." Brooke pulled him away from the window to the chair by the sink.

She gently turned the arm and examined his injury before saying, "It's a through and through wound. You're lucky."

"Yeah. Lucky," Jack said in a sarcastic tone.

"So . . . do you want me to bandage it, or do you want to just act tough?"

"Will I still be able to play the piano?"

She smirked and wet a towel. "Tell you what. I'll use a dirty towel. How about that?"

He held his arm over the sink while Brooke, none too gently, washed the blood off and then poured something over the wound that burned like hell and made him grimace.

"It's not whiskey," she said. "Sorry."

"I'd prefer Scotch," he said through clenched teeth. "But thanks."

She examined his arm and wrapped a clean gauze bandage very tightly around it, tucking in the end.

He admired her work. "You've done this before."

She propped her left leg up on a chair and pulled the pant leg almost to her knee. He could see a perfectly round scar on the side of her calf. It looked old.

"I was eight years old. Fishing with my dad right out there." She nodded toward the lake. "Some hunters didn't know our cabin was back here."

Jack whistled appreciatively. "Eight years old. And you dressed it yourself?"

"Are you crazy!" she said. "My dad took me to the hospital."

He unbuttoned his shirt, opened it, and revealed the thick white scar that ran from below his right ear, across his chest, ending just above his left nipple. "I got that in a knife fight with the nurse when I was born."

Brooke raised her eyebrows questioningly.

"She won, but my mom killed her." He buttoned his shirt.

"No, you got that from Bobby Solazzo. I heard about that," Brooke said. "And you killed him." Her expression turned serious.

"Damn right," he said, and then asked, "You got coffee?"

Brooke took a jar and a mug from the cabinet behind her and made cold instant coffee. She handed it to Jack, and he stared into the black liquid and handed it back. "Never mind."

"I heard your ex got engaged to Eric Manson."

"She did."

"How do you feel about that?"

Jack didn't answer. He walked back to the front room window to watch the road.

She followed him and pulled a cigarette pack from her pocket. "What are we doing here, Jack?"

"They'll be coming."

She would have asked who would be coming, but she had known what his plan was from the beginning.

"They were firing a fully automatic weapon at us. Do you keep any ammunition here? Or maybe a spare fifty-caliber machine gun in the closet?"

She shook her head. "It's a fishing cabin. I've got two extra clips, thirteen rounds each, and thirteen in my Glock. That makes thirty-nine."

"I've got the same as you, plus five rounds in the shotgun," Jack said. They both knew it wouldn't be enough to hold off an assault. *If we call for backup, it will bring the killers here faster, or they will turn tail and disappear—maybe come at us some other time.*

"I saw cords of wood stacked on the side of the cabin. We could bring it in here and put them against the wall for a barrier," Jack said.

"I'll help you carry it in."

Now that he had time to think, the plan to play bait sucked. "You don't have to do this, Brooke. Give this address on the radio and then you can take Moira to the hospital. Just don't call for help. Give me your extra clips."

She shook her head. "I can't do that."

"You know it's the right thing to do, Brooke." She was a stubborn woman. She reminded him of himself. But he was better looking.

"Okay, how about this? We lay the wood along the bedroom wall. You stay in there and protect Moira."

"And you take these guys on all by yourself?" she asked. "You're incredible, you know that."

"If it looks like I'm losing, you call for backup," he said. "Give me one of your clips."

Outside, Brooke spotted headlights peeking through the trees two hundred yards out. Her cabin was the only one on this road. *So Jack was right all along.*

"Too late," she said, drawing her .45.

CHAPTER EIGHTY-ONE

Brooke felt chills run the entire length of her body. She squeezed the checkered grip of her .45 to keep her hands from shaking. She closed her eyes firmly to stop the waking nightmare from coming and robbing her of her faculties when she needed all her focus. But the nightmare came . . .

She's standing at the bottom of the parking garage ramp, both hands on her pistol, pointed into the darkness at the top of the ramp. "Police. Put your hands up. Come down the ramp with your hands up over your head or I'll shoot you!" she yells at the shape in the black leather biker's jacket.

The jacket moves deeper into the darkness. She can make out a flash of something pale against the black. A hand? It's reaching beneath the jacket.

"POLICE!" she yells in a commanding voice. "Come out where I can see you . . . NOW!"

The paleness slips beneath and comes out with something shiny . . .

"Drop the gun!" she screams, and drops into a shooter's stance. She aims to the right of the shiny thing she sees. It seems to be floating in the darkness. Her training has taught her most gunmen are right handed.

Her mind registers a flash, and then a second flash, and she returns the fire. Two center mass, then aim for the head, go for the kill shot. Put the threat down.

The target in black falls straight down. In a heap. Not thrown backward like in the movies. Just straight down, in a heap, and doesn't move.

She crosses the distance—carefully—muzzle of her pistol pointing at the threat. Verifying the kill. And sees the body of a small girl in a huge black biker's jacket. She isn't more than thirteen or fourteen. A silver cell phone is near the dead hand. The dead eyes stare into hers. Her throat threatens to close. She can't breathe.

"They're here," Jack said.

Brooke opened her eyes and stared at the gun in her hand like it was a disgusting object. As she leaned against the wall, he realized Brooke was barely holding it together. He pulled the window shutters together, leaving a few inches of space, and turned back to Brooke. He'd heard about the shooting she was involved in from some of his state trooper friends. She had shot and killed a teenage girl. She was cleared by the state shooting board, but the kid's family had made her life a living hell. He could sympathize with how she was feeling, but he needed her back here. Back in the present. Ready to kill these bastards. They sure as hell weren't worried about killing him and Brooke and Moira.

"Ever shoot anyone?" he asked. He knew the answer, of course, but he wanted to get her mad. "I said, have you ever shot a man before, Brooke?"

Her head jerked up. "Why?" she asked angrily. "What have you heard?"

"I've heard you're good with that thing. I hope that's right because here they come."

The window exploded, and glass and wood splinters showered them like a swarm of angry hornets. He pulled Brooke to the floor.

"Are you hit?" he yelled. The sound of machine-gun fire was deafening. "Brooke, are you hit?"

She lay on the floor, pistol shoved out in a two-handed grip. Tears streamed down her face, and her hands shook.

"You asked if I ever shot someone," she said. "The answer is yes. I killed a young girl." The expression on her face changed to one Jack knew well. Fight or flight. And this was fight.

Another hail of bullets slammed into the walls behind them.

Through clenched teeth she said, "I'll be damned if they get Moira."

CHAPTER EIGHTY-TWO

The boss had given Clint an exact location, down to the dirt track he had just turned left on. Through the trees he spotted the moon's reflection on the lake, and on the other side was the cabin. They were several hundred yards away. He slowed down and pulled off into the grass.

"If the boss knows about this place, why aren't there cops all over the place?" Clint wondered out loud.

"Only one possible reason I can think of."

"Does it have something to do with the female cop we ain't supposed to kill?"

Book nodded. "That'd be my guess. We'll circle around the lake. Come at the cabin from both sides. The boss said there ain't a back door, so they have to come right to us."

"It'll be a turkey shoot," Clint agreed.

Book got out and checked his equipment, adjusted his body armor back in place, and released the slide forward to seat a live round.

"Murphy wants a showdown," Book said. "That's why there's no cops around here." He paused, thinking, then said, "Except for those two inside there."

Clint leaned heavily on the steering wheel, holding his ribs while he got out of the truck. "How are we gonna get out of here? The cops must have a description of our wheels, man."

Book nodded toward the cabin. "They got wheels. They won't be needing them in a few minutes."

But Clint knew it was over. The boss's last instructions were to finish the job, then drive west to St. Louis, where she had already purchased airline tickets for them. She said the police had their names and their military records, so they were to pick up new passports, driver's licenses, and some money from a guy in the parking garage at the airport. She had already purchased round-trip tickets for them to Croatia, and a connection with the airlines had back-dated the tickets, so they wouldn't raise suspicion.

He knew there wouldn't be any passports or money waiting for them. There would be a team waiting to kill them.

"You know there won't be any new identities or passports," he said to Book.

"To hell with the boss, and the client she rode in on," Book said. "And I ain't letting the female cop live. We kill them all."

They stayed in the tree line along the lake, and when they got near the cabin they split up. Book came in from the left, Clint from the right. They took up positions close to the front of the cabin.

Book stepped out of cover holding the MP5 by his side, one-handed, and held the trigger down. The submachine gun sprayed the front of the cabin from left to right, and back. The MP5 was a seriously badass piece of weaponry, capable of laying down eight hundred rounds per minute, with an effective range of over six hundred feet. And Book was a hell of a lot closer than that.

The first barrage struck the windows and door, and when he stopped he could hear glass still falling inside the cabin. And that was just a taste. Clint knew Book would deliberately keep the bullets high. He didn't intend to kill them quickly. He wanted to make a grand entrance and gut-shoot Murphy. And then he would savage the two women before he cut their heads off.

Clint figured they were out of effective range of any weapons Murphy and the female cop might have. This was their last job. They'd already been paid. He didn't care if Book had some fun, but Clint didn't like killing women. He'd made his mind up that this would be the last time he would do one of these jobs.

In fact, this job had gone so sideways that his instinct was to eliminate any witnesses—women or not—and that included the client. They could make their way to New York. Anything could be had for the right amount of money, and they had plenty of that in offshore accounts. They would buy fake identification and passports and go to Haiti or Nicaragua. They could live like kings on the money they already had. Plus, there was a need for someone of their talent. But no more female targets.

Book sprayed the front of the cabin again until he was out of ammunition. While he locked another hundred-round drum of ammo in place, Clint opened up with the UMP submachine gun.

CHAPTER EIGHTY-THREE

Moira rolled off the bed, onto the floor, as all hell broke loose. The air above her head seemed to be alive and buzzing. She didn't know what she could do to help, but she was through being scared. She crawled toward the living room, where Jack and Brooke were.

Jack crouched to the left of the door. He and Brooke just had time to pull the sofa against the wall before the cabin was strafed with more machine-gun fire. Pinned down, he was unable to even shoot back. He rose up, leaned over the couch, and used the butt of the shotgun to hammer the shutters open. It wasn't hard because they were mostly in tatters anyway. Another hail of lead ripped through the open window. Huge chunks out of window frame exploded, driving splinters into his hand and arm.

Gun in hand, Brooke rolled across the floor to the other window.

"You with me?" Jack yelled.

"I'm way ahead of you!" she said. "I'm going to pull the door open so we have a field of fire."

Book signaled to Clint that he was moving in. Clint drove another ammo clip home and opened fire while Book rushed forward, his movement covered by the deafening clatter from the UMP as it poured .45 caliber ACP rounds into the door and door frame.

As in a choreographed dance, Clint slapped another clip into the UMP, and opened fire again on the front window to the west of the door, giving Book an open path to the front door. Book crossed the open ground in large strides, weapon pulled in tight to his body, barrel down.

Clint stopped shooting, and Book launched his two hundred eighty pounds straight through the weakened door.

From the bedroom doorway Moira saw Jack and Brooke crouching behind the ripped-up sofa, heads down. The air around them filled with flying bits of wood and glass and shrapnel.

"Jack!" she screamed, but her voice was barely audible above the gunfire.

Jack slid the shotgun across the floor to her, and she stared at it until he yelled, "Take it! Get back in the bedroom. On the floor behind the bed!"

Moira grabbed the shotgun and began to crab-crawl backward, but the front door was shredded right before her eyes. It was a welcome bulwark one moment and then it was gone, and in its place was the biggest man she had ever seen. He came through the door like it was made of paper. He was holding something long with an explosion of flame erupting from its end. Lamps, furniture, walls, floor, disintegrated wherever it pointed.

Moira screamed and scooted up against the doorway, trying to lift the shotgun, watching helplessly as the figure swiveled toward Brooke.

She saw blossoms of red flower across Brooke's body, hip to shoulder, and she knew Brooke was dead. Then the giant swept the flaming barrel toward Jack, but Jack had disappeared. From the corner of her eye, Moira saw an arm rise, and the top of the killer's head disappeared in a mist of red. The weapon expended itself harmlessly into the floor and then the flame was extinguished.

Jack instantly followed up by dragging Brooke out of the doorway. In slow motion he turned his head toward her, yelling something, but she could no longer hear.

CHAPTER EIGHTY-FOUR

Jack knew the directed fire at the front door for what it was—an assault—and scrambled to his feet. He put his back against the wall on the other side of the door just as it exploded inward and the gunman burst through, sweeping the room with destruction.

Brooke reacted well to the intruder and rolled onto her back. She shot the gunman dead center, four, five, six times, but he didn't seem to react. He continued to sweep the submachine gun across her. Jack stepped close and fired into the man's head.

Like a marionette whose strings had been clipped, the man dropped to the floor, and Jack instinctively went to drag Brooke out of the doorway. He knew another man was still firing outside. She could be hit again. But he was too slow. Too late he heard the crunch of boots behind him, and turned to look into the impossibly huge barrel of Clint's UMP .45.

The butt of the .12 gauge shotgun rocked backward with the blast and broke two of her ribs, but Moira was unaware of the pain. The man who had stood in the doorway staggered backward when all nine of the double-aught buckshot, each projectile the size of a .38 caliber bullet, struck him in the solar plexus.

Then Jack sprang on his feet and raced out the door after him.

Book kicked the door down and began raining down hell inside the cabin, which had been Clint's cue to charge. He started for the cabin, but when Book's weapon went silent, Clint thought that meant all the targets were down. With his UMP .45 at the ready, he rushed into the doorway. Only then did he realize his mistake.

A glance told Clint that Book was dead. All that was left of the big man's head was part of the jaw, a piece of skull, and one eye staring into space. The sight of his dead partner made him hesitate, but he quickly recovered. He began to pivot toward Murphy and then a giant fist smashed him in the chest. When he came to his senses, he was on his back, thrown outside, unable to draw air into his bruised lungs. Murphy was straddling him, knees pinning Clint's arms, and holding a hand cannon against his forehead. Murphy was saying something, but the words all ran together, and in that instant Clint knew he was going to die.

CHAPTER EIGHTY-FIVE

An attractive older woman answered the door. Although it was well after midnight and she was in her robe and housecoat, her makeup was perfect, and not one gray hair was out of place.

"Are you here to see my husband . . . Detective Murphy, isn't it?"

"Yes, ma'am."

She smiled and stood back. "Please come in."

Jack entered a foyer the size of his cabin. A massive chandelier hung overhead, its light reflecting on white marble tile and colorful stained-glass windows that made up the east wall.

"You may wait in his den. Do you know where it is?"

"No, Mrs. Wethington. I've never been here before," Jack said as they entered the front room of the three-story mansion. He heard that Trent had bought it when he decided to run for governor.

Jack followed the lady of the house down a hallway, past a sweeping staircase, and to the back, where she showed him into a room with a massive cherry desk and chair. It was accompanied by two long benches and two heavy chairs made of the same cherry-wood. Cherrywood shelves filled mostly with leather-bound volumes covered every inch of wall space. This room was worth more than Jack brought home in a year. The house must have cost more than he would make in his lifetime.

Mrs. Wethington turned on a desk lamp and indicated that Jack take a seat. He remained standing.

"Would you believe this was a guest bedroom?" she said, as if it were nonsense to ever think it so. "My husband had it built to be fit for a governor. What do you think, Detective Murphy?"

"Cherry," Jack said appreciatively.

Mrs. Wethington smiled. "If you have the opportunity to come back during the daytime, Detective, I'll give you the grand tour. Would you care for anything? Perhaps some coffee?"

Jack declined the offer, and she excused herself with a promise her husband would be in shortly.

Jack looked down at the bloodstains from Moira and Brooke on his shirt and pants. Mrs. Wethington hadn't remarked on it. Maybe she didn't see it. Maybe she didn't see a lot of things.

The door opened and Trent entered the study. Jack half expected him to come in wearing his work finery, but instead he was wearing his sleep finery: pinstripe silk pajamas, matching striped silk robe with the belt hanging around his trim waist. Jack thought all that was missing was a fez, a calabash pipe, and a howler monkey perched atop his shoulder.

Trent took a seat behind the desk without a word or acknowledgment of Jack's presence, or bloody attire. His posture and carriage demonstrated his position in this meeting. The man was the poster child for a governor—or a sociopath.

Without expression, Trent asked, "What can I do for you, Detective Murphy?"

"I'm here about Brooke."

Trent's composure remained unchanged, but he leaned back in his chair, and said, "If you're here to have her taken off the case, I can't help you."

Jack remained standing in front of the desk. "The case is closed."

Trent's complexion turned pale. He leaned forward, hands folded on top of the desk. He took a deep breath in through his nose and slowly let it out

"I thought you would be overjoyed, but you don't seem happy," Jack said. "And you haven't asked why I'm here about Brooke."

Trent locked eyes with Jack. "Of course, of course. That's fantastic news. Congratulations, Jack." He added hesitantly, "How is she? Are you here to give me bad news?"

Jack didn't answer him at first. Instead he asked, "Do you still think you'll win?"

Trent paused, then said, "Do you know who I am? Don't you play games with me, Detective. Is my niece alive?"

"Shut up," Jack said. He leaned over the desk and got in Trent's space. "I do know who you are. And I know *what* you are. You're the piece of shit I've asked the FBI to give me five minutes alone with."

Instead of being insulted, Trent's eyes cut to the door as if he were expecting someone.

"Oh, they're out there, all right," Jack assured him. "The FBI, Sheriff's deputies, state police. It's just too bad Liddell couldn't be here."

"What is this?"

"I arrested your boy, Clint Hallard, for murder and attempted murder. You remember him, don't you? You were the only one who knew where we were tonight. Brooke called you from her cabin. You sent those bastards to kill us—to kill your own niece."

Trent deflated like a balloon, his lungs expelling the breath he'd been holding. His elbows leaned heavily on top of the desk; his face was a frozen mask of defeat.

Jack walked to the study door and said, "But don't worry. I blew the other guy's brains all over Brooke's cabin. And in case you give a rat's ass, Brooke is shot up pretty bad. She's in the hospital, but she's alive and holding her own. Spending the rest of your life in prison is too good for you, and you know something? I'm sure she would agree with me."

Trent's complexion turned ashen. "I would never hurt Brooke. I never wanted this—"

"Yeah, right," Jack said. "You would never hurt her unless you yourself might get hurt."

Trent pleaded with Jack, "I'm not the only one you want."

Jack leaned against the door, and said, "I know. But I didn't think you would tell me."

That's when Trent started talking. He told Jack some of what he already knew or guessed, but the breadth of the conspiracy surprised him. Ten minutes later, Jack walked onto the front porch, where several federal agents and a posse of others waited. Some were on foot and several more were in cars with the engines running. One of the Feds approached Jack. "We've got our warrant, but we'll need Hallard to identify him."

Jack said, "Thanks for giving me a few minutes. He's all yours. We need another warrant, though. I don't think Hallard will be able to identify Trent. There's someone else."

The agent nodded. "We'll have the federal prosecutor get another warrant if you give them the information. I take it you need one ASAP?"

"Sooner would be good," Jack said, and started off the porch.

The FBI agent had started to round up his search team when a loud report came from inside.

"Oh, shit!" the agent said, and a group of men—uniformed and suits alike—rushed inside.

Jack hung his head, and taking a deep breath, walked around the corner of the house to the car where two heavily armed officers were guarding Clint Hallard. One of the officers opened the back door, and Jack slid in beside the killer.

"I heard a gunshot," Hallard said. "Did you kill him?"

"No, I'm afraid that's your business, not mine."

Waiting for the Feds to get their amended warrant was excruciating, but the wait was worth it when two special agents of the FBI led county attorney Bob Rothschild out of his home in handcuffs. They brought a marked county police unit to the edge of the porch, and the car window rolled down.

Clint Hallard looked at the man in handcuffs and nodded at Jack. "That's him. I saw him on TV at that news conference. That's the guy we found at the house. He kept saying we had to help him, and he was crying." Clint shook his head in disgust. "What a pussy."

"He's all yours," Jack said to the FBI special agent in charge. He swiveled slightly to address the county attorney. "Hey, Bob. I'm a better detective than you thought, huh?"

CHAPTER EIGHTY-SIX

Jack was surprised to find Brooke sitting up in the hospital bed watching the *Today* show. It was eight in the morning, and Matt Lauer was just going live to Channel Six television in Evansville with breaking news. Claudine Setera reported:

Thank you, Matt. A shoot-out at a fishing cabin in northern Vanderburgh County early this morning has left one suspect dead and another in custody. In a surprising twist, Evansville Police revealed that a team of killers, hired by Vanderburgh County Attorney Bob Rothschild, are responsible for the recent killings of a man and woman in Illinois and three women in Evansville that had previously been thought the work of a serial killer dubbed The Cannibal.

As the reporter's smiling face chattered on, Brooke pushed her head against her pillows and closed her eyes. A thick bandage covered her left shoulder. Her mouth was set a tight line and Jack could see she was in pain.

"Do you need the nurse?"

She cracked one eye and rolled a finger in the air. "Just turn that crap off."

Jack picked her remote off the bed stand, cut the gorgeous reporter off in mid-sentence, and hit the call button to bring a nurse. He was concerned about how she was taking Trent's suicide. He felt a measure of guilt for not seeing it coming, or more truthfully, not caring if he caused it. He had Trent to thank for nearly getting killed—Brooke and Moira, too—and if he had been in the room with Trent, he could have easily helped him put the gun in his mouth.

The nurse came in, checked Brooke's IV, added pain medication, and said, "You should be feeling better in a few minutes. Do you need anything else?"

"I need a Scotch," Jack said.

The nurse turned to him and smiled. "I get off at three, Jack," and left the room with Jack pleasantly surprised.

"Did you see that?" he asked, grinning at Brooke.

"Yeah, you're such a stud muffin. It's a good thing I'm resistant to your charms. I mean, what with being in a weakened condition and all," she said, and laughed.

"Hey, I saved your life."

She gingerly touched her stomach. "Yeah, boy! But you took your sweet time doing it."

"I had to think about it," he said, and they smiled at each other.

Her smile faded. "Was my uncle really behind all of this?"

Jack nodded.

"I called him when I went for the first aid kit in the trunk of the car. I thought you were being paranoid about Eric, and I couldn't believe Trent would . . . you know? So I told him what had happened, that we were safe." She paused, then said, "He was the only one who knew where we were. I'm so sorry, Jack."

"He was your uncle. How could you know? And he wasn't the only one who knew. You see, I had a chance to talk to Hallard after Moira shot him, and I called the FBI in on this because of what he told me. He and Book worked for a murder-for-hire outfit. He didn't know exactly where they were located, but he had enough information that I thought the FBI would be interested." And it would keep me from having to arrest your uncle Trent, Jack thought.

"When I confronted Trent, he told me about Bob Rothschild and the organization on the East Coast. They were funding Trent's run for governor. There was a fortune at stake for both Trent and the organization. This was all about money." Jack stopped, feeling a familiar bitter taste in his mouth. Most murders were about money, jealousy, or hate. "The FBI told me they were already investigating a gambling organization in Atlantic City. They suspected that the organization wanted Trent to swing things their way on the gambling in Indiana, and if he was governor, they could have it all."

"But why would my uncle get involved with them? He was always a shoo-in for governor. And what was Bob Rothschild going to get out of it?"

"The FBI said Bob was going to get in the witness protection program. He told them the rest of the story. If Trent was elected governor, Bob would become lieutenant governor. He planned to run for governor when Trent stepped down. It was Bob who had contacts with the organization in Atlantic City. It was Bob who called them for help when . . ."

Jack took Brooke's hand and said, "I don't know if you want to hear the rest of this. If you're not up to it, I can tell you later. You already know most of it. Maybe you should get some rest."

She was not going to be fobbed off as a medical patient. "Maybe you should just tell me. I'm just wounded. I'm not a basket case, Jack."

"Okay, I'll tell you," he said, though a part of him still wanted to spare her from truth.

"Trent killed Nina," he said. "She had worked on his campaign with Bob, and everything was fine until she found out about a sexual liaison between Trent and Hope Dupree."

The only reaction from Brooke was a quick blink. "Really?"

"Nina had a diary on her office computer. Moira found it and showed it to me. In the diary Nina said that she had found out about someone in the prosecutor's office trading dismissed charges for sexual favors. Apparently Hope had somehow communicated with Nina and told her about Trent. According to the diary, Nina didn't believe it and did some research."

Brooke said, "The list on the thumb drive."

Jack nodded. "The diary didn't name anyone, but apparently Nina was having an affair with Trent. When I first read the diary I assumed it was Eric." Before she could comment he said, "Don't worry, I don't suspect him of anything more than being a prick. Trent had called him and asked him to go to Nina's to check her welfare. This was the day of Katie's engagement party. So, anyway, Trent told Eric where to find the key to Nina's door. I've talked to Eric and he said he didn't tell on Trent because he didn't want to 'make waves.' Can you believe that?"

"Not everyone is as ethical as you, Jack," she said, somewhat sarcastically, and he grinned.

"So, I questioned Eric at length." He gave a satisfied smirk. "He finally admitted that he, too, was having an affair with Nina. He had his own key to her house, but he pitched it in a dumpster after he discovered she had been murdered.

"He was actually glad Trent had called him because he wanted to make sure that if we found his fingerprints, he would have a good excuse. He did all this after identifying her head at the morgue. So he went into a possible crime scene before we could get there to try to destroy evidence. Unfortunately, I couldn't arrest him. The chief wouldn't let me."

"Felony prickery," Brooke suggested.

"There's that," Jack said. He was glad to not go into the true depths of Trent's sordid sexual past. Brooke didn't need to carry those memories of her uncle, even if he was a scumbag.

"So, what you're telling me is my uncle was dirty, and in bed with the mob? And now he's dead, and Bob and one of the killers get a free ride?"

"I was turning Trent over to the FBI when he took his own life. I'm sorry you had to go through that, Brooke."

She gave him a skeptical look. "I still don't understand how you got all of this from Hallard before the ambulance arrived. In about—what—three minutes?"

"I was very convincing," Jack said. "Do you want to hear the rest?"

She made a vague wave at all of the medical equipment surrounding her. "I'm not going anywhere."

He continued. "Clint said they were sent here to get rid of a woman's body that someone else had killed."

"Was that Nina?" Brooke asked.

"Yes. Clint said they met a man inside Nina's house. The guy was in a panic and Clint got him out of there." He paused. "He said the guy was driving a silver sports convertible."

"Bob Rothschild," Brooke said. "But what about Hope Dupree and the guy in Harrisburg?"

"Clint said that when they were on their way to Evansville, their boss called and said they needed to take care of another job in Illinois. The pimp with Hope was collateral damage. Wrong place, wrong time. Clint said the boss knew about the old MS-13 murders in Harrisburg, and so they were supposed to make it look like gang killings. That's why they left the heads."

"Let me guess. They were supposed to make Nina disappear,

but then parts of her turned up at the dump and that threw a wrench in their plan . . ."

"And so they were told to stay and kill some more women to make it look like a serial killer," Jack finished her thought.

Brooke's painkillers were kicking in and she looked sleepy. She said, "Trent insisted that the killings were MS-13. He knew all along who and why the killings were taking place, didn't he? That's why he brought me in. I was family, so he thought he could control the investigation."

Brooke took Jack's hand, and tears welled in her eyes. "He was my uncle, Jack. He took me fishing at that cabin. Drank beer with my father. Attended every graduation from high school through the police academy. I was so proud to be his niece. I can't hate him. I can't—" Her words were choked off by a torrent of tears.

Jack leaned over the bed and gently held her. No offense meant to Liddell, but she was as good a partner as he'd ever had. He wished he could take her pain away, both physically and emotionally.

Brooke lifted her face and asked, "So what now?"

"Clint Hallard and Bob Rothschild are in a federal holding facility until the FBI decides what to do with them. With any luck they'll costar in a movie, *Desperate Housewives of San Quentin.*"

She laughed at that crack and wiped away her tears with one hand. "What about Cinderella?"

The dog had turned out to be a miracle story. "That mutt should have been a cat. Talk about nine lives. She was found by one of the officers searching around my cabin." He didn't mention that Cinderella had been shot. The bullet had taken out a chunk of scalp, but her hard head saved her life.

"How is Moira?" Brooke asked.

"She's not even going to have a scar," Jack said.

"Well, she's a lawyer. They have nine lives, too, don't they?"

Katie and Moira rode to the third floor in the hospital elevator. They wanted to offer their condolences to Brooke for the loss of her uncle, and to thank her for saving Moira's life.

"Sis, I'm so glad you aren't going to marry that stuffed shirt!" Moira blurted out.

"I'm so glad you approve," Katie said dryly.

"Damn right, I approve," Moira said, and impatiently punched the button for the third floor. "Jack wouldn't tell you, but Eric has a reputation for being a womanizer."

Katie gave Moira a hard look and sighed. "That *is* my fiancé you're talking about, Moira."

"Ex. Ex-fiancé, sis. And he really, really creeped me out."

Katie was grateful that Moira needed nothing more than a tetanus shot and some Steri-Strips for her injuries, but her emotions and self-worth had been sorely tested by what she'd gone through. Katie only wished some Steri-Strips would hold her own emotions together.

She didn't know now why she had fallen for Eric. Sure, he was good-looking, and was charming when he wanted to be, but he didn't have the personality that would allow him to settle with one woman. She had always known that on some level, but she so desperately didn't want to end up alone.

"When I told Eric I wanted to call the marriage off, I think he was relieved," Katie said. She had worried herself to death about how to tell him, and had finally decided that she owed it to him to tell him face-to-face. It had been easier than she thought. When she told Eric that it was over between them, he just shrugged and said, "Your loss." Then he walked away—to his next conquest, no doubt.

Moira hugged her sister.

"Are you going to stay with the prosecutor's office?" Katie asked. She and Moira had had a long talk about that topic. Moira didn't want Eric for a boss, and even with all that had happened, it looked like he was going to take Trent's place as prosecutor. She had decided to move on.

"I'm seriously thinking about hanging out my own shingle," Moira said. "That is, if I can stay with you for a while." The elevator arrived at the third floor, and Moira added, "Katie, you've got to tell Jack how you feel."

"It's too late," she said, although it was her feelings for Jack that made her realize she didn't love Eric. She had known it from the moment she invited Jack to the engagement party, but the thought of being alone, of not having her feelings returned by Jack, was just too much to endure.

Moira put her arms around Katie and whispered in her ear,

"Jack still loves you. He has always loved you. Don't you know that by now? You belong together. Don't let him get away, sis."

The elevator doors slid open, and Moira pushed Katie out in the hall, saying, "Liddell told me Jack is visiting Brooke. I'm going to give you two a chance to talk. I mean you and Jack, of course. I'll come back up and see Brooke in a bit."

"Wait," Katie said, but the elevator doors shut.

Katie stood there for a moment, and then slowly walked down the hallway toward Brooke's room. *Moira's right. To hell with my head. I need to tell Jack what is in my heart.* But her confidence flagged as she approached the door. *What if he doesn't feel the same as I do?*

She hesitated, and then with a smile on her face, she pushed on the door.

"I'm thinking about resigning," Brooke said.

Jack shook his head. "They would lose a great investigator."

"I have a law degree," she said. "I could join a law firm."

Jack stared at her.

"I know. I know. You hate lawyers."

He smiled, leaned over, and gently hugged her. "If that's what you decide, I'll make an exception. I guess I owe you that."

Jack didn't know if it was the painkillers she was on, or the bonding between two people that had just narrowly skirted death, but she began kissing him. He was trying to unlatch from her embrace when Brooke suddenly looked over at the door. She pushed him away, and said, "Oh! I think that was your Katie."

"My God! Katie!" Jack jumped up and rushed out of the room.

He reached the end of the hallway and saw Katie standing alone at the back of the elevator with a hurt expression on her face.

"Katie, wait!" He ran, yelling, "Wait a minute. Katie. Wait."

As the elevator the doors shut, he saw the look of betrayal in her eyes and heard the elevator's descending hum.

ACKNOWLEDGMENTS

This book would not have been possible without my wife, Jennifer. She held my hand from the idea to delivery, listened to ten million versions of scenes, names, dialogue, and unfunny jokes, and never once asked for a divorce. Instead she listened patiently, gave her honest opinion—good or bad—and then brought me a Scotch. She's my jackpot.

To my editor, Michaela Hamilton and all of the staff at Kensington who worked so hard behind the scene. I hope this book meets your approval. Thanks for everything you attempted to teach this old man.

My brothers, Mike and Tim, and my brother-in-law, Jeff Hudgins, offered priceless suggestions during the development of this book and any errors of fact are all mine.

My biggest thanks goes to all of you who enjoyed this book. You are the reason I write.

BONUS MATERIAL

If you enjoyed *The Deepest Wound*,
please keep reading to enjoy an exciting preview of

THE HIGHEST STAKES
A JACK MURPHY THRILLER

Coming from Lyrical Underground in Fall 2016.

CHAPTER ONE

Chicago's financial district

The steady June downpour in Chicago's financial district didn't stop the workforce from hurrying about their daily tasks. The storm came up suddenly, umbrellas sprouted and those women who came to work unprepared held scarves over their head, while men pulled up their coat collars. A hive of worker ants, they streamed along the sidewalks, impervious to the rain, to each other—to Mr. Smith inside the shiny black Hummer.

He punched a number into his iPhone and held it in his lap. From his vantage point at Wacker and LaSalle he could see the Chicago River meandering along on his right, the Sears Building looming impossibly tall just behind him, but, most important, he had a clear view of the Bank of America two blocks distant.

He was of average height, average weight and build. His mousy brown hair was cut not too long and not too short. Only his lifeless gray eyes were remarkable. Dressed in dark clothing behind dark-tinted windows, only the intermittent movement of the wiper blades gave his presence away.

He continued to watch the Bank of America, or more precisely, the telephone booth on the sidewalk next to the bank. In the last hour alone he watched a dozen or more people duck into the booth to hide something in a briefcase or a purse that they didn't want drenched with rain. No one stayed inside the booth for more than a few moments. He wondered if they sensed they were putting themselves in harm's way and thought it not likely. The average person made it through each day by pure luck and not by skill or alertness.

The target would be in the phone booth at noon awaiting a call.

Mr. Smith's employers had picked the location because it would facilitate a hit and run. He thought it had a more appealing feature. One that wasn't so boring.

His eyes gave the barest hint of recognition as a middle-aged gentleman, stepped out of the bank. He pulled the collar up on his twelve hundred dollar Brooks Brothers suit coat, walked down the steps, folded his newspaper, tucked it under his arm, and entered the glass and aluminum rectangle that would soon become his tomb.

It was time. Mr. Smith started the Humvee, put it in gear and hit the cancel button on his iPhone.

The shock wave from the blast violently rocked the Humvee. Mr. Smith watched in morbid fascination as bodies were thrown about like rag dolls, some landing on the sidewalk, some had been hurled into the street, some landed on top of cars. The unlucky ones, those closest to the blast, were now a sticky film on his windshield.

Those lucky enough to live were frantically running away, others crawling or rolling around with their clothing aflame, their flesh melted by the heat, internal organs damaged from the blast. It was beautiful.

A woman staggered out of the chaos and smoke and stumbled against his window. The left half of her face and most of hair were melted. She clawed at the door with skinless fingers and collapsed. He allowed himself a smile.

Washington, D.C.

Three blocks north of the National Cathedral in the nation's capital Mr. Smith waited for Pamela to come home. He could smell her scent in every room. Faint, but it was still there.

He met Pamela last year during an assignment in D.C. She tended bar at a downtown nightclub facetiously named Madam's Organ. He had introduced himself as Alex Stanhope, day trader. When he awoke beside her the next morning he had been surprised. Not by the fact that he'd slept with a beautiful woman, but that he had actually stayed the night.

He found he enjoyed her company and she his, so he rented a condo and let her live there as part of his cover. She worked the nightclub and he stayed with her as often as possible. She had never once questioned his prolonged absences, or his need for angry sex immediately upon his return. His cover job perfectly explained his strange and frequent absences and narcissistic lifestyle. Lying about whom he was and what he did was like taking a breath. Involuntary yet necessary.

In Columbus, Ohio, he was Daniel Whitcomb, who ran a successful consulting business. In Seattle, he was Professor Douglas Levin, on sabbatical from Shoreline College where he taught Criminal Justice. There were many others, and in each location there was someone to complete his cover. But of all these identities he preferred being Alex Stanhope because Pamela was like no one he had ever known, and the Agency didn't know of her existence, or of the condo, and keeping them in the dark was extremely satisfying.

The killing in Chicago had also been satisfying. He was tired of creating accidents and suicides. He truly enjoyed killing. The bean counters at the Agency had become soft, politically correct, worried about public opinion or political fallout or budget hearings or congressional oversight. Only in the aftermath of 9/11 had he been truly happy. He was like Hercules unchained, doing what he was born to do.

But he knew he had stepped over a line in Chicago. The pussies in the Agency were likely wringing their hands and crying like old women. Or more likely, doing damage control, eliminating any thread of connection between themselves and the Chicago incident. He was one of those threads.

The condo was dark. He looked at the luminous face of his watch. It was almost time. He had turned the forced air off, silenced the ticking of the wall clock, sat on the sofa, closed his eyes, and let his senses take over. Pamela would be walking in the door at exactly one a.m. She was very punctual for a woman. He would wait for her. Hopefully spend one more evening with her. And then he would have to kill her and move on. Such a waste.

He heard soft footfalls on the hall stairway. She always rode the elevator. He should have heard the hum of the motor and the clattering noise the doors made when they opened. She was five minutes early. There was no sound in the hallway of someone coming toward the door, but he could feel the slight movement in the floor. *Definitely not Pamela.*

He knelt beside the sofa and retrieved a handgun he had taped underneath the coffee table. He thumbed the guns safety to the "fire" position, stepped into the bathroom, and stood with his back against the doorframe.

A key rattled and the bolt turned. Soft-soled shoes, more than one set, quietly moved into the condo's foyer.

He risked a quick glance toward the living room and saw two black silhouettes. One tall and one short with a faint green glow floating around the heads. *Night vision.*

He reached around the doorway and flipped a wall switch. The town house was immediately illuminated.

He watched gloved hands scrabbling for the night vision goggles, the bright light causing a searing pain and effectively blinding the wearers. Before they could pull the goggles off, he shot the closest one in the neck and chest. He swung the pistol toward the shorter of the two and shot him in the mouth. Both targets were down.

He calmly examined the bodies.

Cleaners. And not very good ones. He was insulted.

The shorter one seemed familiar. He knelt beside the body and pulled the goggles up and for a moment felt something he hadn't felt since he was a child. Embarrassment. Shock. Disbelief.

The face he was looking at had been ruined, but there was no doubt it was Pamela.

He looked out the window for signs of a backup team and there were none or at least they weren't aware of what was happening. These two should have reported in to their team, and so he only had minutes to leave.

He picked up his briefcase from beside the sofa and went to the massive wooden entertainment center where he lifted the plasma television out and tossed it to the side. In the back of the cabinet was a panel to a secret compartment where he had installed a wall safe before Pamela moved in. He worked the combination and opened the inch-thick steel door revealing a silenced pistol, several passports, other identification, and stacks of twenty and hundred dollar bills.

He took the silenced pistol and money. He considered leaving the Identification kits and passports. If Pamela worked for the Agency, she would have found his hidey-hole and may have reported his aliases to the Agency, as he would have done. Perhaps she had recorded the serial numbers on the money, but he would chance it until he was well on his way. The last item he removed from the safe was a small canister that resembled a can of shaving cream except for the metal cotter pin on the top. The incendiary device could be detonated remotely and would create the diversion he needed.

He stood over Pamela and looked down. He knew why he had liked her better than the others. She was like him.

"You broke my heart, Pamela. Let me return the favor." He fired several more shots into her body and left.

The backup team that Pamela brought was sadly disappointing. Had she thought it would be that easy to kill him? He spotted a man by the elevator as he stepped into the hallway and shot him in the throat. As that one lay gagging on his own blood, another opened the stairwell door and was dispatched with a double tap to the face. He shot them both once more in the head before stepping over the bodies and descending the stairs. As he stepped out the service door, he keyed in a sequence of numbers on his cell phone, hit the Send button, and heard a small explosion. There would be nothing left of his presence in the condo, and the fire may even burn the building down.

He walked into the street where an obviously intoxicated man and woman were getting into a DC cab. He walked to the cab's open door and shot the couple multiple times and then shot the barely aware cabbie through the back of the seat.

He pulled the driver's body onto the street and drove away.

CHAPTER TWO

Three weeks later, far west side of Evansville, Indiana

Nineteenth-century military strategist, Helmuth von Moltke, once said, "No battle plan ever survives contact with the enemy."

That statement was apropos of the position Detectives Jack Murphy and Liddell Blanchard were facing. Four robbers armed to the teeth with fully automatic weapons and hand grenades against Jack and Liddell, who were armed with p-shooters compared to the other side of the equation. They weren't supposed to be taking on the team of bank robbers alone. The detectives' job was to direct the takedown from a safe distance while a heavily armed SWAT Team converged on these assholes like ducks on June bugs. But Jack Murphy's Law says, "Anything that can go wrong will, and always at the most inconvenient time."

Jack rode shotgun as Liddell turned off Red Bank Road, whipping the Crown Vic into the lot of Citizens Bank. Three figures in ski masks, black tactical vests and clothing ran toward a waiting car. One robber was as big as Liddell and Liddell was as big as a full-grown Yeti. It was hard to tell the build of the other two because of the bulky weapons vests, but they seemed slighter and were moving slower than the big guy. The robbers made it to their car and looked up, hearing the Crown Vic's engine screaming, coming at them fast.

They were carrying black duffel bags that looked heavy and what looked like MAC 10s or UZIs. The robbers reached their car and began spraying bullets at the car bearing down on them.

"Tighten your seat belt," Liddell said, and they leaned down, trying desperately to get below the dashboard as the windshield imploded and the air was filled with buzzing lead and glass projectiles.

Liddell stomped the gas pedal to the floor. They hit hard and were slammed forward. The impact deployed the Crown Vic's airbags choking them with a cloud of white powder.

"You okay?" Jack asked when the worst was over and Liddell nodded. "You are one crazy mother. Next time I drive."

Coughing, they kicked the doors open and bailed out with guns in hands.

The getaway car had rolled onto its passenger side. Jack ran to the front of the suspects' car and saw one of the robbers about thirty yards away, carrying his weapon and a money bag and limping toward an alley. The other two suspects were down and weren't moving. One had his legs pinned beneath the car's body.

Liddell peeked inside the getaway car. It was an older model GTO, with no safety devices to protect the driver whom was slumped, ass over head, the side of his face covered in blood. "I got these," Liddell called to Jack. "I'll call an ambulance. Go."

Jack heard sirens coming closer. He ran past the two downed robbers, pausing only long enough to kick their weapons out of reach, and then sprinted after the one that was running.

Reaching the mouth of the alley where he had last seen the robber, he pushed himself close to the brick wall and risked a quick peek around the corner. Something was rolling towards him.

Jack fell to the concrete, protecting his head with his arms. A split second later a massive explosion rocked the ground.

"Oh, no, you didn't!" he said through gritted teeth, his voice sounding muted and coming from far away. Without thinking he was up on his feet and running into the alley.

The robber was getting to his feet from behind a dumpster, saw Jack, and turned towards him. Jack's .45 was at shoulder level and pointing at the robber's head from less than fifteen feet away. He could see the eyes behind the ski mask wide with indecision, and then turn to steely determination. *He was going to try it.*

Jack's finger tightened on the trigger, and then the dye-pack in the money bag exploded, enveloping the robber in an expanding cloud of red smoke and tear gas.

The tear gas's effect on the robber was immediate. The money-bag fell to the ground and the robber began rubbing at his eyes and coughing, gun still in hand.

Jack moved forward, gun out front at shoulder level, yelling, "Drop the gun, asshole! I said drop the gun!"

The robber shook his head, but Jack could see their eyes were red and swollen almost closed.

"Drop the gun!" he growled and pointed his .45 at the robber's head. He saw the head turn slightly to one side, eyes slitting, trying to focus, grip tightening on the gun. Jack shot him, lowering the .45 at the last moment, the bullet striking center mass like a sledgehammer. The robber fell straight down but stubbornly held onto the gun.

Jack crossed the distance before he could recover, stomped the robber's wrist and kicked the gun away. The man was gulping for air, like a politician caught in a lie. Jack rolled him over and hand-cuffed him. He patted him down, and then rolled him onto his back.

"You're alive," he said to the still gasping man. "The wind was knocked out of you. Calm down and it'll come back."

Jack knelt and pulled the mask over his head.

"What the . . . ?"

"*You shot me,*" the girl said.

Photo by George Routt

ABOUT THE AUTHOR

SERGEANT RICK REED (ret.), author of the Jack Murphy thriller series, is a twenty-plus-year veteran police detective. During his career he successfully investigated numerous high-profile criminal cases, including a serial killer who claimed thirteen victims before strangling and dismembering his fourteenth and last victim. He recounted that story in his acclaimed true-crime book, *Blood Trail*.

Rick spent his last three years on the force as the commander of the police department's Internal Affairs Section. He has two master's degrees, and upon retiring from the police force, took a full-time teaching position with a community college. He currently teaches criminal justice at Volunteer State Community College in Tennessee and writes thrillers. He lives near Nashville with his wife and two furry friends, Lexie and Belle.

Please visit him on Facebook, Goodreads, or at his website, www.rickreedbooks.com. If you'd like him to speak online for your event, contact him by going to bookclubreading.com.

A SADISTIC
SEX SLAYER'S
GRISLY DESIRES...

INCLUDES KILLER'S
CONFESSION

BLOOD TRAIL

STEVEN WALKER
AND
RICK REED

THE
CRUELEST
CUT

"As authentic and scary
as thrillers get."
– Nelson DeMille

A JACK MURPHY THRILLER

RICK REED

THE

COLDEST

FEAR

A JACK MURPHY THRILLER

"Reed writes as only a cop can ...
impressive and dramatic."
— Nelson DeMille

RICK REED